VOKLANE

GEN-HEIRS: THE GUARDIANS OF SZIVERIA

SARAH WESTILL

VOKLANE

Gen-Heirs: The Guardians of Sziveria – Book 8

Copyright 2024 by Sarah Westill

ISBN 978-1-955293-25-9

Cover Design by For the Muse Designs

Other titles by Sarah Westill

Don't miss all the Gen-Heirs titles

The Guardians of Sziveria
(in reading order)

Levkaseon – A Prequel
Wintersfall
Raiventon
Kynhaven
Asherwick
Ericksen - A Wintervail Special
Survaine
Wolvenguard
Voklane

Bella and the Beast Master
(A novella series)

Frozen Flowers Fallen
Perfect Melody Silenced
Dreams Never Seen
Fiery Nights Tempted
Broken Heart Questioned (fall 2024)

For world maps and to stay up-to-date on the latest
information, be sure to visit www.sarahwestill.com

DEDICATION AND ACKNOWLEDGEMENT

To God, for giving me the inspiration and the ability to create an entire series.

To my oldest son Blake, born of my heart.

To every mother who has a child born from her heart.

To all my readers who have stayed with the series the entire journey.
Thank you.

FOR MY READERS

Dear Readers,

This is it.

The end of the series.

A bittersweet *see you later*, but not a goodbye.

For those who have been along on this journey since the very first book, meeting Sean and Katria, discovering with me all the nuances to a genetically gifted people and a bleak future for humanity, thank you. If this is your very first time opening a Gen-Heirs book, welcome! But please be aware this is the final installment to a serial series and there are spoilers for the previous books.

If you're like me and aren't ready to say good-bye, then you'll be excited to learn I have another series in the works. Don't forget to check out *Bella and the Beast Master*, the start of the rowdy Ralston family. You will be seeing much of this family in the future. *wink*

I hope you enjoy reading Ryan and Delanee's story as much as I enjoyed writing it.

Sarah

Content Warning:

This book contains mature content, including but not
limited to –
Consensual sex (non-graphic)
Kidnapping

Reader discretion is advised.

WELCOME TO THE GEN-HEIRS WORLD

In the distant future, a major cataclysmic event not only reshaped the world as humanity knew it, but left entire lands uninhabitable. As generations of survivors struggled to endure a fight for territory and resources, humanity regressed into what became known as The Primal Years. A dark and dangerous time that lasted for centuries.

Slowly, civilizations formed in the new nations. Limited means of transportation and communication began to develop in a resource-poor world. Powerful countries arose known as Sziveria, Ruthenia, Italyssa, Westica, and Cairo. New cultures, with their own standards of honor, became global powerhouses.

By 830 Post-Cataclysmic Event (PCE), strong talents are now inherited traits, passed down through genetics. The recipients of an unavoidable hereditary legacy are known as Gen-Heirs. Trains, ships, carriages and if one can afford them, small magnetically powered vehicles move people. Radios are the only means of quick communication besides handwritten messages. Heated water is a luxury. Extreme drops in temperature and harsh arctic winds have forced most food growth indoors, in greenhouses. A dangerously lethal virus known as Human Rabies Syndrome (HRS) plagues the globe. The inhabited world is growing at a slow rate, each unique country striving to exist in harsher, cold climates, and those who survive have become ruthless in their quest to thrive in this new, forsaken world...

THE RANKING SYSTEM:

Guardians of Sziveria
Queen/King Elect
Prince/Princess Elect
Arch Guardian
Prince/Princess
Shield Guardian
Master Guardian
Primary Guardian
Key Guardian
Guardian (anyone who serves the realm)

Other Key Terms –
First Intelligence Office (FIO)
Sziverian National Investigative Division (SNID)
Haven City Enforcement Services (HCES)
Medical Science Officer (MSO)
Medical Science Investigator (MSI)
Uninhabited Zones (UZ)
Human Rabies Syndrome (HRS)

ONE

MAY, 2ⁿᵈ, 838, P.C.E. (Post-Cataclysmic Event)
Haven City, Sziveria

"ARE WE GOING TO GO INSIDE?" a soft female voice asked.

Ryan Voklane, liaison to one of the most powerful men in the nation, fought panic.

Because of the woman seated beside him in the small space of the vehicle.

Her scent, a combination of clean citrus and sweet flowers too pleasant to his senses, surrounded him. Had driven him to the brink of insanity since she'd swept into his vehicle. Gripping the steering column of his Ariot, he wondered for the hundredth time what in the arctic he'd been thinking. He stared out the windshield into the dark void beyond. His street had limited lighting, one of the reasons he'd chosen the neighborhood. Privacy. And here he was about to let a near stranger into his *home*.

His refuge.

Where his every secret would be laid bare.

To a journalist.

"Ryan? Hello?"

A feminine sigh of frustration filled the small cab. *Ryan.* She'd never called him Ryan before, only Mr. Voklane. Sweat dotted his forehead and dampened his back. Everything about Delanee Ralston was dangerous to him. From her choice of career to the way she made him think seductive thoughts he had no business entertaining, to the danger currently following her. Having her under his roof would not end well. For either of them.

"It's okay if you've changed your mind," she whispered.

This time, Ryan's heavy sigh penetrated the silence. His hands dropped to his lap. "No, I haven't changed my mind."

"Okay."

Before he could second guess his decision again, Ryan yanked open his door and exited. Delanee didn't wait for him to reach her side, stepping out into the brisk night. The unassuming clothes she wore hid the modest curves she possessed. She rose to her full height, only a few inches shorter than him. Kissing her wouldn't hurt his back from having to hunch to reach her full lips. He blinked and quickly turned his attention to his house. There would be no kissing.

"Wow," she breathed, the sudden thud of the vehicle door closing breaking through the quiet night.

Ryan shoved his hands into his pants pockets and studied his house—a simple, single-story red brick structure. A half-wall and columns made of brick separated the porch from the front of the house. Ivy crept up most of the surface. The recessed front door under an archway was painted a vibrant turquoise blue. Lanterns burned on either side of the door, casting a whimsical light when paired with the vibrant colors and greenery.

"What?" he asked, curious about her thoughts concerning his home.

"I don't know. I guess I expected you to live in something foreboding, like my brother. Not this," she waved at the house, "enchanting property."

Ryan lifted his brows. "Am I foreboding?"

Her lips pressed into a flat line. "You aren't cheery."

He glanced at his house again. "And my house is?"

"It's..." She sighed and dropped her hand. "Perfect."

Someone else had once called the dwelling adequate. A charming stepping stone to something greater. The perception should have been a blaring, red warning sign. Ryan shook his head to dislodge the bitter memory. He didn't know how to take Delanee thinking the place was perfect, which had always been his opinion since the moment he purchased the property.

"Come on." Time to get on with his brilliant plan.

She didn't move.

Ryan paused on the paved walkway and turned. The moon cast her in silvery shadows, leaching the color from her hair to leave it black instead of the wine-red unique to her family. Her clothes, a long navy embroidered skirt and a tan blouse, practical and comfortable, were rich shades of gray. Even the hue of her skin, a stunning dark honey, was washed away. Her eyes, though, he knew those would still hold their melted gold coloring if he were brave enough to venture close and test the theory.

"What's wrong?" he asked.

"Are you certain?" She hugged a worn leather messenger bag. "You want me here?"

No, he was far from certain of his decision. For so many reasons. But he'd made the protective offer and meant to see the choice through. Delanee had made a rash decision of her own, and here they were. She needed a safe, anonymous place, and he was the only one capable of providing said space.

Ryan held his arms out at his side. "Miss Ralston, come inside or don't. It's getting cold and—"

He shook his head and sighed, cutting off his words and heading up the walkway. She'd know his secret soon enough, but he couldn't bring himself to speak the words aloud beyond the walls of his house. The soft fall of her footsteps scuffed the stones. Relief and frustration warred within him. For reasons unknown to him, Ryan needed to know Delanee was safe. The palace would be the only residence safer for her than his house. And therein lay his frustration. Why did her safety matter at all to him? Aside from not wanting another innocent hurt in the secret ongoing war with an unknown enemy, he shouldn't have a reason. Couldn't have one.

Sliding his key into the front lock, Ryan opened the door with more force than necessary.

"You did too cheat, you old hag," a shaky female voice echoed through the foyer.

"Me, an old hag? Have you looked in the mirror recently? Your cheeks are about to sag right off your face."

"I saw that! Put it back. Caught you— oh, hello, Ryan dear."

Ryan leaned against the archway into the living room. "Evening, Evelyn." He nodded and turned to the elderly woman sitting across from her. "Ava."

"Ryan!" Ava clapped and stood. Three colorful tiles tumbled to the carpet. "Come here, come here!"

Smiling, Ryan crossed the short distance. Those same tiles were spread across the long living room table. Evelyn sat in a plush chair while Ava had occupied the couch. A cheery fire burned in the hearth and all the lamps were lit, brightening the room. He knew the ladies couldn't see without the excess light. Both wore matching bright blue shawls, brown skirts, and yellow tops with little brown flowers. Ryan figured they liked keeping people on their toes about which twin they interacted with. Even their hair was coiled in identical, loose silver buns atop their heads.

Evelyn waved a hand and tsked. "I told you he'd know the difference between us. He always knows."

Ava folded him into a warm hug. "Ah, I love that he knows." She gripped his chin and kissed his cheek. "Smart, our boy is."

Evelyn glanced at the floor and gasped. Red blossomed across her cheeks. Sputtering, she pointed at the carpet, her thin frame vibrating. "Oh, oh, oh, I knew it!" Her finger wagged. "I knew it, you-you double-crossing old cow! I knew you were hoarding tiles!"

Ava slid her foot over the evidence, folded her hands in front of her, and turned up her nose. "I don't know what you mean."

Evelyn glared, pointed at her twin, and opened her mouth. Ryan turned and motioned toward the foyer. Evelyn blinked, snapped her mouth shut, and pivoted. Delanee stood in the archway, eyes wide.

Ava laughed and clasped her gnarled hands to her chest. "What an impression you've made, Evie. How wonderful."

Evelyn adjusted the ends of the scarf. "Ryan, I didn't realize you'd cont—"

"This is Miss Delanee Ralston," Ryan interrupted before Evelyn could make the situation any more awkward. "She'll be staying with me for the foreseeable future as a guest."

Evelyn and Ava exchanged glances.

"A guest," Ryan reiterated.

Ava touched his arm, leaned close, and whispered, "I should think one child outside of a contract would be enough of a lesson for you, Ryan."

Ryan's gut clenched. "She really is a guest. She needs a safe place to stay."

Mint, lavender, and the pungent scent of the cedar sticks the women used to *keep away the vermin* invaded Ryan's space. "And her family isn't safe for her?"

"No, not without putting them in danger as well. I offered my home as shelter, and she accepted. Nothing more."

Ava removed her hand and nodded. "Come, Evie, let's head home so Ryan can see to his guest's comfort."

Evelyn raised her finger. "But—"

"No, we will return first thing in the morning." Her dark brown eyes were stern as they met his gaze. "*First* thing."

Ryan smiled. "I would expect nothing less."

Ava nodded. "She had a good day. Ate well. Had two messy diapers. She went to sleep about three hours ago."

Ryan leaned forward and kissed Ava's cheek. "Thank you." Evelyn came around the table for her nightly good-byes. Ryan kissed and hugged her. "Thank you, Evie."

She patted his cheek and then his chest. "Be good, Ryan."

Ava grabbed a cane near the terrace door, and Evelyn took down a coat from a peg. Their exit left the house blan-keted in silence. Ryan sat on the couch and picked up the tiles from the floor. They chinked as he tossed them onto the table with the others.

"They think I'm your mistress, don't they?" Delanee asked quietly, kneeling on the floor across the table from him and sliding the wooden box to store the tiles closer to her. She set the tiles into the container one by one, by color, he noted.

"No, they don't. They're just... overprotective of my imaginary reputation," he said. "Would you care if they did?"

Her chin lifted. "No. We know the truth." She carefully set a handful of tiles in the assigned places, focusing on the task. "Who are they, anyway?"

"My neighbors."

"And they hang out at your house while you're gone all day?"

"Asking as a guest or a journalist?" he couldn't help but question.

Finally, her stunning golden gaze lifted. Such brilliance against her darker skin. "I already promised not to share anything." She glanced around the living room. "You aren't exactly my editor's targeted content, anyway. Sorry."

He rubbed his forehead. "No, I'm sorry. I'm just not used to my privacy being invaded."

Pink stained her cheeks, and her shoulders straightened. "I'm not invading anything. You invited me."

Ryan slapped his hands on his thighs. "I did, you're right."

Folding her arms, she rested them on the table. Tiles clinked together and slid out of her way. "What do you do at all these events I see you attend? Because clearly, ordinary conversation isn't your strength."

He leaned forward. "Are you saying I'm socially awkward?"

"Yes."

No, being alone with *her* was awkward. Ryan stood, not wanting to contemplate the beautiful, tempting, and feisty woman who'd spend the night a few hundred feet away. "I'll show you to your room."

Standing, she gripped the leather strap across her chest. "Ryan, why were two old ladies waiting for you to get home? Are they here every day? Do I need to be careful around them?"

"Yes, they're here daily, whether I need them or not. They insist on feeding me. I can't get rid of them. No, you don't have to be careful around them. They don't leave their house except to go to the market down the street, and they fight the entire time so no one approaches them. Ever."

She lifted a dark, sculpted brow. "Do I want to know how you know that?"

"I've gone at the same time." He smiled. "It's an experience."

Her grip on the strap tightened. "And why were they waiting for you?"

The smile faded. Answering the question warred with his deep need to cling to his secrets. But this wasn't a secret he would be able to keep, no matter how hard he might try. Taking a deep breath, he revealed his most precious confidence. "They care for my daughter when I'm not home."

DELANEE BLINKED, all intelligible words fleeing from her mind. Ryan Voklane had a daughter. He was a father. Her gaze immediately fell to his unadorned left wrist and hand. Not that the lack of jewelry meant anything. She wanted to collapse on the couch, stick her head between her knees, and breathe because what felt a lot like panic was wanting to take over. All this time, she'd been secretly pining for a married man?

"Will your wife be okay with my staying here?" she somehow managed to get out of her dry mouth.

A sad smile toyed at his lips and didn't reach his pale, silvery blue eyes. "I don't have a spouse."

Instant relief almost made her take a deep breath, but confusion replaced the relief. No one had children outside of a contract; they resulted from one. "I don't...." She licked her lips and tucked a curl behind her ear. "I don't understand."

He held his arms out, his way of showing frustration she was learning. "What is there to understand, Miss

Ralston? I wasn't contracted to a woman I slept with and she had my baby."

The blunt words made her flinch. Shocked, Delanee realized she didn't want another woman to know Ryan in such intimate terms, which was ridiculous. He'd likely taken many lovers in his life. Unlike her, she had never been interested in a man enough to do much more than kiss, and every attempt had been such a disappointment that anything more seemed a waste of time. Still, the last thing she wanted was a former lover re-staking her claim when she discovered Delanee staying in the house.

"Where is she?"

"I have no idea. My daughter was delivered via a courier and a note." He clenched his jaw and looked away from her, red darkening his neck and cheeks. "With the state of things, I'm lucky she cared enough to give her to me instead of selling her."

The situation embarrassed him. Perhaps it even brought him shame. Such a contradiction to the steady man she'd known every other encounter. Delanee didn't want to be the reason he experienced any humiliation. "Okay, so you're a single parent, and your elderly neighbors help you. Anything else I need to know?"

His jaw flexed. "Not that I can think of at the moment."

"Great, I'll see my room now, thank you."

Ryan nodded and led her to a long, narrow hall. Only one lantern burned, making the space darker than the living room. She tried not to stare at his butt, perfectly molded in pale gray slacks, or the way the navy sweater he wore stretched tight across his broad shoulders. On appearances, Ryan worked a desk job, but his fit physique spoke of physical training, an unseen part of his career. Delanee dragged her attention from the intriguing man sand took in her surroundings.

Framed colored sketches of ruins lined the walls, which were painted a calming shade of sage green. Delanee wanted to stop and examine the art, wondering where they were drawn and what they showed. A carpet runner in greens, golds, and deep browns ran the length of the hall. They passed three doors on the left, and he opened the last one.

A match flared, and a gentle light filled the room. Delanee looked around her short-term home. Comfortable like the rest of his house, the space was decorated in more masculine tones. All the furniture was walnut. The carpet was tan with the same style runners as the hall on either side of the bed. The walls were a shade of lighter sage. The comforter on the bed transitioned from cream to dark green in a smooth gradient. Delanee stood in the appealing room and only wanted to know what his space looked like. The same with subtle differences? Larger? She eyed the full-sized mattress and then slid her gaze to him. The mattress for his bed would be bigger. Something she should not be thinking about, not with images of him with another woman dancing through her mind.

His former lover had probably been the Sziverian standard of beauty. Full curves, on the shorter side, with luscious hair laden with the appropriate number of baubles, and pale skin. Delanee saw the same characterization in hundreds of the same dresses at every party her editor made her attend. Probably the daughter of a ranked guardian who moved in his circles. Who had seduced whom, she wondered? And had he loved her? Jealousy speared a hot path straight to Delanee's heart. She had needed a reason to give up her teenager-like infatuation with the man. Now she had one.

"The bathroom is through that first door on the left. The second door is to the closet. Logs for the fireplace are in the basket. If you need more, they're stacked on the terrace in the greenhouse." He pointed out everything and then set a book of matches on the hearth to the right. "I'll bring you a t-shirt to sleep in."

"Thank you."

He rapped his knuckles on the wooden hearth and then nodded and left. Delanee huffed a long breath and pulled the strap to her shoulder bag over her head. Sitting on the bed, she pulled out her notebook. She flipped to the first page of her interview notes, which were the reason for her sitting in a near stranger's home. A trusted stranger, at least, or her older brother Deklan wouldn't have allowed her to leave with Ryan. Sighing, she held the journal in both hands and dropped them to her lap.

Tonight, she'd made the fortunate— or perhaps unfortunate, considering her situation— discovery of identifying the assassin plaguing the country for years. Once he learned she was a journalist, his only goal would be eliminating her. Her ten siblings, parents, and grandmother would also be in jeopardy if she ignored the threat. Delanee wouldn't allow anything to happen to her family. Ever. Ryan had offered safe shelter. Rejecting the offer would have been foolish. He'd disrupted his life for her.

A life that included a daughter.

Delanee tossed the book aside and stood. Would her presence endanger the child? Placing an innocent life in the path of danger was an unthinkable risk Delanee couldn't allow. She left the room and knocked on every door, easing them open and calling Ryan's name, only to discover dark spaces. An empty bedroom decorated in shades of muted pink and the same sage green. It must be his favorite color. Another door led to a dark study, bookshelves lining every wall, and, in the center, a spacious desk in the same walnut wood as the bedroom set in her room.

Delanee wandered through the living room, the foyer, and a quiet dining room. She peered around the corner, finding a stunning kitchen and breakfast nook with a built-in bench table. Beautiful counters in a sea foam green marble texture, and pinewood for all the cabinets and furniture created an elegant space. Striking bone tile with ornate curves painted in taupe covered the floor. Delanee slowly ventured to the large island in the center, her fingers caressing the cold, smooth surface. She gasped. Not painted wood after all, but natural marble. A luxury she'd only heard about being in the kitchens of the high-ranking guardians.

The muffled whimper of an infant drew her attention to the opening leading to another corridor. How big was his house? Light bled through a partially open door at the end of the hall. Another small wail had her heart clenching. Being part of a large family meant babies. She knew the distressed cry, the unhappy quiver of a tiny voice that no amount of soothing seemed to fix. The question was, would Delanee intrude, and would he allow her to help if she did?

Louder and more distraught, the infant screamed. Delanee's chest constricted, and her feet carried her to the door before her brain could argue. Using her fingertips, she pressed on the door. The hinges squeaked, and gravity opened the way into the room. Ryan stood in the center of the dimly lit space, bouncing on his feet, attempting to soothe a red-faced baby in pink pajamas. A navy t-shirt was slung over his shoulder, messy with spit up, and a damp spot bloomed on the shirt he wore. The baby's tiny feet pumped up and down. Her little fists trembled.

"Let me see her," Delanee whispered.

Ryan hesitated for a second before handing over his daughter.

Delanee arranged the tiny girl in the crook of her arm. She stuck a finger into her mouth. Confused, the crying stopped while the infant tried to figure out if something edible had been placed in her mouth. Delanee swept her fingers along the baby's gumline during the quiet lull. The telltale lump of an emerging tooth had her sighing. "Where's your medicine chest?"

"In the bathroom. Why?"

"She's teething." Delanee glanced around the room. A door in the left corner appeared to lead outside, so she turned and headed toward a door on the right that'd been behind her. "What's her name?"

"Inara."

Pretty. A small-minded part of Delanee wondered who had chosen the girl's name, Ryan or his former lover. Inara gummed Delanee's finger, her whimpers building up to another cry session. "Shh," Delanee implored, bouncing the fussy baby in her arms. "It's okay, sweet girl."

Ryan followed her into the bathroom, lighting two lamps near a huge mirror. The same stunning marble from the kitchen created the bathroom counter and two sinks. Ryan crouched down and dug around beneath the counter. He set a wooden box with a medical scientist emblem on the counter.

"Anything specific?" he asked, rising and opening the box.

She listed a few essential oils. He set them out with a coconut oil container and a small mixing bowl.

"If you'll wait for me to change, I'll help."

Delanee cuddled Inara, her hand splaying across the baby's torso. She was always amazed she could span an infant's abdomen from chin to hips. A baby belly pressed into her palm. Inara blinked up at her. Silvery-blue eyes and the pale blonde fuzz on her head left no doubts about her parentage. Fabric rustling drew Delanee's attention. She glanced up in time to see Ryan peeling his shirt off and tossing it, and what he'd used to catch spit-up, into a basket in an open linen closet. Delanee froze. Men in top physical form were nothing new in her life. Her brothers kept themselves in excellent condition. But they were her *brothers*.

Ryan Voklane was not her brother.

The ember flames of the lantern reflected off his alabaster skin and platinum blond hair. With each step, muscles rolled from his shoulders to the small of his back. Metal jangled, and leather hissed as he undid his belt and pulled it free, his defined biceps flexing. A curious tingle raced through Delanee.

He was male perfection Delanee should *not* be admiring.

Inara gurgled and whined. Delanee tore her gaze away from Ryan and returned her attention to the baby in her arms. She grasped the tiny fist, and Inara immediately latched onto her thumb, her pale eyes widened, and she kicked her feet. "We're going to fix the ouchies."

Pulling on a shirt, Ryan stopped next to her. His normally styled hair stood at odd angles. He motioned to himself. "I can take her now, thank you."

Delanee handed her over, frowning at the loss. Ryan made big eyes and a goofy face. He held Inara under her armpits and helped her stand on the counter. Pain seemingly forgotten, she squealed and bounced on her chubby little legs. Drool dribbled down her chin to soak the front of her pajama top. Everything feminine in Delanee melted. She blinked. *Nope, nope, nope.* She could not get attached to this man or his child. She wasn't here to find romance. He wasn't even her type, she reminded herself.

"She's what, six months?" Delanee asked, dropping precise amounts of oils into the mixing bowl.

"Almost, yes. Spend lots of time around babies?"

Delanee paused mid-drop of chamomile. "You are aware of who my family is, right?"

He laughed, helping Inara bounce while she babbled

incoherent noises and slapped her hands on his forearms. "Fair enough."

Delanee stared and then quickly looked away. She'd never heard him laugh before and had never really seen him smile, either. A dimple peeked out on his right cheek. Picking up the coconut oil to make the final mixture, Delanee caught herself sneaking glances at Ryan in the mirror. Handsome was an understatement where he was concerned. The man looked chiseled from stone, an artist's flawless rendition. Strong jaw, high cheekbones, and arched brows. A nose perfect for his face and full lips that no doubt knew how to kiss. There'd be no slobbery, half-terrified pecks from him. Not that she wanted to know how he'd kiss, she reminded herself. Again.

Finished with the concoction, Delanee slid the small glass container toward him. "Rub this on her gums when she gets fussy. It'll help soothe the ache of her first tooth coming in."

"Thank you." He lowered his head until he was level with Inara. "You're getting a tooth, baby girl? Getting so big." Hefting her onto his left hip, he grabbed the container in his free hand. "My dresser is on the other side of the bed. Grab a shirt for yourself if you'd like. I'm going to change her."

Making baby talk, he turned and headed back to his closet. Delanee rubbed her hands on her skirt and returned to his bedroom. A crib sat to the right of a huge bed. A navy comforter with sage green and gold embroidery covered the mattress. A masculine contrast to the pink baby blanket and pastel stuffed toys on the bed and in the crib. Delanee debated going to the dresser. Opening any of the drawers felt like an invasion of privacy. Ironic, considering she had no issues invading other people's privacy when her editor made such demands.

The wall above the dresser didn't have the usual mirror.

Instead, notes, a long timeline in various ink colors, drawn images, and what appeared to be shipping manifests were all tacked into an organized arrangement, spanning the entire space from the window to the corner. Curious, Delanee inched closer and took in the information. Above everything, in large bold letters, was The V Alliance. Delanee crossed her arms and leaned closer.

"What are you doing?" Ryan asked behind her, making her jump.

She spun around. "What, or who, is the V Alliance?"

Two

Ryan ignored Delanee's question. No good would come from answering the inquisitive journalist. He laid his daughter in her crib and searched the mattress for her pacifier. She waved her arms and pumped her chubby legs, her eyes wide. Blowing noises between her lips, little spit bubbles popped and sputtered into the air. Ryan smoothed a hand over her belly, amazed once again he'd created such a precious life, a responsibility he both feared and treasured. Gently, he eased the pacifier into her mouth. She grabbed at it, sucking, her eyes fluttering closed.

He watched her closely, making sure the astonishing medicinal rub Delanee had made continued to work. "How often can I use the rub you made?"

"Whenever she fusses. Something to chew on also helps." Papers rustled, and Ryan glanced up to catch her lifting a few of the manifests he'd tacked into place. "These were from the job you sent my brother to Mark Inland for? The kidnapped passengers?"

She leaned closer and tapped at the timeline Wintersfall had made years ago when they'd first become aware of a cohesive situation endangering the nation. "Oh, and look, Deklan's wife Lucianna is on here. That's because of the assassin, right? The one I saw tonight? And... Cora Dandridge?" Straightening, she looked over her shoulder, meeting his gaze across the crib. "Why is Cora on here? I know she was murdered in Westica, and her brother needed help when he returned home, but what does her death have to do with anything?"

Ryan's chest tightened at the mention of Cora. The vivacious woman hadn't just been murdered. She'd been tortured and raped. All because she'd been a journalist on the hunt for a story and trying to help her twin brother learn the depths of corruption lurking here in Sziveria. Ryan went to the dresser, yanked open the drawer with his shirts, pulled one free, and slammed the drawer closed.

He held the clothing out to her. "Here. It's late, and Inara is going to fall asleep any minute. I'd like to get a few hours myself."

She accepted the dark orange t-shirt, the cloth sliding slowly from his grasp. "You aren't going to answer me?"

"The answers will lead to nothing but trouble." He tossed a hand at his notes. "Forget about all this."

Delanee clutched the shirt in both hands, pressing it to her chest. "Cora was my friend. My mentor. What really happened to her?"

"You were what, twenty-one when she died?" Ryan asked, crossing his arms over his chest and leaning his hip against the dresser.

"Twenty," she whispered.

"You took over the society pages after her death."

"As I said, she was my mentor."

Ryan leaned close. The light caught the brighter golden hues of her irises. Genetic inheritance eyes that didn't belong to a writing talent. Ryan wasn't the only one keeping secrets. "Cora died chasing a story. I promised your brother I'd keep you safe. Forget what you've seen here. I don't need another journalist's death on my conscience."

Fire ignited in her beautiful gaze. "Is that all I'd be to you? Another dark stain on your conscience?" She closed the distance between them until the warmth of her breath caressed his lips. "Tell me, Ryan, how many regrets are running through that mind of yours?"

More than he cared for, but probably not as many as most would believe.

Ryan tried hard to live an honest life, both personal and professional. Sometimes, he failed on both accounts. His single-parent status attested to one of his failures. He met her stare. "How many are in yours?"

She recoiled, immediately averting her gaze. "None."

The urge to use his talent and uncover all her secrets tingled along his skin. If he weren't careful, the energy of his gift would bleed into his eyes and crackle in the air around him. Not a problem if he were touching his target and engaged. They'd never remember. Right now? She would witness his hunger to uncover the truth, a compulsion he'd forced himself to overcome. To date, Delanee was the only person who could elicit enough of an emotional reaction in him to trigger his ability. He still hadn't figured out why. What about her tugged at his very essence? A dangerous mystery.

"And would you want to be more than a failed duty for me should something happen to you?" he pressed, knowing he shouldn't. He reached out and feathered a finger along the corner of her jaw. His light skin was such a contrast in comparison to her honeyed brown. Tiny arcs of electricity leaped across his fingertips. The sparks danced in her eyes, but not enough to draw her into his web. Not yet. He wanted her to remember the answer. "How much do you want me to care?"

•   •   •   •

ALLURING AND STARTLINGLY SENSUAL, the teasing flutter of his touch on her skin left Delanee breathless. Any time he touched her, a simple caress on her hand or across her wrist, she was left with an unwelcome awareness of him. As though he'd somehow managed to brand his presence on her nerves. Something she did not need nor want where he was concerned, she reminded herself. Again.

Taking a step from him, breaking the delicate contact, took an effort that made her want to hiss. The bigger issue, she acknowledged, pressing her lips together in frustration, was her answer. What to say, what to say? Be flippant and shrug away her remark made in the heat of the moment. Or be honest and admit that maybe, perhaps just a little, how he felt about her mattered. She wanted to be more than an obligation. More than a job well done.

"Would my answer matter?" she asked, surprised at her breathy voice. She swallowed and glanced at the years of research affixed to his wall. "Whether I was impetuous and spoke without thought, or—"

The tip of his index finger glided under her chin, shifting her attention back to him. "Or? Don't lose that nerve on me now, Miss Ralston."

Miss Ralston. A subtle reminder that only professionalism had ever existed between them. Except for the one time she had insisted he take her home so she could escape a rather aggressive pursuer. And even then, standing in the dark in her dining room, he'd been aloof. Always civil, regardless of her many barbs she had sent his direction. Delanee wanted to break that façade, see the real man beneath. The one he'd hinted existed in the bathroom.

But perhaps not in the intimate space of his bedroom.

The feisty side of her personality she usually showed him cowered beneath reality. She would reveal more than she could afford if she allowed their banter to continue. In the limited time she'd known Ryan Voklane, she had to force herself not to allow him into her midnight fantasies. She didn't want or need another alpha male in her life, especially not as a forever spouse.

Whatever man she ended up marrying would be tame. Quiet. Unfortunately, those types of men tended to be terrified of her. Delanee knew Ryan would never shrink from her temper. He'd never fear her hidden nature, which constantly wanted to rise to the surface whenever she encountered him. Delanee took another step away.

"You aren't going to tell me anything about your research, are you?" she asked, kneading the soft cotton of the shirt in her hands.

"No. You aren't going to tell me why you want me to care, are you?"

Delanee's breath burned in her lungs. She shook her head.

Inara cooed in her crib. Delanee resisted the urge to go and check on the infant. Ryan had no such hesitation. He crossed the short distance and leaned over the railing. Seeing an opportunity to slip away, she eased past his spacious bed to the open door.

"Running isn't like you," he said.

Grasping the doorframe, she half turned and looked over her shoulder at him. "Oh? Do you not remember helping me escape Mr. Ingerman?"

Slowly, he moved around the crib. "You don't run from *me*."

No, she didn't. Rather, she hunted him down and liked to see what he'd do if she challenged his authority. But when she did so, they weren't standing near his bed, in a room that smelled of him. Like sandalwood and the sharp tang of the ocean. She had some separation. A reminder that kissing him, discovering what all the muscle hidden beneath clothes would feel like, would be a very bad idea.

"Goodnight, Mr. Voklane," she whispered, turning from him.

"Miss Ralston, wait."

Delanee stilled but didn't turn back around. Her heart thundered in her ears. "Yes?"

"We should have gone by your apartment tonight and gathered the things you'll need for at least a week. Here." Blinking, she turned around and found him holding out another t-shirt and a pair of cotton pajama pants. "I'll take you when I return home after dark tomorrow night."

Delanee accepted the clothes, her gaze shifting over his shoulder to the papers and images tacked to the far wall. Immediately, she began planning how she'd explore the material he had gathered and where to search for additional information in the study she'd discovered earlier. "You're leaving me here by myself tomorrow?"

"You're going to snoop, aren't you?" he asked, resigned.

"I prefer to call it investigating," Delanee answered, smiling sweetly.

The smile he returned was tight. "Not an invasion of privacy?"

"I promise not to look through your bedside table."

His mouth flattened. "How considerate of you."

Delanee couldn't help but wonder what she *would* find if she snuck a peek. Boring, everyday things, or perhaps something a bit more salacious. From her limited understanding, men didn't go without physical pleasure, even if they were alone. Most women didn't, either. Mr. Harold's Book Emporium's lusty book section was always busy with citizens of Haven City searching for their next visual fix. A heated flush blossomed across her cheeks. She'd never been brave enough to venture there herself but had written about plenty of others being noticed among the bookshelves.

Inara shouted an inarticulate noise and then blubbered. Delanee glanced at the crib. The baby girl grabbed at her toes, giggled, and then kicked her feet away, shouting another unknown word only she knew.

"I think she's ready for bed," Delanee said. She held up the clothes. "Thank you. I'll see you in the morning."

Ryan grasped the top edge of his door. "I'll answer your questions before I leave for the day."

Delanee raised her brows. "All of them?"

"All that I can without revealing secrets, yes."

"I won't share them," she promised.

He touched his chest. "Guardian of Sziveria. I guard her secrets, as well as her people."

A shiver raced up her spine. Indeed. How could she argue with that statement? Three of her brothers were guardians, one so high-ranking that only the queen-elect had authority over him. In fact, it was information her brother Deklan's wife had uncovered that had led Delanee to identify the assassin.

Her attention shifted to the wall again. "I still won't share anything."

"I know how desperate you are to break free of the social pages," he said quietly.

"I am, yes." He had no idea. No one did, not really. How could they? The determination to see her name on an article of value had led her to all manners of exciting investigations. And each one had been rejected by her editor. He'd shaken the paper at her and told her society gossip was her job, and if she wanted to continue to write for *Haven City Chronicle,* she'd better stop bringing him anything else to review. She wasn't giving up, however. Someday, she would write something her editor wouldn't be able to turn away. "But not at the expense of my personal morals. I said I won't share anything. You can trust me."

Something close to regret filled his eyes and subdued his smile. "I know."

All the senses Delanee tried to keep buried prickled with awareness. She knew without a doubt Ryan Voklane had another personal secret.

THREE

GOLDEN MORNING LIGHT spilled into Ryan's kitchen, reflecting off the pale green marble and pine cupboards. He blew on the hot cup of tea between his hands and smothered a smile as Delanee stumbled through the archway from the living room. The dark orange cotton shirt, while too big, revealed she wore no underclothes. Her modest breasts were perfectly outlined. The gray sleep pants he'd give her to wear for the day hung off her slender hips but, thanks to her height, didn't drag on the floor. Chaotic dark, wine-red curls framed her face and tumbled over her shoulders. She shielded her eyes from the bright room.

"What time is it?" she asked, her words husky and a little fatigue-slurred.

"Didn't sleep well?" he asked, turning, and pouring her a cup from the stove. "Sugar? Milk?"

Her hands pressed into the marble as she slid onto a stool across from him, still squinting and blinking. "Both, thank you. And I slept fine for being in a strange bed."

Ryan hadn't slept much. He'd wanted to check on her, ensure she was comfortable and not getting into trouble sneaking around his house. At least, that's what he told himself. It had nothing to do with knowing she slept in nothing but his t-shirt. Nothing at all.

He slid the prepared tea across to her. "It's eight in the morning."

She grumbled, dragging the cup closer. "Terrible time."

"I've been up for three hours."

She hissed. *Hissed.* Her golden eyes glared at him as if he'd committed some great offense. Well, that was unexpected. Then again, he'd had suspicions where she was concerned. Her uninhibited beast-like reaction added to his hunch about what her eye coloring really meant for her genetic inheritance. Ryan kept his features carefully schooled, not wanting her to realize what she may have revealed.

"Why would you *ever* get out of bed so early?" she asked.

"Not all of us rule the nights. Inara is a morning baby, and the twins arrive at dawn to pick her up. I go for a swim—"

"Swim?" she interrupted, staring at him as if he'd lost his mind. "Where do you swim? You don't even have a bathtub."

"There's a lap pool in the greenhouse."

"And you don't freeze?"

He smiled and took a sip of his tea. "This entire street shares a natural hot spring for water. You'll notice a difference when you shower."

Her jaw worked, and she tapped her fingers on the marble counter. "This is real."

"Yes."

"Your house is beautiful."

"Thank you."

"And hot spring fed."

"Yes."

"How did a liaison for an arch guardian afford a place like this?"

He set his cup down and turned. "Hungry?"

"Curious. Answer the question."

"You first."

She growled, but conceded. "Fine. Yes, I could eat."

A knot formed in his chest. He gathered the ingredients for a simple egg and potato dish and heated a pan on the stove. "My parents owned three houses, one here in Haven City, another at Evanmoore Lake, and the third is up in the Northern Boundary, in Mysthaven."

"Why would anyone want a house up there?"

"Privacy. No one bothers anyone in the Northern Boundary. There are a few communities that make life seem mostly normal when there is no access to items we take for granted. My parents were part of such a community. When we traveled up there, they'd bring chests filled with wares. They were like a traveling general store. Summers in the Northern Boundary are... special." The simplicity of life in a part of the country where winter made only the hardiest Sziverians brave the land on the other side of the Tabria Mountains was something Ryan found himself missing at the oddest moments. Like now, while he chopped the jarred potatoes, remembering his mother doing the same thing in a humble kitchen.

"I've never been," she said. "I never thought I'd want to go, but now... perhaps it'd be worth a trip. I could write about it."

"Cora was going to, before she died. Write about the Northern Boundary." He swept potatoes into a cast-iron skillet and set them on the stove. "Raiventon has a house there, and his wife wants to provide a better life for the inhabitants. Access to medical scientists, basic medicine, and even clothing."

"There's no clothing?"

Ryan added salt, pepper, rosemary, thyme, and powdered garlic to the potatoes. "There is, but clothing is a bartered item. Most everything is. If you need a new pair of pants, you'll have to find something a seamstress needs to trade. There aren't any clothing shops."

"So, three homes. Your parents are wealthy?"

"My mother inherited the house on the lake. My father inherited the house here in Haven City. They bought the residence in the Northern Boundary. Or rather, they staked out the land and built a house." He stirred the potatoes, checking to ensure they were browning evenly. "I only still own the Mysthaven house." And only then because he'd helped build the cabin. The family memories had made parting with the home impossible. "The other two I sold after...."

After they disappeared, too many years passed for Ryan to believe they would ever return home. "Anyway, with the raimarks from both the properties, I was able to purchase this house."

"You're very lucky. Even in winter, you'll have access to fresh, warm water."

He glanced over his shoulder. "You do, in your apartment building."

"Yes, we're lucky, too. Most people in the depth of winter are thawing snow to drink, cook, and bathe with." She set her elbow on the counter and dropped her chin on her palm. "Would you move if offered a ranked guardianship with a property?"

"No." He returned to the potatoes, cracking two eggs over the top and then covering the pan.

"Can you do that?"

"No, I won't ever accept a ranked guardianship position."

"Whyever not?" Exasperation filled her words.

Because no one could know what he was capable of

except the two who already did. He lifted the lid and checked on the eggs. "I have my reasons."

"I don't think I've ever met anyone who would reject a ranked guardianship."

"Hasn't your brother...." He lifted his head to the ceiling, snapping his fingers to jog his memory. "Which one was it again? Oh yes, Drayke. Hasn't he rejected multiple offers from both the SNID and the FIO to take a ranked position, but he's chosen to stay with Haven City Enforcement Services?"

"Well, yes, he has, but that's because he's happy where he is." Ryan looked over his shoulder, brows raised. She huffed and slapped her hands on the counter. "So, you're happy in mediocre, understood."

"Who said my job was ever mediocre?"

She gave him an *Oh, please* stare. "You communicate orders from Arch Guardian Synintel to his intelligence teams."

"Important orders. I'm also responsible for making sure the teams are healthy and functioning without strife and that any safety concerns are addressed." Ryan checked the eggs, found them ready, and spooned the meal onto two plates. After getting a fork and napkin, he slid Delanee her half and leaned on the counter to eat his.

She poked at her egg, breaking the bright yellow yolk over the crispy herbed potatoes. "I still can't believe you'd say no to a ranking, especially with your experience."

"I'm content where I am." Not a choice, but one he accepted.

They ate in silence, Delanee seeming to be lost in thought. When she finished, she picked up her plate and went to the sink. Her plate clinked with all the other objects.

"I'll wash these today," she said.

"That won't be necessary," Ryan said quickly.

"I'll need something to do. I don't mind. I'm usually on dish duty with my grandmother. She loves to cook."

Ryan shook his head. "You're a guest. I'll do the dishes in my home."

She braced both hands on the lip of the sink. "I'm a favor for you to hold over my family, not an invited visitor."

Allowing her to think she was nothing more than a means to get into her family's good graces would be the wisest course of action. However, the misconception reflected badly on them both. On him because she believed he was using her situation for his gain. On her because she'd reduced the value of her safety to what her family could provide him in return. Both were lies he was unwilling to allow her to believe.

Ryan straightened and grasped her chin between his fingers. He leaned close enough to see the flecks of gold and dark amber in her irises. If he shifted his touch, he could discover if her full lips were as soft as they looked. A dangerous urge. "Once again, you're making me wonder why you care. But to clarify, you aren't a means to more power for me. You aren't here because I'm playing some dominance game. You're here because your safety matters. You matter. And no one is going to hunt you. Understand?"

"Y-yes," she whispered, her eyes luminous.

Ryan dropped his hand. "Good." He set his teacup and plate into the sink. "Come on, we'll go over what you wanted to know last night before I leave for the day. Evie and Ava have said they'll come over around lunch."

"I don't need a keeper," she groused.

"They insisted, I don't argue with them." Managed to be a complete waste of time when he tried anyway. Being well into their sixties, the twins had mastered the art of manipulation.

In his bedroom, he stopped at his dresser. Worry

gnawed at him and tightened his gut. He didn't want to share the information with her. Didn't want to put her further in jeopardy with more knowledge. However, data without proper understanding could indeed be dangerous, and she'd come in here while he was gone and try to figure things out on her own.

"I won't be able to answer all your questions, but I'll answer what I can."

"Can you wait? Just a second?" she asked, her expression bright with excitement.

"Wh—"

"I'll be right back. Just give me a minute!" she shouted over her shoulder, racing from the room, her dark curls bouncing along her back.

Ryan released a puff of air and looked over the countless notes he'd pinned and clipped to canvas an entire wall. A map on the right side of his room had colorful threads pinned from Sziveria that led to other nations in the known inhabited world.

Delanee rushed back in, a notebook and pen clutched in her hand. He quirked a smile. Always the journalist. Ryan really hoped he wasn't making a huge mistake.

"All right," she huffed, tucking an errant curl behind her ear. "I'm ready." She waved her hand in an elegant roll. "Proceed."

Ryan moved to the start of the gathered materials. "Primary Guardian Wintersfall created this timeline for me over three years ago, in 835. He started at the first event he knew about, Katria Nachemir's family being assassinated in 832. I added another event I knew about, which also occurred in 832. Then, in 836, we learned of an additional event in 832."

She scribbled. "So, 832 is definitely a point of origin for...."

Ryan swallowed back distaste. "The V Alliance." He loathed saying their name.

"Who are they?"

"Not sure, but I'll get to more on them in a minute." He touched the timeline. "In 832, this is what we're aware happened. Chances are high there are other victims, other situations we won't learn about until all the truth is uncovered. Alexandrov Nachemir, a known Gen-Heir assassin, is targeted by an assassin. They killed his wife and his youngest daughter. His eldest daughter, his genetic heir, agrees to come work for the FIO. In the spring of 832, a rapid acting form of Human Rabies Syndrome is introduced via an addictive powder. The culprit was discovered to be the former Sheild Guardian Levkaseon, who was after the arch guardianship of Terravine. The situation was contained, but the non-infectious form of magic lily dust has continued to plague our country."

"How would introducing a rapid onset version of HRS lead to a shield guardian taking over an arch guardian's rank?" she asked, the pen cocked in her hand.

"Because he thought he could make it seem like Arch Guardian Terravine wasn't doing her job. He ran into trouble when his daughter, an honest woman, discovered and promptly foiled his plan."

Delanee blew out a long breath. "How did you keep that secret?"

"We didn't necessarily. The Levkaseon rank had to go before the Endowment and Revocation Council, where the rank changed hands due to the scandal. That the former shield guardian was after the arch guardianship didn't need to be mentioned; he'd done enough to tarnish the family name by releasing HRS." Ryan slid his finger down the line. "835, Jonathon Hunter investigates the Nachemir murders. He learns Katria was meant to be the only survivor, and whoever committed the crime wanted her because of her talent, to separate her from the ones she loves."

Delanee's gaze narrowed. "But you made it to her first."

Ryan inclined his head.

"Did you know? All the time, did you know?"

"I knew about her, and I knew someone had approached another genetic heir for sharpshooting. It was sheer luck I beat them to her," Ryan admitted. "And I had no idea who we were dealing with. No one did." He tapped his finger under the year. "During the same time in 835, Primary Guardian Wystone is murdered after he reveals to Wintersfall someone is forging manifests. Master Guardian Raiventon then learns his wife—"

"Who is the daughter of your boss," Delanee cut in.

"Yes, Arch Guardian Synintel's daughter was being used to alter goods manifests. Shield Guardian Enbrackon was behind the ruse. He lost his ranking over the deceptions." Ryan let out a long exhale. "We learned most of the falsified goods were coming from either Westica or New Columbia, with a few others scattered globally, but the bulk were to and from these two nations."

Delanee's jaw clenched. "And that's when Cora went to Westica."

"Yes. She went to learn what was being stolen from Westica, to where and how they managed to move so much product without the knowledge of the local government. And that's where she learned about the name of the V Alliance. The group in charge of everything."

"Primary Guardian Kynhaven returned from Westica with a wife," Delanee said. "He asked me to be the personal reporter for the events introducing her. Was she part of the V Alliance, and she turned?"

"No," Ryan sighed. "No. She was a victim, like Cora. We learned her father is Arch Guardian Praekasdeon. He was coerced into forging prisoner transfers after Jessalyn was kidnapped and presumed dead in," he tapped the time-line, "832. When he refused, they kidnapped his wife, brought her to Sziveria, and threatened her in front of him. He submitted, took his wife, and disappeared into the Northern Boundary."

"But he still did the prisoner transfers?"

"Yes. For years."

She stared at him, incredulous. "And no one noticed? How is that even possible?"

"Our maximum-security prisons are shrouded in ice for nine months a year. No one south of the Tabrias goes there and does a prisoner inventory. We trust the prison keepers that their population is what they say it is."

"Fair enough," she blew out.

"In 836, Sylphine Seartavos—"

"The Italyssian shipping heiress?"

"Yes," Ryan smiled. "I believe you wrote an article about her while she was in Haven City."

A flush darkened her cheeks. "I wrote several. She did contract with Key Guardian Asherwick in the fall of eight hundred thirty-six."

"Yes, she did. One of the reasons for that contract needing to be fulfilled was the owner of Cyrano Shipping hoped to marry Sylphine and gain access to her father's trade empire. Leone Cyrano was the main person respon-sible for the human trafficking we experienced for several years."

Her pen scratched on the paper. "And that's been stopped? The trafficking?"

"It'll never be completely stopped, but we know what to look for now, and Leone Cyrano was taken into custody in Italyssa in the spring of 837." Ryan moved down the dresser to point to a new area on the timeline. "Also, in the fall of 836, Lucianna Castien was kidnapped after her mother and young brother were murdered. The family was out picnicking in a park."

"These people are horrible," Delanee said, anger burning in her eyes. "I hope you find him, Ryan."

"I will," he stated, trying to ignore the funny sensation in the pit of his stomach at hearing his name from her lips again. He moved on to the next event. "Vayden and Melody Dossett rescued her and dozens of other children, mostly kidnapped from—"

"Orphanages."

Right. Delanee was working on a story about the orphanages. She'd been interviewing a former resident of an orphanage when she learned the identity of the assassin. "As you already know, I sent your brother and his team to Mark Inland to help recover those who hadn't been rescued before the ship departed in the spring of last year."

"And they were successful."

"Yes. The bulk of the passengers weren't from Sziveria as we'd originally thought, but New Columbia."

She pointed the pen. "Which is where Deklan's wife Cia went, right?"

"Yes, and also discovered where many of the escaped prisoners had gone."

"What is New Columbia's stake in all this?" she asked, glancing down at her notes.

Ryan looked at his watch and winced. On a normal day, he was already in his office. "I'm not sure they have one. But I can't answer any more questions right now."

She laughed. "Is that your line to all the journalists?"

"I don't speak to any other journalists. My routine is off today, which is abnormal. I don't need anyone keeping a close eye on me to suspect anything."

She puffed out her cheeks and blew. "That's fair. So, I can ask questions when you get home?"

Home. He liked believing she'd already become

comfortable enough under his roof to consider the dwelling hers. Which was ridiculous. Hadn't he learned a harsh enough lesson with Inara's mother? Giving an internal shake, he grabbed his ivy cap from a peg near the door to the greenhouse. He had several in various colors.

Slapping on the hat with one hand, he grabbed a navy, cream, and sage green scarf from another peg. "Sure. I'll answer what I'm able."

She looked over the timeline, and he could see her mind working and formulating. He wondered what her thoughts were. Perhaps he'd have some questions of his own tonight.

"Let me cover this story," she whispered, facing him.

"Excuse me?"

"When it breaks, and it will, and the people have a right to know, let me be the one to cover it."

"That's not up to me," he said quickly.

She scoffed and waved a hand. "That's a lie. It's entirely up to you."

"I really do work for Arch Guardian Synintel."

She stared at him.

"I do!"

"Then ask him on my behalf. Or I will. It's not like I can't get access to him."

Ryan shook his head. "A story of this magnitude won't be up to him, either."

"Then who?" She laughed and glanced at the wall again. "Queen-Elect Arnita?"

Now Ryan did the staring.

Delanee's eyelashes fluttered. "You're kidding."

"No."

"The queen-elect?" she breathed, pressing a hand to her stomach. "I'd... have a story approved by the queen-elect?" She covered her mouth with a trembling hand. "Mr. Levin would have to run my story then. He wouldn't be able to say— it wouldn't matter what he thought. I'd have a story approved by Queen-Elect Arnita." Her attention swung back to him. "Ryan, please let me do this. *Please*."

Her pleading reached deep into Ryan and wrenched something free. He *wanted* to be her hero. Someone she didn't need more of in her life. Heroes surrounded Delanee. Her father. Her brothers. But they didn't currently have the means to help her achieve her dream of leaving the social pages behind. He could do that for her, and how badly he wanted to shocked him.

"If I agree," he said slowly, "you may be stuck with me—"

"Deal." No hesitation. She didn't even let him finish, just held out her hand, her gaze wide and expectant. "I'll stay here for as long as I need to. I'll follow whatever rules you lay out. I'll obey whatever orders you give while on our pursuit of the truth."

"It's going to be—"

"Dangerous. I know." She thrust her hand further toward him.

Ryan slid his fingers along her smaller, softer ones. The electric spark he couldn't contain around her crackled between their palms. She gasped but didn't break contact as he closed his hand around hers. He wanted to pull her into his chest, discover how she'd fit against him. If her curves were soft or perhaps firmer. She looked athletic and lithe, though he had no doubt all the parts he loved to explore on a woman would still entice him on her.

His gaze dipped to her chest, to the gentle swell of her pert breasts. Her nipples were large, erect, and outlined through the dark orange fabric. Touching her would be as simple as sliding his hand underneath. Would she let him? Ryan tore his attention away and to the evidence wall.

"This is a bad idea," he muttered more to himself than to her.

She yanked her hand from his. "I won't compromise anything, I swear."

No, but he worried he'd compromise *her*. The inexperience she displayed at his obvious slip ogling her chest had him wanting to rake a hand down his face. If he needed any indication of her innocence, he'd just been handed proof. He wanted to ask because he knew she'd been courted. However, the sharing of personal information could be dangerous. Could lead to an intimacy he wasn't ready for yet, and may never be again. Best to keep things professional.

Impersonal.

He refused to reflect on why that disappointed him when he only should have felt relief.

Four

Delanee stared at the chart next to the map on Ryan's bedroom wall. He had a comprehensive list of genetic traits, categorized by class, and then listed in subclasses beneath. Most Sziverians knew about the different types of genetic inheritances, but she'd never seen them in a clear and concise table like the one he'd created. Some of the talents he had listed she'd never even heard of and wasn't sure they existed. Perhaps at one time? Or maybe among the kidnapped victims, or transferred prisoners, someone had displayed such a talent? Delanee made a note. That theory made sense to her, but she'd ask him all the same.

Her gaze kept skittering to the beast master trait, a category listed under touch-based. Beneath the talent were all the known beasts with which a master could potentially bond. Two were written. A wolf and a falcon were the two known animals her family had revealed, though a wolf had already been known. Her older brother Dominik's ability to pair with a falcon and his promise to serve Sziveria had led to a new ranked guardian position. Master Guardian Scythian. If only they knew about the others....

Ruthenia kept her secrets close, and all the missing

animals for the beast master talent were a glaring omission Delanee had the crazy urge to remedy. She wanted to tack a piece of paper underneath with an updated list, but to do so would lead to questions she wouldn't answer—ever.

Moving on, she shifted to the map, noting the colors of thread, some with multiple lines running to the same country. Westica had five colored threads alone. New Columbia also had five, while Ravenna had two. Others were a single color or two. Delanee made another note. Whatever his color coding, he'd left the key for what the colors meant off or in another location. She assumed they had to do with imported or exported goods, perhaps both.

Excitement thrummed through her as she explored all the evidence he'd amassed. She found a few consistencies with her research into the orphanages, making additional notes on those because she was determined to finish the story. Even if her editor rejected her work. Again. Knowing he wouldn't, couldn't, reject the story she'd get to write for Ryan had her being extra diligent in her questions and what she needed to research. She couldn't make a mistake with this opportunity.

"I'm not saying it was nasty, but—" an elderly female voice floated past the glass door to the greenhouse.

Delanee leaned over and looked through the glass. Evie, or was she Ava? One of the women carried a happy Inara while the other followed. Seeing the beautiful infant caused an odd fist to tighten in her chest. Delanee pressed a hand over her heart and rubbed.

"If you aren't saying it, why are you implying it?" Evie — or Ava —said.

"I'm not rude. I'm not going to say you can't cook."

"I cook just as well as you do!"

Ava –or Evie –nodded. "Exactly."

The one not holding the baby disappeared from Delanee's sight. "So, you're insulting yourself, then?"

The voices were inside now. Delanee squeezed her notebook in both hands.

"I wasn't insulting at all. You simply took my comments that way. Not my fault you have thin skin." The cadence of their voices was the exact same. If Delanee hadn't known there were two of them, she'd have believed a woman was carrying a conversation with herself.

Their disapproval of her residing with Ryan hadn't been lost on her last night. Would they express that same censure this afternoon? Not that Delanee really cared, she had more than a few skills in dealing with overbearing opinions. She had ten siblings, a matriarch grandmother who delighted in meddling, and an editor who'd never been concerned over feelings.

"Where is that girl? Do you remember her name? I know Ryan told you."

A loud sniff echoed along with their words. "I think *that girl* works just fine. She won't stay around long enough for us to worry about her name."

"I am not referring to her as such. It's rude."

"Oh, so you don't care about being rude to her, a complete stranger, but your sister—"

"I wasn't rude to you."

Delanee took a step, intent on marching right into the kitchen and introducing herself. Then she realized where she'd be coming from. Dressed in *his* clothes. Stomping her foot, she cursed under her breath. Multiple times. Attempting to sneak around would make the situation worse if she were caught. She considered her options, glancing around the room.

If she grabbed a few of Inara's toys from the crib, she could claim she'd seen the women in the greenhouse and wanted to help, making sure the baby was entertained. Always important. Or, or... Delanee clicked her teeth together. Or she could return to her research and be caught *in* the room, with no mistake for the reason why.

Then again, what did she have to hide? Nothing. She knew the truth of the reason why she was in the room, and so did Ryan. If the two old biddies voiced their disapproval and wrong assumptions, why should she care? Lifting her chin up, Delanee marched down the long corridor to the kitchen archway.

"Oh, there you are, girl," one of the twins said, unpacking a burlap grocery bag on the counter.

"Good afternoon, dear," the other said, a warm smile on her face. She bounced Inara on her hip, her hand caught by the baby's tiny fingers holding tight. Her watery dark brown eyes looked over Delanee. Silver eyebrows shot upward. "I guess Ryan changed his mind about providing only protection."

A sniff left the twin putting away groceries. "I knew it. Didn't I tell you he was a hussy magnet, that one? Can't seem to find the good ones."

The twins' sole focus shifted to Delanee.

Delanee blinked and looked between them. They both wore bright yellow, blue, and white plaid dresses with a blinding pink scarf around their neck. Both had silver braids wound into tight knots at the base of their necks. Pink slippers graced both their feet. With faces containing the same expressions, Delanee wanted to slowly ease away. Her family had two sets of twins, and neither was identical. This odd same-person situation was a little freaky.

"I'm Delanee Ralston," she said. "And my grandmother would be appalled to learn I'm considered some sort of hussy. I recommend you keep that to yourself."

"We never go anywhere," the twin holding Inara said.

"Did your grandmother raise you?" the other asked.

"No, I live with her, though. It was Ryan's idea to bring me here, to keep her and the rest of my family safe."

"How lovely." The older woman set a jar of cinnamon apples off to the side. "Well, I suppose since you'll be around for at least today, you should know our names. I'm Evalyn or Evie."

The other twin lifted her hand. "And I'm Ava."

Evie snapped her fingers. "Wait, I'm sorry, I was wrong. *I'm* Ava."

"Ha!" the other twin smirked. "Yes, and I'm Evalyn. I prefer Evie."

Delanee sighed, looking between their confident smirks again. "Fine. That's fine. I'll just call you both Evie Ava."

"Why does Evie get to be first?"

"You twit, now she knows you're actually Ava." Evie glared. She shook her head while folding the empty bag. "Never mind, doesn't matter. The second she turns her back, she'll forget which of us is which."

"Aren't you two a little old to be playing childish games?" Delanee asked, exasperated.

"Old?" Ava barked.

"Childish?" Evie snapped.

Delanee wanted to smack her forehead. She'd tried polite. They'd thrown that in her face. She'd tried to be the adult in the room. Their offense seemed to have reached new heights. Fine. If they *wanted* to play games, Delanee would play.

She arched a brow and looked them both over. "I mean, who picks out your clothes for you? Because I know two mature women did not choose to wear dresses made for teenagers to wear on park walks. Or maybe you haven't been shopping since seven-eighty?"

Ava's head snapped back as if she'd been slapped.

Evie glared. "Just how old do you think we are, girl?"

Delanee tapped her finger on her chin in thought. Part of her job requirement was to keep up-to-date on the latest fashion trends, as well as those in the past. After all, mocking someone for committing a fashion mistake only held weight if she knew what she was talking about. Thankfully, the charms in the mile-high hair phase were giving way to the more modest and elegant long curls held back from the face by ornamental clips. Now, just *how* ornamental was up to the wearer. Delanee had commented on several clips that looked more like sculptures than accessories. As for clothing....

"The last decade for plaid fashion was around seven-seventy-five. However, the trend continued for walking dresses and men's vests, finally dying a not-so-quiet death around seven-eighty-five, when the more subtle pinstripes came into fashion. Today, we still accept very thin pinstripes and florals on our clothing. Plaid has been completely phased out, and with no return in sight, for which all of us fashion-forward women are most thankful.

"So, either the dresses were purchased prior to seven-seventy-five, which makes you quite old, or you purchased them nearer the end of their fashionable period when they would have been a bit more prevalent and cheaper in the seven-eighties. Which is it? Really old, really cheap, or behind on the times?" she asked, eyes wide and curious.

"Oh, my stars, she's *that* D. Ralston, Eves," Ava gasped.

Evie glared. "*What* are you talking about?"

Ava handed Inara across the counter. "Here, take her."

Inara's pudgy little legs kicked over the top of the counter. Gurgles left her as she gnawed on her fist, drool soaking the bib fastened to her neck. Evie settled the infant on her hip, swaying back and forth in a gentle rocking motion. Ava left the room faster than Delanee figured a woman her age could move. Though really, she shouldn't be so surprised. Her grandmother could keep up with the toddler in the family.

Ava returned to the kitchen, waving a newspaper.

"*Haven City Chronicle*. I knew Ryan would have it. He always has the latest edition delivered on publication days."

He did, did he? Delanee kept her expression neutral. Since he worked in intelligence, wanting to know what the news sources were reporting on wasn't so odd. And everyone knew the *The Havener* only printed gossip and sensationalist pieces. If you wanted respectful and authentic journalism, you read *The Haven City Chronicle*. Delanee couldn't help but straighten her shoulders in pride.

Ava set the news on the huge counter and quickly turned to the social section. She stabbed her finger at the delicate paper. "See! Right there. D. Ralston. You're her, aren't you? The person who writes these articles?"

"I am," Delanee confirmed.

Ava fussed with the bright pink scarf around her neck, her cheeks turning a comparable shade.

Evie scoffed. "Oh please, like she cares what we're wearing. It's not like she will write about two shut-ins on Hawkins Street South, Ava."

"Ba, ah, ah!" Inara shouted and blew her lips together.

"That's right," Evie cooed. "Silly, silly Aunty Ava."

"We aren't shut-ins," Ava retorted, snatching off the scarf. "We go to the store weekly."

"And speak to exactly no one," Evie said.

"I speak to you, harpy," Ava snapped, then gave a curt nod. "And we go, we don't have a delivery made or ask Ryan to get things for us. We leave our house. That counts. We aren't reclusive."

Evie rolled her eyes. "Well, our fashion sense is certainly of no concern to a high-society tart, now, is it?"

"Okay, you two enjoy your afternoon. I will be in Ryan's office if you have any need of me that doesn't include insulting or belittling." Delanee waved and gripped her notebook a bit too tight in her other hand.

"And this is why no one talks to us!" Probably Ava said, her words echoing through the living room.

"Oh please, you aren't exactly a piece of candy. You put on the same dress and said the same rude words. Don't be a pretender. It makes your face extra wrinkly."

"Oooh, who are you calling wrinkly, you old hag!"

Delanee sighed, easing the door to the office until it was open a crack, enough for her to keep a partial ear on the sounds of the house. Two bickering old women didn't interest her, not when much more fascinating information awaited her research.

Light streamed in through floor-to-ceiling windows set between bookcases. Every wall in the room was lined with shelves. A door to the right drew her attention, and she investigated. A quick self-tour revealed a laundry room and a bathroom that connected with what appeared to be an unused nursery. Made sense. Inara was still too small to be on her own. What would the single father do when his daughter was old enough to be across the house? Safety gate everything, she figured, unable to stop a smile. She still couldn't believe the far too serious man had a child.

Back in the office, she set her notebook on the organized desk. Everything was arranged perfectly, right down to the two pens and three pencils lined up beside the writing mat. Delanee had the ridiculous urge to mess up the surface. Her own workspace, the dining room table since she and her grandmother took their meals at the kitchen bar or breakfast table, was a disheveled, chaotic mess of papers, books, newsprint, and writing utensils. All she had to do was reach if she ever needed something, be it research or a highlighter.

Hands on her hips, she wandered the bookshelves. He must have kept his family's collection from the other houses. Only a few of the shelves weren't filled with tomes. Some weren't even in a language she recognized. Could he read them, she wondered, plucking one free and opening the cover. The text was beautiful, almost picture-like with lines and curves and dots. She returned the volume back to the slot and searched the others. A few caught her attention as useful in her research and she pulled them free, a sliver of excitement tickling in her belly. Ryan had his own library. How marvelous.

The familiar rush of a story taking shape had Delanee hurrying back to the desk. Already, her mind swirled with hooks to begin her article and draw the reader into a journey of intrigue, good versus evil, and the eventual moment of reckoning, which she'd possibly be present to witness firsthand. Mr. Levin could choke on his previous rejections of her work. And if he denied her this story, despite the queen-elect's approval, she'd... well, Delanee didn't know what she would do.

The orphanage editorial was supposed to be her big break. The story, no matter what Curtis felt about her personally, he'd not be able to ignore once she placed it on his desk. She'd been working on the piece for over a year, gathering evidence, conducting interviews, and researching the history of the buildings and those who'd run them. Having learned someone was treating Sziveria's children as nothing more than commodities to be bartered had angered her into action. Every child was precious, and a nation unaware could never fix what was so clearly broken. If the youth relegated to a community house were cared for by the community around them, perhaps their fate would be different. They would be more than a future forgotten. The story wouldn't go to waste, but she figured their misfortune would have more impact when told with everything else. An opportunity she now had and would not waste.

Delanee opened every drawer in Ryan's desk, finding paper, more pens, some wax highlighters, and even a few crayons. She pulled out everything she'd need and placed it within easy reach. For hours, she organized her thoughts and wrote notes to slide into the books she wanted to research until her stomach growled in protest. The house was quiet, making her wonder if the twins had returned home. She rose and stretched her aching back and shoulders.

The plush runner kept her footsteps silent as she stepped from the room. A quick peek through the archway into the living room revealed the reason for the silence. Both women were passed out on the couches. Inara rested on Evie's or Ava's chest. Evie hadn't been joking, Delanee had no clue who they were. Both had kicked off their shoes and hung their scarves on pegs near the greenhouse door. A collapsible playpen was set up by the windows over the softest pink rug Delanee had ever seen. Wooden enrichment toys and stuffed animals were scattered in every direction. Some in the play area, some on the living room table, some on the floor between the table and the couches. A chest she hadn't noticed last night was open near a shelving unit by the fireplace. The space under the shelves was just the right size for the chest to slide into position.

Delanee tiptoed to the kitchen, wishing there were doors instead of archways from the living room. If she woke either of those women or the baby.... She shuddered at the thought of what they'd say. How did Ryan tolerate their constant wagging tongues? Then again, what choice did he have? They cared deeply for the infant, that much she couldn't deny. Delanee supposed if the welfare of her child rested on someone else, she'd tolerate quite a lot, too.

In the kitchen, she carefully searched all the cupboards, learning the layout of where he kept things. When she didn't find any food items, she went searching and discovered a pantry the size of her bedroom off the corridor to his room. He used the space for more than food. Unmarked boxes made her fingers twitch to explore. She tapped on the lid of one and bit her lip.

To look or not?

The investigative journalist in her chimed in a with a big *yes, look, look, look*! The rational, honest side of her argued Ryan would be more than angry if he caught her going through his private things. Yet, how private were they being stored in the pantry? One little peek under one lid wouldn't hurt— *No*! She fisted her hands. She needed to be honorable if she wanted him to trust her with information. Sneaking around his house and prying into his personal life wouldn't accomplish that. Spinning around, she resisted the urge and searched for something to eat in the dim space.

A jar of vegetable soup caught her attention. She snagged the glass container and shook the contents on the way back to the kitchen. Cold soup would have to do. She didn't want to make the noise gathering a pan and heating the stove would create. Grabbing a spoon and a lid opener, she headed outside. Gray stone and the same style of pillars from out front that were lamps since they had no roof to support created a beautiful patio space. She imagined the space was stunning at night, with all the lamps burning.

Rock footpaths branched from the porch through thick ferns and dwarf fruit trees. Delanee followed one and discovered they all led to the same place, the lap pool Ryan had told her about. A narrow stretch of crystal-clear water flowed from a small burbling waterfall. Tendrils of steam disappeared into the already humid air. She leaned down and tested the pool. Heat enveloped her fingers, and she groaned. To be immersed in that and never get cold? Paradise.

Rolling up her pant legs to her thighs, she sat with her butt on the edge and kicked her feet into the water. She looked at her jar and wondered how long it'd take to warm the contents if she set the soup on the narrow ledge running the edge of the pool. Shrugging, she placed the jar on the ledge, leaned back, and looked up. The sun sparkled through the canopy covered by glass. Nothing obstructed the rays. Not green algae or built-up grime. Even here, in this outdoor space, Ryan kept everything immaculate.

Delanee sighed and lay down, resting her hands on her stomach. Did he have such control over everything? No, she figured not since he'd had a baby outside of a marriage contract. *Something* had gone out of his control. Terribly, from his reaction when she had asked if he had a wife. What must that have been like for him, a man who kept everything in a state of tidy perfection, to have failed?

The sun slid a lazy path across the sky, and Delanee found the peaceful space lulling her into sleep. Warm water lapped at her knees and cocooned her lower legs. The gentle heat of the afternoon seeped up from the stones beneath her. Her rumbly stomach and warming lunch were forgotten, and her eyes fluttered shut.

"Delanee."

Her name spoken low, and a gentle shake, roused her. Blinking, she stared into pale irises that competed to be classified as silver or blue. Delanee had never seen eyes like Ryan's before, and they never failed to make flutters tease her stomach. She wanted to touch him.

"Are you okay?" he whispered, leaning closer.

Grogginess made her slow to process his question. She reached up out of habit and grazed her face, finding a cooling trail of drool running from the corner of her mouth to her chin. Gasping, she launched herself upward, almost slamming into Ryan's face, not caring because, gross, she was *drooling* everywhere. A million needles suddenly prickled into her feet, and she twisted to try to grab at one, only to remember too late that she wasn't lying on a flat surface. The awkward jerk upward and attempt to grab her limb sent her teetering into the pool.

Warm water enveloped her, closing around her head, shoving up her nose, and filling her mouth. The pain in her feet competed with the sting up her nose, and she flailed. Her head broke the surface long enough for her to choke, gasp, and gag.

"Stand up!" Ryan shouted.

"I—" Water swirled over her head, and Delanee tried to reach for anything to grab onto, but she only encountered more water. The pool, which had seemed small, now felt like an ocean.

Strong arms banded around her chest and hauled her upward. Solid muscle slammed into her back. She grabbed his forearm and held on tight, her nails catching on his skin. Water sluiced over her face and down her shoulders. She coughed and gulped in the air.

"I've got you," he whispered, moving them in slow inches toward the other end of the pool. "Relax."

A tremor raced through her body. Blood continued to rush to her lower legs, now throbbing. She still couldn't move her toes. "I c-can't feel m-my feet," she managed to get out through her trembling.

"All right, it's okay," he said evenly. "Just hold on."

He was the epitome of calm. Controlled. Delanee didn't know whether to be grateful or annoyed. Did nothing break his composure? Then he sat on the wide stairs leading into the pool and situated her on his lap, and *her* composure almost had a meltdown. She didn't know what to do. A handful of times, she'd leaned close enough to a man for him to kiss her. Well, attempt to kiss her. Delanee wasn't sure if she could quantify the timid press of lips she'd experienced as actual kisses. How more than one man could be so awful at kissing was beyond her.

But this, sitting on his lap, her shoulder pressed to his chest, the solid muscle of his thighs beneath her butt, his hands... she squeezed her eyes closed and tried not to hyperventilate. His hands were touching the bare skin of her waist beneath the water. No other male, except her family, had ever been so close to her. Had touched her bare skin.

His breath teased across her cheek, a little rushed. She still clutched at his forearm, and she couldn't make herself release her hold. Turning her head, she looked him over. A mistake. Water spiked his dark lashes and pale hair. Droplets chased each other down the perfect planes of his cheeks, where a faint stubble grew. Also dark. How interesting. Delanee couldn't help herself. She reached up and traced a finger along the coarse texture across his jaw.

"Do you grow a black beard?" she asked, whispering.

He blinked at her. More beads trickled down his nose and temples. "It's more a golden brown."

"But darker than your hair?"

"Yes." His fingers tightened on her waist. Little prickles of awareness tingled across her skin. "My pale hair is an odd anomaly."

Which meant what? His hair wasn't so pale anywhere else? The instant the thought entered her mind, heat flamed across her cheeks, and she tore her gaze away.

"Are you having naughty thoughts, Miss Ralston?" he whispered into her ear. A shiver raced up her spine.

"N-no."

"How disappointing," he muttered.

Or at least, that's what she thought he muttered. When she snapped her gaze back to him, he no longer focused on her but rather down the length of the pool. Frustration clenched in her gut, and she refused to examine why. Instead, she once again reminded herself any attraction toward this man was *not* in her best interest. Or his. She wiggled her toes, grimacing.

"I can sort of feel my feet again," she said.

"Can you stand? The entire pool is five and a half feet deep. You'll be able to without any issues."

Yes, she would. Both her parents had gifted her with tall genes. Twisting on his lap, she touched a prickling toe to the textured tile bottom. She wobbled, but Ryan's hold on her waist remained. He supported her effort, gliding her through the water to stand between his knees at the bottom of the steps. Uncertain of her footing and not wanting to sink under again, Delanee grasped at his forearms. She was able to get her first good look at him and wondered if she looked as pitiful.

He'd kicked his shoes off before jumping in to rescue her, but that was all. The fabric of his blue shirt plastered to his thick shoulders and upper chest. Delanee couldn't help but trace the contours revealed with her eyes. The water seemed to gently sway her closer until, without thought, her hands eased up to grip his shoulders. Water lapped between them, a quiet buffer she had the urge to eliminate.

"Bad idea," Ryan whispered.

"How do you always know what I'm thinking?" she asked quietly.

"I already answered that a long time ago."

"Remind me."

His focus shifted to her mouth, and Delanee's heart almost pounded free of her chest. Why, oh why, did she want to know his kiss with such desperation? Really, the need to experience his lips on hers bordered on the ridiculous.

The subtle graze of his fingers along her jaw made her gasp. His eyes remained fixed on her mouth. "Your thoughts are obvious by your expressions."

Curious, she raised a brow and inched closer. "And what was my expression?"

"The same one you have now, telling me you want *this*."

And then he kissed her.

FIVE

BAD IDEA. Bad, bad idea. Ryan brushed his lips over Delanee's in a soft, pulling kiss, testing her reaction. Gauging his. The gentle flutter of her breath skated across his mouth in a rapid gasp and an excited exhale. He should stop. One simple kiss was enough. He didn't need to compound the situation by succumbing to the urge to taste her.

Except... the too-big shirt she wore floated around her body, revealing tantalizing glimpses of the flat stomach, rounded hips, and tea-with-cream skin he'd had his hands on moments before. The water catching the fabric and sending it drifting up further to expose more taunted his fingers and tempted him to forget he'd sworn off intimacy. Of any kind. Including kisses.

Worse, he had no one to rescue him from the temptation. When he'd found Delanee sleeping, he'd sent the twins with his daughter back to their place. No one would interrupt his aquatic misbehavior.

The golden light filling the greenhouse glimmered off the water and cast long shadows between the trees. Darkness would soon fall, a reminder of his plan when he'd awoken her—a plan that did not involve seduction.

Her mouth pressed to his again, an uncertain exploration that had his eyes sliding closed. Oh, sweet summer sun, the inexperience in her kiss should have been enough to launch him from the pool and far away from her. Innocence hadn't been Ryan's to claim in so long he'd almost forgotten what it felt like. The curious slide of her mouth across his, the hesitant probe of her tongue along his bottom lip, undid any rational thought he may have managed to grasp.

Ryan *wanted* to be Delanee's first real hint of passion because he knew, without a doubt, no one had kissed her properly. No one caused a burn to ignite, so deep within, she'd do almost anything to discover what came next. Ryan should not be that man. But his mouth opened, and her tongue eased inside, and he groaned at the sensation.

Careful not to spook her, Ryan slid a hand along the small of her back and floated her closer. Her feet lifted from the bottom of the pool, her weightless form bumping into his as he eased from the stairs. In a semi-crouch, he encouraged her to alleviate the remaining distance between them. Her knees moved to cage his sides while her arms wrapped around his shoulders. Warm water swept her hair along his neck, and wet, the length was much longer than he realized. Falling midway down her back, the curls flowed in graceful strands around him.

Ryan took over the kiss, needing more than she knew how to give. His mouth slanted over hers. His tongue plundered and explored. Tasted and experienced. She clung to him, her nails biting into his back the way they'd dug into his forearms, but for a different reason entirely. Desire flared hot and hard through his entire body.

Back off. His inner voice of reason whispered through his mind. She was too inexperienced to understand where this could lead. Her tongue danced with his, her body pressed closer, mashing her breasts to his chest. The hard points of her nipples tempted him and made him want to taste her in a new, exciting way. Made him want to caress and discover what sounds she'd make when he touched her just right.

Back off!

Ryan yanked his mouth from hers. His breath heaved. She continued to cling to him but leaned away, her beautiful golden eyes vivid in the dying light. Her desire left the irises little more than rings of gold around black. The gilded light honeyed her skin, and the aroused flush of her cheeks made her seem so very vital.

Beautiful.

Pure.

Swallowing against the urge to slam his mouth back on hers, he gently eased her from his frame. "We should get out and dry off. I want to take you to your apartment once the sun sets."

She floated away, reaching for the nearest edge. She made several failed attempts before finally catching hold and clinging. He missed her nearness and ignored the absurd sensation.

His eyes narrowed. "Can you swim?"

"I never learned, no," she said, breathless.

"You really can set your feet down."

"So, we're just going to pretend this didn't happen?" she asked, the quiet words stopping him mid-turn to climb from the pool.

"No point in discussing something that won't happen again," he said. Harsh, but the truth.

"I agree," she said, surprising him.

"Then why did you kiss me?"

Her chin rose. "You kissed me first."

"And you're the one who stuck your tongue in my mouth."

The pink deepened across her cheeks, and a brighter fire ignited in her eyes. Ryan's pulse kicked back into an excited thrum. He didn't think he'd ever seen a woman more gorgeous. Hair in damp curls around her face, skin dewy from the moisture rising from the warmth of the water, color high, and an honesty in her gaze so many in his circles lacked. She was annoyed and not afraid to let him know. She never had been. Her authenticity was dangerous to him, for her integrity made her all the more attractive.

"So, I did." She glared. "And as you said, it won't be happening again. We both acted on impulse, and what's done is done."

Why did the words spark anger in him? He *wanted* her to keep her distance. "Good. Have we *discussed* it to your satisfaction then, Miss Ralston?"

"Yes," she snapped.

"Excellent." He turned, the water a heavy resistance against his need to escape.

Hopefully, she wouldn't notice the raging erection he'd be unable to hide when he left the pool and his clothes stuck to him like a second skin. Water slid down his frame in a rush as he took the steps out, the sudden loss of the heated pool chilling his skin.

"Whoa," Delanee said. The single word somehow managed to convey shock and reverence.

Ryan's hands fisted, and he kept walking, unsure what she'd seen to garner the reaction. The little-left-to-the-imagination condition of his clothing from the back, or something more personal to his anatomy that she'd somehow managed to see of his front. Water splashed and slopped from the pool. *Do not look*. He kept his straight march forward. With each step he took, the loose stones of the pathway crunched beneath his wet socks.

"I don't want to walk through your house soaking wet like this," she said behind him, teeth chattering.

Do *not* look. "It's not far from the door to my bathroom. I have to get you dry clothes anyway."

"The water won't ruin your carpet?" she asked, closer. A few stones kicked past him from her hurried steps.

"It'll dry."

Do not look! Though, now he'd been out long enough for his clothes to bag instead of cling. The stubborn desire he hadn't been able to shake had dissipated some in the cool air. He couldn't risk a relapse. Not with her so near. At his bedroom door, he pushed open the glass and stripped his shirt from his damp skin.

"Um, should I just wait here, or...."

Ryan finally chanced a glance over his shoulder. She stood hunched into herself, arms crossed, wet clothes more like a tent around her than anything revealing. Relief almost made him trip. "You can follow."

"All r-right."

"I'd start a fire, but since we're leaving—"

"I'm okay. Really. Thank you."

The quiet snick of the greenhouse door closing seemed loud. A final *boom* to his precarious control. They were alone in the empty house, his blood much too heated for the bed to be so close. He hurried past, refusing to look and yet unable to stop the maddeningly sensual fantasy of tumbling her onto the soft mattress. Would she let him peel the cold layers of fabric from her body and savor her chilled skin? How quickly would she combust beneath him? And would she be a quiet lover or loud? He opened and closed his hands, took centering breaths, and forced the tantalizing thoughts away. She'd never be his lover, so the internal musing was pointless.

Ryan tossed the sopping shirt and socks into his shower. He left a wet trail to his closet, closing himself in enough to kick his wet pants onto the tiled bathroom floor but not display his nudity. Naked, he squinted in the weakening light coming through the textured glass block windows that ran the entire length of his massive closet. Most of his lounge clothes were in his dresser, but a few looser bamboo blend pants he wore around the house on his days off were hanging near his work pants. He tugged a pair free, stepped into them, and pulled the drawstring tight. The soft, dry material instantly warmed his legs. He found a large, dark gray knit sweater and yanked it on over his head. He grabbed another one in pale blue for Delanee. The garment would swim on her, but at least she'd be comfortable and warm.

In the bathroom, she waited, leaning against the marble, palms braced on the ledge, her attention wandering the luxurious space. The damp clothing displayed the curves he'd hoped to avoid seeing. Long, long, slender legs, generous hips, flat stomach, small, pert breasts with large nipples, erect from the cold fabric molded around them. Her hair was a wet, curly mess around her face and shoulders. Ryan clamped down his reaction. The new pair of pants would obscure nothing.

"Here," he said, unable to hide the gruffness of his voice.

She accepted the sweater, frowning. "Do you own anything in actual colors?"

"Blue is a color."

"It's close to a shade of gray. You only wear shades of gray, pale blues, and boring beiges. Why?" She set the shirt away on the counter. "Is it to remain unmemorable?"

Ryan shrugged and slid past her, resisting the urge to reach out and touch her. Anywhere. "I'm not big on colors."

"Except in your house," she said, following him.

He glanced over her shoulder. She'd stopped at the edge

of the carpet and grabbed the doorframe. Small favors. The movement caused the wet outfit to once again billow around her. "What about my house?"

"Did you make any changes after you moved in?"

"No. I liked what the previous owners had done. Everything... worked for me." The muted, elegant colors and simple lines of all the spaces had made him fall in love with the home's nuances.

"Maybe some color variants for your clothes would work for you, too."

Ryan grabbed a pair of cotton pants from the dresser from among a stack of black and dark gray. He shifted a few plain t-shirts neatly folded nearby, all in shades of gray and subdued blues. He tried to imagine something brighter, more vivid among the stack and almost shuddered. "I'm fine with my fashion choices."

She accepted the pants. "I've never met anyone who works so hard to remain hidden."

His gaze met hers. "That's because you've never met anyone like me."

Six

The bedroom door closing was Delanee's cue to change out of the frigid clothes and into something warm and dry. Yet she found her feet glued to the tile, her eyes staring at the space Ryan had occupied. When he'd made his chilling declaration about never having met anyone like him, a warning had raced through her, a sensation she imagined prey would experience when staring at a predator. Which was absurd. Delanee came from a family of predators, could in fact be considered one herself in some circles.

The only threat he posed to her personally were her wayward desires concerning him. If she allowed, the yearning could risk the future she'd mapped out for herself with a beta male. Nothing about Ryan could, or ever would, be considered *weak*. Now, she had to reassess. A dangerous man lurked beneath the calm and controlled exterior of Ryan Voklane.

Ryan posed a mystery the journalist in her wanted to uncover, but the woman in her needed to stay far away from.

Licking her lips, she took a slow step backward and closed herself in the opulent bathroom. The simple luxury of his house appealed to her, and she hated to admit she was pleased they'd be returning. She didn't want to leave, yet another internal warning she needed to heed regarding him.

She met her reflection in the mirror. "You want a mate who won't dominate you, who won't be perceived as a threat to anyone, especially your alpha brothers, remember?" she asked herself and then waved a hand of annoyance and turned away. No, she hadn't forgotten. She just didn't know if the man she'd envisioned for herself was what she wanted anymore.

Men were the biggest obstacle to the box she'd created for her future spouse. They were... pathetic and weak to her Ruthenian half, an inferior offering for her future. Ruthenians detested weakness, so much so that until her parents had produced genetically superior children, they'd barred marriages outside of the nation. Her father had given up his country for her mother and then had shown them what they'd so casually thrown away. Ruthenia's loss had become Sziveria's gain.

However, the repulsiveness of obvious weakness remained a fixed part of her, no matter how much she longed to be attracted to a passive man. Their nervous attempts at kissing had made the act a waste of her time. Their timid attempts at groping had made her wonder how anyone could enjoy sex enough to create children, let alone risk a deadly virus for the act. She couldn't imagine having to endure sweaty palms on her skin, sloppy kisses, and what was sure to be an inadequate experience all around.

Until Ryan.

There was nothing timid, nervous, or sloppy about the way he'd kissed. He'd allowed her to be curious and had taken over to show her how aggressive pursuit could be exciting. Indulging in another round would not be a waste of time. And sex... Delanee's heart skipped, and a curious, almost pleasurable ache throbbed at her center. The sensation was new.

Peeling the sopping clothes from her body, Delanee took note of the sensitive changes. Her breasts ached. Her legs were shaky and not from the cold. An odd sense of empty need had her inner muscles clenching, which only seemed to make things worse.

Again, the investigator in her wanted to catalog the unfamiliar awareness. She'd be writing about the experience in her journal. Perhaps she'd even seek out one of her previous suitors and do a little experiment. Maybe she'd been too clinical and needed to let go, like she had with Ryan, and the encounter would be different. Yes, that's what she'd do. All was not lost.

Except, the thought of anyone else touching her made her stomach rebel. Delanee threw the wet clothes into the shower with Ryan's pants a little too hard. They landed with a solid *plop* and splash of water. Stupid, stupid kiss! Why hadn't she let well enough alone and pushed away when his lips had pressed to hers? No, she'd had to stick her tongue in his mouth and wrap around his muscular body like she had the right to be so familiar with him.

Yanking on the dry clothes, she ignored her wild, tangled curls. She didn't care about her appearance. She wasn't trying to entice him. She clenched her teeth. She. Was. Not. Determined to ignore any lingering attraction between them, Delanee stalked from the room to find him.

In the process of tying his shoes, he glanced up when she entered the living room. "The sun should have set fully by the time we arrive."

"My shoes are in my room. I'll be right back."

"And your keys," he said, standing.

She nodded. "I'll grab my bag."

"Leave the bag, it's recognizable to you," he said, crossing the room to where his scarves and hats hung.

A sense of vulnerability made her cross her arms. The assassin *had* seen her with the messenger bag. Had stared right at her while she'd hurried, packing away her notes. "All right."

"I'm not going to let anything happen to you."

A vow. One that didn't curb Delanee's attempt to see him as anything more than a guardian. She foolishly wanted the promise to be personal. Ducking into the hallway, she squeezed her eyes closed and took a moment to clear away her wayward desires. Really, the inappropriate and unwelcome fascination with him had to stop.

She toed into her shoes while digging around inside her bag. Metal jingled as she palmed the keys. Desperately, she wanted to ignore his warning about the messenger bag and sling it over her shoulder anyway. Her fist tightened over the keys, the sharp edges biting into her hand. All the research she'd be collecting to continue her work would fit inside, where it belonged. Spinning on her heel before she acted like a petulant child, Delanee left the leather satchel on the bed.

Ryan waited in the foyer, a slate gray scarf wrapped around his neck and a navy ivy cap on his head. He held another head covering, a huge, wide-brimmed hat with a crease down the crown and two dents on either side. Delanee had heard of the hats, had seen them in a museum once, and stared at them in paintings, but she'd never seen someone *holding* one.

"An actual Westican hat?" She reached for the head-wear. "Where did you get this?"

"My father wore them. He had several styles, one at least for each region of Westica."

The style had been popular over fifty years ago. Before her time, and even her parents. The expensive felting process and large surface had made it a silly choice for all but the most affluent or those who worked outdoors a lot.

Which weren't many in Sziveria. How old had his parents been?

"He enjoyed the style?" she asked, smoothing her fingers along the worn edge. A leather band braid of blue, maroon, and ochre yellow added decoration.

"It was a practical choice for him. He was an archaeologist." He motioned for her to turn. "All your hair will fit under it."

"If I wear this, everyone will notice me."

"In the shadows, you'll look like a slender man wearing an unusual hat. I don't have anything else to contain all your curls."

"I look like a man?" she asked, blinking. She knew she lacked feminine curves, but hearing him confirm her absent physique hurt. She shouldn't care. After all, she wanted him to stay far away from her. But she couldn't help the reaction.

"No," he replied. Quick, without a doubt. "You didn't hear *in the shadows*?" His fingers brushed along the curve of her jaw. "No one would mistake you for anything but a beautiful young woman up close."

Warmth blossomed through her. "I can braid my hair."

"No need. The hat will work fine." He made the turn around motion again.

Delanee obeyed, the hat clutched in one hand, keys in the other. The gentle sweep of his fingers through her wild hair caused her heart to kick. She closed her eyes. He gathered the curls together, twisted, and piled the mass atop her head.

"Hat."

Delanee held the Westican hat over her shoulder. He shoved the crown over her hair and wiggled the brim into place.

"How's that?" he asked, adjusting it a bit along the back.

Delanee reached up and patted the crown. "It's awkward."

"I'll help you avoid knocking into doorways," he said, his rare smile peeking out across his lips.

She touched the brim. "It's not that big, is it?"

"You won't be used to the size when you get in and out of the Ariot."

Right, his vehicle. Delanee released a breath.

"Ready?" he asked, keys clinking together in his pocket. "I'll keep you safe."

Her hesitation must have shown. Delanee lifted her chin and squared her shoulders. "It's my grandmother I'm concerned about."

"We'll only be in the building long enough for you to pack a bag."

"And get my research for my article."

"Yes."

"And I have to go to the paper tomorrow. I have a piece due from the Danellis party."

"Can I deliver it?" he asked, opening the door.

"Won't that defeat the purpose of no one knowing we're acquainted enough for you to be hiding me away?" she asked, stepping past into the cool evening.

"I'll use an FIO courier."

She chewed on her lip. "I guess I can write a note about why I'm not there in person."

Ryan locked up. "Will you need to make corrections?"

"No, Mr. Levin does that."

The soft lamplight on the front porch cast a warm glow over his skin. "Is that normal? An editor rewriting an article that isn't his?"

Delanee went down the stairs. "He isn't rewriting anything. He only fixes grammatical issues. If he hates the article, he'll use another written by the woman who's the backup social journalist."

"There's a backup?"

"Of course. People get sick, or...." She couldn't bring herself to finish the sentence.

"Right," he said quietly. "I don't think I've seen anyone else's work in your section, however."

Delanee beamed. "I have a high approval rating."

For the social pages, at least. If she had her way, that'd all be changing. Soon.

DELANEE SORTED through the piles of paper on the dining room table. She discarded several while adding others to a growing stack.

"How can you find anything in this mess?" Ryan asked, turning a paper front and back, looking it over.

Delanee leaned across the distance and snatched the paper from his hand, adding it to the pile. "It's my mess. Leave it alone."

"She's always been a bit chaotic," her grandmother said, handing Ryan a cup of tea.

Delanee launched herself back across the table, reaching for the steaming cup. Papers crumpled beneath her stomach and slid along the wood surface. "No, wait, *Baki*, he's—"

Madeleine chuckled. "Driving. I know, child, I'm not foolish."

Delanee sighed in relief and eased off the table. Ryan glanced at the cup and then at her, confusion beetling his brows. "She likes to add whiskey to her tea."

"Ah," Ryan said and took a test sip. "All good."

Madeleine tsked. "I said I didn't. I wasn't lying."

Delanee gave her a pointed stare. She knew her grandmother very well.

"What?" Madeleine raised a defensive hand. "I want you to arrive safely wherever you're going, and I know you can't drive. He'll be a hundred percent sober."

Delanee couldn't help but wonder what Ryan would be like, slightly inebriated. She doubted he'd ever allow himself to get completely drunk, but a little tipsy? Perhaps.

"Won't happen," he said casually, taking another sip. "Alcohol and I don't get along well."

Focusing on the papers in front of her, Delanee kept her growl internal. "I guess I need to practice schooling my features if I give my every thought away so easily."

"That'd be a shame," he whispered.

Goosebumps rose across her skin, and she slowly raised her eyes to meet his intense stare.

"Such honesty is rare in this world."

Averting her gaze, Delanee stacked several books together. If only he knew. Some things she'd become very, very good at hiding. Her immediate thoughts were proving to be a problem around him. She wasn't sure how to conceal those. And if she weren't careful, she'd reveal she had a secret. Couldn't happen.

"That's a matter of opinion, I suppose," she said airily. "I think this is all I need for my research. I'll go pack my clothes."

"Do you have a box I can put all this in for you?" he asked, setting his cup behind him on the kitchen bar.

Madeleine lifted her age-spotted hand. "I'll get one for you."

Delanee headed to her room, which was off a long hall to the left of the living room. When her parents first married, the apartment was their family home. But after Deverick and Drayke, the second set of twins, the Ralstons had officially outgrown the five-bedroom apartment. Her grandmother had kept the Haven City dwelling, and as each grandchild came of age, they'd lived here, getting used to adult life in the busy city. Unlike the others, Delanee had never desired to leave. She loved the apartment, the memories, the family history, and residing in the same space as her *bakishka*.

At least, she hadn't wanted a change in her living situation until she'd stepped foot into Ryan's home. The realization she'd soon leave all the comfort of her childhood behind for an extended period of time made her pause outside her bedroom. Why had *his* space felt so right? So familiar and secure?

A firm hand grasped her elbow and propelled her into her room. Delanee squeaked and tried to keep from tripping. Her grandmother's cool fingers dug into the tender flesh of her inner arm.

"*Baki*, what are you doing?" she asked.

Madeleine closed them in together. Her dark gray and silver-threaded hair fell in a braid over her shoulder. Despite her advanced age, her cheeks were a healthy pink, her skin still beautiful. Intelligence and a hint of annoyance glimmered in her sandy brown eyes. "That is precisely what I'm wondering, Delanee. What *are* you doing?"

"What?" she asked, confused.

A wrinkled finger pointed. "That man out there? The one who's been to this apartment a single time that I can recall is perfect for you. I told you then, and I'm telling you now, all those weaklings you keep trying to be compatible with will be epic failures compared to him."

An ache pounded behind her right eye. Delanee pressed her fingers to her forehead. "*Baki*...."

"Don't *Baki* me. You're the one who keeps dragging men home to me to sit with and endure their constant listing of all their stellar attributes. And I keep telling you sure, if you yell at them enough, they'll be what you *think* you want, only you'll end up miserable."

"I wouldn't yell at them," she grumbled. "I'd caringly suggest."

"You'd demand, Delanee," her grandmother corrected.

"You'd demand until they were crying, and you know it. That isn't a partnership."

"Women in Ruthenia—"

Madeleine slashed a hand through the air. "This isn't Ruthenia. And these men you've convinced yourself will allow you to hide, to maintain control because they are calm and non-threatening to your dominant half, will be nothing more than a glorified servant to you. Is that really what you want?"

"Yes," she hissed. "I want normal, *Baki*, I don't want —" She snapped her mouth closed.

Compassion softened her grandmother's features. She swept a cool hand across Delanee's cheek and to her jaw. "My dear girl, you will have normal as soon as you accept strength is a blessing, not a curse. In you and your future spouse. And don't lie to me and tell me you aren't attracted to him."

She pulled her jaw free and yanked the silly hat from her head. Her curls tumbled down her back and over her shoulders. "Of course, I'm attracted to him. I mean, you've seen him, he's—" She growled and then sucked air through her teeth before she said something she'd regret. "He's a single father."

Madeleine's brows rose. "Really. How old is the child?"

"A daughter. Inara. She's six months old. Just started teething." Delanee tossed the hat onto her unmade bed. "He's not interested in a relationship, and he's all wrong for me anyway, regardless of what you say."

"I can't wait to meet her."

Delanee lifted her head and stared at the ceiling. "*Baki*," she whined. "I'm serious."

"I am, too." She patted Delanee's cheek. "I will meet her. I can't wait. Now, let me go find your guardian a box."

The door opened, and Delanee fisted her hands. "He's not my guardian!"

Her grandmother's chuckle followed her out. Delanee growled.

"Who's not your guardian?"

Ryan's deep voice snapped Delanee's attention to the door. She blinked. He leaned across the jam, hands in his pockets, his wide shoulders filling the narrow space.

"You," she said before she could stop herself.

He shrugged, his gaze sliding across her room. "Technically, I'm everyone's guardian, including yours."

Delanee stilled, her attention shifting to the disaster area known as her bedroom. Clothes were strewn over every surface. The top of the long, chest-style dresser against the wall near the door was buried beneath old journals, books, beauty products, hair pins, and half-finished yarn projects. Balls of colorful thread, knitting needles, crochet hooks, and sewing circles littered her room. She had a weakness for the vibrant string and no patience to finish any of the projects she started. Dozens of them were crammed onto shelves and laid on open surfaces. A mound of sheets, pillows, and a comforter were a wrinkled mess on her mattress.

Ryan slowly walked into her room, his nostrils flaring. "You live in this—in here?"

"Yes," she answered slowly.

"Huh." He poked at a pink, layered skirt with a dark green bra dangling by an eyehook caught in the lace slung over her reading chair.

Delanee rushed over and grabbed both articles of clothing, balled them up, and hugged them to her chest. "It's my space. Not everyone is obsessed with cleanliness."

"Do you get dressed off your floor?" he asked, toeing a pair of amber slacks and an ivory tunic with a wide leather belt she'd dropped on the floor three days ago.

"No, I have a closet." She motioned to the half-open folding doors behind him.

He turned and reached for a panel. Hesitated. "I'm afraid to know."

Delanee rolled her eyes and went to find a bag for her clothes. "It's just a closet," she said.

She sank to the floor and dug around under her bed. Dust plumed, and she coughed.

"Oh, sweet summer sun," Ryan breathed.

Rising onto her haunches, Delanee rested her hands on her thighs and looked at the closet. Both Ryan's arms held the doors open to the disaster contained within. Fine, maybe *utilizing* her closet was a misnomer. The space was more of a void for her to shove things when she didn't want to look at them anymore. She chewed on her bottom lip.

"Delanee," he said in horror. "What... how... I mean, I'm not...."

"Oh dear," Madeleine said from the hall. "I'll take care of this. Come on, child." Her grandmother grabbed Ryan and guided him away from the closet.

He pointed. "How?"

"Yes, I know. It's a gift she possesses. Her parents gave up on teaching her organizational skills a long time ago. The mess works for her."

"But—" He motioned at the floor.

Madeleine threaded her arm through his elbow and patted his forearm. "It'll be all right. She knows where everything is that she needs, I promise."

"What—"

"No, come on, I found a box."

Her grandmother's soothing words faded from the hall, and Delanee let out a rush of air. She'd drive Ryan crazy with her sloppiness. Delanee could keep things clean. She just didn't prioritize housework. Gathering her favorite clothes off the floor, she tossed them onto the bed. She would use the laundry room she'd found earlier in the day at his house.

Sitting on her heels, she looked around the room again. Ryan was the first man ever to set foot into her personal space, and the mess had been too big of a distraction for her to appreciate the moment. Maybe there was something to keeping things clean after all.

She found a crumpled overnight bag near her dresser from the last time she stayed with her parents and held it open, cramming her clothes inside. She tossed in a few beauty and hair essentials. In her bathroom, she grabbed her shower supplies and shoved the bottles into the external pockets. By the time she finished, the bag was a misshapen, bulging mass.

Back in her room, she tried to recall her schedule, which was on her desk at the office. She snapped her fingers. At least one formal dinner, a theater show the diplomat from Ravenna was supposed to attend, and a blooming party for a master guardian who grew a greenhouse full of *Bougainvillea glabra*, and at peak bloom were a crazy riot of colors. The party always started in the late afternoon to see the flowers in full light and carried on into the night when the hostess lit paper lanterns. She encouraged her guests to experience the greenhouse in a very romantic setting. The nature of the party always provided Delanee with social page fodder for days. Yes, she'd need to grab a gown or three, which meant another bag.

With two bags in her hands and a dress draped over her shoulder, Delanee went to the dining room. The space was empty, but the low murmur of voices led her to the living room. Her grandmother sat on the couch near Ryan. Alarm raced through her, and she hurried her steps. The satin of the gown swished around her legs.

"And they went to this place?" Ryan asked, a page turning. Delanee slowed.

"They did. They were invited to return when the entire cavern was formally dedicated to the archaeologist who discovered the ruins a few years after the initial excavation," her grandmother answered.

"Did they attend?"

"Well, Bella was pregnant with Deklan, I believe, at the time. She doesn't travel well, so they waited until after he was born and done nursing."

"They went with the kids?"

"No, I kept the babies. I told them being parents didn't mean they had to stop enjoying travel. I was here, we had this huge apartment, and Markus's parents were coming for a visit around that time. They needed the break."

"He didn't want to see his parents?" Ryan asked, another page turning.

"Oh," Madeleine hummed, "they tended to linger. Markus was their only child, and his having so many children was unheard of in Ruthenia. They absolutely basked in their grandparent status. I didn't do much but make sure we had enough food in the house when they visited."

Delanee had mixed feelings about her paternal grandparents. Yes, they'd loved all their grandbabies, but at first, it'd been a struggle as they waited to learn whether they'd be genetic heirs or genetically common. In the end, Delanee knew it wouldn't have really mattered, her Ruthenian *bakishka* and *dakishka* would have come to accept their grandchildren, but the stigma was there all the same. And she hated that about her father's culture.

"Ruthenians usually have one or two children per family, right?" Ryan asked.

"If they're lucky. They're too proud to acknowledge they're a dying nation, and if they don't accept fresh blood, they won't be around in a hundred years."

"I'm ready," Delanee chimed, wanting to stop the conversation of family and genetics.

If Delanee married a Sziverian, her situation would be

different than how her parents had been gifted with offspring. She'd be lucky to conceive even a single child. A large family would be out of the question without a Ruthenian mate. The experiences of her brothers who'd attempted to find mates in Ruthenia had been so horrific, Delanee refused to put herself through the ordeal. If the women were cold and cruel, how much more so would the men be? She wasn't willing to learn.

Ryan closed the book. A large ten-by-thirteen tome filled with artistic sketches of underground ruins of a pre-cataclysmic city in Thanzia. Delanee loved that book. She loved exploring it with her parents, who had so many vivid stories about their time spent in the caverns. The album had a permanent space on the coffee table. Framed sketches from the same collection were hanging in the living room and library at her parents' house, along with several treasures uncovered from the depths.

He stood, took in her overloaded frame, and frowned. "Why the dress?"

"Master Guardian Silverhill holds an annual *Bougainvillea* bloom party. I can maybe miss my other commitments, but I can't miss that one. It's almost exclusively a list of ranked guardians," she said, ruffling the sheer plum layers of the cascading skirt.

"Might not be the be—"

"No, nope," she said, arcing a finger through the air and shaking her head. "I will have Deklan attend with me if necessary."

"And his wife," Madeleine said, nodding. "She'll keep you safe, Delanee."

Delanee beamed at Ryan. "See, I have my own guardian team, too."

He picked up the box from the couch. "Hopefully, it'll be a non-issue by then. Her party is in a week?"

Her smile faded. "Yes. Right. Hopefully."

"You're going to be gone a week?" Madeleine asked, her gaze narrowing.

"Maybe." Delanee forced a smile back into place. "I'm investigating a rather tricky article."

"About the orphans? Are you traveling?"

"Um," Delanee looked to Ryan for help. She didn't want to lie to her grandmother.

"She discovered some information that might compromise her," Ryan said. "I'm keeping her safe."

Madeleine touched a hand to her throat. "I see. And your brothers know?"

"Deklan knows," Ryan answered. "And I'm working to eliminate the threat."

Madeleine held her hand up. "No, I don't want to know. I will just worry. As long as one of the boys or your father knows, that's good enough for me. Are you somewhere safe?"

Delanee nodded.

"Good." Her grandmother patted her cheek. "Make smart choices, child. You still have three siblings who have to leave the nest. Don't ruin it for them."

Incredulous, Delanee could only stare at her grandmother. Mischief sparkled in Madeleine's eyes. Great. Just wonderful. All the things Delanee *thought* she'd been hiding about how she felt concerning Ryan, her grandmother had figured out.

"Where's my hat?" Ryan asked.

Still speechless, Delanee pointed at the hall.

He groaned. "I have to go back in there?"

He disappeared down the hall, and Delanee glared at her grandmother. "Nothing is going to happen between us."

"You keep telling yourself that." She gently swept curls over Delanee's shoulder. "I have a blank contract, when you're both ready."

Delanee stepped away, sputtering. She glanced over her shoulder to ensure their conversation remained private. "Absolutely not. I can't believe you just said that."

Humor fled Madeleine's features. Delanee's heart skipped at the sudden seriousness in her grandmother's gaze. "Do not miss this opportunity to discover something beautiful because you're scared, Delanee."

Delanee shook her head. "Neither of us—"

"I've heard all the arguments before. None of them matter when the heart is involved."

SEVEN

RYAN EASED the Ariot around a corner, driving slower in the darkness. The nights were becoming warmer each evening, the traffic increasing after sunset due to Haven City's burgeoning night life. By summer, the sidewalks would be filled with pedestrians enjoying the temperate weather the evenings offered. For now, only vehicle traffic had increased.

Delanee sat quietly beside him, her gaze fixed out the window. The slide of streetlights washed over her pale brown skin, illuminating and concealing the beautiful curves of her face. Ryan had to keep reminding himself to look at the road to drive safely.

"Do you really think I'll be in danger if I attend the blooming party?" she asked quietly.

Ryan's hand tightened on the steering column. "I can't say you'll be safe, but I'm not certain how much danger you'd be in, either. I know the assassin is aware of you, but to what extent is he willing to go to locate you? I'm not sure. Hopefully, I'll be able to find him before he makes any real effort to find you."

She turned to face him. Her fingers twisted in the oversized sweater pooled on her lap. "Did you learn something today?"

Ryan contemplated how much to share. He didn't want to give her false hope. However, it was her life being placed on hold while stuck in a strange home. "I was able to discover where he lives."

"From the companion house owner?" Delanee asked, skeptical.

"Yes. The paid companionship house was my only lead to the assassin since that's where you saw him. Where else would I go?"

"And she shared that with you?"

"Of course," Ryan said as he turned left.

Delanee shifted her attention to the window again. "She didn't seem the type to share information while I was there. She barely tolerated me talking to Fione for the orphanage interview. She was probably hoping you'd sign up to sponsor one of her women to become a patron of her establishment."

"Not part of our discussion, actually." The second the words left his mouth, Ryan realized his mistake. He wasn't dealing with an average woman. Delanee's curiosity would demand a deeper explanation. One Ryan didn't have to offer.

"You asked, and she answered? Without any persuading?" She twisted to face him again. "You have something over the house, don't you? Did you threaten to reveal her to the SNID? Or maybe you lied about what you wanted the information for?"

"That I can't say, sorry."

She huffed and crossed her arms over her chest, facing the windshield. "Well, does he live in the city?"

"Kind of," Ryan hedged, slowing to a stop as a carriage crossed an intersection in front of him. "He's hiding out in Old City Ruins."

Delanee gasped. "No wonder you haven't been able to track him down. People go there specifically to disappear."

Checking to ensure no other vehicles were about to cross, he eased through the juncture. "Yes, but the ruins lack any civilized comforts or safety."

"But I've heard once the community accepts you, you *are* protected. They take care of their own."

Ryan inclined his head. "To a degree, yes."

"You think you'll be able to find him in the ruins somehow?"

"I'll do more than locate him."

"How?"

Ryan pulled into his driveway. "There's one thing you never, ever do in our country, regardless of what subculture you belong to. City, outlying towns, the Rows, the Ruins, or even in the Northern Boundary." He turned his head and met her shadowed stare. "You don't hurt children, and you certainly don't take them from us."

"And he has," she whispered.

"At least twice that we know of. The moment I reveal that fact to whoever oversees Old City Ruins, they'll do anything to help."

"You hope."

Ryan shook his head. "No, I know. Even the uncontrolled interior of the Ruins has standards. Perhaps higher than our own in many ways, as they only have their rules to allow them to survive."

"Do you know why that area was allowed to become so lawless?"

"It's dangerous. The buildings are crumbling. The roads are long gone, little more than muddy trails. The people who live there know where to go and what parts to avoid. Haven City Enforcement Services had no hope of knowing the same. Venturing after criminals who disappeared into the Ruins became impossible. Many of the accused's crimes never happened again once they disappeared into the Ruins. It became obvious the people were either handling the issue, or the criminals changed their ways enough to integrate, knowing it was freedom in the Ruins or conviction beyond."

"They became self-governing and helped reduce crime in their own way," Delanee mused. "Would make an interesting story."

Ryan smiled and opened his door. "No one would talk to you long enough to learn the full truth."

She shrugged. "Maybe. I have my own ways, you know."

He leaned over his seat to grab her bags from the small back area, handing her one and her gown. He took the second bag and the box, using his foot to close the Ariot's door. "I imagine you have many ways to get the information you seek, or your editor wouldn't have you mingling among the highest echelons of society."

Delanee hugged the bag to her chest, frowning. "I think having Deklan in the highest ranking possible landed me the position after Cora. No one would dare deny me entrance into one of their parties. Cora was in a similar situation as Kynhaven's sister."

"And she wasn't shy about using her family status."

"No," Delanee said with a sigh. "I'm still uncomfortable with my family's name getting me through doors that would otherwise remain closed, but I like my job. Someday, I won't have to rely on parties to get my work published."

"Have you written other articles not related to the society pages?" he asked, stopping at the bottom of the steps to the front porch.

"I have," she said quietly.

"What happened?"

She shrugged and looked out over the shadows of the

front yard and dimly lit road. "He said they weren't compelling enough."

"What were they about?" he asked, sitting on the steps and letting her bag drop while resting his arms on the box.

She joined him. "The first one I wrote was about magic lily dust arriving in Kyn when all the Haven City guests were at Kyn Manor. I was asked by Kynhaven to write about the parties and made the discovery when I went to town."

"Someone brought it with them to sell in town," he said.

"Yes. It quickly became popular among the people my age. Mason was not happy."

"No, I imagine not. The town of Kyn has been the Dandridge's responsibility for a very long time." Ryan drummed his fingers on the box top. "And your editor felt a large city drug appearing in a small town at the height of guest arrival wasn't worth mentioning?"

Delanee shook her head. "He said the antics of the party were enough. *That* is what people wanted to read."

"I'd expect such a response from the editor of *The Havener*."

"Right?" she proclaimed, holding out a hand. "I guess part of me should be flattered he feels my social page work is popular enough to carry the print, but I want to contribute to the serious articles, too."

"What else have you offered?"

She pulled the hat off her head and laid it on the porch behind her. She shook out her curls and Ryan fisted his hands to stop from helping. "Over the years? I investigated magic lily dust in greater depth after the Kyn situation. I figured if the small town wasn't good enough, maybe looking into the problem here might."

"And he wasn't interested?"

She picked at the sweater's thread. "Well, another journalist was writing an article about Princess Verica's efforts to help those addicted. My editor felt it'd undermine the other piece and the princess's work."

A tingle of unease slid through Ryan. "Can't have that. What else?"

"There was an unusually high amount of HRS incidents over a year ago. I researched and discovered most of the infected had attended the parties of the same ranked guardians."

Ryan tried to recall hearing about the incidents. "Were the ranked guardians infected?"

"No, only the guests who'd attended. It was all very odd. Anyway, I wrote the article more like a social piece since it involved ranked guardians. My editor said my theories were all conjecture and rejected it. That's when I decided to focus on the orphans."

"Do you still have the articles?" he asked.

"Of course. I was going to submit the magic lily dust article to *Haven City Journal*. They publish quarterly and accept more serious pieces." She smoothed her hand along the ruffles of the gown draped over her shoulder.

"Why didn't you?" he asked gently.

"I don't want to have another serious piece of work rejected. And I need to update the information."

"Would you mind if I read them?"

Her attention snapped to him. "Why?"

"I'm curious."

Her gaze narrowed. "About what?"

"About why your editor keeps rejecting issues that go hand in hand with the goals of the mysterious alliance."

Delanee blinked, her shoulders straightening. "You think he's been sabotaging my work to protect someone?"

"I think it's an interesting coincidence. Did he ever ask you to stop investigating any of the subject matters in the articles?"

"No."

"Did he ever ask about your sources?"

Her face scrunched in concentration. "All of us have to cite our sources. That's not an odd request."

"Even if he rejected the article?"

"We must list our informants or where we witnessed the events ourselves when we turn in the article."

Ryan rubbed his fingers together to ease the urge to touch her and speed up the conversation. A familiar urgency to acquire information made the compulsion difficult to resist. "And did you notice any of your usual sources disappearing or becoming unavailable?"

"I've never tried to contact any of them again after the articles were rejected," she admitted, chewing on her bottom lip.

Ryan didn't have time to investigate if anything had become of her informants, and he didn't want her digging deeper if there was even a small chance her editor was part of the group causing so much chaos in the country. However, he needed to know if their media was under the control of the nefarious alliance.

"Who do you trust at the paper?" he asked, rising.

"Our illustrative journalist, Sarkis Filosa." She grabbed the hat from behind her before standing. "He's tried to help me with every article I submitted by providing a sketch or two. He figured it might appeal more to Curtis if it were print-ready."

Jealousy tried to rise within him, which was ridiculous. He knew nothing about this Sarkis, nor did he have any reason to envy Delanee's trust in the man. "Would he be able to look into your informants from the articles?"

She hugged the bag to her chest. "You really think something may have happened to them?"

"I think it's worth looking into," he hedged. "You want the queen-elect to approve of your writing an article. I can't make that request without knowing the publication is honest."

"He didn't like my work—"

"Your editor likes your work just fine, or you wouldn't have a job."

"I told you, my family—"

"Isn't your talent."

Her lips pressed together, and she glanced away. "I guess he feels I'm good enough for the flippant pieces, but serious isn't where my gift lies."

"Or it's not you." Ryan picked the bag off the step. "Are the articles at your apartment?"

"I have copies in my desk at the paper."

Ryan didn't want her to go to the paper for multiple reasons, but he knew he wouldn't win the argument. "Does the illustrator work daily?"

"Yes, I'll speak with him."

Worry pinched her beautiful face, and Ryan wished he had a free hand to smooth the lines away. "You won't be in any danger."

She waved her fingers. "Oh, I know. There won't be time for anyone to contact someone. I plan to turn in my article, get the papers from my desk, talk to Sarkis, and then leave."

Ryan lifted his brows. "Where do you plan to go?"

She considered his question. "Terravine, I think. Then, if I am followed, it won't be back to your place. I trust them, and you know where it is, right?"

"Every guardian knows where Shield Guardian Terravine lives," Ryan stated. "She holds the largest annual gathering outside of the HCES in the city."

"For ranked guardians, yes." Delance's gaze turned speculative. "But you aren't a typical unranked guardian."

Time to retreat. Ryan smiled and headed for the door. "Sure, I am. Amari Dossett just likes me."

. . .

"AMARI DOSSETT LIKES EVERYONE," Delanee said, trailing after Ryan into the house. What was the infernal man hiding from her? She knew it was something. "But she's firm on the ranked guardians only attending her Wintervail Iris bloom party."

"You attend."

"Yes, in my journalistic capacity. She's a very gracious hostess. And if she wouldn't let me, I'd just go with Deklan or Dominik. Neither Darius nor Drayke receives an invitation to attend because they don't hold rankings."

He shook his head and held open the door. "I think I need you to write down the names of all your siblings. I know Darius, I've worked with him on several occasions. And Deklan. Dominik, I've heard about but never personally dealt with. I believe one of your brothers works in finance? And a sister married an Icekutian breeder. Another sister is a matchmaker, like your grandmother. I'm not certain about the others."

"Dominik holds a ranking that was created specifically for him. He does assignments for anyone who needs his specific talent with his raptor," Delanee said, entering the foyer. "Dalila is the matchmaker. Deverick is indeed in finance. He handles investments for import and export businesses. My brother Drayke has my mother's talent. He works for the HCES and occasionally the SNID. Damira married into the equestrian dynasty. Not really unexpected since she has an affinity for horses."

"She can bond with a horse?" he asked, surprised.

"Not like Deklan can with his wolves or Dominik with his hawk, no. She describes it more as a medical scientist but for horses. She can touch them and learn what may be going on inside them. The family hired her when several of their horses became mysteriously sick."

"And fell in love with the son."

Delanee smiled. "Yes, very much so."

A love Delanee envied. Dalila had also found love, but the intensity didn't seem to rival Damira's match or what Deklan had with Cia. An experience Delanee believed she'd never really want, despite the ache she suffered when she watched the couples together. Ryan's explosive kiss was changing her mind. Unfortunate since she couldn't have him, and shouldn't want him.

"My younger brother, Donovan," Delanee continued, "is a wolf talent like our father and Deklan. Dustin will probably be another raptor talent, and Dyna is associating with a cat."

"A cat?" Ryan raised his brows.

"Yep," she said, gliding past him. "Rarer than a wolf, but not as rare as the raptor talent."

"How does that work—"

"Da-ba-ba-ba!" an excited baby squealed.

Thankful for the interruption, Delanee kept her expression carefully devoid. Some family secrets she wouldn't divulge, and hers had more than a few. Ryan went through the archway off the foyer and set her things on the dining room table before continuing to the living room. He clapped his hands and held out his arms.

"Baby girl is still awake," he proclaimed, a huge smile on his face that changed everything.

Delanee's heart lurched. She stopped in the shadowy alcove and leaned against the wall. One of the twins was passed out on the couch. Her arm flopped over the side while her head was tilted at a grimace-worthy angle. The other twin sat on the opposite couch and handed the infant to Ryan.

"She had a long afternoon nap and is very alert tonight."

Ryan held her high in the air and gently twisted her

back and forth while her legs kicked out. She laughed, and he faked dropping her, catching her against his chest. Delanee smiled at Inara's squeal of delight.

"She knew I'd be home late," Ryan said, cuddling her against his broad shoulder. "Do you need me to wake Ava or leave her on the couch?"

Ah, so that made the awake twin Evelyn.

"Inara's bottle should put her down for the night," Evelyn said, rising. "And I don't care if the old sleepyhead stays the night."

Ryan turned. Delanee's stomach trembled at the sight of him holding the precious bundle of life to his chest. One hand supported her little bottom, while the other engulfed her small back. The pale blonde curls gleamed near white atop her head. "Do you mind holding her while I walk Evelyn home?"

Evelyn waved a hand. "Pah, I don't need help. I'm not incapable."

"I never said you were, but it's late, and I'd feel more comfortable knowing you made it home safe," he stated, his voice calm and patient.

Delanee moved to set her things on the table with the other bag and the box. The gown flared across the wood surface, the intricate beadwork on the bodice shimmering in the dim light. She went through the archway and smiled at the baby girl. Inara's big, silver-blue gaze watched her every move.

"Can I hold you?" Delanee held her palms out.

Inara scrunched her nose and leaned back. "Mmm ba-da-da!" she shrieked.

Delanee knew an impending meltdown when she saw one if the girl was handed off and glanced at Ryan. "I can walk Evelyn home."

Evelyn lifted her nose. "Absolutely not. I don't need any help getting to my house. It's twenty feet away."

"Do you mind a crying baby?" he asked, his gaze conveying an unspoken apology.

"Not at all," Delanee said, plucking Inara from his hold. A wail of displeasure echoed through the living room. Tiny hands reached for Ryan.

"Ryan," Evelyn snapped.

He motioned toward the back of the living room. "She'll be fine. I'm coming right home. Come on."

Ava stirred on the couch. Ryan went to help her rise.

"What has gotten into that girl?" Ava asked, her voice gruff from sleep.

"She wants her daddy," Evelyn sniffed and glared at Delanee.

"And she'll get him," Delanee replied. "When he's assured himself you're safe. So don't make him wait, hmm?"

Delanee tucked a squirming, kicking, straining Inara into her side. Fat tears raced down her red, chubby cheeks.

Ryan frowned, his hold gentle on Ava's elbow. "Are you sure you'll be okay?"

Little legs kicked against Delanee's side. Inara arched her back, attempting to dislodge herself in her fury. Delanee rested her hand on Inara's back to keep her in place. "I'll be fine."

Ryan nodded and motioned for the ladies to exit the house via the greenhouse. Evelyn attempted to argue, but Ryan urged her forward with gentle guidance on her back. He glanced over his shoulder, eyes wide, and made a face of annoyed disbelief. Delanee pressed her lips together to keep from laughing. Inara's squalls of displeasure joined the twin's whines of Ryan leaving his daughter behind.

Alone with the baby, Delanee swayed her hips and bounced the girl on her way to the pantry she'd found earlier in the day. As a single father, Ryan would have milk jars for his infant. Evelyn had said Inara needed a bottle before bed. Now seemed a fantastic time to help her calm down. The bottles were arranged in perfect order on a middle shelf to the right of the door. Delanee grabbed one, shaking it on her way to the kitchen. She searched the kitchen for how he heated the milk and had to raise a brow at his fancy stove that had a built-in warmer.

Setting the bottle in the holder, she continued to sway back and forth. The kicking and bowing had ceased, but the infant still screamed, her chunky cheeks shiny with tears.

"You are a vocal little thing, aren't you?" Delanee cooed, using the soft towel near the sink to wipe away tears and snot. She tossed the rag on the counter and checked the bottle.

Inara murmured, her little chin quivering, pale eyes glossy with unshed tears.

"Yeah?"

Delanee opened and closed drawers, searching for nipples. She found them in a drawer near the sink, divided into neat compartments for all Inara's required kitchen supplies. Little bowls for her cereal. Small spoons for small hands. Bottle cleaners. Folded bibs and cloths for wiping her down after she ate solids.

"Your daddy has a problem, I've decided," she said, plucking a nipple from the set. "Does he twitch when something is out of place?"

Having become gifted at one-handed bottle-making before her seventh birthday, Delanee made quick work of preparing Inara's evening meal. She glanced around the kitchen and breakfast area and shook her head. Nope. Perhaps Ryan had something more comfortable to sit in his bedroom. Sloshing the milk back and forth to ensure an even heat, she carried the baby to his room.

To her delight and surprise, she discovered he'd turned the right corner of his room into a comfortable nursery setting. This morning, she'd been too immersed in the information tacked to the wall to look around. The bed had been the only place she'd continually found herself glancing, so she'd stopped looking anywhere except at Ryan's research. A sweet pink rug contrasted with all the shades of navy. A single shelf floated at sitting level to the left of a rocking chair in the same pine wood. To the right, a stand with a candle under glass and a children's picture book left no doubt about the purpose of the space.

Delanee crossed the room and took a seat in the chair. The wood groaned beneath her weight and rocked back. Inara hummed, her bottom lip pouting. "Shhh, here we go."

She worked the nipple between Inara's gums, smiling when the baby instantly latched on and accepted her meal. Delanee arranged her more comfortably, the baby's head resting on her left breast, her little feet sliding along Delanee's right hip. Using her toes, Delanee gently rocked and found herself unable to look away from Inara's beautiful silvery blue eyes. Exact replicas of her sire's. Beautiful.

A tight warmth gripped Delanee's heart. Her fingers constricted on Inara's thigh, hugging the child closer to her torso. Such a perfect baby. How could anyone have walked away from her? Inara's little hand waved, her fingers opening and closing as if reaching for something. Delanee shifted and maneuvered until she could hold the bottle and the baby and offer her a finger to latch onto.

The second Inara's strong grip wrapped around Delanee's finger, something cracked inside her. Inara's feet kicked, and her bottom wiggled. The baby smiled around the bottle and cooed happily. Her grip remained firm, a sensation mimicked in Delanee's chest. Tendrils of white crackled to life in Inara's eyes, a curious phenomenon Delanee had witnessed on occasion within Ryan's gaze. Usually gone so quickly, she often wondered if she'd mistaken the sight.

Delanee's skin tingled where she held the infant. She had the urge to wrap around Inara and never release her. Protect her no matter the cost. Love her always, even though she wasn't technically Delanee's to love. The detail of the baby not being hers made no difference.

Denying the sudden truth was impossible and yet unachievable. No matter what her heart dictated, she could never be this child's mother. Delanee pressed a soft kiss to Inara's forehead.

"I wish, baby girl, I do," she whispered, shocked at the sincerity of her words.

This moment was as close to motherhood Delanee would ever achieve. Her chances of conception outside of a Ruthenian mate were slim, if not impossible. Her body would reject all but the strongest genes for her future child. And while Sziveria had genetic heirs of Ruthenian descent, they'd likely never be good enough for the genetic half she'd inherited from her father. She thought she'd made peace with a childless future. Had accepted the inevitable the day she'd decided to find a Sziverian mate. Yet, here she sat, clutching a baby and... what? Imagining she could claim Inara as hers? Perhaps she hadn't resigned herself as she'd believed. One explosive kiss and one simple feeding did not create a future.

But they could....

The notion drifted through her mind, igniting a spark, shifting the foundational blocks Delanee had laid out for what she believed she'd wanted. A soft creak broke the serene silence in the room. Delanee glanced up and found Ryan staring at her from the greenhouse door across the room, arms crossed, shoulder braced against the jam. His expression was indiscernible. Blank. Had he once again guessed at her thoughts and didn't like what he'd perceived? Not that she blamed him. She was little more than a stranger, one that could bring any amount of trouble to his door. She had no business contemplating a scenario where she helped raise his child.

Flushing, Delanee dropped her attention back to Inara. "She's almost done."

"Thank you for taking care of her," he said over the *snick* of the door lock engaging.

"She's so beautiful." Delanee tilted the bottle to ensure no excess air made it into Inara's belly.

"Thank you."

Delanee glanced up again and found Ryan perched on the edge of his bed across from the rocking chair. The weak light in the room bathed him in heavy shadows, making it impossible to know if his closed expression had changed. Delanee returned to watching Inara. Either the baby didn't care her father had returned, content in Delanee's arms, or hadn't noticed.

Again, amazement struck Delanee as she stared down at the baby girl. "What happened with her mother?"

Eight

Ryan slid to the floor and braced his forearms on his
raised knees. How much to reveal about his personal failure? And not just his. Oh no. The failure was so epic, he'd
cost his daughter a mother. The inability to see the truth
about his ex-lover before she'd stomped all over his heart
and abandoned a family he hadn't even known they'd
created still left him raw. Bitter. And yes, more than a little
humiliated and ashamed that he, Ryan Voklane, the great
sifter of truths, had been so thoroughly deceived.

Delanee pulled the bottle from Inara's mouth. The
infant released the nipple with a loud *pop* and hummed,
grasping for the empty glass. Ryan leaned forward and
opened a small drawer on the side table. He removed a pink
clay and rubber pacifier and handed it over. A pricey import
from Perazil, for which most parents were willing to
scrounge the raimarks to have on hand. Delanee inspected
the rubber portion to ensure no cracks and nothing was
pulling free of the clay base before touching it to Inara's
lips. His daughter pulled the pacifier into her mouth and
sucked.

The rhythmic creak of the rocking chair and squeak of

the binky being enjoyed filled the silence. Delanee seemed in no hurry to relinquish her hold on Inara, and Ryan wasn't in any hurry to make her. Walking into the room and spotting Delanee holding his daughter with obvious tenderness had stopped him. The twins loved Inara and cared for her, and Ryan would be lost without them, but they'd never fill the void left behind, the true love of a mother.

Ryan had no plans to seek a relationship, which may have led to such a bond eventually forming. He'd resigned himself to singlehood and Inara knowing only him as a parent. Seeing Delanee with his child made him question his decision. Not that she wanted the difficult job.

Continuing to look at them together, he realized his baby girl in *her* arms was right. A content glow radiated from them both as a mutual happiness. And yes, he noticed as he leaned forward and narrowed his focus, Inara's talent, inherited from him, was crackling in the air around her, wrapping Delanee in a subtle cocoon. He should break the contact. But unlike the twins, who entered a strange sort of inert phase until something distracted Inara and the connection was broken, Delanee remained attentive, aware of her surroundings. How intriguing.

Ryan knew from using his talent on Delanee in the past, she *could* be manipulated into falling under his influence. But he'd also discovered by touching her last night, and this afternoon, she could manage a hint of his gift without succumbing. What that meant, he didn't know. Apparently, she could also handle Inara at her happiest and not fall victim. However, if she hadn't already, she'd notice the odd glow in Inara's eyes at some point, which meant he'd have to reveal more than just his relationship mistake.

"What I share remains between us," he said softly, loath to break the peaceful mood.

"I have no plans to write about you, Ryan," she whispered, maintaining an even back-and-forth with the rocker.

"It's not just writing about me. What I reveal about myself to you...." He took a deep breath. "I'm trusting you with information only two people know."

"About Inara's mother? Was she a spy or something?"

A smile cracked through the seriousness. "You and your writer's imagination. She was an ordinary woman. At least, as far as I'm aware. But, if you're going to be in my home, occasionally caring for my daughter, there are a few other things you need to know."

A dark brow arched upward, and he didn't miss how her hold tightened around Inara. "Occasionally care for?"

"She isn't your responsibility," he said gently. "And I'm not asking you to make her one."

"You don't have to ask," she said, then pressed her lips together as though the admission had come forth unbidden. "I mean, I'm more than happy to help when I can."

Ryan wanted to touch her. Skin-to-skin. He didn't care where, he just wanted the physical connection. Her foot was close. A gap between her shoe and the sleep pants revealed her ankle. Sliding his fingers along the skin of her calf would be easy. The urge was so great he'd found himself leaning forward, hand reaching before he realized his intent. He carefully eased back and shifted his weight.

"I will ask for any help I need," he stated slowly, a reminder to himself. "Always. And you can tell me no."

"I won't," she said so softly he almost missed the words.

"But you can. I didn't bring you here to care for her. I don't need another babysitter. I already have two."

Delanee smiled. "Two crazy old biddies."

"Not denying that," he agreed. "I just want you to know there's no pressure or requirement for you to care for my daughter."

"Noted."

Ryan nodded. "All right, good."

"Now, you'll tell me about her mother?"

He shifted again. He loathed thinking about her, let alone speaking the truth that he'd been involved enough to have an intimate relationship with the wrong woman. "I met Renelle at the records department. She was crying and trying to get a guardian to help her skip the line."

Delanee snorted. "If only that worked."

Ryan stared at her.

Delanee's eyes widened. "It worked? You're joking."

"I was in a weird place. I'd just learned about human trafficking being a definite problem in our nation, and a vulnerable woman was more than I could walk away from," he admitted.

The moment of weakness had cost him. So much. He ran a hand through his short hair. No one, not even the twins, knew all the details concerning his shameful behavior concerning Renelle. Evelyn disapproved of the relationship for obvious reasons, but she'd only guessed at his mistake. She didn't know the specifics.

"I helped her get what she needed. Documents supposedly proving her ownership of an inherited apartment so she wouldn't be evicted. Afterward, she wanted me to go with her for a meal. I agreed." He rubbed the back of his neck, his attention shifting to the spines of colorful children's books on the shelf. "Things moved fast after that. She'd show up at my work for a walk or inquire about my weekend plans. If I had an event and she was able to attend, she accepted without hesitation but didn't want to be introduced as anyone but a friend. She said her commoner status might hurt my reputation."

"And you agreed?" she asked in disbelief.

"No, I didn't agree with her assessment, but I respected her request. To her, at least from what she told me, she wasn't proud of her origins, and she didn't want me to have to explain our relationship. As friends, her being at my side was nothing more than my not wanting to attend alone."

"Which is ridiculous. Anyone who knows you would know you never cared about going solo." Her gaze narrowed when he met her stare. "In fact, I'd say having a plus one made your reason for attending the party in the first place more difficult."

He inclined his head. Later, he'd dissect how Delanee knowing him in a way others hadn't noticed affected him. "And you'd be correct. I don't go for the fun of them. Like you, I go for the information I can obtain. Renelle usually disappeared on me within minutes of our arrival, but I couldn't work normally with her around. She cried the first time I didn't take her. I should have called off the relationship then, but—" He locked his jaw.

"But one of you had already seduced the other," Delanee guessed, her voice flat.

"I'd say seduction is a mutual event regardless of who begins the process. The end result is the same between two consenting adults."

Delanee shrugged. "I've heard some women are very gifted at getting their way in that arena."

Renelle Maxton had indeed been very, *very* gifted in the art of sexual persuasion. Mortification still filled Ryan when he remembered how easy it'd been for her to get him naked. He'd barely managed to make sure she hadn't been with another lover within two weeks before they'd become intimate. In the small window of his asking and her answering, he should have come to his senses and walked away. But the second he knew she wasn't potentially infected with human rabies syndrome, he'd given in to the lust she'd woven.

"A few weeks later, she wrote me a letter telling me she had a family emergency and didn't know when she'd return. No contact information. Not where she was going. Nothing. I went by her apartment and was told a month-to-month tenant had vacated, and the place was available if I was interested."

Delanee frowned. "She'd lied to you."

"Yes."

"And you're certain you were her only lover then?" Delanee asked. "I know Inara is yours. I'm just, the risk you took—"

"I know," he breathed, shaking his head. "Trust me, I know. But yes, I'm sure I was her only lover. At least at the beginning. If she took another before she sent her note, I have no way of knowing. Since she had no doubt Inara belonged to me, I'm assuming she didn't."

"It's a little hard to deny your genetics at work," Delanee said lightheartedly.

"When she was delivered to my door, her eyes were dark blue, and she was completely bald. Her hair came in around her first month, and her eyes changed about two months ago." Leaving no doubt about her parentage. Not that Ryan would have denied her. The instant the swaddled, tiny infant had been placed in his arms, she'd become his daughter, blood or not. "The note with her asked I not search out Renelle. What happened to the baby was entirely up to me. Renelle wanted, written in the entire note, simply as 'her mother,' no rights or responsibility."

"I'm sorry, Ryan."

Ryan stared at his beautiful daughter. A sense of sadness filled him, not for the first time. "Her loss."

"A loss I can't fathom choosing voluntarily," Delanee whispered.

Ryan propped his arms back on his knees. "I wish I knew her better to even guess at her reasoning. And what does it say about me that I don't?"

"That you're human?" she asked, focusing on Inara. She gently wiggled the pacifier, testing whether Inara would let the binky be removed. Inara's eyes fought to stay open, but she sucked more aggressively, pulling the clay guard tight to her face. Delanee smiled. "All right, sweet girl, you can keep it a little longer."

That weird flip sensation turned in Ryan's chest again. He rubbed the spot over his heart. The subtle, crackling glow around his daughter began to fade as she lost her battle with consciousness. "Single parenting is so rare in our society. Children aren't born out of marriage often, and when they are—"

"The children are treasured, but the parent...." She blew out a long breath.

"The parent remains single," he finished, smiling without mirth. "How can someone be trusted to remain faithful after a contract is signed if they couldn't even wait for a contract to have a child with someone?"

"I'd imagine if two people had a courtship, as is customary, the reasons for a baby out of contract would be discussed." Her gaze lifted. "You don't seem the promiscuous type, but I've discovered in my job that people can hide their true selves very well."

Curious, he leaned forward and rested his chin on his folded arms. "What do you consider promiscuous?"

"This Renelle, I assume she wasn't your first lover?" Delanee asked, confident, despite the sudden flame of pink across her cheeks.

"No. So, more than one?"

"Why would anyone need more than one?" she asked, then squeezed her eyes closed and shook her head. "I'm sorry."

"No, you are right. But, even Ruthenians take lovers to learn if a bond can be formed. Sometimes, intimacy happens first. Sometimes," he said softly, "the person just needs a connection that feels real right then because anything more is impossible."

The rocking chair stilled. "Why would more be impossible?"

Ryan rose onto his knees and leaned forward, closing the distance between them. He caged her in to ensure Inara stayed safe. His fingers slid along the silk of her inner arm, igniting his talent. White sparked from his fingertips, crackled along her skin, breached the barrier, and rushed through at lightning speed to overtake her consciousness. Colored leeched from her irises until only white remained. An odd phenomenon showing his talent had indeed engaged, and nothing would be remembered. She sat motionless. She'd hate him when she learned he'd done this to her, not for the first time.

Three times before, he'd tested her loyalty to her nation. Tested her reason for investigations and questions. She'd never believe him unless she saw him use his talent in person on another. Not a possibility at the moment. He had to show her a different way. He had to reveal her secrets. Carefully, so as to ensure he didn't delve too deep and completely strip away her sense of privacy. A delicate balance.

"Who was the first man you kissed?" he asked.

"Victor Heidel," she answered without any infliction. A straight answer, unable to be false.

"Did you like the kiss?"

"No."

"Why not?"

"He had terrible breath, and he tried to stick his tongue in my mouth. I gagged."

"Have you enjoyed anyone's kiss?"

"Yes."

"Whose?" His hand tightened around her forearm.

"Ryan Voklane."

Don't ask, don't ask, *don't*— "Why?"

"He didn't make me gag."

Well, that was something, Ryan figured. And he should stop. Should remove his hand and put distance between them. "Would you allow Ryan to kiss you again?"

"Yes."

Stop, stop, stop! Ryan's heart pounded in his ears. Excitement he had no right to feel coursed through his veins. The pressure to absorb more information from her rode him hard, not just because he needed more but *wanted* more. He wanted to crawl inside her head and learn everything about her. Every secret. Every desire. Every lust-filled fantasy.

Sweat beaded along his hairline and dampened the skin under his clothes. He lost the battle of self-discipline and asked one more question. "What else would you allow Ryan to do besides kiss you?"

"Anything."

Ryan squeezed his eyes shut. The word was devoid of emotion, yet he could imagine her whispering the sultry reply into his ear. He snatched his hand from her and fell back on his butt.

She blinked, the stunning gold flooding back into her irises. She glanced at her arm, at him, and back to her arm. A clear frown of confusion pinched her face. Had he followed his own rules, she'd have perceived his touch as a quick stroke of his fingers on her arm, nothing more. Not the confusing sight of him stumbling away soaked in sweat, when in her mind, a mere second had passed since the question she had asked. In reality, minutes had passed. An entire conversation of which she had no knowledge.

Ryan swallowed, his mouth dry, his breath heaving. "You asked why a relationship is impossible for me."

She blinked again and slowly eased the rocker back into motion. "Yes."

Ryan sagged against the frame of his bed. He'd never disliked his talent before and hadn't really lamented his fate. Right now? He found himself hating the gift. "Your first kiss was with a man named Victor Heidel. You despised it. His breath stank, and he tried to take the kiss further than you wanted."

The chair slid to a halt. "What? How do you know that?"

Ryan couldn't meet her gaze. He picked at imaginary loose threads on the carpet. "I asked, and you answered."

"You asked me no such thing," she snapped, rising from the chair. She swayed, maintaining motion while carrying a slumbering Inara to the crib on the other side of his bed.

Ryan stood and braced his hands on the soft mattress. "I did. How else would I know?" He eased along the edge. "How else would I know you didn't feel the same about *my* kiss?"

NINE

Shoulders stiff, Delanee stopped in front of Inara's crib. A tremble shivered in her stomach and threatened to knock her knees together. If he spoke the truth....

How else would I know you didn't feel the same about my *kiss?*

The words echoed in her mind. She swallowed away the burn of anxiety and gently laid Inara in the crib. The baby's small limbs twitched, and she sucked faster on the pacifier but stayed asleep. Delanee rested a hand on the infant's round belly, unable to bring herself to face Ryan. Not yet.

"I'm not lying," he said, close enough for his voice to wash over her skin like a caress.

Delanee lifted her hand slowly, brushing her fingers along Inara's brow before turning. She braced her hands on the railing and placed her back to the crib. "I never said you were. I'm trying to understand how. How did I answer your questions? I have no memory. And why would you ask something so... personal?"

He'd sat on the corner of the bed, too far to touch but close enough to make his words soft. "If I'd asked your favorite color, you'd have said it was a guess. If I'd asked anything simple or neutral, you would have been able to criticize my words."

Delanee gripped the thin rail until her knuckles hurt. She couldn't deny the logic of his confession. She *would* have scoffed at his claim to have somehow burrowed into her mind and divined an answer to questions only he had known he'd asked. Would have denied the disturbing intrusion.

No one, not even Victor himself, knew she'd almost thrown up after he'd kissed her. For months after, Delanee questioned if she even liked men, the negative reaction to his kiss had been so severe. A crush on a quiet man over the summer erased the doubt. Though she'd felt no excitement at the simple kiss they eventually shared, he hadn't repulsed her either. None of the suitors who'd pursued her and attempted to woo her enough to brave a kiss had managed to thrill her. Until Ryan. The memory of their earlier embrace made her want to relive the experience.

"You can, what, pull thoughts from my mind?" Something she'd suspected with how easily he knew her every contemplation.

"No, you answer. You speak just as you are now."

"Impossible," she said, her chin lifting. "I'd remember."

He reached out, the quickest of brushes along her wrist. A lingering tingle remained, and she brushed away the sensation.

"Your most embarrassing memory while on the job happened to be your first assignment," he said confidently.

Oh no... oh no, no, no.

"In fact, the evening was so terrible, you told your editor nothing worth writing about had happened." He braced both his hands on the bedspread. "In a drunken moment of self-pity, Candace Washmore stripped in the guest bathroom to prove she wasn't fat, where you walked in on her. She latched onto you, sobbing, and wouldn't let you leave. Her husband found you both tangled on the floor and believed the worst. The only reason either party said nothing was because he didn't want the disaster in the paper, and you didn't want anyone to know it'd happened in the first place."

Delanee tried to swallow, but her mouth was too dry. The memory of Mrs. Washmore clinging to the point of scratching, demanding to be told how beautiful her breasts were, still made Delanee shudder. She'd never attended another party at such a late hour again. The minute anyone showed signs of being drunk, she left, except for a few she was asked to cover where getting drunk was the sole purpose of the evening. Those she attended relishing her sobriety.

"How?" she managed to croak. "How can you possibly know anything about that night?"

"I already told you." He lifted his hands. "You gave me the information."

Delanee looked away from him. Heat flooded her cheeks. "When?"

"Just now while you stood there. I asked you."

She shook her head. "You asked me nothing. You barely moved, let alone spoke any words."

His lips pressed into a firm line. "I won't keep asking your secrets. You'll crack under a different strain."

She crossed her arms to hide the tremble she could no longer resist. "Explain to me what you're doing. What's happening."

"You're very calm," he said, gaze narrowed.

Panic seared her insides. If he could learn those secrets, he could learn them *all*. Stars above, she couldn't allow him to do whatever strangeness he utilized to get the answers from her again. "I'm trying to be rational."

"How very professional of you." Emotion fled his

features. "Please remember you promised not to reveal any part of this conversation to anyone."

"And I'd appreciate it if all the little tidbits you stole from me would also remain in confidence," she bit out.

"I would never betray your trust."

No, only her sense of privacy. She needed to sit but refused to do so beside him on the bed. Not a good plan. Even angry and a little scared, his nearness still managed to elicit a sensual awareness.

"Can we go somewhere else to have this conversation?" she asked.

"Where would you like?" he asked, rising.

"The kitchen. I need some tea." She stalked past, not really caring if he followed.

He did, easing around her once they entered the kitchen, preventing her from banging pots and pans while searching for tea supplies. A task that would have allowed her to vent. Instead, she planted her butt on a barstool and dropped her head into her hands.

"What kind of tea?"

"I don't care," she answered and realized her rudeness. She sighed. "Anything will be fine, thank you."

Minutes later, the sweet scent of peaches and spice wafted under her nose. She wrapped her fingers around the warm mug and dragged the cup closer, breathing deeply. When Ryan didn't join her on a stool, she glanced up and found him leaning on the counter, his forearms braced, and his fingers braided together.

Delanee opened a palm. "Help me understand."

"I'm...." He straightened, jerked a hand through his hair, and stared up at the ceiling. "I don't know of anyone else who is capable of what I am. I don't know if my gift is unique or if it eventually evolved into some other type of genetic ability we see today."

Delanee drew her brows together. "The list of genetic inheritances on your wall—"

"Yes, I'm mapping talents, trying to learn what may have started as an original gift, or what may have even been lost in the hundreds of generations that became the nation of Ruthenia. Your father's nation is so secretive, however, it's impossible to know."

"Why does that matter?"

"Because, like I said, I'm unique." He took a deep breath and braced his palms on the edge of the counter, letting his weight fall forward, attention on the floor.

Clearly, he struggled to reveal something, and couldn't Delanee relate? She wanted to lean across the distance and touch him. Assure him anything he shared would remain between them and be free of judgment. A revelation that shocked her. She *should* allow her suspicions to rule to protect herself. However, she came from a very powerful family who'd been judged and feared because they, too, were rare and, in some instances, the sole Gen-Heir of their kind.

Going on instinct, she stretched forward and caressed the tips of his fingers. He lifted his head, his gaze an intense arctic fire. "Tell me," she urged softly.

"When I touch someone, I can put them in a sort of stasis and ask questions, any questions, and they answer with complete honesty. Time stops for them, and they don't remember anything."

Delanee slowly pulled her hand back to her tea. "And you've done this to me twice tonight?"

He gave a jerky nod.

Delanee licked her dry lips, clutching the warm mug. "Have you done it before tonight?"

Again, a sharp nod.

Okay. So. Her privacy had been invaded on multiple occasions, and she had not only no memory but no idea the situations had even occurred. Whatever he did, he managed with a thoroughness not even a Sympath could achieve. Doubt had Delanee shaking her head.

"I would have noticed missing time," she said.

"The other times, it was quick, less than a minute," he admitted. "Tonight, time wasn't a concern."

Which meant the previous instances were done when time wasn't a luxury. Delanee tried to remember all the times she'd been in his presence. "When you walked by me and accidentally touched me—"

"Nothing accidental about when I touch you," he said.

Goosebumps prickled along her skin. She took a sip of her tea to help compose herself. "They felt unintended."

"Yes."

"All those times you were asking me questions?"

"Yes."

"About?" she asked, proud her voice remained calm.

"I needed to know you were loyal to Sziveria."

She tapped her nails on the mug. "Had I ever given you a reason to suspect my allegiance?"

"No, but some surprising betrayals have happened. I couldn't risk it, not when I was telling you things I shouldn't have."

Fair enough. She'd badgered him into sharing information about her brother and his travels, some of which could be considered national secrets. "Do you have a watch?"

He reached into his pants pocket and removed a silver watch, sliding it across the counter. Delanee used her index finger to pull the timepiece closer. Anxiety threatened to break her resolve, but her curiosity wouldn't be denied.

She needed him to ask her something safe that wouldn't spark additional curiosity on his part and deviate from the original topic. *What to use, what to use....* She almost snapped her fingers. "Ask about my memories of my father's wolf, Lunah."

"You *want* me to use my talent on you?" he asked, skeptical.

"Yes." She held the watch in her palm, noting the time. "Memories. Lunah. Now go."

He leaned forward, hesitated, and then gently slid his fingers along hers, half curled around the watch. The tingle of awareness and the sensation of his fingertips on hers made her breath catch. Then his touch glided away, and she blinked, glancing up at him. He grinned, and she frowned, shifting her attention back to the watch. Twelve minutes. She jerked, almost falling off the stool.

"How?" she demanded.

He held up his hands. "I told you." His smile remained. "Your father's wolf, she's...."

"Amazing, I know." The watch clattered to the counter. All right, your talent is touch-based. What is it called?"

"There's no name. As I said earlier, I've never heard of anyone else who can do what I can."

She tried to wrap her mind around his confession. "You should be in an arch guardianship position, Ryan. Why aren't you?"

"Multiple reasons."

"Like what?" she asked before she could stop herself. Stupid curiosity. "Sorry, I'm just trying to figure out why you wouldn't want to be in a higher position of power. Everyone seems to crave it in the guardian world."

"Not me," he whispered. He straightened and opened his arms. "Does it look like I need *more*?"

"No," she replied. "But what you could do—"

"I already do. Two, now three, people are aware of my talent." He held up a finger, adding one with each name. "Arch Guardian Synintel, Queen-Elect Arnita, and you, Delanee Ralston. To be in a higher ranked guardian position, I'd have to reveal my gift to the Endowment and Revocation Committee."

"And that would be bad," she said carefully.

"Yes, because then everyone, and I do mean *everyone*, would be asking me to reveal hidden secrets and agendas. To question suspects, forgetting they have rights. To interrogate diplomats, forgetting we could lose vital relationships if it's discovered. I choose who I elicit information from, no one else."

"Synintel has never asked?"

"He can ask, as can the queen-elect, but I decide if it's worth the risk. I always interview new recruits coming into the FIO who will be placed on an intelligence team, but that's usually the extent of using my talent."

"Who did you inherit your gift from?" she asked, wondering if his parents had similar talents and had somehow managed to create a new hybrid in Ryan. "And does Ruthenia have any clue about your genetic ability?"

"No, and no one in Ruthenia ever will if I have my way." He crossed his arms and leaned against the counter behind him. "I don't know what they'd do."

"What do you mean?"

For a long moment, he stared at her, expressionless. Delanee's heart thumped hard, knowing without any doubt he was about to unleash something catastrophic on her.

"I am what the scientists and archaeologists who found, or rather rescued, me and a handful of others have named Generation Zero," he said without emotion.

"There are more like you?" she asked in wonder.

"I don't know what the others are capable of, only that they exist. My parents, the people who raised me, told me about them, but I haven't met any."

So many questions popped into her mind, and she didn't know where to start. Ryan rounded the counter and parked himself on the stool one away from her. He folded his hands on the counter.

"Here's the thing," he began as if knowing the thoughts

racing through her mind. Maybe he did. She wasn't completely convinced he couldn't read her mind with his weird gift. "Ruthenia's lore, about being some genetically modified race, is based entirely on fact according to the research my parents conducted."

"Why hasn't that been released? Scientific and medical journals would have fought over the rights to publish that information," Delanee said, turning to face him.

"Because when they made the discovery, the lives of eight infants were on the line. They all agreed to wait until they could determine the legal issues that would arise from raising us."

Delanee waved a hand at him. "You're grown now. Why has nothing been said?"

Seriousness darkened his features. "Because our gifts, if mine is any indication, could start a war. Ruthenia is obsessed with her place in the inhabited world. They were the only nation to thrive in the primal years, and that's because they didn't have any sort of primitive degradation in their society like everyone else. The people who founded the nation kept their island private and isolated and built the first society that all others are basically modeled after.

"Their people, for whatever reason, left the island generations ago and created the first genetically superior offspring in other nations. Which led to a sort of global stabilization as the inheritors took their roles seriously, using their talents for the good of their society."

Delanee shook her head, not understanding his line of reasoning. "We're the only country that places Gen-Heirs in a guardian-type hierarchy."

"Yes, that's true, but Westicans vote for theirs to run their government. Cairo used theirs to begin an empire where the talents were rented out for others to utilize. Italyssa is still discovering the abilities born on their land, but already we can see the positive effects in the capital their gifted can produce, either through agriculture or commerce. I'm not surprised botanical and financial talents settled on the island."

"And why would Ruthenia care about you when, like you've said, their people and genetics are all across the inhabited world now?"

He sighed and then pressed his lips together. Another difficult admission, then. Delanee's head already swam with all he'd divulged.

"According to my parents and Queen-Elect Arnita—"

Her brain seized. "You know the queen-elect personally? Like, personally, *personally*?"

"Focus, Delanee," he said, his hands pointing in an arrow on the countertop. "My association with the queen-elect is irrelevant right now."

"But—"

"No, listen, I'm only going to say this once, and then we'll never speak of it again, understand?"

She gnawed on the inside of her bottom lip and nodded.

"Good, thank you. Now, according to Arnita—"

First name basis! He was on a first-name basis with the *queen*! Stars above, she'd be getting that article for certain. She almost bounced right off the stool.

"Delanee." Her name growled pulled her awareness back.

She snapped her attention to his eyes. "Yes?"

"Should we finish this in the morning?"

She flattened her hands on either side of the teacup and took a long, bracing breath, wrangling in her wayward excitement. Chances were, he'd change his mind in the morning. For whatever reason, he'd decided to share tonight. Best not to risk a reversal. "I'm good."

"You're sure?"

"Yes. Please, continue."

"No one knows how Ruthenia founded their nation, only that the purity of their genetics is vital to their sovereignty in their eyes."

"I'm well aware of their standards," she said, failing to hide the disgust from her voice.

"I know. And if they can look at the stunning results of your family line and change a law, imagine what would happen if they learned the original form of their genetics is alive today."

Delanee tried to process his statement and drew a blank. Original genetics? "I don't understand. Don't all Ruthenians have original genes?"

He shook his head. "Not like mine."

That's when his previous words finally coalesced in her mind as something tangible. *Generation Zero.* As in none previous. The very first, like patient zero in an infection. And he'd been rescued, not born, by his parents. Rescued from what? From where?

Delanee stared at him, and he stared back, once again devoid of emotion. He expected her to see a monster, she realized. And the temptation was there, the fearful impulse to put distance between them. But she had what many considered atrocities in her family. The too-powerful. The freakishly gifted. Deklan's ability to bond with three wolves *and* pull a bond from another wolf master was dreaded. Donovan.... She shook her head. Donovan's capability hadn't been seen in over a hundred years. Beast masters panicked in his presence, and for a good reason. Her brothers were *not* monsters. What they were capable of needed respect, not fear.

"You're human," she stated. A fact.

"I—Yes." He gave a quick nod, but doubt flickered in his pale eyes. "Yes."

"But?" she urged, knowing there was more, knowing

he'd questioned his humanity at one time. She saw what he tried to hide.

He opened his palms. "But they found me, and others, in a sort of incubator. Only it was unlike anything they'd seen. We were encased in ice."

"Ice?" she asked, shocked. "Like frozen? You were frozen and *lived*?"

"It wasn't normal ice. I can't explain it well because they couldn't. But, yes, I was alive."

"Where was this? In Ruthenia?"

"No, deep in the UZ, far outside of Siber. Over two weeks of walking in freezing conditions. My parents and a handful of scientists, and other archeologists went on an expedition to try to discover what was in the land. They found an underground laboratory with babies. Intrigued, they took an incubator to their camp. When it thawed...."

Delanee covered her mouth. "A live infant."

He nodded. "They returned and rescued as many of us as they could find, eight in total."

She perched on the edge of her stool. "Are there more? Have there been more?"

He glanced away, but not before she caught the sadness in his gaze. "My parents ventured back about ten years ago. They never made it home."

Delanee grasped his bicep and squeezed. She couldn't imagine losing either of her parents, let alone both at the same time. "I'm so sorry. What happened?"

He shrugged, the movement causing the muscles beneath her hand to flex. "I don't know, and I couldn't learn anything. After everyone went missing, Siber forbade guides from entering the UZ again. Anyone caught helping is locked out and will starve or freeze to death."

Delanee let her hand fall away. "I am so very sorry."

"Anyway," he sighed, "no one can know the truth about

my origins. Ruthenia could potentially lay claim to my genetics, and I refuse to become a prisoner or property."

Delanee's focus shifted to the archway leading to the hall to his room. "And Inara."

"Yes, and Inara."

Keeping her attention on the archway, Delanee asked, "Why did you tell me all this? Why are you trusting me with something so dangerous to you?"

TEN

"I DON'T KNOW," slipped from Ryan's mouth before he could stop himself.

Truth was, he *did* know. He wanted her to be aware of him, *all of him*, as a man. Illogical, and yes, as she stated, dangerous, and he couldn't explain the need. Other than sitting with her while she'd held his baby, hearing the answers to all the questions she hadn't known he'd asked, learning *her*, he wanted her to have the same sense of familiarity. Even out the flow of information. Now she knew more about him. And surprisingly, he was okay with that. Because Ryan had also discovered another startling truth.

He wanted Delanee.

All of Delanee.

For a very long time.

She hadn't run screaming from the room. Hadn't demanded to be returned to her brother. Hadn't stared at him as though he'd grown a second head and was planning to murder her. Hadn't been repulsed in any fashion, only curious. Always curious. He could be himself around her, his true self, and the knowledge was a potent mix of hope and lust that left him on fire for the woman seated inches away.

"Why aren't you—"

"Freaking out? Shocked? Distressed?" she asked.

Ryan waved a hand. "Yes, all those things."

She shrugged. "Most of us Ralstons, even the non-beast talents, have what some would call inexplicable qualities. Being a powerhouse of a genetic heir isn't something unusual in my family."

"But not you," he said and wondered at the sudden press of her lips. Or perhaps she did have some secret gift. He flattened his hands on the cold marble countertop, suppressing the urge to pry.

"But not me," she said, sighing. In longing? Or, in relief that he didn't touch her? "Is this your reason for believing you need to be alone?"

Ryan straightened from the barstool. "Trust is hard when you know someone can invade your privacy on the level I can. Perhaps impossible. No relationship can be built without trust."

"You said I'm the first to really know."

"Yes, you are. And again, if I don't trust someone enough to reveal what I'm capable of, why would I be in a lifelong relationship with them?"

Her jaw flexed. "Only short-term sex is acceptable?"

Very short term. Renelle had been his longest affair, spanning weeks. Prior to Delanee, he'd never really given much thought to his intimate life. "Most of my lovers were widows, not wanting to be tied down themselves."

"And human rabies syndrome?"

He held up a hand and wiggled his fingers. "Isn't a concern for me. One touch, one honest answer."

She rubbed her arms as if chilled. "Stars above, your talent in the wrong hands... you could do anything to anyone, and they'd never know."

"My talent in the wrong hands of an authority figure is a bigger concern for me," he admitted.

Her beautiful golden eyes regarded him, and he sat still and silent, letting her contemplate without interruption.

"How did your parents keep you a secret?" she asked, arms still crossed.

"When they realized what I was capable of, they took me to Arch Guardian Synintel. My parents trusted the guardian system and went to the highest authority they could think of to ask what would happen if Ruthenia learned my history. Henry advised them never to say a word and to let him work with me."

Suspicion narrowed her gaze. "Were you forced to work for the arch guardian?"

"No, he left the choice up to me. I agreed on the condition my talent would remain between him and me and never be recorded. He asked if he could inform the queen-elect. I agreed, but with the understanding that any requests from either of them were to be completed at my discretion. They were never to order me to interrogate anyone." He rubbed the back of his neck. "The queen-elect doesn't know exactly how my talent works, just that I can get an honest reply from someone without their knowledge. That was another requirement."

"They know what you can do, but not specifically how?"

"Synintel is aware of what I can do. I've known him almost my entire life."

"Second father, hmm?" she said, a faint smile toying at her lips.

Ryan couldn't stop a sarcastic snort. "More like a strict uncle who always looked for ways to be disappointed."

The smile faded. "I'm sorry."

Ryan reached for her cold, unfinished tea. The action placed him close enough to catch her delectable scent.

Clean, citrusy florals. "Don't be. He didn't want me to think I was above the others around me or above the laws everyone had to follow. Never wanted me to become arrogant enough to lose my integrity."

She shifted on the stool to close the small space between them, taking his hand and lacing their fingers. Ryan's pulse raced, and he gripped the porcelain so hard, he was surprised the cup didn't shatter. How did this woman make him feel like a teenager again? Like intimacy and romance were unexplored concepts with the boundaries waiting to be broken and experimented upon. Each touch a new and tempting experience.

"You used your gift today, didn't you? To discover where the assassin lives?" she whispered.

"Why are you touching me?" he asked, shocked by her action, intrigued to know her reason, glancing at their joined hands and then her face.

She stiffened but didn't pull away. "Do you want me to stop?"

"No."

Angling her head, her focus on their joined hands, she twisted her wrist until her fingertips danced along his. "I figured the best way to show you I wasn't afraid of what you can do, who you are, was to show you."

Her touch wasn't meant to seduce. Yet the casual glide of her hand along his had the same effect on Ryan as if she'd trailed a slow path down the front of his shirt toward his pants. He shifted, bumping the stool behind him, thankful he wore a sweater that covered the sudden bulge in his trousers. A sense of wonder softened her face, her attention remaining on their clasped fingers.

Realization slammed into him. Everything felt new and thrilling because, for Delanee, it *was* new. The innocent, almost sweet examination of entangled fingers shouldn't be an aphrodisiac. Ryan wanted the unrushed exploration to extend to the rest of her. To ease his hands down her sides and reveal the satin smooth expanse of her stomach an inch at a time. But the awareness of her inexperience demanded a slower pace. Needed to allow the nuances of each moment to be fully appreciated. To be slow, to savor and devour, a luxury Ryan didn't think he'd ever had himself.

"Yes, I used my gift today," he answered her question from earlier. "The woman let me right in, thinking I was a potential customer. Didn't take much to get her isolated in her office and ask a quick series of questions about Berk Pherson."

Her motions stilled, but she continued to hold his hand. "What will you do next?"

Ryan took a deep breath. "I'm going to have to find someone in Old City Ruins who will work with—" He caught himself before he said *my team*. "Who will agree to allow an intel team inside to search for him."

"And my brother's team, too, right?" she asked.

"I'll ask Wolvenguard, but—"

Her fingers squeezed his. "No buts. Deklan's new mate won't allow herself to be left out of the hunt, nor will he. Not with the dangers posed to both his wife and now his sister. Consider him part of the team, at least for the Old City Ruins task."

"I figured as much, but it's not up to me."

She yanked her hand free and glared, her eyes sparking with her anger. Would her gaze be as vivid with a different passionate fire burning behind them? Oh, the temptation to find out....

"*Desymda*!" she snapped and slashed her hand through the air in front of him.

Ryan raised a brow. He'd never heard her speak a word of her father's native tongue. That she spewed one now, a curse word at that, shocked and thrilled him. Shocked because this was Delanee, the epitome of a Sziverian woman. Thrilled because this was *Delanee*, who perhaps wasn't all she tried to portray. Then again, she'd given him a glimpse of the fiery woman hidden beneath all the composure she maintained.

She seemed to realize her slip and poised her features, smoothing a hand down the front of the too-big sweater engulfing her slender frame. "That's nonsense, and you know it. Why do you insist on keeping up the ruse when I know everything else?"

"What ruse?"

"The one that you have no control over the intel teams."

"I don't," he said easily. "I am just a liaison."

"That's—"

"All I am, and trust me, it's enough. Do you think it's easy to make sure Synintel, and by proxy the queen-elect, treat everyone beneath them fairly? That's what I do. When Wintersfall demanded the terms of his contract with his bride be honored the instant their marriage became genuine and not just a paper contract between them and Sziveria, I had to ensure that happened. When Raiventon, whose father-in-law is Synintel, refused to leave his wife's side when she learned of her last two pregnancies because he'd already missed the birth of his first child, I had to fight for him. When Lucianna agreed to be on a guardian team, I had to make sure with her heartbreak and anger, that she was placed on one that would not only train, but support her while she healed."

The determination remained in her gaze and hardened her features. "Right, exactly, they are *your* teams. They'll follow you before they ever follow an arch guardian. *You* instruct them to allow Wolvenguard to accompany them to the Old City Ruins, and they'll agree."

"I still work under Synintel, and I *can* be relieved of my position if I overreach my authority. Which I will not do."

The teams who relied on him were worth more than any power struggle. An authority he did not want. Ever.

Her arms crossed, fully revealing the modest curves of her breasts. Ryan forced his attention to the tea he'd been in the process of picking up before distractions— such wonderful distractions— had abounded.

"Admirable of you," she grumbled and tossed her wayward curls, tucking a strand behind her ear. "Will you, though?"

"Make sure your brother's team can participate?" Mug in hand, he stood and rounded the counter to the sink.

She nodded, swiveling on the stool to face him.

A quick twist of a knob poured water from the faucet. "I'd like him there. The wolves would ensure a victory, which we desperately need."

"Will you go?"

His gaze lifted. Had a hint of concern laced her words? None showed on her face, only the inquisitiveness she never seemed to be without. Ryan returned to washing the few dishes in the sink. "No. I don't lead any teams. Liaison, remember? I'll be waiting outside the ruins to learn of their victory."

"You're that confident?"

"Absolutely. They can't fail, not when it comes to eliminating the assassin."

"And what if they do?" she asked, worrying her lush bottom lip between her teeth.

Ryan held a dish under the warm, flowing water, meeting her gaze. "They won't. Trust me."

Her palms pressed flat against the marble. The creamy stone, combined with the low flicker of the only lamp in the room, made her honeyed skin glow. "I do. Trust you."

Ryan braced his wet hands on either side of the sink and regarded her. "Why?"

She traced the mossy green lines snaking through the

marble. "Because you trusted me. You trusted me not to share what you revealed with anyone. Trusted I'd be honest when I said I wouldn't do so. And I trust *you* not to use your talent against me, not to burrow around in my head without my knowledge. If you want to know something, ask."

"And you'll answer just like that?" he asked, snapping his damp fingers.

"Maybe, maybe not, but we'll have a conversation all the same, won't we?" Her head angled as she regarded him. "Have you ever been able to have a normal conversation?"

"Of course."

"Without the use of your talent?"

"Yes." Now, whether he could resist the compulsion to keep from using said talent was another situation. "I can't use my ability in the presence of witnesses."

"Ah." She lifted her chin and motioned between them. "And one-on-one, you still have a normal conversation, knowing some things may remain a mystery?"

"Depends on whom I'm speaking to. I trust Winters-fall's team implicitly. If they're keeping something from me, they have a reason. And if I suspect and ask, they'll answer me honestly. Another guardian? Depends on the conversation." He turned off the water and dried his hands. "The thing is, once I feel the need to receive an authentic response, I can't really stop myself from getting one."

Her jaw flexed, and she dropped her hands onto her lap. "What do you mean?"

"Discovering the truth becomes a sort of obsession until I have the answer. Sometimes, it may take me weeks, not necessarily a discussion, to reveal what I'm searching for."

"All the unknowns in your search for answers about the, what are they called again?"

"V Alliance," he supplied.

"Yes, them, must be driving you nuts."

Ryan rehung the hand towel, making sure all the edges were aligned. "The last few years have been a challenge."

"But you've managed not to enthrall every person you encounter."

Ryan wavered a hand back and forth. "Eh."

She laughed. A beautiful sound of joy and light. All he could do for a second was stare, transfixed by her stunning grin. She had dimples. Adorable and, wow, sexy. How had he never noticed a genuine smile on her face before?

The humor faded, and she watched him, confused. "What?"

Ryan opened his mouth to tell her the truth. To tell her how gorgeous she was to him, how her laughter had brought an ache to his chest. Instead, he scrubbed his hands down his face and sighed. "Nothing. I'm just, I'm tired."

Which was also the truth. Exhaustion seeped into his veins and tugged at his muscles. He had to remind himself he hadn't brought Delanee Ralston into his home to seduce. She wasn't the type anyway. She deserved forever after. And even if she claimed to trust him, their first big fight would bring about suspicion. What could Ryan do to defend himself? Never touch her? Deal with the distrust when it reared its ugly head? An inevitable occurrence. Another reminder as to why he and relationships were destined for failure.

He dropped his hands and grabbed the dishes to put away. "How do you normally get to the paper?"

"I take a shared carriage for the morning business commute. My stop is the seventh one."

"Have you ever taken Deklan's carriage before? Or his Ariot?"

Delanee shook her head. "No." She tapped her nails on the marble. "What if you drop me off two blocks away, and I walk?"

"Too exposed. And someone could be waiting for you near the entrance."

She straightened. "I can use the news crier entrance. It's off a narrow side street that runs behind—"

"I know where the crier entrance is located." Ryan knew the exit locations of any building he'd been inside. Since there were few in Haven City he hadn't ventured into, he knew the layout of almost every major structure in the city. "And that may work. I could even drive you. My Ariot will fit down that road."

"The criers leave on their bikes around nine when the sun has melted most of the ice. The road is empty after they head out."

He leaned against the counter and crossed his arms. There would be no going near her again. Too many temptations. "Do you need to arrive before nine?"

She nodded. "Yes. I have to get Curtis my article in time to print it if he's happy."

"And you're sure I can't take it in? We'd talked about it yesterday."

Patience smoothed across her face, and he fought a smile. "That was before you wanted to know if anything was missing from my desk, remember? Since I need to go anyway, I can deliver the article."

"All right, what time?"

She gnawed on her bottom lip. Ryan wanted to launch across the counter, take over, and then kiss the sting away. He pressed his butt into the edge of the counter until pain grounded his wayward concentration.

"Seven?" She held her palms open. "I don't normally go in the morning. I work in the afternoon. I should have gone in today."

Ryan straightened. "Seven it is. Let me check on Inara, and I'll help you bring your things to your room."

"I—okay," she whispered, sliding off the stool.

Ryan wondered what she'd stopped herself from saying but opted not to push. The hour *was* late, and with an early morning, they needed to sleep. In their separate rooms. Far apart. He repeated the mantra in his head over and over while checking on his sleeping daughter, starting a fire to warm the room, and grabbing her empty bottle to wash and put in the box to return to the vendor.

Delanee was nowhere to be found when he finished, but a box and her gown were still on the dining table. Ryan debated leaving the gown and setting the box in the office, which was in the process of being overtaken by her anyway. The last place he needed to be anywhere near was a room with a bed and her in the same vicinity.

No, what he *needed* was to remind himself he had self-control, knew how to use it, would act like a grown man, and carry the things to her room. She could decide if she wanted the research in the office or the bedroom. An office he'd ignore for the time being. The top of his desk had disappeared in a single day. The woman had a gift with her inability to clean up after herself.

Faint light spilled from the office, and he stuck his head in to investigate. Empty. Frowning, he continued down the corridor to her room at the end. No Delanee. He set the box on the dresser beside her empty bag and contemplated laying the gown on the mattress. A reading chair sat adjacent to the bed, and he imagined the elegant gown thrown over the arms and altered course, heading to the closet. He secured the dress on a hanger and then carefully smoothed the flowing layers to keep the gown from further wrinkling.

"Is keeping *everything* neat a compulsion for you? Because I promise no one is going to notice or care if my dress looks like I picked it up off the floor and put it on. They'll assume the rumpled fabric is part of the design. Trust me on this," Delanee said behind him, throwing an armload of clothes onto the chair he had hoped to avoid becoming a laundry basket.

"Do you tell yourself that so you can treat the floor as a dresser? Because the drawers work much better," he said, closing the closet. Then he changed his mind as he looked at the pile she'd unloaded a few feet away. His fingers twitched. "Where did those come from?"

"It's what I wore yesterday. And I'm not sure when the clothes I grabbed were last washed, so they're soaking now."

Ryan could only stare. "How often do you wear dirty clothes?"

Her shoulders squared. "I make sure they smell clean. If they don't stink, then they are clean. The clothes I grabbed didn't smell fresh."

"Sweet summer sun," Ryan muttered, swiping a hand down his face. "Nothing smells right when you walk over it all day long."

He grabbed the shirt and skirt, shaking them both out before draping them over his arm. "Try putting things where they belong for a week, for me, and see the difference it makes."

"Yeah, no. I mean, if it's a requirement for me to stay here, I'll do my best, but I make no promises."

Angling his body to still see her and hang up the clothes, he frowned. "Why? I mean, why won't you clean up after yourself?"

"It's not a matter of won't. It's a matter of I have better ways to spend my time than sorting and hanging all my clothes," she said, shrugging. "My parents tried for eighteen years, and they failed. My *baki* has also tried and gave up after six months. I... like my chaos."

Ryan shuddered at the memory of her bedroom. He pointed at the floor. "This room will never look like that."

Her expression remained neutral. "I've figured that. I'll do my best to keep the floor clean."

The compromise should have been good enough. After all, he rarely ventured down this hall, let alone into this bedroom, except to dust twice a month. Now, though, his imagination would be getting the better of him. The need for his home to remain free of clutter would be a driving pressure to check in here and ensure the space hadn't exploded into disarray.

"Uh oh," she whispered, grabbing the bag off the dresser and dropping it into the top drawer. What had his expression shown? His panic at the mere thought of a mess? "Is it part of your talent? This need for control?"

"It's not control. It's order," he said, shifting the hangers in the closet. "I prefer things to be organized. And no, I can't explain it."

His parents had theorized perhaps a military-like strictness had been ingrained in his genetics since he'd maintained a clean space without instruction since he could first relocate objects on his own. Ryan didn't like to think of himself as being fully programmed despite possibly being an experiment. He wanted autonomy, a sense of self.

"You're messy, and I'm neat. We both have quirks. Everyone does," he said, closing the closet door.

"Mine will—would—" she quickly corrected, her hands fisted at her sides, "drive you crazy."

Ryan liked *will*. He liked the slip that revealed she'd imagined a future with him, though he shouldn't. Liked it so much he didn't think before speaking. "Maybe I need to be driven crazy."

ELEVEN

DELANEE COULD ONLY STARE at Ryan, unsure how to reply. She wasn't some charming socialite, the type of woman he was probably used to associating with. He'd admitted most of his lovers had been widows. She'd imagined, with a jealous fire she hated to acknowledge, that they'd been quick meetings of spent lust at dinners, evening events, or other such social functions. The women had known how to seduce with a glance. How to entice with body language. Delanee had never lamented not knowing how to use feminine wiles, but now she wished she'd at least taken a little time to learn.

Because she really, *really*, wanted to kiss him again.

She had no illusions about what would happen once the assassin situation was handled. Ryan would usher her out his front door so fast she would wonder if she'd managed to grab all her possessions. Time was not on her side to discover more about attraction or to learn about herself as a woman. His response felt like the invitation she'd never had before, and she wasn't sure what to do about it.

Men didn't flirt with her. They listed their attributes in

the hopes of getting into her social circle. The few who had stolen kisses had been so unpleasant, Delanee had made no efforts to allow a repeat, let alone encourage another attempt. Kissing Ryan again wouldn't be another attempt, it'd be another experience. One she wanted. Desperately.

Ryan appeared to come to his senses, realizing in the taut silence what he'd said, clearing his throat and shifting to leave.

No.

Delanee panicked. She did the only thing that came to mind.

She launched herself at him.

Wrapping her arms around his shoulders, she meshed their mouths together. While he was tall, so was she, and the action propelled him backward, slamming his back into the wall between the closet and bedroom doors. The collision of her body into his hard chest expelled a gasp from her and he took advantage, his mouth opening, his tongue seeking entrance. Delanee didn't hesitate. She opened wider, her grip tightening in the velvety fabric of his sweater and burrowing into the softer hair at the base of his neck.

His hands did a little exploring of their own, right up underneath the sweater she wore, and Delanee couldn't stop a moan from escaping. Little arcs of pleasure tingled everywhere his fingertips danced. Along her hips. Her back. Up her spine. Around her rib cage. Back down. The gentle study of his touch mapping out her curves caused a throbbing ache to develop deep inside. Delanee squirmed, seeking... something. She didn't know what, only knew she wanted, needed, more.

Inside her mouth, his tongue danced and glided. Their breaths mingled in rapid bursts of excitement. He moved to grip her hips, pulling her tight to his lower body, where a telltale solid mass pressed, oh stars above, exactly where she craved. Pleasure sizzled through every nerve in her body.

Wow. She wanted more, and she wanted more *now*. The revelation sobered her and had her yanking free, stumbling back a step.

He froze, his hands outstretched from where they'd been holding her. Delanee touched her damp and swollen lips.

"I'm sorry," she sputtered, holding out a trembling hand. "I didn't mean, I shouldn't have—"

He shook his head. "No, I should be apologizing. You-you're not—"

"No," she said, straightening, not wanting him to finish the phrase. She knew she wasn't sexually accomplished. She didn't need a reminder. "You're right, I'm not. And I'm not going to use you like others have."

His mouth snapped shut, and he blinked. Passion still flushed his cheeks and made him appear so vital, so alive, so absolutely beautiful... so *hers*. Delanee didn't want to consider another woman ever having the man in front of her again. Right now, the heat in his eyes was for her, and her alone. But to accept the pleasure she had no doubt he'd deliver and then walk away as if it meant nothing would make her no better than all the others before her. Would make her no better than the hussy Renelle. Thinking her name made a hiss rise in Delanee's throat. She didn't want to be like any of them, but especially like the one who'd dealt such an awful blow. Ryan deserved better. Inara did, too.

"You're worried about me?" he asked, having started a statement, but ending on a note of uncertainty. Like he couldn't quite believe she'd be concerned about his feelings. Confusion pinched his face and flooded his eyes. "I assure you, any using was mutual. They didn't force me into anything."

"I know. Because you believed you couldn't have more." When he opened his mouth, she lifted her hand higher. "No, I'm not insinuating anything should happen between us. I know better. However, I'm not looking for a quick memory."

"What if that's all I can ever give?" he asked softly.

Delanee shook her head. "My brothers have been down that road, and it has led nowhere good. I promised myself I'd treat my body and anyone else I respected the same."

Ryan took a deep breath and braced his hands on his thighs. "Admirable, Delanee, if not a bit naive."

Her chin lifted. "I'd think you, of all people, would understand."

He smiled, though as usual, the action didn't reach his eyes. "I am grateful for your sense of propriety. I seem to lose my own where you're concerned. But I'm far from innocent and don't need protecting. You, however, do." He moved to caress a line along her jaw to her chin. "You have something very precious worth saving."

Delanee wanted to scoff, but she *did* have something prized. He was correct. She couldn't imagine being with someone who didn't have her whole heart, and she agreed, her heart was precious indeed. No matter what he'd told himself, he had a heart worth loving as well. She wrapped her hand around his thick wrist, holding his touch in place, her gaze searching his. "You do, too."

He leaned forward and ghosted a tender kiss to her lips. "Goodnight."

The moment he pulled away, she wanted to argue. She compressed her lips tight and swallowed the urge as he slipped from her room. In her mind, she knew his walking away was necessary. Her heart still cried out for the loss. Not good, not good at all.

When she'd agreed to come to his house, a deep, insatiable need to explore a physical relationship had never crossed her mind. Yes, she'd been drawn to him. No sense in denying the truth, but the startling surge of desire was new.

And, much to her disbelief, not unwelcome. What that meant exactly, she wasn't sure.

Deciding to worry about her puzzling attraction to Ryan later, Delanee readied herself for bed. She showered, untangling her hair with conditioner. Afterward, wrapped in a towel, she started a slow-burning fire. Ryan hadn't given her anything to wear to bed tonight, and she'd thrown what she'd worn last night into the soaker with her other clothes. Nibbling on her bottom lip, she considered her options. Sleep naked, or in the clothes hanging in the closet she planned to wear tomorrow. Not wanting to smell like a bed all day, she opted to slide between the cool sheets nude.

Bang, bang, bang.

Exhaustion pulled at Delanee, and she struggled to open her eyes. Hadn't she just crawled into bed? On her stomach, a pillow tucked under her arm, another beneath her head, and yet another for her knees, she inhaled and burrowed deeper into the warm cocoon.

"Delanee!" a masculine voice called on the other side of the door.

She groaned and flopped onto her back, dropping an arm over her eyes.

"Delanee, we need—" His words cut short, no longer muffled.

"We need what?" she mumbled, sitting up and stretching.

"To um, to leave. It's six-forty-five."

She collapsed back onto the pillows. "Too early."

"No, it's not. You said you needed to be at the paper by seven?"

The paper. Her article. The deadline to get her work to her editor before the first print. Gasping, Delanee flew up and tossed off the covers. For the first time, she finally focused on Ryan, who stood motionless, grasping the doorknob, eyes wide, a faint white glow bleeding into his irises.

"What?" she asked.

He choked.

Cool air brushed her skin. *All* her skin. Breath lodged in her throat, and their gazes clashed before he stepped back and slammed the door shut. Delanee remained frozen, wondering what all he'd managed to see before fleeing. Thighs spread, she had one leg off the mattress, the other still tangled in the sheets, which she'd tossed to the side to leave the bed. So, okay, yes, he'd seen *everything*. Mortification burned through her chest and teared in her eyes. She forced herself to stand instead of diving beneath the covers and hiding. Forever.

At least he hadn't stood and gawked or spoken when she realized she wasn't wearing a scrap of fabric. Only now, she had to figure out how to proceed when she saw him again. Which would be in... less than ten minutes. She took deep breaths to relieve the urge to cry.

Delanee dressed as unhurriedly as possible but not slow enough for her sanity. Wearing what she'd had on when she'd conducted the interview, a simple yet professional skirt, tunic sweater with a wide belt, and leather boots, Delanee held her head high and marched from the room. Ryan waited at the front door, glancing at his watch, a paper bag in one hand and a travel mug in the other. The impulse to fidget and avert her gaze from his had her hands fisting. White tendrils still brightened his eyes, turning his stare more silver than blue.

"I presumed you'd wish breakfast to go," he said, holding out the bag and mug.

Delanee slowly accepted both, her cheeks on fire. "Thank you?" She'd expected him to be embarrassed, like her, not considerate and acting as if nothing happened.

"You can eat in the Ariot." He glanced at his watch again. "It's at least a twenty-minute drive this time of morning."

"I'm sorry I overslept," she whispered, following him into the cool morning. Frost sparkled on the lawn and shrubbery.

He sucked air through his front teeth, locking the door behind her. "You know," he said thoughtfully afterward, palming the keys and jogging down the stairs. "I'm not going to complain."

Delanee's grip on the bag tightened, crinkling the paper. She didn't know how to decipher his words. Did that mean he liked what he saw? Did she even want him to appreciate her body? She wasn't beautiful by Sziverian standards. Too thin and too flat everywhere men wanted curves. Except for her butt, which seemed plenty round enough. Now, she wanted to know, but the conversation wasn't exactly appropriate. Then again, exposing herself hadn't been either, even if by accident.

Ryan disappeared inside the Ariot, and Delanee rushed to join him. The sun kissed the roofline, making her squint once she left the shadow of the house. Her breath puffed out in glowing vapor clouds. He'd popped the door for her, and she slid inside, setting the bag on her thighs and gathering the length of her skirt before shutting the door. The magnetic engine purred as Ryan eased them onto the quiet street.

Contemplating the best way to approach the indignity of her morning, she gnawed on her bottom lip.

"Wait, please," he said, making a right at the end of his road.

"Wait for what?" she asked.

"Just eat your breakfast. If you still want to talk when we reach the paper, we'll talk."

"Why?" She glanced at him.

His grip tightened on the steering column until his knuckles were white. "Because I don't want to wreck my vehicle. It was expensive."

She blinked and focused on the travel mug. "Oh, um, okay."

"I made you tea, and the twins brought orange blueberry scones when they picked up Inara."

"How nice, thank you."

Delanee ate, enjoying the complement of honey-sweetened pastry with hints of orange and bursts of plump blueberries. The tea Ryan made her was equally surprising in flavor, orange, something tart, and a trace of creamy vanilla. The silence should have been tense, but she found herself relaxing at the lack of awkwardness he exhibited. He acted like nothing uncomfortable had happened between them. His driving easy, his expression pensive, as if contemplating his day ahead.

Traffic was congested near the paper. Most of Haven City's government buildings were in the same area, and her paper happened to be adjacent to two official locations. Ryan kept driving where the carriage she normally took turned, taking two additional streets before turning down a narrower side road. He took two more alley streets, pulling up behind the paper. A few criers were parking their bikes and grabbing their empty bags to fill with today's print run.

"Did you still wish to talk?" Ryan asked, his deep voice breaking the silence.

Delanee licked her lips, dislodging crumbs. She wiped at her chin and considered taking the coward's way out, thanking him for the ride and hopping from the vehicle. But then she would think about what happened all day and get nothing accomplished, wondering what he thought.

"I don't normally sleep naked, just to get that out first," she said, folding the edges of the bag between her fingers. "I didn't have anything to wear last night."

"I wasn't offended, and it's okay if you do. There's no right or wrong way to sleep."

Heat flared across her cheeks and chest. "I know. I wanted you to know it won't happen again."

"I'll knock next time."

She chanced looking at him. He was still relaxed, staring out the windshield. His fingers tapped on the steering column.

"I don't know if that would have mattered," she admitted. "I wasn't altogether awake yet."

"I noticed, but I'll still be knocking."

Maybe he hadn't liked what he saw after all. And what was she thinking? She didn't want him to see her naked again. Did she? *No.* No, she did not. Her emotions were all mixed up, a confusing blend of curiosity and mortification. She wanted to know if he'd appreciated what he saw while at the same time being appalled he'd seen her in the first place. Her bottom lip began to sting from her chewing.

"Delanee," he whispered, and she jerked her head to face him.

"Yes?"

"You're beautiful."

Everything in her stilled. "I am?" she breathed.

"Yes. I'd say more, but I'm afraid I'd shock you, not in a good way. I need you to stay with me for a few more days." He smiled that shallow smile.

Challenge accepted. "I'm not so easy to shock. I do write the social pages, you know."

"What you witness in others and what someone says about you to your face are completely different things." He sighed and shook his head. "I won't offend you or make you feel uncomfortable. Let's forget what happened, okay? It's not going to happen again."

"But I want to know," she said before she could stop herself. "You said you weren't complaining about what you saw and that I'm beautiful. Does that mean...." She licked her lips and gathered her courage, trying again, "Did you think what you saw of me was... beautiful?"

His nostrils flared, and he braced an arm on the steering column and another on the back of her seat. Leaning forward, his breath fanned across her lips, and the sharp, woodsy scent of him invaded her space. Those white striations bled into his irises, making her wonder what the onset of his talent meant when he wasn't touching her. Then again, Inara displayed the same gentle glow while Delanee fed her last night. An emotional reaction?

"Are you sure you want my answer?" he growled.

Her heart kicked, and warmth blossomed along her entire body. "Yes."

"You won't run?"

"No."

His pupils expanded, gobbling up any color until only a thin, pale rim remained. Delanee stared, fascinated, her body tingling with a new awareness.

"Seeing you perched on the edge of the bed, open to me, made me want to drop to my knees on the floor and taste a woman for the first time," he said against her mouth. "Do you know what that means? What I want to do to you? What seeing you did to *me*?"

Delanee's heart pounded so hard she wondered if the thunder of her pulse filled the Ariot, not only her ears. Her breath sawed past her lips. The throb she'd experienced yesterday flared between her legs, and she almost moaned. "You've never done that before?"

"Tasted a woman?" he asked, his lips fluttering across hers, a tease of sensation.

"Y-yes."

"No. I've never had the opportunity, nor have I cared to. But this morning? My mouth craved to know what you'd feel like against my tongue, how you'd taste."

Delanee trembled, her eyes closing as his erotic words painted a visual in her mind.

"Would you ever like a man to do that to you?" he asked, delivering another far too brief kiss.

"You," she admitted on a breathy exhale.

He groaned, and his lips took hers in a searing kiss. His tongue twisted and glided. His mouth consumed, dominated, and demanded. Delanee needed to be closer, arching her torso and shifting to the edge of the seat. He didn't disappoint. His arm wrapped around her waist, pulling her near until their upper halves met. Still not enough.

The kiss ended as fast as it'd begun. Ryan panted. Delanee struggled to find her own equilibrium.

"Delanee?"

"Yes?" She touched a trembling hand to her damp lips.

"We're in so much trouble."

TWELVE

Delanee couldn't concentrate. Somehow, she managed to get her editor the article he'd needed, though she still couldn't recall how. Sitting at her desk, she stared into the drawer full of unpublished works, some in progress, others fully completed, trying to remember what she needed to search for. Ryan's seductive confession kept replaying in her mind, robbing her of intelligent thoughts.

My mouth craved to know how you'd feel against my tongue....

Delanee didn't know much about intimacy other than the glimpses she'd caught at parties and the few lusty books she'd been brave enough to crack open. Ryan's words were both confusing and tantalizing. She wanted to experience what he'd whispered, and yet she worried her sense of modesty would inhibit her. Shaking her head, she tsked. Why was she giving his words any regard? They wouldn't reach that point in a relationship. Ever.

Why was she digging around in this drawer again? Ah, yes, rejected articles. Papers shifted beneath her fingers. One by one, she removed the more frivolous pieces hidden away in folders that had been rejected. Frowning, she dug deeper, placing loose papers and files on a separate stack on the desk. Where were the serious articles? After reaching the bottom of the drawer, she sat back and chewed her bottom lip. Maybe she missed them. She opened each folder and placed individual papers back into the drawer. All her deep research pieces were indeed missing.

Paranoia had her taking a quick glance around. No one watched her or seemed out of place. Delanee picked up three folders with rejected articles. They were all inconsequential things her editor had felt weren't compelling enough. Of course, when she'd submitted substantial journalistic efforts, they'd been rejected for various reasons. Their absence added weight to Ryan's suspicions. Could someone at the paper sabotage attempts to expose the darkness creeping into the city?

Folders secured under her arm, Delanee navigated the maze of desks and took the stairs for the art floor. The department was a modest attic room, the ceiling angled, beams exposed. Three artists shared the space, their workstations chaotic, colorful messes of papers, easels, and inclined drafting tables. Unframed sketches, watercolors, and even a handful of oil canvases were taped or tacked to every reachable surface. Delanee loved this room. Others did too, which was why sawdust-filled lounge bag chairs were tossed anywhere they wouldn't hinder the moving artists. Many employees spent hours in the room, writing or relaxing on breaks.

Windows set into the vaulted ceiling filled the space with warm light at each corner. Sarkis's workstation sat beneath a window. He hunched over the table, his arm at an odd angle, his hand making sweeping strokes. Delanee stood off to the side of his table, within his line of sight but not blocking any of the precious light.

"Morning, Delanee," he said, still sketching.

"Good morning," she answered, angling her head to figure out what was taking shape on his paper.

"What can I help you with today?"

Delanee took a step back and leaned against the wall, hugging the folders to her chest. They were alone in the room. "When are Jules and Hailey working?"

"Tomorrow, I think. Neither Curtis nor Amanda had assignments for the next two prints."

Delanee glanced at the open door. If she closed them in, people would wonder, and at this office? The gossip would never end. She'd have to risk an eavesdropper. "Do you have any copies of the drawings from the articles you helped me with?"

Sarkis paused mid-sweep and looked at her. The length of his blond ponytail slid across his back. Vibrant blue eyes regarded her in confusion. "Did you lose them?"

"They've been taken from my desk, along with my work."

"And they haven't been published?"

Delanee shook her head.

He straightened from the desk. Shorter than her, the top of his head came to her nose, and he had to continue looking up to meet her stare. "Let me check."

"Thank you."

The loose cotton of his pale brown pants and dark blue shirt flowed around him as he rushed to the other side of the room, where a tall wooden cabinet took up the wall between windows. He opened the section with his name painted on the front, the doors sliding outward. Hanging onto the tops, he peered inside, hummed, and then began digging around. "The last article you tried to publish was what, ten months ago?"

"Eight," Delanee corrected. "Right before Wintervail."

"Ah, that's right. Before the last print due to the arctic

season." Papers shuffled and fluttered. Sarkis's entire head disappeared into the cabinet. "Huh."

His muffled exclamation made her shift closer. "What is it?"

"My originals are missing as well."

Delanee gnawed on her bottom lip. Not good.

Sarkis slowly closed the segment. "What's going on, Delanee?"

"I don't know," she whispered, anxiety slamming her heart into her ribs. "I came to ask you to check on my witnesses from the rejected articles, but with everything missing?"

"Why would anyone care? I mean, they're research pieces, not...." Color bleached from his already pale skin. "You didn't do anything illegal, did you?"

"No! No, of course not." She glared. "You know better than that."

A long exhale left him and he pressed a hand to his chest. "I know, but everyone has a price for success. *You* know that."

She sniffed. "Well, I didn't do anything wrong. Someone wanted to make sure my research, and by association your artwork, disappeared. I don't know why, but it can't be anything good."

Speculation furrowed his brow and shone in his eyes. He crossed his arms and leaned against the cabinet. "What made you look in the first place?"

Uneasiness caused chills to slither over her skin. She rubbed at the bumps. "Like I said earlier, I was going to ask you to speak to some of my witnesses. A... friend is worried that my investigations are being suppressed. On purpose."

Sarkis leaned forward and whispered, "Censored?"

"Maybe," Delanee admitted.

He pointed at the floor. "Here? At this paper?"

Delanee pressed a hand to her forehead. "I don't know,

and I hate this. But my friend is concerned because of the nature of my articles."

"I would have to agree. Who is this friend?"

"A guardian at the FIO."

"Ranked?"

"Does it matter?"

Something in her tone must have revealed her frustration at his question, for he held out his hand in supplication. "I only ask because maybe Tyler knows this person?"

Tyler, the ranked guardian with whom Sarkis had contracted two years ago. Delanee racked her brain, trying to recall the man's rank and position and whether he knew Ryan. She didn't want to say either way, she realized. She didn't want anyone at the FIO to be aware of her investigations, except for the one guardian under that roof she trusted.

"I doubt it," she said easily. "He's just an assistant."

"Ah. Then why is he interested in your articles?"

Delanee scooped up the files she'd grabbed as props. "He's a friend of my brother's and was curious why I only wrote fluff pieces. I told him I wrote other things, but nothing else had been published. He was curious and a little suspicious."

"Warranted, I agree. Do you remember any of your witnesses' names?"

Delanee shook her head. "No, that's why I needed the articles. I know I met one at that bakery on East Street."

"The one that sells the huge cinnamon rolls?"

"Yes. And I met another...." Her words died, and her cheeks flamed. "Near The Rows."

Sarkis raised his brows. "The only place to meet anyone near The Rows is at a curtain show house."

"Yes," she agreed. "But we stayed in the lobby. I left after the interview."

A sultry smile curved his lips. "Sure you did. Delanee, I didn't know you had it in you."

"I don't," she assured. "Not that he didn't try to talk me into attending a show with him every other sentence."

"They are an experience. But, not for everyone."

"Anyway," she drew out, wanting to change the subject off the erotic curtain shows. "I don't remember what either of their names were."

"The bakery interview was about...." He waved a hand.

"HRS incidents happening at ranked guardian parties. And the curtain show house was magic lily dust."

He hummed and returned to his work table. Picking up a charcoal pencil, he twirled the thick black stick between his fingers. "I'm not surprised about the magic lily dust at the curtain show. The drug is said to enhance sexual experiences."

"The drug is said to enhance any number of things," Delanee stated, frowning. "It seems to be a wonder substance, according to sellers."

"It is a product to them," Sarkis said, smudging some of his art. "I will check the other shelves. Maybe someone misplaced the artwork."

"I appreciate it," she said but knew nothing would be found.

Back downstairs, Delanee fought to act normal and not suspicious of every person she encountered, including her editor. She popped her head into Curtis's office. "Did you need anything else from me?"

The lamp light flashed off his silver hair as he raised his head. He propped his arms on the desk littered with open newspapers and loose sheets of print. The sleeves of his ivory shirt were rolled up to his elbows and black ink stained his hands. An unlit cigarette dangled at the corner of his mouth. He pulled the slender rollup free and pinned her with his dark blue eyes. "You're going to the...." He snapped his fingers in question.

"Master Guardian Silverhill's *Bougainvillea* Gala, yes."

He returned his attention to the sheets before him, his too-long hair shielding his face. "Good. That works. I'll need the article on my desk before the first print run."

"Understood."

He popped the cold cigarette back into his mouth and mumbled. She'd been officially dismissed. Delanee hesitated momentarily, taking in the disheveled office and the over-worked man behind the desk. Could he be silencing infor-mation for a detrimental cause? She really didn't want Curtis to be a bad guy. Yes, he could be gruff and rude, and all the other irritating nuances that came with a powerful position, but she'd never considered him her enemy, rather an obstacle she needed to overcome to advance her goals. She was determined to see her name associated with more than fluff, whether by impressing him or going around him and submitting what he'd rejected elsewhere. Ryan was correct. However, they needed to know if the *Haven City Chronicle* could be trusted.

Delanee eased away from the doorway before Curtis noticed her lingering and questioned her. Returning to her desk, she checked every drawer and slender shelf for the missing articles. She didn't know if she had copies of her documents back home. One of the exposés, in her opinion, was the best piece she'd ever written, and losing it hurt. After digging through the piles of fashion journals, old invi-tations, and whatever else she hadn't thrown away, Delanee found the current invitation she'd need to the gala. She read the fine print and sighed with huge relief. Ryan could attend as a plus one if he wished. Normally, she'd bring Miriam, the journalist who covered articles in the event of an emergency, but she wanted Ryan's presence.

With a messenger bag slung across her chest and a hat

on her head, Delanee used the crier exit to leave the building. She walked down two alleys before braving the sidewalk and hailing a carriage-for-hire. After giving instructions, she climbed inside the simple wood frame interior. Without calling for a specific service, hailing a decent cab streetside was a rarity.

The city slid from tall, granite buildings to businesses and finally into large residences. Terravine took up nearly a block. The shield guardianess' greenhouse rivaled the size of the mansion. The driver stopped at the end of the curved drive and tapped on the window. Delanee slid the partition open, paid her fare, and then hopped out. The brick driveway absorbed the sun's heat, the rising warmth a nice contrast for her walk to the front door in the chilly breeze rustling leaves and toying with the length of her skirt.

Halfway to the front of the house, the door swung open, and the shield guardianess herself stood in the entrance. A sincere yet concerned smile graced Amari Dossett's face. Faint age lines and streaks of gray in her rich auburn hair hinted at her age. She met Delanee at the bottom of the stairs, hands outstretched.

"What is going on, child? Why are you here?" the shield guardianess asked, taking one of Delanee's hands.

"I need a safe place to wait until Ryan Voklane can pick me up," she said, trusting Amari with the truth.

"Voklane? Not one of your brothers?" she asked, her brown eyes wide in shock.

Delanee shook her head. "No. I made a discovery that could place my family in danger. Mr. Voklane is...." Driving her crazy in the best ways didn't seem appropriate. Delanee cleared her throat and tugged her hand free. "He's letting me stay with him until the threat passes."

Amari's gaze narrowed. "That's very noble of him."

"I'm in a room across the house from him. Promise."

Delanee took a few steps closer to the house. "No one knows I'm there except now, you, Deklan, and my *baki*."

Relief softened Amari's features. "Ah. Wolvenguard is aware. That is good."

Delanee forced a smile. Providing her older brother didn't become aware of very specific moments of Delanee's time spent under Ryan's roof, all would remain well. "I don't know how long I'll need to wait."

Amari waved a hand and headed back toward the house. "You know you're welcome here whenever and however long you need to stay. You can stay with us if you'd prefer?"

A surprisingly not-so-tempting offer. Delanee *should* be elated to have a chance to stay with the man who was wrecking all her preconceived notions of what she desired in a mate. "My association with Mr. Voklane is limited right now. If someone *is* following me and notices him continuing to pick me up, that won't remain the case. Also, if someone is following me and realizes I'm staying here—"

"Might place us in danger," Amari sighed. "Yes, I can see that being a problem. Grayson might bristle at the perception he can't keep his family safe, but I'll not risk my babies."

"I won't either," Delanee said. "I'm only going to stay the afternoon. If I need another place, I'll figure it out."

"Are you really in so much danger?"

Delanee explained as best she could without revealing too much. Yes, she trusted Amari, but not everything was hers to tell.

Amari shook her head and sighed again. "How did you get yourself into such a mess?"

"By accident," Delanee said.

They entered the foyer just as Grayson rounded a corner, papers in his hands.

"Amari?" he shouted.

"I'm right here, love," Amari said, a smile glowing in her eyes.

"What?" Grayson lifted his gaze from the documents in his hand. "Oh, there you are. Do you know why—" His attention shifted to Delanee. "Ah, makes sense now."

"Why what, and what makes sense?" Amari asked, moving to touch her husband's forearm. She gently pulled the papers free of his grasp.

"A Mr. Voklane called from Arch Guardian Synintel's office. He asked if he could use the back entrance for a brief visit."

"Ah, yes, he's coming for Miss Ralston."

"I figured that." Grayson's unique gold wrapped in gray irises settled on Delanee. "My question now is why."

"Is Ry—Mr. Voklane on his way?" Delanee asked, hoping her excitement at seeing Ryan again hadn't been revealed in her voice or the near slip of being too familiar with his name. She closed the front door behind her.

"He made it sound as if he was," Grayson said.

"I will explain everything later," Amari promised. "Right now, I'm going to get our guest some food. Has Henry eaten yet?"

Grayson blinked. "Patti was bringing a tray to leave outside his room last I checked."

Amari shook her head and sighed. "Will you talk to him again, please?"

Grayson nodded. "Yes, of course. I don't like him hiding any more than you do. And he should be joyous, not more upset, over his daughter marrying."

Amari glanced at Delanee. "Well, we all want different things for our children, don't we?"

Who was this Henry, and why did Delanee suddenly feel they were tiptoeing around the conversation because of her presence? Before she could ask, a housekeeper dressed in navy pants and a pale gray tunic with large navy buttons down the front entered the foyer.

"Shield guardianess? There's a radio call for you," the woman said.

Amari held up the papers. "Were these for me?" she asked her husband.

"For both of us," he moved closer to her. "These are the bids for the new road improvements."

"Oh, perfect. Perhaps that's what the call is about." Amari glanced at Delanee. "Would you excuse us?"

"No problem."

"Good luck, darling," Amari said, smiling. "Patti, will you please escort Miss Ralston to the family room? A man will be arriving to see her home shortly. Bring whatever she needs while she waits."

Patti inclined her head. "Of course, shield guardianess."

"Thank you."

The couple disappeared down a corridor to the left, and Patti guided Delanee to the right. Terravine Manor was massive, though much homier than Deklan's monstrosity of a mansion. The family room the housekeeper guided Delanee to was lined with bookshelves, toy bins, well-worn couches, and throw rugs. The comfortable space immediately relaxed her. Delanee tossed her messenger bag on the nearest couch and plopped onto the soft cushions.

"Tea or lunch, miss?" Patti asked.

"I'm fine, thank you."

"Nothing is off limits in this room. Any book, magazine, or game you wish to use is for you."

The woman left the door halfway open. Delanee slouched until her head rested against the back cushion and stared at the elegantly tiled ceiling. Only one wall had windows, and the soft glow of daylight made the shadows cast by the floral pattern on the tiles stand out in harsh relief.

The ceiling in her parents' formal living room had similar insets, and a rush of longing to be home with her family had her eyes closing. How much would Deklan tell them, if anything? Knowing all the Ralstons, they'd turn the family home into a fortress and dare anyone to try to take one of their own away. A situation Ryan was hoping to avoid.

Her family might be the only ones capable of taking on a nation and winning.

Subtle, pleasurable prickles danced along her skin, and Delanee took a deep breath and opened her eyes. Ryan stood over her. Had she fallen asleep? He straightened, and the sensation faded, making Delanee frown.

"Did you touch me?" she asked, her words slow and rough. She rubbed her neck and tried to smack away the dryness. Yep, she'd fallen asleep. At least when he woke her up this time, she was clothed.

"No."

Her frown increased.

"Why?" he asked.

"It just—" She shook her head and rubbed her hands down her face. The sensation of his talent must have been imagined. If he said he hadn't touched her, she believed him. "Never mind."

"I already spoke with Shield Guardianess Terravine. Are you ready to leave?"

Delanee straightened and patted the couch cushion for her bag. "Yes, we can go."

He helped her stand, a hand on her elbow, and though the touch was simple and polite, the heat of his skin still tingled along hers. She clutched the bag to her chest to keep from grabbing him and smashing their mouths together like she'd done last night. A mistake. Why did she have to keep reminding herself?

Because he tempted her. Made her curious to know where the physical awareness he elicited would lead. What he could make her experience. All dangerous. All to be avoided. Delanee stepped away and hugged her pack tighter, refusing to look at him. One glance and she'd crumble. She'd... missed him in the short time they'd been apart.

"I parked on the other side of their property. We'll have to walk through the yard and down the service alley," he said, rounding the couch, putting more space between them.

Delanee lamented the distance and clenched her jaw at the silly reaction. Space is what she wanted, and why he'd moved, she had no doubt. "I'm fine with walking."

She followed behind him. They didn't speak anymore, a tense silence stretching between them. Outside, the sun shone high in the sky. A faint breeze ruffled leaves and flowers hardy enough not to need the shelter of a green-house. Curls brushed across her cheek and stuck to her lips and eyelashes. Ryan glanced over his shoulder and then stopped so suddenly, Delanee almost slammed into his back.

She fought with another breeze, swiping the hair from her face only for it to return. Ryan grasped her chin, angled her into the wind, and gently swept the stands into place, readjusting the pins. When he finished, he didn't move away. His thumb swept a teasing path along her jaw, chin, and bottom lip, where his gaze locked.

"Did you find your articles?" he asked, still staring at her mouth.

Delanee licked her lips, the tip of her tongue catching the end of his finger. He dropped his hand, his gaze dark. "N-no," she managed to whisper.

His focus lifted to her eyes. "No?"

"They're missing. All of them, and Sarkis's art."

Thirteen

Ryan handed Delanee a small bowl of mashed carrots and potatoes in beef broth. Inara slapped the wood surface of her highchair table and yelled.

"I'm coming, I'm coming, no need to get upset." Delanee pulled the highchair closer to her. She stirred the mashed mixture and made num-num sounds. Inara watched her with big eyes, then grinned and squealed, slapping the table again.

Ryan's heart almost burst free. He rubbed his sternum and turned away from the domestic scene, returning to the stove. He couldn't keep Delanee, no matter how badly he or his child wanted her to stay. When the threat had passed, and he was hopeful that would happen soon, Delanee would return to her family, where she belonged. Safe from him and the naughty, inappropriate, lust-filled thoughts he couldn't seem to control where she was concerned.

The arousing image of her naked, legs open to give him the best view of his life, repeatedly flashed through his mind. Her breasts would fill his palm and had enough weight to allow him to plump while taking a dark chocolate nipple into his mouth. And oh, the textural feast her breasts would be on his tongue... the smoothness of her skin to the hard points of the tips. *Yes*. While exploring her breasts with his mouth, his fingers would discover all the erotic secrets between her spread thighs. How fast she'd get wet for him. What made her arch her spine, moan, and beg for more. He wanted the experience so badly a shudder raced through him.

Forcing himself to focus on finishing their meal and not the embarrassing erection covered by his sweater, Ryan plated the roasted beef the twins had left simmering. A jar of butter and a small basket of torn bread chunks waited in the center of the table in the dining nook.

"Do the twins often cook dinner for you?" Delanee asked, feeding Inara a half spoonful of mash.

With easy glides of the spoon left and then right, she scooped excess food off the baby's chin and waited for Inara to open her mouth again. Ryan raised a brow. Usually, the dribble plopped to the highchair, and he'd clean it up afterward. He set a plate down on the table across from her and moved to her side.

"How did you do that?" he asked.

"Do what?" She pressed the spoon to Inara's bottom lip. His daughter's mouth popped open.

"That swipe thing with the spoon." He pointed at Inara's chin. "For the food."

"You just scoop it off," she answered, scraping the edge of the bowl for another small bite. "Nothing special."

Ryan disagreed. Inara's little fists opened and closed, now coated in smashed carrots and potatoes. She hummed as she chewed. When Delanee didn't bring the spoon with the next bite fast enough, Inara squealed, kicking hard enough to bounce the tray.

"Hey," Ryan said and touched his daughter's nose. "None of that."

"Mmm, ba-da-da-da!" she yelled.

Delanee laughed. "You're going to have your hands full when she gets older and can actually form words." Delanee popped a bite into Inara's mouth and cooed. "Yep, trouble, trouble, your daddy will be in."

An understatement, Ryan figured. He didn't like to consider too far into the future what raising a daughter alone would entail. All the things he'd have to handle and talk about that a father would rather *not* have to think about, let alone discuss. A day at a time was about all he could handle without panic threatening to take over.

Excess again collected on Inara's chin, and Ryan closely watched Delanee's technique with the spoon.

She laughed and fed Inara the bite. "You look so serious."

"I didn't know I could do that." Worried, he frowned. "Has she been getting enough food? I'm realizing so much has been wasted."

"Yes," Delanee assured, smiling, "she's been getting enough. She may stay full longer now that she's getting a full serving."

Ryan collected the second plate. Delanee smiled in thanks and continued to feed the baby. He settled on the bench across from her. "I can take over if you'd like to eat."

"She's almost done." The spoon paused halfway to Inara. The baby opened her mouth. When nothing happened, she growled and shouted again. "Unless you want to?"

Part of him did. He enjoyed every minute with his baby girl, and she changed on him each month. Her face, size, and mannerisms all morphed into the person she'd soon become and continue to grow into. So many moments were missed because of his job, meeting her needs was important to him. However, he enjoyed watching Delanee care for her. Liked the attention she gave to his precious daughter. Many essentials had to be met tonight. Bath time, bedtime bottle, and a story, all those would be for Ryan.

"If you wish to keep feeding her, you can." Ryan smooshed butter into his carrots and potatoes.

She smiled. "I do."

"To answer your earlier question," Ryan said, needing a distraction from the ache taking residence in his chest once again, "yes, the twins often prepare food for us. Especially on the nights they've asked not to be disturbed."

Delanee set the empty bowl to the side. "Do you know what they're doing?"

Ryan cleared his throat. "I prefer not to speculate."

She laughed, rising. "That's probably for the best."

Ryan stood and moved before she could turn the high chair around. "Sit. Eat. I'll clean her up."

In the kitchen, he dampened a washcloth and grabbed a wooden cup and spoon. Sitting across from Delanee, he hooked a foot around the leg of the high chair and dragged Inara to his side of the table. Inara chortled and slapped her hands on the tray. Ryan quickly wiped her and cleaned the surface. He set the cup and spoon in front of her for amusement. Happy squeals soon joined the bang of the cup.

"So, was the artist unhappy about his missing pieces?" Ryan asked, mixing his smashed carrots and potatoes until the blend resembled what he'd given to Inara. He scooped the mixture onto his fork with a hunk of roasted beef.

Delanee squashed butter into potatoes and carrots but kept them separate. She took a chunk of bread and spread the carrot mash on top. Ryan plucked a small jar of honey with a pour spout from the condiment box he kept in the center of the table and gently pushed it across. The smile she beamed at him brought him a sense of contentment he'd only really experienced when he made Inara happy. He *wanted* to please Delanee in so many ways.

"Sarkis," she began, drizzling honey over the carrot

spread, "was more baffled than upset. He's hoping the sketches were misplaced."

"He didn't find it odd they were missing along with your articles?"

"Yes, he did, but he didn't want to jump to conclusions just yet. His spouse works at the FIO in a guardianship position, and I didn't want to draw attention to you."

"Who's the spouse?" Ryan asked, soaking up the broth with some bread.

"Tyler Filosa."

Biting into the bread, Ryan kept his face neutral while inside he did a fist pump. Sarkis was contracted. Ryan would have to plan a little hallway collision to ensure the spouse wasn't part of the V Alliance, but otherwise, he could let go of the possessiveness he had no business feeling in the first place.

"Do you know who he is?" she asked, bending down to pick up the spoon Inara had thrown on the floor.

"Filosa?"

Delanee nodded.

"No, I've never heard of him or worked with him. He's not part of Synintel's intelligence teams. He must be supporting staff."

All the various positions played through his mind. Only a few were guardian roles that weren't assigned to intelligence specifically. After all, an accountant assigned to ensure funds were being spent according to the delegated budgets wasn't a guardianship role. Perhaps Filosa was an investigator.

"Ryan?" Delanee asked, her voice a whisper.

"Mmm?" Or maybe the guy was an auditor, except no, those weren't guardian roles either.

"Why is your daughter glowing?" Another whisper.

His attention snapped to Inara, who, yes, was indeed

surrounded by a hazy white glimmer. "She's happy. Last night, she did the same thing. You weren't bothered."

"I...." She blinked and slowly traced a finger down Inara's plump little arm. "I do remember wondering what the faint glow was, but I don't recall it being *this* bright."

"It was," he said, shifting to the end of the bench to stand. "She'd surrounded you both. Maybe you didn't notice as much, then."

"Do you glow, too?" She licked her lips, her gaze moving from him to his daughter.

"I have no idea. No one has said I do, so I must not."

"Or you've never been happy enough," she whispered. "Or felt safe enough."

Ryan went to the trash and scraped off bits of food. He didn't know what to say or how to act. The freaky ability to light up like a lamp would have sent most people running for the front door. Once again, Delanee reminded him she wasn't *most people*. "Perhaps both, yes. My parents said that's how they knew I was different. Some of my emotions were externally projected."

"Must have been alarming for them."

"That's when they brought me to Synintel." He turned on the water and rinsed his plate.

A gentle touch brushed along his shoulder, and Ryan flinched. When had she moved, and why hadn't he noticed?

"But they still loved you."

Ryan bit his tongue to keep from asking if she thought she could ever love someone like him, too. Love had never been a prospect for his future. Not until his daughter. Romantic love still remained an elusive experience outside the realm of possibility. He wondered what about Delanee made him want to consider an alternative to the bachelorhood to which he'd become resigned.

"Yes, they loved me," he answered, taking her plate from her.

"Do you think the other children were as lucky?"

Ryan froze. Water rushed over his hands and the plate. Slowly, he looked at her. "I never thought about them. What their lives were like."

"You must be curious. You're charting talents. You've never tried to find any of them?"

He shook his head and finished washing the plates. "My parents were adamant about them remaining a secret. They said for my and the other families protection. I never considered anything beyond that."

The echo of a wooden cup bouncing on the floor chased Inara's unhappy squeal. Delanee cleared the rest of the table, bringing Ryan anything that needed to be washed, and then plucked his daughter from the highchair. She plopped Inara down on the counter next to the sink, caging the baby between her forearms.

"I wouldn't have been able to stop myself from finding them," Delanee said, playing with Inara's wiggling toes.

Inara shouted and grabbed Delanee's hands, her tiny fingers pale against Delanee's cream-in-tea skin. Each small fist wrapped around one of Delanee's fingers. Chortling, Inara pumped her arms, and a new toy was found in Delanee's hands. The white haze returned, wrapping around Delanee's fingers and wrist like spidery threads. Once again, Ryan watched Delanee carefully for any sign of impairment. Delanee laughed and made Inara's arms wiggle. A happy shriek bounced through the kitchen.

"You're going to be an amazing mother," Ryan said, the internal opinion blurting from his mouth.

The smile faded from her face. "Thanks, but I doubt I'll get the opportunity."

Ryan grabbed a dish towel. Wiping his hands, he turned toward her, propping his hip on the counter's edge. "Why?"

She shrugged, her focus remaining on Inara. "I'm half Ruthenian, and any man I marry... won't be."

Imagining anyone except him marrying Delanee caused an uncomfortable anger to bubble up within him. Since Ryan planned never to marry, he had no right to be jealous of her future spouse. Which would not be him. He rolled his shoulders and forced away the emotion. "Some of your siblings have married. Do they have children?"

"Yes, but it wasn't easy for them. Except for Deverick. He and his wife have two, and I'm certain number three will be announced any week now."

"Then children *are* possible. They just take a little planning. Sean and Katria were able to have a daughter, and Katria is full Ruthenian," Ryan said. "Mason's wife, Jessi, is half like you, and they're expecting their first sometime this summer."

Delanee took a deep breath, her hands settling around Inara's tiny torso. "Perhaps I'm not certain I'll want to try as hard as they must have."

Ryan tried to decipher her words. "Try as in...."

She stuck her chin into the air and met his gaze. Defiance blazed in her golden irises. "As in, I don't expect to feel much passion for whoever I marry."

"That'd be a waste." He caressed a knuckle down her cheek to her jaw. "You're full of passion. Why would you keep that from your husband?"

"I am?" she whispered, her eyes wide.

Ryan dropped his hand and returned his attention to the dishes. Talk of making babies and passion, especially the fiery desire Delanee expressed, led to dangerous thoughts. Inara's hands slapped the marble, and she tried to rock forward onto her knees. Delanee lifted her and helped her do the cute baby wiggle of legs learning to take on weight.

"Yes," Ryan said, keeping his tone neutral. "And it'd be a loss for you to accept anything less for yourself, let alone any marriage you find yourself in."

• • •

HALF OF DELANEE wanted to ask if Ryan was willing to sign up for the job of helping her discover what a passionate marriage would entail. The other half wanted to hand him his baby and run. Hide in her room or maybe the closet. Ignore the flutters in her stomach and the excited tingles along her skin.

Subject change needed. Immediately. Except the faint white haze returned around Inara as she chewed on her fists, bounced on her unstable, pudgy little legs, and drooled all over the front of her clothes. Delanee glanced at Ryan from the side, wanting to know at what age he'd stopped revealing his happiness as an external manifestation and if she, or the baby, could make the grown man exhibit the feature. Or perhaps it was a childhood situation, like the association phase eventual beast masters displayed of the animal they'd one day be capable of bonding with.

At moments of heightened emotions, the children acted like animals. Growling, hissing, snarling, even barking. Dominik had squawked. She'd heard from her father the first time Dominik displayed raptor traits, Markus had cried. He'd laughed so hard at his son. As adults, only the strongest surge of emotions brought the actions to the front. Deklan still had a habit of growling when frustrated. Darius had roared in anger in the safety of their family home after a difficult case, shaking the walls. Their mother had wrapped her oldest son in a tight hug afterward.

Delanee looked the content baby girl over, wishing she had the right to claim her, to introduce the beautiful infant to the huge, loving Ralston family. Nothing about the baby's emotional displays would concern anyone.

"You said earlier I wasn't bothered by her talent trickling out of her. What did you mean by that?" Delanee drew the baby into her arms and propped her on a hip.

"Aside from you not freaking out?" Ryan asked, wiping

down the counters. Always in motion. Could he ever just sit still and exist?

"Yes."

"If either of the twins are holding her when it happens, they go into a trance similar to what I put people in to answer questions."

Delanee recoiled and looked down at Inara. Her big silvery-blue eyes met her gaze, and she smiled, lifting slobbery hands to pat Delanee's cheeks. "That doesn't worry you? What if they both are touching her when it happens?"

"The instant she's no longer happy, it disappears like snapped fingers. She's never in any danger of being forgotten."

"And the twins?"

"Never knew anything happened. It's rare." Ryan's expression twisted, and he blinked and then shook his head. "It *was* rare."

Did that mean Delanee made Inara happy? She wanted to preen and squeeze the baby to her chest. "She's not content often?"

"I'm not sure if it's from happiness now." Ryan rubbed at his jaw, his fingers catching on the faint stubble growing. Delanee wanted to touch. He shook his head and dropped his hand. "I don't know."

And he had no one to ask. Again, Delanee couldn't help but think of the other children found with him. She nodded, resolved. "You should try to find them. The others like you. Learn more about yourself and what to expect raising Inara."

He shook his head. "I wouldn't even know where to start. My parents kept no records, and I never found any letters between them and the other parents."

"Start with the travel logs. Discover who went on the expedition with them and inquire."

Or maybe Delanee would. To write about such a

discovery? The found infants could be left out of the article, along with the exact location of the ancient laboratory, but the excursion itself into the great unknown? Completely article worthy. Familiar excitement bubbled within her. After the exposé on the V Alliance, she could—

"Oh no," Ryan said, snapping before her face and disrupting her contemplation. "I know that look, and the answer is no. Do not start investigating my past."

She nipped at his fingers and glared. "The past isn't yours alone to claim. Others share it, and adventures into UZs are so rarely written about. People enjoy learning about them, what historians find."

"Uninhabited zones are rarely written about because most people don't return from them."

"What are you afraid I'll find?"

Ryan took Inara from her hold. The baby fussed until Ryan gobbled at her cheek, his eyes remaining hard and serious. "No one can know about me, Delanee. I meant that. And no one can know about them."

"I'd be careful." Her fingers twitched to return the infant to her arms.

"Someone would be too curious to leave your article as the end of the information. They'd dig. There's a reason the expeditions were never recorded or shared." He propped Inara's chest against his, her little legs dangling over his stomach. "Do not make me regret sharing with you."

A hard reminder he'd trusted her with knowledge about himself he'd never confided to anyone else. Including those on the teams he helped run. "I still think you should find them. The others like you," she said.

"Why? So I can feel even more removed from the rest of the human race?" He shook his head. "No, thank you."

Delanee couldn't stop from reaching for him. Her fingers curled into the fabric of his sleeve and forced him to turn. "You're just as human as I am."

Harsh lines bracketed his mouth and pinched between his brows.

"You are." She smoothed her fingers along his prickly jaw and rested her other hand above his on Inara's back. "If everything you say is true, your generation is responsible for an entire nation. You're just stronger than them. Than all of us. You wouldn't have made this beautiful life if you weren't human."

"It's hard enough knowing I'm different from every Sziverian, even every Ruthenian. I don't like dwelling on it, and I use my talent only when necessary. I don't...." He sighed and leaned forward, resting his forehead on hers. Compelled by an emotion she didn't want to examine too closely, Delanee wrapped her hand around the base of his neck. "I don't need more reminders."

Delanee pressed her lips together to keep from saying she understood. She did. More than she wished. But she didn't want to explain how she knew the discomfort of being *different*, even from those deemed unique. "Consider the subject dropped."

His breath rushed across her lips in a warm tingle of sensation. "Thank you."

If Delanee lifted her face just a little, her mouth could press to his. Oh, how she wanted to. Wanted to experience the heady rush of his lips devouring hers while his tongue did delightful things inside her mouth. Her breath hitched, and her fingers tightened on the back of his neck. A quiver of excitement danced in her belly.

Inara babbled, and a sharp pain sliced across Delanee's scalp. She yelped and tried to jerk back, only for the discomfort to increase.

Ryan grasped the back of her neck to hold her in place. "Whoa, wait, she has her fingers all tangled in your hair."

Delanee should have known better. She'd been around

enough babies to know the temptation her wild curls caused once an infant noticed them.

"Inara," Ryan fussed on a long sigh, releasing his hold on Delanee, "how did you do this? Where in the inhabited world is your hand?"

Delanee's hair shifted. Inara squealed.

"No," Ryan barked.

"Na-ma-ma-ma!" Inara shouted, and another tight pull yanked across Delanee's scalp.

"Do not grab any more of her hair." A frustrated exhale fluttered across her ear. "Inara, stop. I mean it."

The moment Delanee was freed from the baby's clutches, she stepped out of reach. Inara launched an unhappy wail, bucking in her father's arms. A chime echoed through the house. Ryan tilted his head back, his eyes squeezed shut.

"Can you please hold her for a minute?" He handed the writhing infant back to Delanee.

"Of course." Delanee grasped Inara around her small torso and tucked her into her body. "What is that noise?"

"My radio unit." He sped from the kitchen, disappearing.

Inara sniffled and grabbed for Delanee's hair again. Delanee opened the drawer with baby objects and grabbed a pacifier. She waved the two-toned pink binky in front of Inara's face, switching her focus. Her pale eyes widened, and she reached for the item, missing by inches. A sound of frustration burst from her mouth. Little legs kicking, she tried again. Grabbing the pacifier with both hands, she shoved it into her mouth, humming.

Smiling, Delanee carried her into the living room, going to the toys tucked away beneath the shelf near the fireplace. Both Inara's hands clutched at Delanee's top. Ryan rushed from the hall, rounding to the foyer. He grabbed his hat, popped it on his head, and threw his jacket over his arm.

"I'm so sorry, but can you watch her for a bit? I have to go."

Delanee straightened, alarmed. "Go where?"

"To—" He pressed his lips together. "Work. FIO situation."

"Be careful?"

He paused mid-step to the front door and glanced at her. "I will. If anything happens, go next door to the twins."

"And interrupt their uninterruptable night?" Delanee shook her head. "I don't think so. We'll be fine."

He hesitated, his face pinched, then shook his head and stomped to the door. "I'll be back as soon as I can. I'm so sorry again and thank you."

"Ryan," she called as he opened the door. He met her gaze from the shadows of the foyer. "I don't mind taking care of her. Just be safe, okay?"

He nodded and left. Cold air drifted in his wake and then the lock snicked into place. Inara whimpered, and Delanee spun her around. "Oh, no, we're going to be a happy baby, right? No sadness allowed. Let's see what fun things you have to play with."

After dragging the playpen and a few toys into the study, Delanee settled Inara inside and lit enough lamps to conduct her research. Inara babbled and tossed toys around, content for the moment, and Delanee quickly went to work. Two hours later, her focus drifted to the clock for what must have been the hundredth time. Worry twisted in her stomach, forcing her attention back to the papers before her.

Something about the missing orphans nagged at her, but she couldn't figure out what. Inara had toppled over a half hour ago, asleep. Delanee flipped to a blank sheet of paper in her notebook and made a detailed list of all the missing children from the orphanages. Next, she found the missing person reports Ryan had collected and isolated only the minors, adding them to her list. Sitting back, she looked over the list. The pen fell from her fingers. A clear pattern had emerged. The traffickers had a desire for a specific type of child.

Shaken, Delanee pushed away from the desk. She gathered a peaceful Inara into her arms and held her close, needing the contact to assure herself the infant was safe. How many more children would be stolen in the night, no one caring because no one even knew they were missing? The orphanages were understaffed, and from the interviews Delanee had managed to conduct, no one looked very hard when a child disappeared. They did their duty and reported the loss, but nothing else happened. Delanee had a sickening hunch most staff members were relieved not to have to worry about caring for one more ward.

After dousing the lamps, Delanee left the study and the troubling discovery. She made a bottle for Inara and then went to Ryan's room. Settling into the rocker, she fed the baby, who latched on despite being asleep. Delanee didn't know what her discovery meant and hoped Ryan had an answer. Although, whatever the reason turned out to be, nothing would be good enough for why the young sons of Sziveria were being stolen.

FOURTEEN

RYAN RETURNED HOME TO SILENCE. He hadn't anticipated a mostly tidy living room, the kitchen showing signs of a bottle having been prepared, and not a sound from his daughter. His fear had been Inara wailing and his houseguest frustrated. Instead, all was calm. Frowning, he doused the lamps in the living spaces, checked on the fireplace to keep the main rooms warm overnight, and then eased to his bedroom.

The door stood open, and a single lamp burned on the wall between the bathroom and bedroom doors. A chill hung in the air, the fireplace dark. Neither woman nor infant seemed to mind the cooler temperature. Delanee slept under a throw blanket on the side of the bed nearest the crib. Ryan paused at the foot of the bed, unable to stop looking over Delanee's resting form. She'd braided her hair, the long, dark length resting over her shoulder to curl around her small breast. The warm hue of her skin glowed against the darkness of his blankets. She looked good in his bed. Too good. He imagined her as naked as she'd been this morning, sprawled over the navy sheets, gripping them tightly while he.... Ryan tore his gaze away and went to his daughter lying in the crib. Yes, fantasies of a writhing, begging Delanee in the throes of passion were a welcome distraction, but much too dangerous.

Inara's fingers twitched, but she remained asleep as Ryan looked her over. Delanee had dressed her in a single piece outfit that covered her from head to toes. A binky lay beside Inara's head, no longer needed to soothe. Ryan removed the pacifier. He'd wash it for later in the night if necessary.

After starting a fire and making sure Delanee remained asleep, he closed himself in the bathroom and showered away the emotional and physical remnants of the evening. The hot water pounded on his back as he leaned forward, arms braced on the cold tile.

The assassin was no more.

Relief should have come when the combined teams of Wolvenguard and Wintersfall emerged from the Old City Ruins. But as Ryan stood alone, the body of the man who had caused so much damage to so many families at his feet, dread had crept within him. Would the V Alliance retaliate? Would the knowledge that one of their key players had been eliminated cause someone to make a mistake and reveal themselves, jeopardizing the people he cared about?

He didn't have to worry about anyone discovering *who* had executed the mission. The location meant nothing would be investigated. No one ventured into the Old City Ruins without authorization from the residents, and no one revealed information to outsiders.

Ryan would contemplate the myriad of potential issues later when exhaustion didn't want to drag him under. He finished showering. Wrapped in a towel, he exited the steamy bathroom, did a quick confirmation check of Delanee still sleeping, and then crept across the room to his dresser. He opened the drawer for his pajamas and removed a soft pair of bamboo pants. Cloth rustled behind him, and he froze.

"Ryan?" Delanee asked, her voice lethargic from sleep.

Ryan shoved his feet into the pants and pulled the fabric beneath the towel. "Yes, I'm home."

A faint grunt sounded. "I didn't mean to fall asleep in your bed."

"You're fine," Ryan assured, draping the towel across his shoulders. He grabbed the ends and moved to stand beside Inara's crib. "Thank you for watching her."

"Can you talk about why you needed to go?" She swung her legs over the edge of the bed, draping the throw across her lap.

Ryan wanted to sit beside her for the conversation but knew better than to get any closer to her and the bed. Especially when all that'd be between him and her touch was a pair of thin pants.

"The assassin has been handled."

Her eyes widened, and she stood. "Is everyone okay? My brother—"

"Wolvenguard is fine. Katria took the shot after Lucianna shoved the assassin out a window. Your brother and the rest of the team were support, nothing more."

A heavy breath left her as she leaned forward, bracing her hands on her thighs. The blanket fell to the floor to puddle around her feet. "I am so glad you didn't tell me before you left. I would have worried myself sick."

"I didn't want to get your hopes up," he admitted. He'd never considered she would worry about her brother, though he should have. After all, the first time he had seen her outside her apartment had been when she arrived at his office, demanding to know where he'd sent her older sibling.

"How long before you think they realize he's gone?" she asked, wrapping her arms around herself.

Ryan shrugged. "Depends on how often they check in with him or require his services. With him living in Old City Ruins, communication may have been sparse. We may get lucky, and they won't notice for some time."

"What about his..." She pressed her lips together and waved a hand. "You know."

"Body?"

She nodded, displeasure scrunching her face.

"I had Sheild Guardian Levkaseon come pick up the body and place it in a morgue drawer only he knows about. As the guardian over Haven City's Health Services, he can ensure no one snoops. He can also tell me what he finds from a medical perspective."

"You want an autopsy?" she asked softly, moving to stand over Inara's crib.

"I'd like to know if there are any similarities to other members of the V Alliance, yes."

"I found something," she whispered, licking her full lips, and Ryan found himself mimicking the action. He wanted to kiss her again. So badly. "While you were gone."

The words made him lift his gaze to hers, where she watched him with a mixture of unease and longing. What did she have to be apprehensive about? The threat was eliminated, unless she worried about his attraction. Though, if that were the case, she wouldn't be looking at him with desire. Ryan's thoughts tangled together until he had to sift through the chaos to figure out what she'd said. "Found something...."

She motioned at the wall covered in papers. "From your research."

"Our research," he muttered before he could stop himself.

Apparently, the right words to say, for she glowed in pride, the unease fading. "Yes, our research now. Anyway, what I discovered is in the office."

"Let me grab a shirt. I'll meet you in there."

Her attention shifted to his bare chest, and her delectable tongue made another appearance, tracing the full shape of her lips. Ryan almost groaned. He moved past her, not waiting to hear her reply. If he remained in her presence a second longer, he'd be unable to hide his reaction. In the privacy of his bathroom, he palmed the thickening length bulging at the front of his thin pants. He needed to control himself before joining her in the study.

He grabbed an old sweater, stretched and faded, the weave too soft from age for him to discard, and yanked it on over his head. After confirming the hem obscured the evidence of his lust, Ryan went to the study. The playpen was assembled next to the desk, toys scattered around inside and a few outside. The desk... he shuddered. Not an inch of wood showed beneath the documents and books strewn across the surface. Two lamps burned, one beside the door and one behind the desk.

Delanee pulled an open journal and several loose sheets of paper closer and tapped at the journal. "Look."

Despite knowing he shouldn't get any nearer, her scent already chasing away lucid reason, Ryan rounded the desk. He braced a hand on top of papers over her shoulder and leaned closer, breathing deep. Summer sun, but she smelled *good*. He wanted to lick her neck and discover if her skin tasted like sweet flowers and candied citrus. Found himself reaching for the braid hanging over her shoulder to slide away the thick mass and fisted his hand along the back of the seat instead. No one had ever made him forget himself like she did.

"What am I looking for?" he asked, the frame of the chair creaking beneath his grasp.

"I compiled a comprehensive record of all the kidnap victims over the last three years, from your list and from mine that I'd managed to get from the orphanages that agreed to talk with me."

"The victims ranged in age." He shifted until his chest brushed her shoulder.

"At first glance, they do, yes. But look closer."

She tapped at the page where row upon row of ages and... colors? Ryan touched the journal beneath her hand. "What does this mean?"

"Age, hair, and eye color."

Ryan picked up the book, straightening. Sprinkled throughout the data was an adult here, a teenager there, and random looks. The bulk of the missing persons were boys, ranging in age from five to nine years, with brown hair and brown eyes. Not an uncommon color combination. "Brown is the most common hair and eye color. It'd make sense the bulk of the kids would fall in that category."

"I would agree if not for the specific age group," she said.

She turned in the seat, grabbed the back of the chair, and braced her other arm on the desk. The action pulled the shirt she wore tight across her breasts, reminding him of their perfect shape bared to him earlier in the day. Ryan's fingers tightened around the hard edges of the journal.

"Someone is targeting boys of a precise age and appearance. Why?" she asked.

Ryan forced his attention back to the research. Why indeed. Delanee's curious nature had led her to seek answers, researching a source everyone else, Ryan included, had figured was nothing more than convenience for human traffickers. After all, stealing where no one would be missed seemed opportunistic rather than coordinated. But what if the kidnappings were part of a bigger, more sinister plan?

"Three years since we started documenting the kidnappings, and no one caught the pattern," Ryan said, laying down the journal.

He crossed the room to the bookshelves housing the Directory of Ranked Guardians. He slid his fingers over the binding, searching for the newest edition. Not much changed annually, a few new additions or name changes as new blood took over a ranked seat, and.... He flipped to the opening pages. Ages. Delanee's seductive scent preceded her joining him.

She jerked back when she realized what page he'd stopped on. "The royal family?"

Ryan touched the page beneath words that described a now familiar look and a sketched image of an innocent, smiling face. Delanee gasped, snatching the book from his hold.

"No way," she whispered, taking the book to the desk. "You don't really think—"

"Prince Jaiden. Age nine. Brown hair. Brown eyes. It fits," he said, frowning. Unease tightened in his chest, chasing away any lingering lust from earlier. "The question is, why target a prince? He'd be near impossible to abduct."

"Ransom?" She looked up from the book.

"Why do three years' worth of trial runs just for ransom?"

"The payout they have in mind must be worth it to them."

"Or maybe it's all by chance, and Prince Jaiden has nothing to do with the kidnappings," Ryan mused. "Either way, I can't ignore the coincidence. I have to tell Synintel."

"I'm going with you." She snapped the journal closed and held it to her chest. "Please."

Ryan glanced at his watch. "I'm not going now, but first thing in the morning, before he arrives at the office." He looked back at her, unable to stop the rush of heat. "Will you be able to get up on your own?"

Vivid pink darkened her face up to her hairline. She

shifted her feet. "I promise to be wearing something to bed tonight."

Ryan let his gaze wander the length of her body, remembering the delicate brown of all her exposed skin. He wanted another viewing. Soon. Even though he shouldn't. Scratch that, even though he couldn't.

"How disappointing," tumbled from his mouth anyway.

The delightful blush deepened, another reminder of her inexperience. An innocence he had no business— or right — to claim. He squeezed his eyes shut. Why did he have to keep reminding himself of that fact?

"I mean...." He tried to think of something more appropriate to say.

She inched closer. Halted. The book, still clasped to her chest, rose and fell with each shallow breath she took. Her irises were pools of liquid gold staring at him. Ryan skimmed his knuckles along her jaw, tracing the gentle curve. Before he realized his own intent, he'd wrapped his fingers around the back of her neck beneath her braid and hauled her closer.

"Is it wrong that I like you appreciating what you saw?" she whispered, her gaze flickering to his mouth and back to his gaze.

"It should be," he rumbled.

She licked her lips. "I think, maybe...." Another swipe of her tongue along her bottom lip had Ryan suppressing a groan. "Maybe you might be the only man who does."

Leaning close, inhaling her sweet, feminine scent, Ryan whispered into her ear, "Any hot-blooded man would have savored."

He traced his lips down the long column of her throat, pleased when she tilted her head to give him easier access. The little hitches in her breath encouraged him more. Gently, he grazed the backs of his fingers along the side of her breast. When she didn't jump away from his touch, he did it again, only across her pebbled nipple straining against the fabric of her shirt, begging to be caressed. Her ragged gasp fluttered across his neck. What would she do if he slid his hand beneath the shirt and cupped her breast fully? Stars above, he wanted to learn.

"Tell me to stop," he murmured against her skin.

Something clunked to the floor, and her hands grasped his shoulders. "W-why?"

"Because I—"

The faint echo of Inara's wail drifted through the house. Ryan froze. Delanee's fingernails bit into his skin through the sweater before she released him and backed away. Ryan cursed internally, reaching down to retrieve the journal she'd dropped.

When he rose, he met her uncertain stare. "Be ready in the morning."

She nodded and accepted the book. "Don't forget her teething ointment."

At the door, he hesitated. There were so many things he wanted to say. Praise over her passionate responses to him. A warning to keep her distance. The promises for what would happen to her by his hands, mouth, and body if she didn't. In the end, he offered a curt nod, an abnormal act on his part. Ryan wasn't usually such a coward. But he knew if he challenged Delanee, she'd accept. And then his need to control the situation, to dominate, would leave him no other option. Delanee Ralston would be his.

FIFTEEN

THE PALACE LOOMED large at the end of a long, wide, stone walkway. An imposing gray structure in the style of nearly every other official Sziverian building, lacking in any warmth, or creative architecture. Like most official buildings, the palace and been erected during a time when structural engineering was necessary versus aesthetic. Delanee swallowed, trying to remember why she'd insisted on joining Ryan.

"I thought we'd be going to the FIO," she said, keeping pace with him as they walked to the front doors.

"Synintel has his weekly meeting with Queen-Elect Arnita and her security team today," he said, jogging up the wide stairs to the front of the public half of the palace. The private half was on the other side of a massive greenhouse and accessible only to those who knew the royal family.

"You're allowed to interrupt that?" she asked, huffing as she fought to keep up.

"I am for this."

A guard opened one of the six doors into the entrance hall. Each door had a sentry on the outside, and the doors leading into the entrance foyer had another set. Two tables were set up with baskets, and Ryan motioned for Delanee to place her messenger bag in one of the containers. She clutched at the leather strap and debated stepping back outside.

"It's okay." Ryan pried her fingers from the strap and swept the bag over her head. "They're professional."

"Why do they have to go through my things?" she asked, craning her neck to watch a stranger rummage through her belongings. The invasion of privacy bristled.

"To ensure you aren't here to harm the royal family or any guests they may have."

At the second set of doors, Ryan produced some kind of identification. The guard stood at a pedestal and opened a well-worn book. He ran a blunt finger down a page, nodded, and motioned them through the doors. Yet another guard patted down Ryan's chest, sides, pants pockets, and around his ankles. A woman stepped forward, and Delanee jumped. The same action was repeated on her own body.

The weight of the messenger bag dropping against her chest had her jerking a second time. She grabbed the thick leather strap in both hands and held tight. "Is that all? Are we done?"

"Yes, we're free to walk around." He moved with purpose through the spacious foyer.

A white marble floor gleamed from the light streaming in from above. The Sziverian national seal was a colorful work of art in the center. Plush, emerald rugs led to long, wide corridors branching off either side. Wooden benches for sitting and large potted trees gave the space a welcome yet professional feel. Men and women bustled across the vast space, all dressed in subdued attire. Shades of gray, muted blues, and browns. Delanee glanced at Ryan, wearing dark gray slacks and a pale gray collared sweater. He fit right in.

"Is it a national requirement to dress boring?" Delanee asked, stepping closer to him.

"What?" He turned down the corridor to the right, easing to the left as a large group of men wearing baggy brown pants and light brown tunic-style shirts passed. Silk sashes draped across their chests were a bright pop of contrast. Every man wore a different color. Golden or silver threads and beads the same color as the sash created intricate, unique patterns, each a work of art.

Delanee stopped and shifted to watch them. Their skin was a rich cinnamon, hair black and wavy, and eyes equally dark. They were all shorter than her. Ryan's hand on the small of her back urged her to move again.

"Vativarsans," he whispered. "The sashes are to set them apart from other cultures and showcase the rich textiles they offer. A lot of our embroidered fabrics are from Vativarsa."

"And our people wear boring, depressing colors," she muttered.

He plucked at the sleeve of her burnt orange shirt, which she'd paired with a sky-blue skirt and a sheer cream vest. A sash of the same creamy fabric wrapped around her waist twice, accenting her slender build, and draped in a long tail from her left hip. The outfit was bright, airy, and feminine, and she hoped professional enough to meet with an arch guardian who was not her brother.

"I can't speak for everyone, but I prefer non-distracting colors when dealing with potentially tense situations. Plus, I never have to worry about matching. Everything I own can be worn together."

Delanee scrunched her nose. "So boring."

He shrugged. "Convenient."

An area they'd likely never agree about. Following behind as he walked down the long corridor lit by lamps and decorated with portraits of the royal families through the generations, Delanee was torn between taking in her surroundings and watching Ryan's confident gait. Oh, how he twisted her up inside. When he'd walked away last night, Delanee had almost chased after him. Her curiosity about how only he could make her feel, what happened between a man and a woman, was reaching critical heights.

For half a second, she'd even contemplated following her new sister-in-law's lead and asking Ryan if he'd be interested in contracting. The shocking thought had snapped her out of the lust-induced haze. When Delanee contracted, she wanted the relationship to be longer than a year. She wanted a lifetime. A commitment she doubted Ryan was willing to consider. Besides, she hadn't changed her mind about needing to settle with a non-dominant man. She flexed her hands. *She hadn't.*

Ryan nodded to people who greeted him in passing but never broke his stride. At a tall mahogany door on the left, he stopped and opened without knocking. He led her into a spacious sitting room decorated in pale gray and dark blues. A glittery chandelier illuminated the elegant space.

"Wait here for me?" he asked.

Delanee nodded, stepping away from the doorway. He disappeared down a narrow corridor to the left. Taking a deep breath, Delanee glanced around the lobby-style room. Fresh flowers on all the tables in muted pinks, oranges, and greens added a subtle brightness to the windowless space. Landscape paintings offered views of distant lands. Delanee was drawn to a desert scene, the contrast of red rocks and yellow sand against an azure sky captured in breathtaking detail. Not for the first time, she wished she'd inherited her mother's ability to touch an image and be mentally transported into the picture. Only one Ralston had been gifted with Bella's unique talent, her older brother Drayke.

Muffled masculine voices echoed from the narrow hall, and Delanee licked her dry lips and took a centering breath.

She turned to watch Ryan exit the corridor with Henry Edmond, the arch guardian of Synintel, at his side. The two were deep in conversation, leaning close together. Gray streaked through the arch guardian's cropped, chestnut brown hair. A face distinguished by age was clean-shaven and drawn in tight lines. A charcoal suit paired with a pale yellow shirt showed off a figure still powerful. Unlike many ranked guardians, Synintel hadn't softened or grown lazy within his position. The man took the arch guardianship seriously, and no one who met with him, foreign or domestic, would mistake him as weak.

Delanee squared her shoulders and resisted the urge to pat her hair. She'd tamed the curls as best she could, but they tended to do whatever they felt like. Not that she needed to impress anyone. Her role here was to observe for her potential article. To understand the process and help her readers know the people they trusted did indeed care about their well-being. Butterflies danced in her belly despite her self-assurance.

"Delanee has the full numbers if you want to see them." Ryan stepped fully into the room, Synintel at his side.

Delanee scrambled to get her bag open and the journal out. She didn't know who to give the information to, so held out the book. Ryan grasped it with a nod and flipped to the last pages. Synintel shifted close, leaning over her research, and Delanee's heart almost burst from her chest. Evidence *she* supplied was being reviewed by an arch guardian with a direct link to the queen-elect. Delanee grabbed the strap of her bag to keep from punching the air. Curtis would have to take her work seriously now.

"Two hundred and sixty-three?" Synintel snapped away from the book and swiped a hand down his face.

Ryan returned the notebook to Delanee. "Yes, over double the reports for other kidnapping victims, children, and adults, which appear to be random."

"I admit there's reason to be suspicious. I just don't see the reason, however," Synintel said, crossing his arms over his broad chest. "No threats have been made, or ultimatums issued."

"Perhaps because they haven't made their move yet," Ryan said.

"Maybe. Or the young prince's looks are common enough, and he has nothing to do with this." Synintel waved a hand in the air.

"Except I've seen too much involvement in the V Alliance from ranked guardians to believe that. Someone can get close to Prince Jaiden if he is indeed a target of the group," Ryan said, his words low.

Synintel's pale brown gaze flickered over Delanee before returning to Ryan. "Who is she again?"

Ryan glanced at her, and she fought the urge to squirm. "Delanee Ralston."

A muscle jumped in the arch guardian's jaw. He grabbed Ryan's elbow. "Can I talk to you in private?"

Delanee clutched the book to her chest. She went to assure the high-ranking guardian she could be trusted, but at a curt shake of Ryan's head, she snapped her mouth closed. He'd trusted her with his dangerous truth, she would trust him to defend her, if necessary. Taking a deep breath, Delanee sank onto the couch, hoping the arch guardian didn't burn her dreams to ashes.

"Delanee Ralston?" Henry whispered harshly. "As in *the* Ralston family?"

The unexpected question took Ryan a second to process. He'd assumed Henry was upset about Delanee's career choice, not her family ties. Uncertain, Ryan answered, "Yes?"

Henry's hold on Ryan's arm tightened. The arch

guardian dragged them deeper into the narrow corridor. "How is she related to Wolvenguard?"

"Younger sister."

"She's one of Markus Ralston's eleven?"

Ryan blinked. "Yes."

Synintel cursed and dragged a hand through his cropped hair. "Does anyone know she's researching the V Alliance?"

Ryan held up a hand and went to say no, then remembered her missing investigative pieces. He made a fist and dropped his arm. "Maybe."

Another litany of hushed curses left the arch guardian, and Ryan raised a brow. "Listen to me very carefully, Voklane. Nothing can happen to that young woman. Do you understand?"

"I wasn't planning on allowing anything to happen to her, Arch Guardian."

"Her family will start a war, and we can't afford to lose their allegiance to Queen-Elect Arnita."

Of course, powerful allegiances mattered more to him than the welfare of one young woman whose only value lay in her remarkable family. Ryan didn't know why the knowledge led to disappointment. Henry Edmond's priorities would never change. "I'm aware. It's why she's with me. She discovered the identity of the assassin we eliminated."

"With you?" Henry's gaze narrowed.

"She's staying at my house as a guest."

The arch guardian's shoulders straightened. "I have blank marriage contracts here and in my offices in the other buildings. I can—"

"No," Ryan snapped. "Her family knows she's with me. She's safe and will return to them as she left them. Not every issue can be solved through contracting."

"Most of them can," Henry stated, smoothing his hand down the front of his shirt.

He and Delanee would not become another casualty of Henry's contracting game. Even if all the couples to date *had* found love, Ryan wouldn't force Delanee into a marriage against her wishes. No matter how much he wanted her or the glimpse of a future she alone could offer.

"No."

Henry sniffed. "Very well. If anything happens to her, or her family takes issue with her being in your home unmarried, you'll take responsibility. Are you sure you don't want the full benefits of a spouse for your duty?"

"If I ever marry, Arch Guardian, it won't be for duty."

"Sometimes that's the noblest sacrifice you can make. For your country and your future spouse," Henry said softly.

"Are you going to inform the queen-elect of the danger to her son?" Ryan asked, changing the uncomfortable subject.

"I'm going to investigate a bit more before I worry Arnita unnecessarily," Henry said. "But don't worry, nothing will happen to the boy."

"I'll see what I can learn, too, now that I have more specific information to utilize."

Synintel nodded. "Let me know if you require invitations to specific events or any tickets. And keep me informed, no matter how small you think the detail may be, I want to know."

"Yes, Arch Guardian."

Synintel hesitated, then nodded. "All right. Anything else?"

Ryan shook his head.

Henry took a few steps, then stopped and turned. "Be careful, Ryan."

The arch guardian didn't give him the chance to respond, simply pivoted and strode down the hall, returning to the meeting Ryan had interrupted. Henry had never expressed concern before, and Ryan had to wonder the reason. Did the arch guardian worry more than he let on about the situation, or did he care about Ryan specifically? Needing a second to process, Ryan remained in the hall for a few quiet moments. The rustle of fabric from the sitting area forced him into motion.

Delanee stood the second she spotted him, the journal still held in both hands. "Everything okay?"

Ryan opened the door to the main corridor. "Fine. He was concerned about your family."

"What about my family?"

"Burning Haven City to the ground if anything happens to you," he said, the corner of his mouth quirking into a smile at her wide-eyed stare.

"Oh." She gnawed on her delectable bottom lip. "He wants me to go home?"

Ryan tore his gaze from her mouth and focused on the busy hallway. "No, the opposite. He's worried your safety has been compromised."

"Like Deklan was worried."

"Yes, and it's possible you've been in danger longer than you realize with the articles missing." Ryan urged her out of the room. "Someone may have been watching what you were doing next before deciding if you were a threat. Your family is crucial to the security of our nation."

"And he's concerned that'll somehow change if something happens to me?"

"Yes, and how they'd respond."

"Well," she huffed while shoving her journal into her bag, "don't I feel important?"

Ryan grasped her arm and shifted them near the wall, out of the main flow of traffic. "You are important, Delanee."

"Because of my last name and what my brothers can do," she stated, her jaw clenching.

He slid his hand down her arm to her hand. The public display of affection was probably the last thing he should be doing, but he couldn't stop the need to touch her. "No, because you, *Delanee,* are important. Not what your family provides."

"Why do I have a feeling that's not how the arch guardian felt?" she asked, squeezing his hand.

"Does it matter? How your family feels," *how I feel*, he silently added, "is all that matters. And to them," *to me*, "you are...."

Everything.

The word went off like a bomb in his skull. Ryan blinked and pulled his hand free.

"I'm—" Delanee gasped. She grabbed his hand again, tugging him down the wall. "I'm going to need you to calm down."

Ryan blinked. "What?"

She tested a knob as she walked by and opened a door. Before he could realize her intent, she'd yanked him into the dark room and shut them inside.

"What are you—"

"You were starting to glow. I didn't think you wanted anyone else to see," she said in a rush. Quieter, she asked, "Are you okay?"

"I'm fine," he whispered and tried to stop panic. Damn it! How did this woman affect him so deeply? Guess that answered her question of whether he still manifested like his daughter. He'd have to be much more careful in the future with his emotions where she was concerned. "Do you think anyone noticed?"

"I didn't see anyone staring, although I'm sure they noticed us disappearing into this room. What upset you?" Her hand still clasped his, her thumb caressing over his knuckles.

Ryan wanted to yank her into his frame and hug her

tight. Kiss her. Instead, he shoved the desire down deep and released her hand to open the door back into the corridor. No one really knew him. Not by name, anyway. He'd worked hard to appear to be a nobody, an errand runner for an arch guardian. Hopefully, their disappearing act would cause a few snickers, but no one would ask who they were.

"Just too much going on, I guess," he answered.

Doubt clouded her golden eyes, the brighter light of the hall washing over her face. "All right."

"Thank you," he said, not leaving the doorway. He hadn't had anyone watch over him in a long time. That she protected him, kept his secret safe, humbled, and honored him.

She nodded but didn't reply, slipping past him into the busy thoroughfare.

Ryan lingered, making sure his emotions were contained before following her. She slipped through the crowd, her tall, slender form a bright beacon weaving through the mundane. The graceful beauty of her once again hit him like a punch. How had any of her suitors walked away? Let alone made her feel as though she weren't desirable? Criminal.

Outside, a crisp breeze swayed the stalks and blooms of daffodils and ruffled the leaves and petals of the colorful primroses lining the walkway to the palace. Delanee's skirt rippled around her legs. Ryan remained purposefully behind, enjoying the view. The colorful flowers comple-mented her colorful attire and wine-red hair. He jogged to catch up with her near the parking area, not wanting her weaving through the parked Ariots and carriages without him. A driver walking his horse to the stables waited for them to pass by.

At his Ariot, Ryan opened Delanee's door before entering on the driver's side. Her long, heavy sigh echoed around the interior. Ryan paused before starting the magnetic engine process.

"What's wrong?" he asked, shifting to face her.

She stared out the window, her reflection in the glass troubled. "Where do we go from here? How can we possibly learn anything more without making it obvious?"

Ryan punched the button to start the Ariot. A quiet hum filled the cab. "Carefully. But, we're in a unique position to gather information."

She turned, blinking, and met his stare. "We?"

Ryan nodded and slowly inched through the congested parking area. "You don't go anywhere without me. And since you're a social columnist, you'll be at many events where the people I'm concerned about may gather."

"How will you keep your association with me secret if we're seen together at every function I normally attend alone or with a colleague?"

He smiled and eased onto the road. "We won't walk in the front door together. I've learned over the years how to blend. Most people don't even realize I'm around."

Her pretty golden eyes narrowed. "You're over six feet tall with pale hair. How exactly do you *blend*?"

"Boring clothes, limited conversation. I have perfected the art of the wallflower," he said, waggling his brows.

Laughter burst from her, brightening her face. Like the sun breaking through the gloom of clouds, her smile lightened him from within. His next breath became easier, and he flexed his palms over the steering column.

"Well," she said, still chuckling, "this is something I'll need to see for myself."

"Your next event is the blooming party for Master Guardian Silverhill, right?"

She nodded, smoothing her fingers along her skirt. "Yes. Have you been before?"

"A couple of years ago. I needed information, and it was

the largest gathering of guardians in one location that week."

"Are all your activities based around intelligence gathering? Do you ever do anything for fun?"

The last time Ryan had done something *fun*, just for him, he'd ended up a single parent. Somehow, he didn't think she wanted to discuss his colossal relationship mistake. He sure didn't. "Not really."

"That's a shame," she whispered.

"I don't have much time for fun right now," he admitted, turning onto a less crowded street. "At least, not outside my house."

"I suppose that's fair. You do have a lot to enjoy at home."

Ryan agreed, especially since a whirlwind known as Delanee Ralston had swept into his personal space. He tapped his fingers on the steering column. What in the arctic was he going to do after she left?

SIXTEEN

RAINA MERRICK TUGGED on the small hand of her oldest son, practically dragging the wailing four-year-old through the front door of her father's house. The guard at the entrance gave her a sympathetic smile while a footman held open the door, pretending a shrieking child wasn't disrupting the quiet.

Ignoring the burn of mortification and Tanis's clawing fingers along her wrist, Raina adjusted Silas on her hip. The toddler mumbled, his pale brown eyes wide, pointing at some fascinating object only he knew about.

Raina nodded. "Yes, very pretty," she agreed. The arch guardian's house contained any number of shiny, bright, or otherwise interesting sights.

The front door closed, darkening the expansive foyer. Raina released her son, who immediately plopped onto his butt and screamed. Raina squeezed her eyes closed and rubbed a soothing hand over her swollen belly. Her growing baby kicked. Hard. Big brother being upset wasn't something the little one liked. Silas squirmed and Raina sighed, bending slowly to set him down. He crawled to her father's office, used the closed door to help steady himself while standing, and slapped the wood. Raina straightened, arching her back.

Tanis rose on his knees and reached for the diaper bag. She pushed his hand away. "No," she said. "You knew better than to throw your train at the driver. That was mean."

He screamed again and flung himself on the marble floor. Raina ignored him. Silas rose on his toes and tried to grab the office doorknob. A grunt of effort left him, his fingers barely skimming the bronze knob. He lost his balance, fell on his butt, grumbled, stood, and tried again. Exhausted, Raina had the urge to let her son succeed in his quest to reach his grandfather. But a closed office door meant do not disturb, and that included family. She scooped him up and backtracked to the wide staircase.

"Pa-pa-pa-pa!" Silas demanded, pointing at the closed door.

"I know." Raina arranged him on her lap, a small foot on either side of her thighs, and bounced her knees. "Tanis, that is enough of that."

Sniffling, her oldest pushed off the floor and sat on his haunches. His gray eyes gleamed with unshed tears. Sandy blond hair promised to darken to his father's shade, the locks as untamed as Kevin's. Raina's heart squeezed. Seeing her husband in her son never failed to make love expand. Being pregnant? Tears burned behind her eyes, and her bottom lip quivered. She took a deep breath and kissed Silas's soft hair. Getting pregnant so soon after having Silas hadn't been the plan, but Rose, her women's and infant's medical scientist, assured both she and the baby were healthy. Then again, none of their pregnancies had been planned. She brushed her fingers along Silas's dark curls and smiled. All her children had been happy, little surprises.

Shoes slapping on marble, and the unmistakable laugh of a child echoed from the back of the house. Raina's spine straightened, and she leaned to the left to try to see around the columns of the open-air ballroom. A young boy raced into the foyer, skidded on the marble, and grabbed the knob to her father's office.

"Jaiden!" a woman shouted. "Don't you dare op—"

Snickering, the boy twisted the knob and cracked the door open.

"Jaiden!" the woman hissed. Shoes squeaked on the marble seconds before a heavy-set woman marched into the foyer. Her large breasts bounced with each firm step. Arms pumping, hips swinging, she raced toward the child, a glare tightening her flushed face. "You know not to open that door."

Everyone knew better than to open that door. Raina looked between the two. Perhaps this was the child's first time in the arch guardian's home.

The boy named Jaiden lifted a narrow chin. "I want to see my father."

The woman motioned toward herself. "Come back here, and let's return to the greenhouse to play. You can see him when he's finished. I'll let one of the guards know to tell him."

Jaiden lowered his chin and pouted. "But I want to see him now."

"Pa-pa-pa-pa!" Silas shouted, holding his arms out.

Both Jaiden and the woman slowly turned. The woman's face flushed a deeper shade of red, and Jaiden blinked at them.

"Who are you?" the boy asked.

"Jaiden!" the woman scolded, then rolled her eyes and sighed. She wiped her hands on the long navy skirt, straightened, and smoothed her fingers along the pearly buttons of her navy and white striped shirt. "Excuse us. We were unaware the arch guardian had visitors."

Raina shifted Silas to one arm and used the banister to

help her stand. "I'm Arch Guardian Synintel's daughter, Raina."

Interest lit Jaiden's gaze. He looked between her and the other children. Behind him, the door opened completely, and Henry filled the entryway.

"What is going on out here?" Henry asked.

"Pa-pa-pa-pa!" Silas squealed in happiness and wiggled, arms outstretched, legs kicking.

Henry's gaze softened, and he held out his arms. Raina moved close enough to hand off the infant. A tug on the diaper bag had her swiping Tanis's hand away. Again.

"I want my train!" he shouted, stomping his foot.

"No."

Henry glanced at Tanis, raised his brows, and met Raina's stare, a question in his pale brown gaze.

"He threw his toy at the driver who brought us here," she explained.

"Ah." Henry nodded, then looked at Tanis again. "That was wrong."

Tanis crossed his arms, lifted his chin, and turned his face away. Raina's gaze narrowed, the action eerily familiar.

"Well, since I was interrupted, let's go to the greenhouse." He wrapped a big hand around Jaiden's shoulder and guided him. "How long have you been here?"

Jaiden spoke before Raina could. "About an hour. Miss Margie wouldn't let me come see you."

"Not long," Raina said when Henry looked at her.

"Miss Margie knows the rules, as do you," Henry answered, his grip tightening on the boy's shoulder before releasing. Jaiden didn't let Henry's hand get far before latching on. Silas chortled happily in his grandfather's hold, clapping his hands.

Raina glanced at the office doorway. No one followed behind her father. She rubbed her belly with both hands and tried to ignore the flare of unease.

"Did Raiventon ask you to come here?" Henry asked, nodding at a guard who opened the greenhouse door for the group.

"Yes. He'll come get us when he's finished doing whatever you asked of him," she said. While Raina respected the work her father required of her husband, she didn't appreciate the danger Kevin often faced, and the not knowing.

Henry adjusted Silas on his arm and went to the large, outdoor sectional couch arranged around a firepit with a grill in the center. A low-burning fire crackled and warmed the nearest seats. Tanis ran to the toy chest her father had placed in the space he usually only allowed family or close friends to venture within. Any social gatherings at his house were kept in the ballroom or game rooms. Jaiden joined him. Silas remained content on his grandfather's lap, engrossed by the glittering onyx buttons of Henry's dark red shirt. He poked, twisted, and attempted to pluck them free, muttering when nothing happened.

"How are you feeling?" Henry asked, sitting and taking one of Silas's small hands.

Raina sat adjacent to him and adjusted the length of her peach skirt. "Fine. Rose expects I may deliver a little earlier than I did with Tanis and Silas, but it's common, and the baby should be fine."

Concern tightened Henry's brow. "Should?"

Raina patted her belly. "I'm not worried if Rose isn't."

Jaiden handed Tanis a box with wooden building pieces and grabbed a second set. The two boys sat across from each other and began building with the interlocking pieces. Raina watched them, noting how the sun glimmered off the tops of their heads, highlighting Tanis's paler shade to Jaiden's richer locks. Jaiden's earlier words echoed through her mind.

I want to see my father.

Raina flexed her jaw and glanced from Jaiden to Henry.

The older boy scooted around to be closer to Tanis, showing him how to connect two trickier blocks. He glanced up, the light catching the pale brown of his irises. The same shade as Henry's. Same shade as hers. He smiled and returned to building.

Henry watched the boys. "I should have had you bring Tanis over more often. It's good for Jaiden to have someone to play with."

Margie patted her hair and shuffled on the other side of the firepit. "If you tell me when Jaiden can be expected home, I'll radio Arnita to inform her and leave you to your family, arch guardian."

"I've already told Arnita my plans. You can return to the palace or remain here and return with us. The choice is yours. I appreciate you escorting him here," Henry said, moving Silas to his leg to bounce the toddler.

Margie squared her shoulders. "That's my job, arch guardian. Jaiden is my charge."

Henry smiled. "Of course. Thank you."

Raina chewed on the inside of her cheek, the unease returning with enough force to aggravate her baby. Raina rubbed a soothing hand over her stomach. She waited until Margie left to ask the questions now burning within her. "Palace? Is... is that *Prince* Jaiden?"

Henry sighed and nodded. "Yes."

Raina blinked, her mind wrapping around the impossible facts. "And he's... your son?"

Henry stared at the two playing children. Silas squirmed, and Henry carefully set him down. Using the couch for support, Silas ambled over to the emerging city. Tanis fussed at the toddler's presence, but Jaiden handed Silas a block and showed him how to stack a few squares. Silas plopped down, taking a block from the prince to inspect.

"He is," Henry said quietly. He turned to meet her

stare, his gaze bleak. "No one can know, Raina. He's already in enough danger."

Hurt made her look away. "How could you keep this from me?"

"It wasn't entirely up to me." He shifted closer and touched a hand to her knee. "You would have had questions Arnita didn't want answered."

"I'm your daughter," she whispered to keep the emerging conflict between the adults. Raina pressed a trembling hand to her chest. "Did she not respect the family you already had?"

Henry clasped his hands between his legs, his shoulders sagging. "When she found out she was pregnant, she was terrified. We both were."

"How long?" Raina asked, her jaw clenched.

Henry didn't pretend to misunderstand what she asked. "About six months before her husband died." He touched her leg again. "Not something I'm proud of, but he'd been long gone before he passed, you know that."

She did. Raina also knew the arranged marriage had been fruitful but not loving. Unless required, the couple had never done things as a pair, and the citizens of Sziveria had never considered the man anything more than a consort to the queen. Arnita had and continued to run the country on her own, with the help of her closest advisors and arch guardians.

Jaiden's birth would have coincided with her father's impulsive protective streak. "You married me to Kevin to—"

"No," he quickly cut in. "I married you to Raiventon to keep you safe. Always to keep you safe, Lorraina. Not because I wanted to start over with a new family. Don't even speak that lie."

Raina took a shaky breath. "Why allow the truth to be known now?"

Henry looked back at the playing children. "He's going to be here a lot more. Arnita, too. I told her I wouldn't keep them a secret from you any longer, nor would I ask you not to visit when they're in residence."

Raina bristled. The Synintel house was as much her home as the Raiventon house. "She asked you to do that?"

"I didn't give her the opportunity to."

"But she would have?"

"I don't know. Jaiden is our baby, and...." He ran a hand through his short hair.

Raina looked at the little boy patiently helping her youngest son build a lopsided something. Her anger melted away. "And he's the only child both of you have conceived in love."

Henry shot her a startled glance. "I cared for your mother."

"But not like you care for the queen-elect," Raina surmised. "And we both know Mother hurt you. Something you and Arnita had in common since her husband also wasted away from addiction abuse."

"Yes. I understood her distress. Was perhaps the only one who did."

Which led to an affair, that might have started as a means of comfort for them both and morphed into something more. "You're still together in secret?"

Henry nodded. "If it were appropriate, I'd contract with her. But I can't as an arch guardian, and she's not ready for me to publicly give up my position. Not until the threat of the V Alliance is eliminated."

Until Kevin and grandchildren, Henry hadn't engaged in much conversation with Raina, especially nothing of a personal nature. Raina didn't want to push too hard for more information, but her world had tilted on its axis. She had a royal brother and may, in the future, have a royal step-mother and father. "Do you love her?"

"Yes," he whispered.

Raina looked at her beautiful sons, unable to imagine their conception outside of the love she shared for their father. An experience her father and the queen-elect didn't understand until Jaiden. The boy would always hold a special place in their hearts. Henry gazed at him with the same open happiness he did with his grandchildren.

Blowing air out her cheeks, Raina collapsed back against the couch cushions. Now she had to figure out how to tell Kevin, who never appreciated being the son-in-law to an arch guardian, that he was the brother-in-law to a prince....

SEVENTEEN

"Recognize any of the names?" Ryan asked, leaning back as Inara splashed and babbled in the huge kitchen sink half filled with soapy water.

Delanee braced her forearms on either side of the open folder Kevin Merrick, Master Guardian Raiventon, had delivered a few minutes ago. He'd been in a rush to return to his family and had practically tossed the folder of authorized radio numbers at Ryan and left. Delanee couldn't help but wonder if the young prince would soon be staying with the interceptor and his family. Or maybe Deklan and his wife. Cia also carried the interceptor gene. Add the wolves, and no one would dare break into Wolvenguard.

"Is this country-wide or just Haven City?" she asked, flipping through what amounted to a book's worth of information.

"Nation, including the Northern Boundary."

"Whoa. That's a lot of radios." Delanee sighed and flipped back to the beginning. "I figured there weren't many because of how expensive they are."

Ryan shrugged and gently poured water over Inara's head, shielding her eyes. He soaped his hands and then softly ran them over her little head, shoulders, and arms, all the way to her fingers, which she attempted to yank free, shouting at him. Once free, she chased around a large floating ball. Delanee smiled. He bathed her effortlessly, comfortable in the familiar task. Witnessing him caring for his child never failed to make Delanee want him just a little bit more. A temptation she needed to shove far, far away.

"You figure businesses have them. Hotels. Apartment complexes have at least one, though most have multiple. Government officials who hold important positions have radios in their offices and homes. Those all have to be registered."

Delanee flipped through the bound file until she spotted his name. "You have three?"

"Yes, I did. I have one here in the house and one in my office. The third is no longer valid. That one was at my parents' house." He frowned and leaned closer. "I wonder how outdated this registry is."

"There's an entry from three months ago, so whoever records the numbers is adding, but maybe not removing?"

Ryan washed between Inara's toes. "Except what happens to the radios that are no longer in use? Is there a code or anything to mark they've been deactivated?"

Delanee ran her finger down the page with Ryan's name and numbers. "Ah, yes, there's a tiny X next to this one that I'm assuming used to be the radio at your parents' home. Perhaps that means no longer assigned?"

"Why not cross the number out? They reuse radios. I had to turn that one in."

Delanee shrugged. "You could call it, maybe? See what happens?"

"Not a bad idea." He pulled the drain on the sink and Delanee straightened, grabbing the small towel with a little hood to hand to him.

"Can you radio from here? Or can it be traced somehow?" she asked, helping him wrap Inara in the soft fabric to carry her to the bedroom to be dressed for bed.

"No. The only way to know a specific location is if someone gives it during the transmission. I have to know who I'm radioing to have their frequency, but on my end, they'll have no idea where I'm even located, let alone if I'm nearby."

Delanee tucked the edges of the towel up under Inara's kicking feet, her fingers brushing Ryan's chest. The heat of his skin bled through the cotton of his shirt. Delanee wanted to press her hand flat and discover the full texture of his muscles sliding beneath her palm. Instead, she pulled her hand back and tried to force the sudden pound of her heart to return to normal.

"I have a book with radio numbers but no names. I'll hopefully be able to reconcile them and learn who they belong to." He adjusted Inara on his hip. The hood flopped off, and he quickly slid it back over her damp hair. "We'll see if any of them have the small Xs and no names. With my luck, most of them will be outdated numbers with no known assignments but still logged, like my old radio."

"That's rather negative."

Ryan shrugged. "Would be typical for this group."

Delanee paused in the hall to his room. She gnawed on her bottom lip. "Do you want to meet me in your office, or...?"

"The book with the codes is in my room. After I'm finished with Inara, I'll bring them out."

The urge to say his room would work just fine had her pressing her lips together. Not following to help with Inara's nighttime routine felt somehow wrong. Like a rejection. Shaking her head at the ludicrous notion, she returned to the kitchen, setting down the thick file of radio numbers on the breakfast table. Inara wasn't her daughter. She didn't even have a relationship with the infant's father. And at no point had Ryan even hinted he wished otherwise. Yes, he admitted to wanting to do wicked, sensual things with her. Delanee wanted more than a few stolen moments.

Easing onto the bench, she sighed and propped her chin on her palm. When had she begun to consider a future with Ryan? Because sitting here, the sting of dismissal still burning in her heart, Delanee couldn't ignore the wish that things were different. That she had the right to go into his room whenever she wanted. Pick up Inara, cuddle, care for, and love her. Slide between Ryan's sheets and show the man a different kind of love. A shiver raced up her spine at the desire.

Would he glow? Biting on her bottom lip, she realized she wanted him to. Wanted him to become so lost in her, in them, he let everything go, including the chains on his talent. Another conundrum. When had she wanted a man, *any man*, to lose control? Never. In her limited understanding, a lack of restraint meant domination. A partner who required the same sense of abandon from their lover. Someone always surrendered, allowing the other to do what they wanted. Perhaps needed. Too absorbed in the moment to care. Delanee wanted no part of uninhibited passion.

At least, she hadn't before Ryan's kiss.

Delanee couldn't deny she wanted to experience his mouth on hers again. Had an aching curiosity to know how he'd touch her. He was knotting her up inside. Making her question every relationship plan she had for her future.

"What has you thinking so hard?" he asked, sliding onto the bench across from her.

Startled, Delanee straightened and blinked. She glanced at the kitchen, where he had to have walked through to get to her. She was used to her brothers and her father walking on silent feet and considered the trait a beast master phenomenon. Perhaps it was more of a Gen-Heir gift all around. "How are you so quiet?"

He smiled without teeth and pushed a thin-bound book across the table to her. "Do you want to look for numbers?"

The binding creaked as she opened the cover. Row upon row of numbers stared back at her. "Might be easier if we both looked. This is... a lot."

His fingers drummed on the wooden surface. "We need paper and a pen, too, for notes. The office might be easier."

Delanee scooted out from the table, dragging the books to the edge. "All right. Did Inara go down okay?"

He looked at her, an odd expression on his face, then he nodded and slid out from the bench. "She's probably still talking to her feet, but yes, she laid down without fussing tonight."

Delanee grabbed both books and hugged them to her chest. She shouldn't have asked how the infant's nighttime routine played out. Inara's well-being wasn't any of her concern, or business, probably why he had given her such a strange look. Once Ryan figured out what he needed to do regarding the V Alliance and neutralized the threat against her, Delanee would return home. The notion of never holding the baby again brought physical pain to her chest.

"Good," Delanee somehow managed to get out, her hold tightening on the books.

"Delanee," he whispered, his fingers ghosting along her elbow.

Stopping at the living room, she waited but didn't turn.

His heavy sigh ruffled the curls around her shoulder. "I know Inara would have loved to have you tell her goodnight, but—"

"But someday I'll leave, and she won't understand," Delanee cut in, hating the tears burning her eyes.

"Yes," he said softly.

Delanee had wanted a denial. Had wanted him to... to what? Profess feelings for her and ask for forever? She blinked. Evidently, her internal peptalk about not wanting an alpha mate had been ignored by her heart. Again. She barely stopped a growl from escaping.

"I agree," she somehow managed to get out, pleased her voice remained neutral.

"Good. Thank you."

His steps faded from behind her, and he appeared on the other side of the living room through the entrance. Delanee wove around the living room table and followed him to the office. He lit lamps, then grabbed a chair in front of the desk and deposited it beside the other seat. All her research still covered the surface, and she flushed, knowing the mess must drive him nuts. She set the folder and journal on the chair and then gathered all her papers, books, and dailies into piles.

"Sorry," she muttered.

Ryan chuckled while helping. "No, you're not. Just like I'm not sorry for needing everything organized."

Another reason they'd be no good for each other. Messes didn't bother her, which meant she rarely cleaned up after herself. The reminder didn't stop her nostrils from flaring to take in the crisp aroma of sandalwood and ocean. The scent of *him*. She wanted to rub her face against his neck and coat herself in his essence. Ignoring the urge took an effort she hadn't anticipated. Her heart pounded in her ears, and her stomach quivered. A tremble raced along her spine and shook her shoulders. She cleared her throat, moved the radio information to the desk, and sat, hoping he didn't notice her odd behavior. Her reaction to this man needed to stop.

"Are the pages easy to remove from the folder?" he asked, sitting.

Delanee opened the file. "Yes, they're held in place by tabs."

He grabbed the journal and opened it to the first page. "We can work at the same time to find numbers."

"We aren't doing them all tonight, are we?" she asked, noting the time on the clock near the door.

"No, there are a few I want to check specifically. If you can just begin a general search, I'd appreciate it."

"Who would have helped you if I wasn't here?" she asked, sliding a clean sheet of paper closer.

He shrugged and found a note page of his own among the scattered mess. "No one."

Delanee leaned her forearms on the desk and looked at him. "No one?"

"And I'd probably have done all this at my desk at the FIO."

While Inara stayed with the twins. Delanee straightened, not sure how she felt knowing how lonely his life truly seemed to be. "Why? You have entire teams who'd help you."

"They help in other ways. Too much evidence has gone missing over the years. Not because of anything the teams have done but because the more people involved, the higher the chance of someone learning we have damning information. I've become cautious over the years when I finally get my hands on something that could help us identify key players."

"You also don't have to explain how you obtained additional information when you learn whom you can interrogate in your special way," she surmised, tapping her pen against the blank paper. "That's a lot on you."

"No more than any other crucial talent being utilized in this land. Look at Sheild Guardian Levkaseon. As a MedPath, Terran Kaine is responsible for identifying contagious pathogens and, in some cases, isolating human rabies syndrome victims for the entire city. There are nights I know he's sleeping at the morgue, making sure everyone in Haven City is safe."

Delanee had never met the medical empathic pathologist, but she'd heard of him and had read articles other journalists at *Haven City Chronicle* had written about him when reporting on active HRS situations in the city. Being immune to all infections, including the deadly sexually transmitted disease, meant he was called for containment situations whenever possible. A bite or splashed bodily fluids from a victim wouldn't hurt Terran.

"But his wife assists him whenever possible," Delanee said. "He's not alone in his burden."

"I've been doing this alone for a long time, Delanee," Ryan said quietly. "I'm used to it."

"You should let someone help you. Mason Dandridge wouldn't mind, I'm sure," Delanee said, having worked with the primary guardian on multiple occasions. He was a good man and, from her understanding, one of the best strategists in the nation.

"Kynhaven has enough going on right now with his wife, who is due to give birth soon. And you're correct about me not having to explain when I go in search of additional information. I really am serious about no one knowing what I can do with my talent."

Delanee shifted on the seat and stared at him, understanding dawning. "You don't trust them."

He jerked back in response and turned to look at her. "I do. Especially Wintersfall's team."

She shook her head, grabbing the back of the chair to face him fully. "No, you don't, or you would have trusted them with your secret. You would have let them help you gather information." A knot tightened in her chest. "Why did you tell me, Ryan? You know each of them far better than you know me."

White striations bled into his irises, catching Delanee's

breath. He blinked, and they faded, making her wonder if she'd imagined them.

"I don't know," he whispered.

Rational thought fled, and emotion took her over. Delanee wrapped a hand around the back of his neck and closed the short distance between them. Her mouth pressed to his, and thanks to him and the way he knew how to kiss, she had learned if she touched her tongue to his bottom lip, he'd.... Stars above, *yes*. Open and let her inside. Allow her to glide her tongue along his and experience the taste and sensual textures of his mouth.

For a few delightful moments, he let her be in control. Her fingers flexed along the corded muscles of his neck. Wanting to get closer, she squirmed to the edge of her seat. The arms of both their chairs created a frustrating barrier. A sliver of sanity reminded her the barrier was good. Necessary. But then his mouth slanted over hers. The kiss deepened and drowned her in a burst of need she felt straight to her core.

Delanee didn't protest when he broke the kiss long enough to pick her up and deposit her on the desk. Papers slid beneath her butt. Important documents she couldn't bring herself to care about were being wrinkled and scattered as his mouth sought hers again in aggressive demand, and his frame leaned over hers. She wrapped her arms around his wide shoulders, her legs parting to accept his hips. This time, when he surged forward, and the hard evidence of his arousal nudged her center, she didn't cower. No, she gasped, her eyes practically rolling into the back of her head at the rush of pleasure that accompanied the press of their bodies.

Her breath caught, and she clutched tighter to his shoulders, wanting to feel whatever he'd done again. He didn't disappoint, rolling his hips in a manner that sent another swell of bliss across her nerves. At some point, he'd grasped her hip, hauling their lower bodies closer together. She braced a foot on the arm of the nearest chair, her skirt sliding to pool on the desk. His fingers tangled in the fabric, further exposing her leg and leaving his touch much too close to her bare skin. She had the sudden, unexpected desire to be stroked by him. To learn how an intimate caress would feel. Then he ground against her again, and she didn't care what he did, provided he never stopped. Summer sun, if this is what he felt like between layers of clothing, how much better would actual sex be?

He tore his mouth from hers. The heavy pant of his breath tickled her neck as he hugged her close, his heart pounding against her breast. Whispered curses left him, every muscle in his body tense. A tremble wracked his entire frame.

Delanee squeezed her eyes tight. A matching tremor raced through her body. Unspent desire and confusion at how they'd gone from her simple kiss to her lying beneath him on the desk so quickly.

"We can't keep doing this," he breathed against her throat, his nose nudging her ear.

She kept herself from crying *why*, and instead, took a deep breath. "I know. I'm sorry, I shouldn't have kissed you."

He straightened enough to look down at her. His large hands framed her face, and he softly kissed her lips. "Not your fault. I'm the one who made things get almost out of control."

She raised a brow. "Somehow, I doubt that."

Straightening, he helped her rise, a small smile on his lips. "Fine. I knew better but did it anyway."

"Why?" she asked, unable to stop herself from asking this time.

He sighed and caressed his thumb over her swollen bottom lip, his gaze dark and intense. "To be so innocent."

He dropped his arm and stepped away. Her cheeks flushed as she scrambled to fix her skirt. A silly modesty, considering he'd already seen everything she had to offer. Not wanting to damage whatever papers were beneath her further, she let him help her down.

The instant her feet touched the ground, the dampness in her panties caught her attention. Her eyes widened, and the burn in her cheeks intensified. How could she sit next to him now? She couldn't exactly ask him to wait while she changed into dry underwear. Or maybe she could. He didn't need to know why she needed to be excused, right?

Delanee cleared her throat and kept from squirming. A heady pulse still drew attention to a part of her body she hadn't known could become so excited. "I'm going to um...." Her mind blanked.

Suddenly, he was in her space, so close she could make out the sliver of blue ice outlining his pupils. Her breath hitched, and her eyes widened. His scent and heat enveloped her once again, burning away any of the calm she'd managed to instill. The faint caress of his fingers on the underside of her jaw sent more tendrils of lust straight to her core. A fascinating, yet frustrating, development.

The desperate need coursing through her made her aware of why human rabies syndrome continued to plague the inhabited world. How temptation could override common sense. Hopping back on the desk, spreading her legs, and allowing him to relieve her of the pressure, loosening her inhibitions, would be so easy. But how many women had done just that for him? How many had demanded he service their needs and then walked away? Delanee wouldn't become just another memory. Not for any man, and especially not for this one. They both deserved more.

He leaned closer, his breath fluttering along her ear, and whispered, "You're wet for me, aren't you?"

Her knees almost buckled. She grabbed for the table, fumbling for purchase. What did he expect her to say to such a question? Wildly improper, and yet at the same time fitting since he'd had his tongue in her mouth and his body over hers.

"If I say yes, what happens next?" she asked softly, resisting the urge to slide her fingers through the short hair at the nape of his neck and guide his mouth to her throat.

He sighed and gently kissed the pulse racing beneath her ear. "Nothing, Delanee. Absolutely nothing."

A breath of relief mixed with frustration left her. "That's what I thought."

Both his hands framed her neck, his thumbs rubbing along her jaw. His gaze searched hers. "How do you tempt me like no one else ever has?"

She blinked. Her heart slammed even harder against her ribs while butterflies took flight in her stomach. "I do?"

"Yes. You make me want to protect your virtue and relieve you of it simultaneously," he said, a small smile toying with his kissable lips.

Delanee steeled her nerves and removed his hands from her skin. Cold rushed to replace the warmth of his touch, and she shivered. In the quiet solitude of his office, she came to a shocking realization. She didn't want anyone else to be her first. She didn't want some passionless sexual experience like she'd previously believed. The encounter on his desk had hinted at a pleasure she couldn't fathom. Nothing else would satisfy her now. Deeper curiosity had taken root, and only he could appease the wonder.

Which meant she'd never know because he was still all wrong for her. *Wasn't he?* Delanee didn't know anymore. A warning she better heed because the next time he kissed her, Delanee knew deep in her heart she wouldn't be able to deny either of them.

EIGHTEEN

The crush of too many people grated on Delanee's nerves. For the first time since she'd begun writing for the *Haven City Chronicle*, she didn't want to be at a social function. The quiet comfort of Ryan's home beckoned. She took a healthy sip of delicious red wine, knowing the trouble she'd found herself in two nights ago in his office had grown into a catastrophe.

Delanee wanted Ryan.

Desperately.

The level of her craving had reached such critical heights, she had argued with herself last night in the dark to stop from sneaking into his bed. And he hadn't even kissed her again. Oh no. Instead, Delanee's imagination had filled in all the missing components for her. Yesterday morning, she'd caught him leaving the pool from her bedroom window. All water-slickened muscle and hard male. The swim shorts glued to his lower body had given a glimpse of how very *male* he was. Her day had been thoroughly ruined. Any hope of maintaining sensibility had ceased to exist. Not even the twins' crazy antics or Inara's loud playing had been able to stop her from daydreaming about carnal moments. Made extra sad because Delanee wasn't even sure what completion would entail.

All she knew for certain? Ryan's body was made for touching. Licking. Biting. Though she'd never let herself go so far as actually to give into that particular craving. Which had only made her overactive imagination explode with visions of her teeth sinking into his shoulder while he.... Hand trembling, she took another deep gulp of wine, the sweet floral notes doing little to distract.

If she continued to let her imagination dictate her mental state of being, she could forget her career. Forcing an internal shake, Delanee focused on the party unfolding around her. Chandeliers shimmered with the light of hundreds of candles above the gathering. The doors leading to the greenhouse were all open and draped in fancy fabric and floral arrangements. Paper lanterns illuminated the path. The blooming *Bougainvillea glabra* lined the stone pathway in tall, slender hedges and vining arches. The floras burst with color, and the garden architect had created a maze of wonder through the expansive greenhouse. The whole setup felt romantic, and couples wandered deeper into the maze, taking in the flowers.

Ryan had yet to arrive. At least, that's what she figured, as she hadn't seen him. She needed to work before he made an appearance and distracted her further.

The book of radio numbers had yielded a few positive results. Two of the people she'd been able to reconcile to radio numbers in the registry would be in attendance tonight. One of them had a spouse who often made Delanee's social articles. Every little thing angered the woman, and at some point, she'd throw a tantrum to gain the attention of everyone in the room. Delanee had to wonder if the episodes weren't a means of distraction for her husband to disappear for a covert meeting or some other nefarious purpose. Delanee was determined to pay attention tonight and learn.

The Caraloussa merchant family was introducing their teenage daughter, Eloise, for the first time tonight, and the poor girl looked ready to throw up. Delanee set her wine glass on a passing serving tray, the remaining contents sloshing up the side. She fished a small notebook out from the handbag swaying from her wrist along with a pen. The nib scratched across the paper as she noted the family had opted to showcase the girl's youth, her straight hair unbound and adorned with tiny sparkling crystals. Every time Eloise went to touch the golden strands, she'd quickly fist her hand and drop it back to her side. A baby blue gown embroidered with silver strands covered her collarbone, past her elbows, and draped in elegant waves to the floor. The tight fitting bodice showcased her developing figure. Her mother popped her wrist when Eloise fidgeted with the large bow-tie sash at her hip. Delanee lifted a brow and made a note.

"I just knew I'd see you here tonight, Miss Ralston," a breathless male voice said behind her.

Delanee froze, her grip tightening on the pen. She swallowed and wondered if she could walk away without speaking a word. Rude behavior wasn't her default, but Barnaby Ingerman made her consider forgetting her grandmother's etiquette lessons.

"I had begun to worry about you and planned to visit Ms. Fenwick if I didn't see you. But here you are." He moved to stand in front of her, blocking her view of Eloise and the girl's mother. Barnaby attempted to reach for her, but Delanee stepped back, and his hand met air. He cleared his throat and smoothed the buttons of his shirt. "I have missed you."

"Missed me?" Delanee stared at him, baffled. "You barely know me, Mr. Ingerman."

When a second attempt to reach for her failed, his shoulders slumped. "I'd like to get to know you better, Miss Ralston. I know we're perfect for each other if you'd give me a chance."

Everything stilled in Delanee. Give Barnaby Ingerman a chance? She quirked a brow. The pale, short, faintly round man might have a point. He *was* what she envisioned she desired in a mate. He'd never aim to control her. Never try to dominate. Delanee would maintain the upper hand in their relationship. Yet, looking at him, she couldn't stop her lip from curling in disdain. His dark green shirt hung from his thin shoulders. A paunchy belly brought attention to the lack of girth around his chest. A brown vest with gold embroidery matched his pants, the gold threads shimmering in the overhead light.

The man was the exact opposite of Ryan in every way. For him, Delanee's sole value lay in her family name. Marrying into her family meant marrying into power. And Barnaby wanted power. He practically vibrated with the need to be taken seriously, to hold sway among the ranked guardians mingling around them. The Ralston name would provide a sense of authority he needed to feel important. And would lock Delanee into a boring and unemotional marriage.

She took a deep breath and glanced around the gathering. No one paid them any attention. "I've told you before we aren't compatible."

"But your grandmother—"

"Never said anything," Delanee reminded him. "She only agreed to meet you."

He raised a hand. "No, no. She said I was a wonderful man, and she'd be delighted to give us time together."

Delanee flexed her jaw. She could just imagine the snicker her *baki* delivered after such a statement. "I'm sorry she gave you hope, but I've never been interested in you for marriage. I've made that perfectly clear."

A heavy swallow bobbed his Adam's apple. He smoothed a hand down his shirt again, the dark color drawing attention to his pasty skin. "Would you at least see the flowers with me?"

Delanee craned her neck to see further over the crowd, catching sight of the young debutante she'd been observing. The girl's mother watched the newly assigned guardian for the Key Guardian Rashmira seat in the Hall of Laws like a hawk seeking prey. The man in his early twenties laughed at something his companion had said, and the pair disappeared through the open doorway into the greenhouse. Eloise's mother tugged her after them.

"Sure, let's see the blooms," Delanee said, distracted, her attention on trailing the teenager and her mother.

A firm hand wrapped around her upper arm. "Oh, excellent, Miss Ralston. You won't regret our time together. I'm determined to help you understand why we're a good match."

Delanee figured telling him the chances of changing her mind were a big fat zero would create a scene, so she simply hummed and allowed him to guide her into the humid conservatory. A line moving at a slow pace paraded by the colorful blooms. The hum of conversation and competing scents of perfumes and colognes filled the air, along with a sense of excitement. Navigating the maze of blooms delighted the master guardianess' guests, as it did yearly.

A woman laughed a sharp bark of merriment up ahead. Another woman squealed. Leaves rustled, and everyone in front of them strained to see what caused the commotion.

Barnaby sniffed beside her, sliding his hand into her elbow. "No one can behave themselves anymore. Disgraceful."

Delanee glanced at him, frowning. "You don't even know what happened."

He sniffed again, lifting his chin. "A couple couldn't be decent and fell into one of the hedges. Happens every year. Ruins that whole section for everyone else because all the petals fall off the flowers."

For three years, Delanee had covered the Master Guardianess Silverhill's blooming event. She never recalled anyone destroying a section of hedges. Perhaps she'd never stayed late enough to witness the antics, and they were starting early this year. "You can return inside if you'd prefer."

He patted her arm. "I will endure any damage."

"Great," Delanee murmured.

She rose on her toes to see over the few guests in front of her and noted Eloise's mother pushing others from her path, dragging her daughter along. The poor teen bumped and jostled everyone she encountered, apologizing and attempting to yank her arm from her mother's hold. Delanee pulled free and moved off the main part of the trail to take notes on her observations. She'd need to figure out how to keep the pair in her line of sight.

"Miss Ralston, we're going to fall behind." Barnaby shuffled his feet and squeezed his hands together. "The maze is becoming more crowded by the minute."

"Just a second," she said, writing shorthand on the journal page. "You can go ahead without me if you wish."

"No, no." He took a long, deliberate breath. "I need to support your work. I shall stand here and be your guard so you can accurately describe the splendor of the blooms. Do you see the ones behind us? Such a vivid orange and pink. Did you know...."

Delanee ignored his launch into the history and preparation of the annual greenhouse event. She didn't care, and neither would her readers. No, the people she wrote for wanted juicy moments they could use to gossip over and forget about their own woes and shortcomings for a bit. Keeping to the outside of the shuffling line, Delanee cut ahead. Flower petals fluttered to the ground and spun in the air as her arm and back brushed over them. Behind her, Barnaby sputtered. Whether from indignation because she dared to leave him, or the minor damage she created to the hedges in her wake, she didn't know. Didn't care, either. Eloise's mother had caught up with the key guardian and was not-so-subtly shoving her daughter at the man, who was too old for the girl. In three or four years, their courting would be fine. Now? Delanee wondered why the woman was even attempting to catch the key guardian's attention with her daughter.

Keeping a few guests between them so the woman didn't become suspicious of Delanee following, she kept a close eye on the mother's behavior. The debutante looked ready to burst into tears, ignoring the newly assigned key guardian despite her mother's constant silent pointing and elbow digs. Delanee wrote down some quick remarks of how she'd word the mother's garish behavior, wanting to make sure when she wrote the article, she captured the moment in vivid detail for her audience.

"Miss Ralston, are you... spying?" Barnaby asked in disbelief, his voice hushed.

Delanee glanced over her shoulder at him. "I'm the journalist for the social pages, Mr. Ingerman. I'm observing."

His trembling hand patted at his tidy side part. "Well, I-I knew you wrote for a paper in town. I guess I failed to realize what. Who, um, who exactly do you write about?"

"Anyone of interest," she said, turning her attention back to the slowly moving line.

"Who," he cleared his throat, much closer to her, "who do you often investigate? Just parties like this?"

Investigate. What an odd word choice. Alarm bells went off in Delanee's mind, and she worked hard not to allow any change in her demeanor. "Yes," she answered easily, making another note. "Parties just like this."

His heavy sigh fluttered the curls that had come free at the base of her neck. She fought a shiver of disgust. "That's good. I mean, whatever makes you happy, of course."

Delanee clenched her jaw to keep from saying her happiness wasn't his concern. Maybe if she rushed far enough ahead, the crowd would create enough separation for her to escape him. In the months since she'd met the man, she had become an expert at evasion. But the crowd was too thick, and she would be much too slow to make real progress.

"Oh, look, what a perfect spot," he said a second before she was yanked into a private alcove.

A narrow path across from an ornate cement bench offered an alternate route back to the ballroom for guests who'd experienced enough of the maze. Delanee wondered how many shortcuts were arranged within the labyrinth. Two candles on slender iron holders gave the cozy space an intimate feel away from all the noise and chaos of onlookers. Huffing in frustration, Delanee moved toward the footpath.

"Oh, no, not yet, Miss Ralston. I wish to continue our private moment," Barnaby said.

"I do not," she snapped, her hands fisted.

She put her back to him and clenched her notebook and pen in her hand until the metal holder bit into her palm. His heavy hand landed on her shoulder, and she spun around. She opened her mouth to berate him for not only touching her but dictating her movement when a hot, sloppy kiss landed on her bottom lip and chin. Barnaby made quick work of adjusting his aim, rising on his toes.

Pressing his body closer, he stabbed his tongue between her lips, still parted from the shock of his kiss.

Delanee attempted to disengage, but his arms locked around her, smashing their chests together. Inappropriately she noted their level of padding was about the same. Nothing solid about Mr. Ingerman except for.... *Ack! Eww, no, no, no!* Delanee's mind protested the hard lump behind his pants pressing into her hip. She wanted no part of that excitement and was appalled he felt such lust for her.

Struggling against his tight embrace, Delanee tried to disengage from him. The repulsive taste of wine and some sort of cheese made her gag, and she feared she would vomit if he didn't stop. His fingers dug into her shoulder blades, and his teeth mashed against hers. Left with no other options, Delanee did as her brothers and father had taught. She lifted her knee and slammed it straight into his crotch.

He howled and stumbled from her, tripping over the bench and toppling into the hedge behind. Vivid pink flower petals burst into the air. Delanee scrubbed her hand over her mouth and resisted the urge to spit. She shook out the navy folds of her beaded skirt and hoped no one had witnessed the embarrassing exchange. Leaves rustled behind her, and she gasped, spinning, her grip tight on the journal she held out like a shield.

"Easy," Ryan said softly, holding out his hands.

Heat flamed across Delanee's cheeks. What had he seen? From the angry glint in his eyes, she figured most everything. She lowered the journal and kicked her toes across the laid stone. "Well, this is mortifying."

"Are you all right?" he asked, his voice still low.

"I'm fine. I handled it."

His lips quirked in a near smile. "I noticed."

She lifted her chin. "He should have known better than to take something I didn't permit."

"With your family?" Ryan asked, brows raised. "He really should have."

Whimpering sounded behind her, and Delanee spun on the ball of her foot. Leaves rustled, and Barnaby's fingers appeared on the edge of the bench. He hoisted himself up, flower petals and twigs poking from his hair. The movement must have proved too much, for he howled again, his fingers losing traction, and disappeared from sight. More petals floated in the air. The unease from earlier had her gaze narrowing and she took a step closer to Ryan.

"If I asked you to ask him a question without his knowing, would you?" she whispered.

"What would you have me ask?"

Delanee took a deep breath. "Why he's really been following me."

Nineteen

Ryan turned his focus to a pale hand attempting to once again grasp the edge of the bench to pull up a pathetic form. A whimper sounded in the dense shadows around the hedge. When Ryan had first spotted Ingerman leading Delanee into the greenhouse, he'd held back. A tiny part of him had hoped the persistent suitor would have some luck changing Delanee's mind. Ingerman wouldn't require her to live a secretive life. Not that Delanee had made any indication she desired anything from Ryan, fighting the attraction between them as much as Ryan had been. But that didn't change the very real fact that a life with him would come with challenges, especially since his daughter's gift had to be protected just like his own.

Then jealousy flared through him, and he'd found himself trailing after the pair. When they disappeared from the path, Ryan found another alcove that led to this one and waited, hating himself a little for spying on them. Ingerman's ridiculous attempt at a kiss had sheeted Ryan's vision red, and had Delanee not intervened, Ryan would have, regardless of the consequences. No one kissed her but *him*. The shocking realization left his heart pounding a little too hard.

The request to use his talent also took him by surprise. Delanee would not have asked if she didn't have a genuine concern. "Why are you suspicious?"

She edged closer, the tips of her fingers brushing along his. The subtle contact eased a tension he hadn't known was present. "He asked me what I investigated," she whispered. "To anyone who follows my work, I don't *investigate*. None of my serious articles have been approved by my editor for publication."

His gaze narrowed on the trembling hand, still attempting to find a cement edge for leverage. "Does he strike you as the type to read the social pages?"

She gnawed on her bottom lip. "Maybe," she whispered. "He's interested in pursuing me because of my family connections. Only someone who follows the guardian's lifestyle would be concerned with marrying into a prominent family name."

Ryan took a deep breath and closed the short distance to the bench. He leaned over and took in Ingerman's sweating face, twisted into a grimace. "Here, let me help you."

"Oh, than—"

The second Ryan touched Ingerman's damp wrist, he shot power into the man. White overtook the dark brown of Ingerman's irises, and all movement froze. Ryan leaned close, keeping their conversation contained, though he was aware of Delanee shifting nearer, blocking them further.

"What do you want with Miss Delanee Ralston?"

"I have to get her to trust me," Ingerman replied without infliction.

Ryan frowned. "Why does she need to trust you?"

"I need to convince her to be alone with me."

Delanee inhaled sharply. Unease burned a path to

Ryan's gut. "Why do you need to be alone with her?"

"I have been tasked with obtaining Miss Delanee Ralston."

Delanee's hand grabbed his shoulder and squeezed. Ryan had to focus on keeping his talent contained in Ingerman alone. "Obtaining Delanee Ralston for who?"

"I don't know, only that there is a need for her."

"Where are you to take her once she trusts you?"

"To warehouse one-thirteen."

"Damn it," Ryan whispered under his breath. The danger Delanee had been in well before her discovery of the assassin was becoming more apparent with each passing day. What would have happened if she hadn't interfered and remained on her own, oblivious to so many threats around her?

Delanee's grip tightened. "What is warehouse one-thirteen? You know it? Is it a business or something?"

"No, it's in the warehouse district outside the city."

"Yes," Ingerman replied in response to Ryan's words.

Ryan took a deep breath. "Why are you to take Delanee Ralston to warehouse one-thirteen?"

"I don't know."

Ryan glanced at Delanee, who'd returned to chewing on her bottom lip. She was going to make herself bleed if she didn't stop. "Who asked you?"

"The V Alliance."

Ryan's fingers pressed into the tendons of Ingerman's wrist. "Who is the V Alliance?"

He'd asked this question what felt like a hundred times, and the answer had always been the same. This time, he wondered if finally, the response would be different.

"All of us. We are all The V Alliance," Ingerman intoned, the response extra creepy from his lack of infliction.

Nope. Not different. He dropped his head in defeat.

"Why would The V Alliance want me?" Delanee asked, her voice so quiet he almost didn't hear her over the rustle of leaves, muffled conversation, and laughter. "My articles, do you think?"

"What does The V Alliance want with Delanee Ralston?" Ryan asked Ingerman.

"I don't know."

Ryan glanced at Delanee. "This is the problem with this group. They don't give additional information to the peons. They piecemeal tasks, and no one knows anything beyond their given assignment."

"I am told what I need to know," Ingerman said.

"Right." Ryan sighed and withdrew the tendrils of his power.

"—k you," Ingerman sighed, his clammy hand wrapping around Ryan's forearm to accept help up.

Delanee trembled beside him, and her hands balled. A jerk of her knee glittered the beads across the skirt of her gown and had him snapping his attention to her. He shook his head. Ingerman's weight yanked on his shoulder and Ryan helped him rise, releasing him the second he stood on wobbly legs. Ryan was used to pretending the information he obtained had no effect on him. They couldn't afford to allow Ingerman to suspect anything.

Cheeks dark with anger, she dropped her foot back to the brick, her hands remaining fisted. "Don't you ever kiss me again."

"I will not, I can assure you," he wheezed, stumbling around the bench and plopping down hard. He yowled and grabbed at his crotch with both hands, cupping himself completely through his pants. "When will the pain *ever* end?"

Ryan tsked and patted the man's shoulder. "I recommend ice."

Ingerman whimpered and leaned over, legs spread.

"Come on," Ryan whispered, urging Delanee toward the narrow side path back to the ballroom.

She sighed again, her shoulders slumped. "I was chasing a story, too."

Her lack of concern or fear over the threat revealed against her made Ryan grit his teeth. If Ingerman failed, someone else would surely be sent in his place. Whatever the V Alliance wanted with her, they wouldn't give up until they were successful. He knew that much about the group. "You aren't worried about what Ingerman wanted with you?"

"Of course, I am," she whispered, pushing a flowering branch away from her face. "But they aren't going to snatch me from a busy party, and my story promised to be a real page gripper."

"Hopefully, whoever you were interested in will return to the main gathering."

"Oh, they will," she muttered, "but I will have missed the best part of their evening."

"I'm sure Mrs. Caraloussa will still be chasing down Key Guardian Rashmira, hoping the man becomes so besotted by her daughter, he'll wait the five years for her to contract legally," Ryan murmured, his hand sliding along her low back.

Delanee slowed, her gaze snapping to him in shock. "You were following them, too? Or me? Were you following me?"

"I've been observing. I did follow when Ingerman disappeared with you in here," he admitted, pausing in the next alcove, where they were isolated and alone, the hum of conversation filtering through the hedges.

"Why?" she asked, her golden eyes searching his in the intimate light.

Her single-word question carried so much weight, and he didn't have an answer. At least not a response he was prepared to offer. So, he opted to misunderstand which part of his statement she questioned. "Almost every guardian in the city is in attendance tonight. The chances of some of them being in league with the V Alliance are high. I'm noting who's conversing, who's disappearing, and if anything is exchanging hands."

"I didn't mean—" She huffed a long exhale and muttered, "Never mind."

Shaking her head, she pressed through the barely visible path between hedges to bypass the maze and return to the ballroom. He followed, his shoulders brushing leaves and flower petals. On a right turn, she came to a sudden halt and attempted to backtrack, her cheeks flaming. Ryan raised a brow and pressed between her and the hedge, ignoring the arousing sensation of her body sliding along his.

The faint *clink-clink-clink* of a belt buckle shaking clued him into what Delanee had witnessed. And sure enough, a couple had used the narrow, empty side paths to steal some private time. Their heavy breaths and restrained grunts and moans filled the small space. Facing away from the trail he and Delanee used, they hadn't noticed the interruption. The woman's pale rear end and legs were on full display. Both her hands were lost in the hedges she gripped on either side to maintain her balance while her lover took her from behind while standing. Little yellow and orange flower petals fluttered around them, shaken loose from the constant movement.

Ryan reached back and wiggled his fingers, motioning for Delanee to move forward. Her hand wrapped around his, and she pressed close, her other hand gripping the back of his shirt. The heat of her breath whispered through the fabric a second before her entire face pressed between his shoulder blades. Her uncomfortable reaction spoke once again to her innocence. Or perhaps it spoke to how jaded

Ryan had become. He'd been in the same situation at many parties over the years. The sight was neither unexpected nor unusual.

Another hot puff of Delanee's breath feathered along his back and sent a tremor of lust through him. "How could anyone... do *that* in such a public place?"

"Because passion takes over and where you are no longer matters. In fact, it can be forgotten," Ryan answered quietly, leading her around a turn.

Her head shake brushed curls along the back of his neck. "That's ridiculous."

The need to teach her a lesson in misjudging the power of desire had him twisting hard enough to dislodge her grasp and face her. A dangerous challenge he should ignore. Yet the memory of her lips and tongue against his and her body pliant had him moving into her space. They were alone once more and far enough from the main path for quiet to press in around them, creating the perfect illusion of privacy. Much like what the engaged couple experienced for their guards to drop enough to be overcome by passion.

Ryan cupped her jaw in both his hands, tilted her face upward, and covered her mouth with his before she could utter a protest. The gentle probe of his tongue along the seam of her lips made her open for him. He slipped inside, her whimper of need an invitation to take what she hadn't offered Ingerman.

Ryan accepted.

His mouth slanted over hers, delving deep. Dominating. Her free hand wrapped around his left bicep, and her nails delivered a delicious bite of sensual pain. Ryan kept one hand splayed across her jaw and neck, her pulse a hard pound beneath his fingers. His other hand moved to her rear, drawing her into his frame since he had no wall or surface to hold her against. The beads of her gown scraped along his pants and shirt as she shifted closer. The softness of her low abdomen cradled his growing arousal. He couldn't stop from rolling his hips, lifting her enough to press as close to the heart of her as he'd ever allow himself to be. But oh, stars above, he wanted to explore. Desperately wanted to learn what would make her moan and coat his fingers, perhaps even his tongue, with her desire.

Her gasp of surprise fluttered across his lips before he pulled back and licked his way to her throat. Gently, he bit the sensitive cord where her neck met her shoulder, and her pulse fluttered an excited rhythm. Her heavy breaths panted across his temple, increasing his arousal.

"I want to touch you so badly I ache," he breathed against the skin beneath her ear.

"You are... touching me," she gasped.

He knew he would shock her with the depths of his need expressed vocally, but he wouldn't scare or offend her. Since words were all he had, all he'd ever have where she was concerned, he didn't hold them back. "I want my mouth here," he whispered, skating his fingers across her breast and then sliding them lower. "And here. I want my fingers buried deep. I want to know how you feel inside. How wet you'll become for me."

A full body tremble raced through her, and she sagged all her weight into him.

"Would you let me, right now, if I pulled up your skirt and slid my hand beneath?" he asked.

"Yes," she moaned.

The permission almost had him throwing his own caution away. He couldn't remember ever wanting a woman as much as he wanted her. But the first time Delanee experienced an intimate touch shouldn't be where anyone could interrupt, especially a stranger. And if Ryan ever succumbed to his need, the sounds she made would be for him alone, not a potential voyeur. He'd share her with no one.

Ryan leaned back and waited until her eyes fluttered open. He lifted a brow, running a thumb along her swollen bottom lip. Quickly recovering from passion was a skill Ryan had developed over the years out of necessity. Delanee had no such ability, and Ryan waited for her senses to return. When they did, she blinked a few times, her cheeks darkening and a glare slitting her gaze. She smacked him on the arm, the harsh slap echoing around them.

"You did that on purpose," she hissed and hit him again.

Ryan turned away from her frustration and caught her hand. "Yes. Though I enjoyed every second more than I should have."

She yanked her hand free and slapped him on the chest with her notebook. "I should write about this, show *you* a thing or two."

"Perhaps someday you will," he murmured, a hand on her back to urge her toward the ballroom again.

"Write about you?" She glanced over her shoulder.

"No, teach me a thing or two."

She snorted. "I doubt that."

Ryan held an untrimmed branch out of her way. Pale purple blooms broke free and floated to the path. "Why? I may have more personal experience than you since I'm older, but I have a feeling you've read quite a bit."

"Well, I mean, hasn't *everyone* read a lusty book or two in their adult life? Although, from my understanding, relying on such will leave you disappointed in a lover. The experiences are grossly exaggerated."

Ryan laughed before he could contain the sound. "Most of them aren't based on reality. And that wasn't what I meant."

"Oh." She cleared her throat. "What, um, what did you mean, then?"

Smiling, Ryan brushed his fingers along the exposed

skin beneath her styled hair at the base of her neck. "I think I like your way of thinking better. I have never read one of those books before."

She glanced at him, her eyes wide. "Seriously, you haven't?"

"Nope, never. Haven't ever had the time for reading beyond work. Am I missing much?"

"I'm not sure. Some would say I'm missing something by never having been to a curtain show. I imagine lusty books are similar."

"Do you enjoy them?" he asked, leaning closer.

"I..." She let out a long breath. "I have found some of them intriguing, yes."

"I believe I'd like them if you read one to me," Ryan said. "Would you?"

"I'm not sure they're anything Inara needs to hear," she said, color infusing her cheeks.

"Mmm, probably not. But she won't be in my room forever." As soon as the words left his mouth, he realized his mistake.

She frowned. "I won't be in your house forever, either."

Ryan had to bite the inside of his lip to keep from asking if she wanted to be, if he asked if she'd stay. Enter a year-long contract. But what did he have to offer? He'd never advance beyond his current position in his career, as he couldn't afford the exposure. Her own career also made any relationship between them tricky. Some secrets could never be revealed. While he trusted Delanee, temptation could be a tricky beast. A reminder he needed to keep from giving into the attraction waging between them.

He returned to navigating the narrow pathways, hoping they didn't encounter any more couples seeking privacy. The bright glow of the ballroom filtered over the hedge, and the hum of conversation swelled around them. Ryan paused to ensure neither of them looked like they'd stolen a moment. Delanee blinked at him, her notebook and pen still clutched in her hands.

"What?" she asked.

Gently, he tucked a stray curl into place. "Making sure no one will know I kissed you."

She rolled her lips together, her gaze dropping to his mouth. "Maybe I wouldn't mind if people knew."

Ryan touched her jaw, tracing the elegant curve to her chin. "You are such a dangerous temptation for me."

Her mouth opened on a sharp inhale, but whatever she was going to say was interrupted by the obnoxious laughter of a woman. A couple stumbled through a cleverly hidden opening between hedges. Ryan dropped his hand and stepped from Delanee just as the couple's uneven steps sent them careening to where Ryan had been standing. The man chuckled, wrapping an arm around the woman's slender waist. Her face was hidden in the man's neck, and her body was pressed close enough to hinder her partner's steps.

"My darling, wait until we're further hidden," he mumbled.

"I can't—"

"Excuse me," Delanee snapped. "Then, at least wait until we've walked by."

The couple gasped and sprang apart. Red brightened the man's face all the way to his dark hairline. Immediate recognition hit Ryan for both guests, though the sight of the woman was like a punch to the gut. Renelle Maxton. He locked down his emotion, settling his face into his usual reserved expression.

"Shield Guardian Elkmont. Miss Maxton," Ryan greeted.

"Mr. Voklane," the shield guardian began, clearing his throat and smoothing a hand down his very rumpled pale blue shirt. "I hadn't realized the arch guardian would attend tonight."

"He hadn't decided one way or another," Ryan said smoothly. "You know I often attend on his behalf."

"Yes, of course." Elkmont cleared his throat again.

Renelle lifted her elegantly rounded chin, her gaze a mixture of seductive interest and self-importance. She knew her beauty and never failed to remind anyone who looked her direction. "And you must have missed the announcement of my marriage to Primary Guardian Chatom."

Ryan lifted a brow and kept his shock contained. Though, really, the information shouldn't have surprised him. Renelle had wanted one thing from him, well, two if he were being crude. "No, I must have missed it."

Delanee moved away from the couple, interest lighting her face. He noticed her notebook was now hidden. "Primary Guardian Chatom contracted?"

Renelle's attention shifted to Delanee and she lifted a delicate brow. Her blonde curls piled atop her head, decorated with dozens of dangling baubles, glittered in the weak light. "Yes, to me. Five months ago."

"Ah, during the winter. Understandable you missed the notification," Delanee said to Ryan.

"Yes," Ryan said without inflection.

Renelle's cornflower blue gaze lingered on Delanee, taking her in from the beaded slippers on her feet to her slightly disheveled curls. "And you are?"

"Apologies," Ryan said, interrupting before Delanee could offer her full name. He doubted Renelle had been among ranked society long enough to learn the identity of D. Ralston who wrote the gossip columns, but Ryan didn't want to take the risk. "Miss Ralston, this is Renelle...." The surname of the primary guardian she'd apparently married failed to come to him.

"Hackleburg, if you took the guardian's name." Delanee filled in for him. Alarm made his spine straighten.

Her predatory smile at Renelle meant she'd realized who stood before them. "Did you?"

Renelle licked her full lips, stained with a rich, dark red pigment. "Of course, he is my..." Her gaze flickered to Ryan, and a blush brightened the false pink brushed along her cheeks. "Husband. I prefer to go by Primary Guardianess Chatom."

Delanee leaned in close, though her loud whisper carried to all of them, "I would, too."

The red blossomed to Renelle's neck. "Right, well, we didn't mean to intrude. We were just, um..."

"Looking for the sculptures," Elkmont quickly filled in.

Renelle's gaze widened, and her slender shoulders pressed back, drawing attention to her full breasts spilling between the deep plunge v-neckline of her gown. Diamonds glittered at her neck, and chandelier earrings dangled from her ears. "Yes, the sculptures. Hidden surprises within the maze. Did you find any?"

"No," Ryan answered, trying not to laugh at the absurdity of them pretending they were doing anything except trying to find enough privacy to expose specific body parts to each other. "Just a bench."

"Oh." Her gaze looked him up and down. The familiar heat that had short-circuited his better judgment over a year ago flared in her eyes. "That's unfortunate." She toyed with her necklace before her fingers danced to her cleavage. "I heard they're quite stimulating."

Elkmont sputtered before latching onto her elbow and backing up a few steps. "Well, I suppose we should go see them before we're missed."

Delanee moved forward a few inches. "Wait, don't you want to know about—"

Ryan grabbed her upper arm and pulled her back from the couple, knowing exactly what she was about to ask and needing to stop the train wreck about to happen. "Don't."

"No, it's not okay," Delanee hissed, anger sparking in the depths of her golden eyes.

"Know about what?" Renelle asked.

"Your daughter," Delanee said before Ryan could stop her again. "Don't you want to know how she's doing?"

A fist squeezed in his stomach, and for the first time in his life, he wanted the ground to open and swallow him whole.

Elkmont released Renelle as if she'd burned him. His ex glared at Delanee, her jaw clenched. Anger twisted her beautiful face. She looped her arms around her companion's bicep and pulled him close. "You must be mistaking me for someone else, Miss Ralston. I don't have any children."

"I should say not," Elkmont said, clearing his throat and adjusting his neckline. "You've only been married a few months."

"That's correct," Renelle said smoothly.

"Where is the primary guardian tonight?" Ryan asked, wanting to steer the conversation away from his daughter and the humiliating reminder he'd conceived a child with the selfish woman in front of him. The only good thing to come of his mistake.

Renelle's chin lifted. "Away, overseeing some improvements to the docks at Port Ice Hollows."

"I promised to continue introducing Primary Guardianess Chatom into society for him," Elkmont said, patting her hand wrapped around his arm.

She beamed at him, yet the fire had banked in her gaze. "So kind of you, too. Elmer is appreciative of your support."

Ryan morphed his snort into a cough. Somehow, he doubted the aging Primary Guardian Chatom knew of Elkmont's encroachment or his wife's scheme to increase her social ranking by the end of the year. Ryan needed to get away before he or Delanee, who looked about ready to burst, said something they'd regret. "Enjoy the rest of your evening."

Elkmont nodded. "You as well. Give the arch guardian my regards."

"No, wait—" Delanee sputtered.

Ryan's grip tightened on her arm, hauling her away from the retreating couple. "Stop it," he ground out.

Delanee twisted and yanked her arm free. "You stop it." She grabbed the small handbag dangling from her wrist and pointed in the direction the pair had disappeared. "How can you let her get away with that? Why didn't you confront her?"

Ryan stopped before they entered the flow of guests entering and exiting the greenhouse. He grabbed her arms and leaned close, his nose almost touching hers. "Listen very carefully because I'm only going to say this once."

Her eyes widened, but she remained silent.

"Inara is mine and mine alone, do you understand?"

"Yes, of course, but—"

"No, there is no *but*. She...." How could he say the awfulness of what Renelle had done to them both? "Renelle didn't claim her, Delanee."

"I just saw that for myself," she bit out. "I still don't understand how you can allow her to ignore her own child."

"There is no ignoring when Inara doesn't even exist."

Delanee flinched back. "What are you talking about? Of course she exists."

Ryan shook his head and released his hold. "No. When Renelle sent Inara to me, she sent her without documentation. I can't file a birth record without a mother's signature or a medical scientist confirming the mother giving birth. Therefore, Inara doesn't exist."

TWENTY

"WHAT ABOUT FANELINE?" Delanee asked, an unexpected desperation to protect the innocent in the mess of Ryan's making causing her mind to spin. The last name assigned to a true orphan might be a good bandage, if not an outright fix. "I know the surname can't be inherited, or used by a contracted spouse, but maybe it'll work to at least give her legal documentation?"

Ryan sighed and turned, pushing through the near invisible exit from the side path. "If I gave her to an orphanage and hoped they'd let me adopt her, I could go that direction. But I can't just file her as a Faneline. She hasn't been abandoned at an orphanage without parentage."

"And you won't forge one?" she asked. "I mean, you have access to several medical science officers."

"And list who as the mother?"

"I don't know," Delanee said under her breath, moving closer to keep their conversation private. "Make someone up."

"And again, who would sign it?"

"Another team member. You do have women who work

for you. Isn't one married to a medical science officer?" she asked, certain Sean Blackbain was an MSO, and he was married.

"Then two of my team members would be committing forgery. Absolutely not."

He pushed through the crowd gathered at the stairs to the house. The entrance was different than the one she'd come through with Ingerman. Delanee ignored all the people milling around, no longer caring about the next juicy story. She had two in her mental inventory now, anyway. She was positive she'd be writing about the hunt for risqué statuary in the seclusion of a maze between a certain married woman and her single male companion. Delanee could already see the article forming. Oh, yes. She almost rubbed her hands together in glee.

The more immediate concern was solving the issue of Inara not being registered as a citizen of Sziveria. If anything were to happen to Ryan, no one could help. She *would* become a Faneline – a child with no background or known family. And if anything were to happen to the infant, Ryan couldn't ask for any help. The baby had no records and nothing for officials to work with to protect her. An unacceptable situation.

Delanee spotted a familiar face in the crowd, and a crazy plan emerged. She bit her lip and tapped Ryan's arm. "I'm going to have Tate bring me back to your house. Might be best if we leave separately since we arrived that way."

Ryan frowned and glanced over the room. "Tate from...."

"My brother's Wolvenguard team," Delanee supplied. "I'm safe with him."

Uneasiness pinched his handsome face. "Delanee...."

"No one is going to try to take me tonight, not if they're hoping Mr. Ingerman will come through." Which he wouldn't. Ever. Another thing for Delanee to worry about later.

He sighed. "You know the way?"

"To your house?"

Ryan nodded.

"Yes, I believe so."

He held out his hand. "Let me see your notebook, please."

Delanee dug into her handbag and removed the slender journal. She handed him the book and a pen. He opened it, and the pen scratched across a random page.

"My address and radio number." He snapped the cover closed and returned both to her. "Please don't get lost."

She hugged the book to her chest. "I won't."

His hand lifted as if to touch her before his fingers curled into his palm and dropped. "And please be careful."

Delanee waited until he melted into the crowd, something that should have been impossible with his coloring and height, yet he seemed to just... disappear. She blinked and took a deep breath, anxiety and a curious sense of excitement tightening her stomach. Tate had relocated, walking close with a beautiful red-headed woman in a shimmery, pale green gown who laughed and took his wine glass to drink from, her gaze daring him to object. Well, darn, it appeared Delanee was about to ruin Tate's night.

Tucking the journal back into her bag, she crossed the distance, forcing a smile onto her face. Tate's gaze slid her way, passed by, and then immediately returned, widening. Her smile grew as his faded. Poor Tate. He leaned close to the woman and whispered in her ear. She frowned and then glared at Delanee. The woman wandered off with Tate's wine glass still clutched between her fingers. Tate met Delanee halfway, grasping her elbow once he reached her.

"What's going on?" he asked quietly, guiding her toward the less occupied foyer.

"I need a ride to my apartment," she said. "Please."

"You can't hire a carriage like you usually do?"

"No," Delanee answered and didn't expand. Not yet. Not with all the ears around to hear.

His dark brown gaze searched hers, and then he sighed. "Right. Come on, then."

"Where's the rest of the team?" she asked.

"I was invited here by a guest."

Delanee glanced over her shoulder at the crowded ballroom. "The redhead?"

"Marley Gilbane, yes." He continued to usher her toward the side door, where departing guests were asked to exit to keep the front door clear for arriving visitors.

"I'm a little disappointed," Delanee said. "I expected a medical science officer to be more careful, Tate."

"Spending time with someone isn't dangerous, Lanee." Delanee gave him an oh-really stare. He laughed, shook his head, and rubbed his temples. "Fine. Look, I've known Marley for years. We're friends, and we trust each other."

"Thanks for giving up, you know, to take me home," she said, bumping her hip to his.

He draped his arm over her shoulder and tugged her close, his head resting against hers. "That's what I'm here for. Are you sure you don't want to go to Deklan's? I think he's worried about you."

She patted his hand. "No. I need to go to my apartment and see my *baki*."

"All right."

They walked to his compact Ariot, barely big enough for two. Delanee arranged the yards of beaded fabric from her gown on her side while Tate started the vehicle. The roads were moderately congested, the nights active as the temperatures rose. Soon, night life would bustle well into the early morning hours.

"Your new sister-in-law will be having her bonding ceremony soon," Tate said quietly in the dim interior. "Did you know that?"

"No. Which wolf will she be bonding with?" Delanee asked, a niggle of guilt making her fidget.

"Izia."

"Surprised it's not all of them," she muttered. The last time she'd seen the wolves, not one had bothered to leave Lucianna to see her. Treacherous canines.

Tate chuckled. "Is that jealousy I hear?"

Delanee sighed. "No, I'm not jealous. Everything happened so fast between them. I'm still adjusting."

"Cia's good for him," Tate said softly, making a slow left turn through a wide intersection.

Apartments rose on either side of the street, the faint glow of illuminated windows breaking up the dark night. Delanee propped her elbow on the edge of the window and sighed. Her breath fanned a foggy circle across the glass. "I know, and I'm happy for them."

"You don't sound very happy."

A twinge of jealousy had burrowed into her at the mention of Deklan's happiness. On the surface, Deklan and Cia's whirlwind romance seemed so straightforward and easy for the couple. They met, fell in love, and decided to make a future together. What else was there to consider? Deklan was lucky enough to meet and mate with a full-blooded Ruthenian, who could bond with one of his wolves. Yes, her brother was very fortunate. Delanee had always figured the discovery and contracting of her future spouse would be just as uncomplicated. The situation she found herself in now was anything but simple.

Tate turned into the small parking area for her apartment building. A large carriage house was on the other side of the block. Only a handful of residents needed the lot. Most hired a carriage or stored their bicycles in their flats.

Delanee gripped the handle and glanced at Tate. "Will

you walk me upstairs? I need to ask you something important."

He hesitated, and then stopped the magnetic engine. "All right."

Nervous flutters danced in her belly. She ignored them, lifting her skirt and gripping her handbag tight. Inside, a couple walked close together along one of the many greenhouse paths. Lamps gently illuminated the three-story conservatory, creating an inviting and romantic atmosphere. Delanee led the way to the nearest stairwell. Tate grabbed the door, holding it open for her to enter first.

"Mind telling me what this is all about?" he asked behind her on the stairs.

Their steps echoed off the walls. "I will, in the apartment."

He sighed heavily. "I feel like I should radio your brother. Should I radio your brother?"

Delanee laughed. "No. I'm not in trouble or anything."

Well, no more than she had been, but she didn't know how much Deklan had told Tate, and she certainly wasn't volunteering the information Ryan had learned from Ingerman in the maze. When they were a level below her floor, she increased the pace, a renewed sense of urgency to fix the seemingly unfixable making her anxious to see her grandmother. The weight of her dress slowed her enough to be frustrating. She was almost running when she reached the corridor leading to her door.

Delanee unlocked the door and shoved it open. "*Baki*?" she shouted. "Are you here? Are you awake?"

A door creaked on the other side of the spacious living room. Her grandmother appeared at the opening of the hallway leading to her bedroom and a small office area. A long gray braid fell over her shoulder, and she tied a belt around a fluffy pink robe.

"Delanee? What are you doing here? Is everything

okay?" Madeleine asked. Tate gently closed the front door. Madeleine blinked and grabbed the back of the couch. "Tate, what's going on?"

"I'm as clueless as you, Ms. Fenwick."

Delanee crossed the distance to her grandmother. "Do you have a blank contract and birth record?"

"I do, as always," Madeleine said, frowning. "Why?"

Delanee took a deep breath and turned to face Tate. "I need you to sign a birth record as the medical science officer."

Alarm widened his eyes, and his gaze shot to her stomach. "What—"

She held out a hand and took a deep breath. "I'm not pregnant."

"Then why would you need me to sign a birth record?" he asked, his brows drawn in confusion.

Anxiety rolled through her, clenching in her stomach and making her legs tremble. "I can't tell you that."

Tate dragged a hand through his short, dark brown hair. "Lanee, I'm not all—"

She reached for him, grabbing his hand, and holding tight. "Please," she pleaded. "This is really important. You know I'd never ask you to do something illegal. And I'm not, not really. Please trust me."

"How is forging a birth record not illegal in any capacity?" he asked quietly, despite no one except her grandmother being able to hear.

"Because no one filled one out to begin with," Delanee whispered. She squeezed his fingers. "Please, Tate."

He growled. "This isn't helping someone bypass an orphanage to get a baby, is it?"

Delanee shook her head. "No. Please just do this. I'd explain more, but... it's not my story to tell."

Tate's chocolate brown eyes searched hers. "All right.

But if I get brought before an accusation hearing for forgery, you're explaining why to your brother."

"You won't, I promise." Delanee released his hand and returned to face her grandmother. "*Baki*?"

"All right," Madeleine sighed, smoothing a hand along her braid. "I'll be right back."

"I could use some of your grandmother's tea right about now," Tate grumbled.

Delanee laughed. "I can make you some. I know her secrets."

"Probably shouldn't. I'm hoping to return to the party. Will you need a ride back?"

Delanee shook her head. "No, we'll hire a carriage."

Because if the night went in the way Delanee figured it would, she'd be needing her *baki* present. Or the twins. She'd rather have her grandmother.

Madeleine hustled into the room, papers fluttering in her hands. "The top one is the birth record. I'm assuming the contract isn't necessary just yet."

Might not be necessary at all, but Delanee didn't want to consider the ramifications of a signed or unsigned marriage document for her future. Tate stared at Delanee until she squirmed, and her face heated under his perusal.

"Are you *sure* about whatever crazy plan you're obviously concocting in that brain of yours?" Tate asked softly.

Delanee rubbed her palms over the rough texture of the beadwork along her gown. "I'm sure."

He nodded and sat on the couch, accepting the pen Delanee handed him from her handbag and the birth record from Madeleine. The pen scratching on paper filled the quiet living room.

"Dates?" he asked.

"Can I fill those in?"

He nodded and handed her the pen back. "Yes. It's not uncommon for the parents to fill in all the information and the MSO to sign at the time of birth. Just don't forget anything. And I expect to be told the full story the next time I see you."

Delanee accepted the pen. "Thank you, Tate."

Madeleine saw Tate out while Delanee took his spot on the couch. She stared down at the birth registry, her pulse racing. Was she doing the right thing? She took a centering breath and adjusted the paper for her penmanship angle. Yes, she absolutely was. Inara deserved a future, one only proper documentation could provide. Plus, if she were honest, selfishness played a part in her decision. The sweet baby girl was *hers* and would now be so officially. Delanee filled in all the information she knew and signed her name in the mother's signature block.

The couch cushion sank beside her from her grandmother's weight. Madeleine gently smoothed a curl behind Delanee's ear. "Why does his daughter not have a birth record?"

Tears blurred Delanee's vision. "How did you know?"

"Who else would you do this for but him?"

"Inara. I'm doing this for her, not Ryan," Delanee corrected.

Warmth filled Madeleine's gaze. "Are you so certain of that?"

Delanee returned her attention to the record, filling in her information. "Yes, I am."

Madeleine slid the generic marriage contract in front of Delanee. "Then why are you hoping he'll do the right thing and sign this?"

Unable to stop from staring at the blank lines to be filled in by both parties, Delanee released a long exhale. The basic requirements to make a relationship official and recognized were on the form. There was no distinction between spouse A and spouse B because sometimes a woman initiated, and sometimes a man. A box for one year, a blank line for those brave enough to jump into longer, or an infinity symbol. Forever. Delanee's gaze caught on that little character, shocked to realize she wouldn't mind if Ryan chose that option. And when exactly had that happened? When had her heart whispering *mate* finally convinced her head?

The last line before signatures was if a name change would be involved. Duration of contracts, family dynamics, and guardian positions all played a role in who would take a spouse's name. Delanee belonged to a powerful family; anyone besides Ryan would have likely opted to take her name. However, Delanee knew Ryan would want his daughter to be a Voklane, not a Ralston, and she respected that.

"I'm not. I'm anticipating his reaction when I tell him what I've done," Delanee said, returning to adding the final required details to the record for her.

Madeleine tapped the contract. "And you think this is what he'll demand of you?"

Delanee gathered both papers together. "I think he'll demand I not file the birth record."

"But you won't honor the request if he does."

Delanee carefully folded both papers to allow them to fit inside her notebook. "No, I won't."

Madeleine patted Delanee's knee. "He'll do the right thing, then. Ryan is a principled man, and you taking on the mantle of mother to his daughter will compel him. The question, my dear granddaughter, is will you accept being a duty to him instead of a love?"

Rising, Delanee sighed. "Of course. Wouldn't I have always been a duty to whoever I contracted with?"

Madeleine rose. "No, only if that's what you chose."

Exasperated, Delanee lifted a hand. "You wanted me to choose him, and I am, and now you're trying to talk me out of it?"

"Will you give him a chance?"

"Isn't that what I'm doing? He doesn't have to do anything but accept what I'm offering for Inara. Not contracting with me won't change my decision."

Though Delanee couldn't consider what his rejection would do to her. He'd already seen, touched, and discovered more about her than any other man. For the first time, she wanted to learn what a lover could offer. But she wanted more than random stolen memories, and she needed Ryan to know he was worth taking a chance on. She'd keep his secrets and be someone he could trust.

"I'm talking about letting him into your heart, Delanee."

"You should go change so we can leave," Delanee said, ignoring her grandmother's concern.

Ryan had lodged himself as firmly in Delanee's heart as his daughter, and she couldn't admit that to anyone yet. The knowledge was too new. Too scary. Gave too much power to another. And maybe if she didn't voice her weakness and he rejected her, maybe it wouldn't hurt as badly.

Twenty-One

Ryan adjusted the final stack of Delanee's papers on his desk, making sure all the corners were aligned in the tray he'd positioned in the upper right corner. Bookends supported the handful of books she'd removed from the shelves for reference, and another tray held all her fashion and style periodicals.

When he'd returned home to an empty house, he'd needed something to do to alleviate the edgy energy riding him from seeing Renelle. The twins were keeping Inara for the night since he hadn't known when he would be finished for the evening. Caring for his daughter would have provided a necessary distraction, and he had almost given into collecting her, but he knew the twins would have put her to bed for the night. So, he found another way to keep busy.

He thought the next time he saw Renelle, he wouldn't be able to feel anything except anger. The emotion had indeed been present, but so had betrayal. Although she was married and had been caught in the act of seducing another, her gaze had shimmered with the knowledge of their intimate past and the dominance she once held over his desires. He had been astounded she could give him such a look after all she had done to him. The woman apparently had no shame. And why should she? He'd never call out her transgressions. Would never be able to hold her accountable for her lies or abandonment.

Thankfully, only negative emotions had bubbled to the surface at the sight of her. None of the desire or attraction that had once been present rose within him. Plus, the sense of relief was a knowledge he hadn't known he needed. A small part of him had feared she would always hold some influence over his libido. He had no excuses where Renelle was concerned, only personal failure. One he never wanted to fear repeating. No, scratch that, he would *never* repeat.

The responsibility of being a father had changed him in ways he may never understand but had happened all the same. Epic mistakes were no longer luxuries he could afford to make. Though he would never regret creating his daughter. Someday, she would have questions about her mother, and after tonight, Ryan had no idea how he could answer them without making Renelle sound like a bad person. He wasn't sure if he wanted his daughter to dislike her mother, but he also didn't know what to say that wouldn't hurt on some level. Because if Renelle's decision hurt Ryan, how much more pain would Inara feel?

Feminine voices outside drew away his unhappy deliberations, and he straightened. He'd left the front door unlocked for Delanee. Anticipation thrummed through him. When she had left with Tate, Ryan had found himself following. Watching. Jealousy had taken him off guard, and the second he realized what he was doing, he'd forced himself back into the shadows.

Ingerman had fled after having thrown up on some poor lady in the maze. The event had become the talk of the party. He wished Delanee had been present to witness the man's humiliation. Though she probably would have been tempted to write about it, which would have alerted whoever wanted the Ralston daughter that the plan to use Ingerman had failed. At least, for now, the group may still rely on the man to do his task and buy Ryan time to resolve yet another dangerous situation. Ryan had left shortly after. Too many emotional battles had been raging inside him for him to continue to be useful.

The echo of the front door opening filled the empty house, along with garbled words. Who was with Delanee? Had the twins noticed her late return and walked her in? Rising, wondering if Inara was with them, he called out.

Delanee hesitated at the doorway, and Ryan frowned. She stepped to the side and his brows rose as Madeleine Fenwick trailed behind her. The matriarch offered him a warm smile. A hint of sympathy softened her gaze, and Ryan's frown deepened.

"Is everything okay?" Ryan asked. "Nothing happened at the apartment, did it?"

"Everything is fine, child," Madeleine assured. "But I can't exactly say nothing happened."

Ryan's heart jumped into his throat. "Wh—"

Madeleine raised her hand. "I'm going to let Delanee explain." She looked at her granddaughter. "Would you like privacy?"

Delanee took a deep breath. "N-no."

Ryan sat and braced his forearms on the desk.

Delanee chewed on her bottom lip and dug around inside her handbag. She pulled out a folded paper and clutched it to her chest. She stared at him for tense seconds and then leaned across the desk, holding the quivering sheet out to him. "I need you to sign this."

Straightening, Ryan reached for the paper. The page crinkled as he slowly unfolded, and a strained, uncomfortable silence filled the room. The bold, elegant lettering across the top of the page made him blink.

"What..." he barely managed to get past the lump in his throat.

"It would be helpful if you could fill in the date and time and, of course, your personal information," Delanee said, stepping closer.

He held the paper out to her and shook his head. A selfish part of him wanted to accept what she offered. Take both the woman *and* her good intentions for his child. But Inara wasn't Delanee's responsibility, and Ryan didn't know if the ambitious journalist would accept becoming his. "No. You can't do this. It's illegal, let alone unethical, for me to accept."

She pressed on his wrist, forcing the certification back to him. "If you refuse, I'll just make up the rest and file it without your information. I don't want to because I don't know what happens when you eventually need documentation and you aren't listed as the father." Her gaze searched his, serious yet pleading. "You know Inara needs this record filed."

And he knew she wasn't lying. The stubborn woman would absolutely correct a wrong despite the shady method. Ryan went around the desk and sat. He carefully smoothed the edges of the paper, reading over the information Delanee had filled in, along with, yep, the MSO for Deklan's Wolvenguard team. She had been willing to do for his child what he couldn't – ask a medical science officer to lie. A hard fist gripped his chest, and he took a deep breath.

"I can't...." His voice failed, but he cleared his throat and tried again. "I can't sign this and have it filed and... and...."

Another sheet of paper settled beside his right forearm. He glanced over and found Madeleine offering him a calm smile. She touched his jaw, patting in a maternal gesture his mother used to do when she understood the bigger picture he either couldn't or wouldn't acknowledge.

"Delanee knew you would struggle with this, and you wouldn't accept the offer to be the mother of your child without legal recognition as a family unit. But really, who will know?" Madeleine dropped her hand to his forearm and squeezed. "I will file your daughter's birth record, a task I do all the time for the residents of my building, so they're used to me dropping off both birth and marriage documents. No one will care or notice the names. You won't be gossiped about if that is a concern for you. No one is forcing you into any permanent decisions, but we wanted you to have the option."

Madeleine glanced at Delanee, who stood with her hands gripped tightly in front of her. The beads on her navy gown sparkled in the low light of the two burning lamps, and her slender curves were defined in subtle shadows. Curls had come free of the intricate knot she'd twisted atop her head, many of the once visible glittery pins hidden by the wayward locks. Lipstick no longer brightened her full lips, and rubbing her face had smeared the eyeshadow at the corners of her eyes and faded the blush defining her cheeks. Yet, she still outshone any woman he knew. A beauty she alone possessed. And she looked at him, uncertain of whether he'd accept her offer to not only become the perceived mother of his child but his bride.

Rejecting her was beyond his capability. He didn't know what that made him. Weak? Or maybe strong because *she* would be at his side, helping him navigate life. Stars above, but Ryan wanted such a future.

"Can you give us a minute, please?" he asked Madeleine. She nodded and left the room without a word, the door closed softly in her wake. Ryan leaned back in the seat and stared at Delanee. "Come here."

For a long moment, she kept his gaze, nibbling on her bottom lip in the way she did when she was nervous or unsure about how to proceed. Her normally rich, caramel skin was pale, and she couldn't hide the faint tremble of her legs. She moved to the corner of the desk, and he leaned over and tugged her closer, positioning her between his knees. Looking up at her, he settled his hands on her hips, pleased when her cool hands wrapped around his forearms.

"Do you want me to sign the marriage contract?" he asked softly.

Her grip tightened, and she swallowed. "If you want."

He squeezed her hips. "That's not what I'm asking."

"What do you want me to say?" she whispered, dropping her gaze.

Ryan needed her closer, in his arms. Needed to touch her. He inched up her skirt and tugged on the bunched fabric. Her breath hitched, but she complied, climbing onto the chair with him, her knees sliding to bracket his hips. Her arms wrapped around his shoulders, her fingers sliding into the short hair at the base of his neck. An intimate gesture she didn't even seem aware of doing. The heavy weight of her skirt pooled on his lap. He glided his hands along her back, hating the rough texture, and shifted to her bare arms.

"Eighteen years," he said, caressing a gentle path from her shoulders to her elbows and back.

"I-I know," she whispered.

"You know me, but do you know me well enough to say you'd be okay with such a long time?" When she remained silent, continued to stare, challenging his doubt, he asked, "What if you can't stand me in six months? Or I ask you to remain silent on a subject you feel the public has a right to know about? Or... Delanee, the list is endless."

"I could say the same. I'm a mess, Ryan." She smiled weakly, tears glistening in her eyes. "I have good intentions about cleaning up after myself, but I don't care about disorder. I don't. And I chase power-hungry mothers at parties and write the worst about them for my career while you keep an entire nation safe. I have seven brothers, five of them older, that you're going to have to contend with at some point. Yet, you're asking *me* if I'll be happy?"

She framed his face between her hands and leaned forward until their lips almost touched. "I'm not going to lie and say I'm not scared. But you're an amazing father, and I think you'll be an amazing husband. And... I'd like to be a good mother to Inara." She took a deep breath, her hard exhale caressing his mouth. The gold of her irises seemed to glow in the dim light as her gaze remained fixed on his. "Ryan Voklane, will you contract with me? I promise never to forsake you or your daughter."

The words slammed into him, hitting at the heart of the insecurities he knew on a deep level he fostered but had never admitted. His parents had disappeared, not on purpose, but they had. Then Renelle had used him. Delanee knew more about him than he realized.

He rested his forehead on hers. "What do I have to promise you?"

"Patience?"

He laughed. "All right, Delanee Ralston. I promise to be patient with your messes and...whatever else you throw my way." He pressed a gentle kiss to her lips. "Thank you."

"Is that a yes?"

"Yes, I will contract with you."

She wiggled to stand from his lap, and he released her. "You finish Inara's birth record while I get my *baki* to witness us signing the contract."

Excitement bounced in her steps, and the tightness in his chest eased. Ryan noted the personal information Delanee had revealed on the birth record, little things most people knew before contracting. He filled in his vital statistics and the day Inara had been delivered to him, along with the time, as her birth information. Next, Ryan filled in the contract information, pre-dating it to the day before

Inara's birth record, which made the length of their contract an automatic eighteen years.

He sat back, arms braced on the desk, and sighed at the enormity of the moment. Eighteen years. He couldn't fathom that length of time. And what if he and Delanee had another child? Did she want more children? He ran a hand down his face. He should have asked. They should have had a conversation about expectations. This wasn't a trial relationship for them. No, they were in it for the long haul. An instant family. By the time Sziveria considered them no longer legally bound, Inara would be an adult.

The two women swept into the room. Delight glowed on Madeleine's face, and Delanee beamed a smile at him. Ryan held out the pen. Delanee grabbed it first, signing her name with a flourish and then handing it over to her grandmother.

Madeleine scrawled all the necessary information on her part and initialed next to the years they'd written to show it had indeed been witnessed. "Two spontaneous contracts in less than a month. Your mother will be in a state of shock over yours, Delanee, my dear girl."

"I'm sure everyone will have something to say," Delanee muttered.

Madeleine gathered the pages together and carefully folded them. "Cia is going to be bonding with one of Deklan's wolves. I know he'll want you to be there. That would be a good time to announce your marriage to your parents, at least. Afterward, of course."

Delanee glanced at Ryan, brows raised, and he nodded. "We'll be there."

"With Inara," she said.

Anxiety curled in his chest. Two people had known of his daughter's existence. Now four would know, and soon to be an entire group that could call themselves a clan, they were so large. But his little girl now had something he never dreamt she'd have. A family. All because of Delanee.

"With Inara," he repeated, his gaze still locked with hers.

Delanee smiled. "I'm going to walk *Baki* out. The carriage we hired is still waiting."

He rose. "Why didn't you say something?"

Madeleine waved away his concern. "There is no rushing a marriage contract. The driver was more than fine waiting. It's late, and I'm a sure fare."

Ryan leaned against the foyer wall with his hands shoved in his pockets while Delanee saw Madeleine to the waiting hired cab. The matriarch left with the documents legalizing his daughter and making him a married man. A future he never considered would ever be his. Emotion threatened to overwhelm him. Delanee returned alone. She closed the door and rested against the wood, sighing. Ryan eased around her and engaged the locks.

He didn't expect her to launch herself at him. Didn't expect her arms to wrap around his shoulders, or her body to press into his. Her hips fit perfectly between his, and her breasts, delicate globes he remembered being tipped with delicious brown nipples, pressed into his chest. Almost desperate, her hands shoved beneath the collar of his shirt at his back, tightening the material across his torso until the buttons strained. Her mouth caught his in a frantic kiss Ryan more than willingly accepted.

She broke their kiss and attacked his shirt. Buttons popped free, bouncing to the floor and pinging off the walls. "I just... I'm sorry, I can't wait any longer, I have to know."

Ryan tried to respond, but her lips once again pressed to his, her tongue sliding between his teeth. Her cool hands caressed across the planes of his chest. She leaned all her weight into his frame, her fingers fumbling at his belt, taking him by surprise, and he stumbled back. His heel caught the edge of the carpet in the living room, and he tripped. Delanee followed him down, falling between his legs and slamming into his chest, knocking his breath free. He collapsed onto the carpet and stared at the ceiling, trying to pull air into his protesting lungs.

Delanee straddled his hips, the heavy fabric of her gown covering his stomach, the beads scratching his skin. Attempting to gather his wits and his breath, he grasped her knees and blinked as she worked his belt free, undid the buttons holding his pants closed— oh, *summer sun*— and wrapped her fingers around his hard length...

"Wait, no, Delanee—" he gasped, but not soon enough.

She slammed down onto him, and Ryan roared, his hips bucking off the floor. Pain warred with pleasure as her virgin muscles clamped tight around him from the forced invasion. She'd been wet enough to get him in but not enough for the fierce manner in which she'd impaled herself. Ryan grabbed her hips to prevent her from moving further. Horror widened her eyes, filling them with tears. Damn it. Oh no. No, no, no. Ryan had to fix her mistake before she decided sex was something she could forever live without. Panic flitted across her face. Every muscle in her body coiled to leap off him.

"Delanee, look at me," he ordered.

Her chin quivered, and her breath hitched, but she met his gaze.

"Kiss me," he said, shifting his hands to her back and pressing.

She shook her head, loosening more curls around her face.

"Yes," he whispered and urged her down onto his chest, careful to keep his hips from rolling despite the rampant urge to finish what she'd impulsively started.

Her shaky breaths teased across his lips before she gave

him a chaste kiss. Ryan undid the buttons along her back, lifting his shoulders to keep their mouths pressed together when she would have moved away. He slid the shoulders of her gown down her arms. Fabric whispered and the weight of the bodice sagged onto his stomach, the beads cold and rough against his flesh. She pulled her arms free, and he broke the kiss, breath catching in his throat as he dropped back to the floor and took in what he'd revealed.

Dark brown nipples formed hard points on upturned breasts, just big enough to fill his palm. Growling, he rose, wrapped his arms around her, and sucked one of those alluring nipples into his mouth. Her squeal of shock morphed into a sensual, keening cry as he rolled his tongue across the tip and sucked harder. Wet heat slickened around the hard length of him buried deep within her. Good, but not yet where he wanted her. Ryan moved on to her other breast, pleased when she speared her fingers into his hair and gripped his head, keeping him where she wanted him.

Ryan *needed* more. Had wanted the introduction to intimacy to go so differently for her, though really, he wasn't shocked Delanee had pounced. Curiosity was a core trait of hers, and in time, he figured he'd benefit from her impulsiveness more than he would be frustrated. But he would salvage this particular hasty decision and make her first time memorable for the pleasure, not the pain. He couldn't do what he really wanted. Couldn't feast between her legs while she grabbed at his head for a different kind of need. Couldn't watch as her body took his until there was nothing left to see of him. Not yet. But he could explore her some by touch.

Rolling over, he settled deeper into her. The gasp she gave wasn't laced with distress, another good sign, though not enough. He braced his weight on one arm and looked down over what he'd managed to expose. Her nipples glistened from his kisses, and a faint sheen of sweat coated her skin.

"Pull your knees up further and spread your legs more," he whispered.

Her gaze searched his before she complied, slowly pulling her knees into his flanks and letting her thighs fall open. Ryan lifted his hips enough to slide a hand between them, shoving yards of fabric out of the way. Damn dress. Next time, nothing would be between his body and hers. He found her swollen clit, caressing a finger along the nub and around her folds. She jerked, her eyes widening. Moving only an inch or two out of her, Ryan slowly rolled his hips, continuing to work the sensitive nerves at her center with gentle pressure. Her mouth fell open in shock as he touched where they joined and coated his fingers with her growing desire. Her hips rose to meet the slick glide of his touch, a whimper escaping her.

Tiny pulses deep within her convulsed around him, gripping him tight, making sweat break out along his forehead and roll between his shoulder blades. She was close. He wanted to pound. Take her hard and hear her scream for more. Mild sex had never much appealed to him. However, slow and careful was what she needed now, and that's what she would receive. There was time, eighteen years' worth, for him to take her any way they could imagine. To introduce her to the type of passion she had anticipated when she'd impaled herself.

He caught her bewildered gaze. "Are you ready?"

"For?" she choked out.

"To come."

Twenty-Two

Delanee didn't know what to do. Did she just lay here and let him do all the work? Let him touch her until her eyes threatened to cross from how good he felt? Or, move with him? She was afraid the searing pain and discomfort of being penetrated would return if she did anything except remain motionless. Some of the hurt had dissipated when his mouth had taken her breasts. Even more faded at his intimate touch. Oh, stars above, Ryan Voklane was *touching* her where she never thought a man would. Sure, she'd read a few lusty books and knew foreplay happened between couples, but she had never imagined it for herself. Had never fantasized about how fingers not belonging to her could bring about the most intense sensation she'd ever experienced.

The subtle need at her center grew. He applied more pressure, framing her clit between two fingers and massaging. Delanee's eyes squeezed shut and her hips rose. He started moving a little faster, pulling out more and driving back in. The awareness of his hard length within her no longer felt invasive but necessary, like the breath she dragged into her lungs.

She opened her eyes to find his face drawn in intense lines. Beads of sweat chased each other down his temples to drip from his jaw to her breasts. The muscles she'd revealed when she'd torn his shirt were drawn tight, flexing with each careful thrust. His supporting arm trembled. The tender way he loved her was costing him because she'd been too desperate to experience this very moment.

For her, he denied his nature.

Every emotion she'd kept locked inside, every suppressed impulse to claim Ryan for her own, burst free. Delanee wrapped around him, her heels digging into the base of his spine, her nails sinking into shoulder blades beneath the loose fabric. Her chest pressed to his. Arcs of energy danced everywhere they physically touched. Power licked across her nerves and soared through her bloodstream. Delanee screamed as a wave of unexpected pleasure joined the rush.

He hugged her close and held her through the storm. His hips moved faster, penetrating her deeper as she rose to take all he had to give. His harsh breaths fanned across her ear and caressed her neck. Where their bodies joined became damp. Slick. Making each of his thrusts easier, seeming to add to the heightened pleasure building within her yet again. A part of her wondered if that were normal or if her reaction was somehow gross because the wet slap of their lower bodies made her self-conscious.

"Do you have any idea how good you feel?" he growled, once again always seeming to know what she was thinking. "I can't wait to see how fast you respond to my touch and to learn everything about your body."

She wanted to learn his, too, but couldn't seem to form any coherent words. How could he talk? She tried to garble a response, but the pinnacle she'd reached seconds before threatened to overtake her again. Whatever she'd managed to utter morphed into a high-pitched moan. She wanted to experience that fantastic, carnal climax again. If *this* was what the couple in the maze had been too desperate to wait for privacy over, she understood now. Could anything rival the decadence of his body inside hers?

As he moved over her, instinct had her pulling her knees up higher, tilting her pelvis, and holding his torso lower. He rumbled a curse and ground harder against her, no longer treating her as if she'd break. The new angle zinged pleasure through her and she shattered, her toes curling and her nails sinking further into his back. His body jerked, and his hips slammed hard, sending him so deep she swore he touched her womb. Liquid heat spilled from him and her eyes opened wide at the sensation. Incredible.

Panting, her arms and legs sagged to the floor. Ryan lifted off her and the sudden emptiness made her cry out and try to press her knees together.

"No," he whispered, grasping her legs. "None of that. Let me see what you denied me earlier."

Limbs trembling, Delanee swallowed against embarrassment and her ingrained sense of modesty and allowed him to part her thighs. His palms caressed down the inside of her legs in reverence. He ran a finger along her tender seam and she shivered.

"Beautiful," he said, gliding his finger over her clit and causing her inner muscles to clench.

She realized he was exposed too, and lifted onto her elbows to look him over. His open shirt framed his defined chest. A narrow trail of light brown hair led down his abdomen to his groin. Her cheeks heated at the evidence of their coupling. Damp curls drew attention to his glistening member, hanging thick between his legs, darker than the rest of him. She wanted to touch and wished she hadn't been so hasty to get to the main event, bypassing all the exploring.

He stood and kicked off his shoes, then his pants.

Delanee struggled to rise and adjust her dress, not quite ready to parade around naked. He draped his pants over his shoulder and then leaned over and helped her rise before picking up his shoes. She wondered what room she was expected to sleep in tonight. Her things were in the room she'd been occupying. But her husband... She closed her eyes and took a centering breath. She had a *husband*.

"You'll be sleeping with me. You can grab what you need, borrow something of mine, or just sleep naked. That'd work for me," he said, taking her elbow when she wobbled from his words.

She liked the idea of sleeping in his clothes again, though she didn't know how to process she'd be sleeping *with him*. The beads of her gown scraped her skin as she clutched it to cover her breasts. He released his hold and strode ahead. The tight globes of his butt gleamed in the low light with each step, his shirttail not quite covering them. Delanee licked her lips and followed, her fingers twitching. Another part of his anatomy she wanted to explore.

The bedroom was dark when they entered. Ryan tossed his dirty clothes in the bathroom before moving to the fireplace. The soft glow of a new fire illuminated enough of the room to move around. Delanee eased onto the end of the bed, clutching the sagging gown to her chest with both hands.

"Come on, let's get a shower before we go to bed." He shrugged the shirt off, grabbing the fabric before it fluttered to the floor.

"A sh-shower?" she squeaked. "*Together*?"

He closed the distance between them, completely naked, and leaned over her, bracing both hands on the bed. She leaned back and stared up at him. "I've been inside you. What is a shower?"

"All right," she whispered.

"I won't touch you if you don't want me to." He pressed a gentle kiss to her forehead, then to her lips.

Delanee studied her body. Soreness mingled with a not-unpleasant tingle at her core. "I wouldn't mind you touching parts of me," she admitted quietly.

With one hooked finger, he pried down the loose gown, revealing her breasts. He caressed a knuckle across her pebbled nipples, and her breath caught. "Then touch parts of you I shall."

A roguish smile tilted his lips and danced in his pale eyes as he straightened. He walked to the bathroom and the weak light caught on a familiar tattoo across his back. A perfect replica of the one gracing her own flesh.

"Oh, summer sun!" Delanee shrieked, jumping onto the bed in shock. The gown twisted around her feet and jerked free of her hands. She tumbled onto the mattress on her knees, modesty forgotten.

Oh no, this was bad. *So bad*! Not once did she consider she'd ever bond with anyone, let alone Ryan. She never envisioned she'd have to do anything more than explain the family tradition of tattooing her back. Never worried she would have to reveal her personal secret, a family trait she chose not to embrace. With his super genetics, she should have known better.

Ryan spun around, his gaze searching for a threat. "What? What's wrong? What happened?"

How did she explain? How was she supposed to admit she'd kept a massive secret from him when he'd trusted her enough to reveal everything about himself? She licked her lips and tried not to burst into tears. He was going to hate her.

"Delanee?"

She tugged at the heavy fabric trapped under her knees.

Ryan sighed and motioned to the bathroom with his

shirt. "You don't have to shower with me if you don't want to."

How easy would it be to allow him to believe she was distressed over sharing a small space with him naked? But the second he glanced in the mirror and saw an inked Ruthenarc lynxia, with blue eyes, pink flowers, and blue butterflies.... She rolled her lips inward and frowned so hard her cheeks hurt.

"Well, see, here's the thing," she began in a rush, still fighting with her dress trapped beneath her legs, needing something to focus on besides his bewildered face that would soon morph into fury. "When it was my turn to choose my design, I went with something feminine. I mean, *really* feminine," she stressed, splaying her hands. "I never thought anyone but me would wear it, you know?"

Ryan shook his head. "No, I don't know. What are you talking about?"

"My beast master mark," she blurted.

"Wait... what?" he asked, confused.

Delanee took a deep breath and then twisted around, revealing her back. "My beast master mark. A tattoo beast masters get, that everyone in my family participated in because eight of eleven of us are beast masters."

"It's beautiful," he said. "As is the tradition."

Frustrated, she balled her hands into fists. He wasn't understanding. The yards of fabric tangled between her legs caused her to wobble and fall when she turned back around. She caught herself on her palms, gripping the soft blanket beneath her. Heat filled his gaze as he looked her over.

"That is even prettier," he growled.

A flicker of lust bloomed inside her veins, igniting a need deep in her core. She examined the sensation, a response to... *him*? Shaking her head, she ignored the impression and focused on the more important issue.

"You have it," she said, rising onto her knees.

He halted the step closer he'd been about to take and blinked. "I have what?"

"The mark." When he still looked at her without understanding, she said, "The tattoo." She touched her chest. "My tattoo. I, well...." She licked her suddenly parched lips and swallowed against the dryness in her throat. "I bonded with you."

His head angled to the side in question and then he spun around and stalked into the bathroom. Light flashed as he lit a candle. A strangled curse echoed through the doorway and she winced. Scrambling off the bed, she let the heavy beaded gown slide to the floor, no longer caring about her nudity.

"Delanee!" he shouted, spinning away from the mirror to stare at her, arms wide. "What in the arctic?"

She held out her hands in supplication. "I know you're mad, and I'm sorry, I should have told you, but I never figured it'd happen, ever."

"You're a beast master?"

She nodded.

"Of... a cat?" he guessed.

"Yes," she breathed, averting her gaze. "A specific species known as a Ruthenarc lynxia. I've never bonded to one. I opted not to."

He braced his hands on the counter and leaned his weight forward, dropping his head. "All right. What does this mean?"

"I guess when I um..." Her thoughts scattered as she took in all the subtle moving shadows playing across the dips and hollows of his nude, muscled form. Summer sun, he was glorious. And she wanted to touch. Everything. Looking up at the ceiling, she tried again. "I must have bonded with you."

"Obviously," he stated.

"I didn't do it on purpose," she whispered, looking down at her toes. "I didn't even know I could."

"All Ruthenians bond with their mates."

She glanced up to find him leaning against the counter, arms crossed, completely unconcerned that he stood before her naked. Unable to stop herself, her gaze wandered over his body, catching on the part of him that had brought her such incredible pleasure, now much smaller than it had been. She angled her head. How intriguing.

"Delanee," he said and her attention snapped up to his face. "Keep staring and see what happens."

"Something exciting," she said.

"Yeah, it'll be excited all right." He rolled a hand. "Back to the conversation."

What had he said last? Oh yes, Ruthenians and bonding. "Yes, we bond with *other* Ruthenians. I never planned on marrying anyone capable of becoming a true mate."

Twenty-Three

A TRUE MATE.

The words rolled around in Ryan's mind, intermixing with the odd sensations coursing through him. Panic, worry... curiosity. All of them were weird because they weren't his emotions. No, he felt many things, and they fought for dominance, to establish reality from imposition. There was a rightness to her statement that caused a settling deep within him. He knew some about the bonding that occurred between Ruthenians, but the ingrained sense of certainty about her statement was something more. Perhaps his own genes were at play. After all, he was the alpha generation. The generation to have birthed a nation, an entire race of people from which Delanee descended from.

He glanced behind himself in the mirror. The tips of tufted ears reached to the edges of his shoulders, while the bottom edge of flowers ended at the swell of his butt cheeks. A stunning colorless cat with spots stared at him with vivid blue eyes. The same shade of blue colored in a butterfly flitting near the cat's left ear. Pink, richer along the edges of the flowers and paler near the center, was a startling shade on his skin.

"Turn around," he asked quietly.

She slowly spun, presenting him with her back. The flowers were a deep fuchsia, fading to what looked almost peach on her. Pink and blue were the only two colors besides black. The lynxia gazed at him. The artist had done an amazing job capturing the aloof arrogance and banked hostility within the stare of the feline. The art was bold, yet feminine, like the woman wearing it.

And now the pretty tattoo graced his flesh. A brand to show the world who he belonged to. Ryan was shocked to discover he wanted a means to mark her the same way. To claim. But only beast masters carried such an astonishing ability.

She turned and gasped, reaching for him. Tendrils of white energy stretched toward her. Ryan lifted his hands. An iridescent haze covered his skin as wisps of light arced and danced around him. *What?* Her fingers smoothed up his forearm to his elbow. His power coiled around her hand and licked at her skin.

"Why didn't you tell me about being a beast master?" he asked, taking her hand in his and entwining their fingers. The subtle glow emanating from him continued to swirl around her.

She stepped closer until their bodies almost touched. The pointed tips of her dark nipples seemed to beg for his touch again. Or his tongue. Ryan's body stirred, desire heating his blood and waking up parts of him he figured were sated enough to not cause trouble. A soft gasp escaped her parted lips and she slid her free hand across his side and up his chest, exploring. Ryan caught her hand and squeezed.

"Answer the question, Delanee," he whispered.

Her gaze lifted. The brilliant gold of her irises seemed to glow with an inner fire. "Compelling me to respond?"

He leaned close until their noses nearly touched. "If I were, you wouldn't be asking."

"I didn't ever want to be one," she said so low he strained to make out the words. A flush darkened her cheeks and flared down to her chest. "A beast master," she clarified. "I just wanted to be a journalist, chasing, and writing stories. Something I could never do with a huge cat following me around, pointing out how different I am from every other Sziverian."

Ryan wanted to assure her the genetic gift she carried wouldn't have hindered her, but he couldn't. Hadn't he hidden his own talent? Sure, being forced to use his ability for the wrong purpose was one of the reasons he kept his talent private. Another reason was because of how others would view him. No one would trust him enough to be in a space alone or to get close enough to even shake hands. He'd be treated with fear and perhaps even contempt. Delanee had accepted him in an unexpected way, and that she hadn't trusted him enough to believe he'd do the same for her, hurt.

Settling his weight against the cold marble countertop, he freed his hands and cupped her jaw. He slid his fingers across her cheeks and searched her gaze. She still hadn't answered his initial question. "Why, Delanee?"

Tears filled her eyes before she dropped her gaze. He applied pressure to the underside of her chin, forcing her to meet his stare.

"No hiding," he whispered. "Not from me."

"I...." She visibly swallowed, took a deep breath, and tried again. Her hands wrapped around his wrists. "I can't even admit this side of me to myself. How could I tell you?"

His heart twisted, but he pressed on. "You acknowledged your bonding animal on your body. Now on mine. You haven't always denied what you can do."

"I only accepted the lynxia as an image, never as what could be mine."

Ryan hummed, understanding dawning. "You thought if you ignored your nature, recognized it just enough to appease your family, and married either a gen-common or a weak Gen-Heir, no one would ever know. Are you ashamed of your genes?"

"No!" she said quickly and tore herself free of his light hold. "No. Who I am, what I can do, that I'm part of such a large family filled with incredible talent, is unheard of in my father's land." She pressed a hand to her chest. "But it's not what I wanted for myself. I didn't want to be known as Delanee Ralston, the Ruthenarc lynxia master."

Her arms wrapped around her slender waist, and she hunched into herself. Naked, the action made her appear more vulnerable, and Ryan wanted to gather her against his chest and shelter her from whatever distressing notion had run through her mind.

"Do you know how difficult it's been for my beast master brothers to find acceptance in a mate? Only Deklan has. Darius, my oldest brother, I know he fell in love, but she rejected him. Dominik, like Deklan had before Cia, gave up years ago. Something terrible happened to Donovan when he went to visit our Ruthenian family two years ago. He won't talk about it, but he came back *changed*. I don't want the drama, or the stigma, or..." She sniffled and shook her head. "I didn't want to go through what they have."

"Okay, I can understand all of that," he said, bracing his hands on the counter behind him, uncaring that it opened his entire body up for her perusal. They were going to be together for a long time, let her look. Despite the seriousness of their conversation, he was semi-hard and tried to continue to ignore all the tempting curves on display before him. "But why keep it from me? After everything I shared, did you think I'd not understand, or accept?"

She blew out a long breath. "You'd have asked questions."

"Very likely."

"I don't know how I would have answered them." She shrugged and stared down at her feet, nudging her big toe along the edge of a floor tile. "I never thought that part of me would matter."

Ryan shoved off the counter and closed the space between them. He smoothed his hands up her arms. "Delanee, even if you never bond to a lynxia, being capable of doing so is part of who you are."

"I'm sorry I didn't tell you," she whispered, her attention still on her feet. "And I'm sorry I bonded without your permission."

"I would have said yes."

Her gaze shot up to his, her head almost knocking his chin. "You would have?"

He nodded, tracing a path along her collarbone and down between her breasts. The curious manifestation of his talent reappeared. Goosebumps rose on her skin wherever the arcs of energy flickered. "Yes, without hesitation."

"It's taboo to force a bond," she said, her voice catching. She licked her lips. His gaze snagged on the glossy trail she left behind across her full mouth. "Only a woman can initiate, and a man has to accept. If he's unaware, she can force the bond, like I did."

Ryan dropped his focus from her mouth to her breasts. The gentle glow of the single lamp he'd lit turned her skin a honeyed brown, making the contrast between them so much *more*. He cupped the small globe and ran his thumb across her puckered nipple. She gasped and her breast pressed deeper into his palm.

"I wouldn't have denied you anything," he confessed. "Especially not that." He brushed a gentle, lingering kiss across her lips and whispered, "We're in this for a lot of years."

"Not just years," she whispered in return. "There will be no one else for me."

White lightning arced from him and lashed around her. Her confession meant he'd be her only lover. He was her first true kiss. Her first true taste of passion. The first man to know how she sounded in the throes of desire. The only man to ever know how her legs felt wrapped around his hips, and the way her body strained beneath his to reach the pinnacle of release.

Her gaze widened and she tried to take a step away. Ryan grasped her upper arm, his talent wrapping around her like a cocoon. "Don't be scared."

"I'm not," she said, her hands flattening on his chest. "Just surprised. I shouldn't be, since Inara does this, too."

Ryan leaned around her to reach into the shower and turn on the water. Steam instantly curled in the air as the water cascaded to the cold marble shower floor. Two recessed shelves held his soaps above a bench spanning the entire side wall he could either sit on or lay across. With his home being hot spring fed, he had the luxury of never-ending heated water. An indulgence he couldn't wait to explore with Delanee.

She pressed her lips together, her face flushed. "I'd like you to, um…"

He lifted a brow. "Yes?"

Air puffed from her cheeks and out her mouth. "Can you maybe use your talent? I don't think I can say it. Not yet."

He chuckled and tugged her into the shower. A half-glass wall kept water from splashing. "I can wait until you're brave enough. I don't want to use my talent on you."

"But—"

"No—"

"Please," she implored, her fingers digging into his biceps, her eyes pleading. "I *do* want to say these things, really. I just...." She dropped her gaze. Water droplets beaded in her dark curls and glided a tantalizing trail down her neck.

Ryan gripped her throat in a gentle hold, applying just enough contact for his talent. White striations bled into her irises. "What do you want me to do to you, Delanee?"

Her grip tightened on his arms and he slid his gaze to his right arm, frowning.

"Why won't you, you know, do your thing?" she asked barely loud enough to be heard over the cascading water.

Ryan released his hold, shocked. "I did."

She blinked at him. "Well, try again."

He laughed and shook his head. Relief slid through him. "No. It didn't work, and likely won't again, which makes sense. The bond must have negated my ability, much like Inara's doesn't work on either of us. And I'm glad for it. You won't ever have to doubt me when I say I didn't compel an answer from you."

She crossed her arms over her chest and dropped down onto the bench. "I guess that makes a weird sort of sense. And I can see how, if you were some kind of experiment to create a superhuman, they'd want to ensure a healthy bond with a mate for future generations."

"Yes, I agree. And it worked since Ruthenia thrived until recently."

Delanee shrugged one shoulder. "Their own fault for refusing to allow new genetic material."

"Over time, the genes do become diluted."

"But not in the first generation. My family is proof of that."

"Yes, but they fear the dilution. Ruthenia's power is in their one-hundred-percent Gen-Heir population."

"And they're dying out. Without new blood, they

won't survive much longer. They'll have to accept tainted genes at some point."

The bitterness in her voice had him crouching before her. "You aren't tainted."

"Not to you," she said, her gaze still averted.

"You don't even know if you are to them either, so why put that on yourself? You never attempted to learn how anyone would feel about you in your father's land. Let's get clean and into bed."

His hands glided up her wet thighs and he gently pressed them open. She allowed him, hesitating only a little before widening her legs on her own. Ryan kept his attention on her face, wanting to look. Touch. Taste. But knowing now wasn't the right time. They had many more nights to explore. He stood and grasped a removable shower head, using a switch to redirect the flow from one of the two rectangular shower heads raining water from the ceiling. Crouching before her again, he moved the spray between her legs. She groaned and laid her head back against the marble wall, her butt shifting to the edge of the seat.

"That feels nice," she sighed.

"Sore?"

"Yeah," she admitted shyly.

He couldn't stop his body from responding as he gently cleaned away the remnants of her first intimate experience. She was still slightly swollen from the encounter. But she winced as he sprayed her opening, too tender for anything his enthusiastic burgeoning erection wanted.

She touched his wrist and he glanced up, meeting her unsure stare. "May I?"

Ryan handed her the shower head and rose, stepping into the water to attend to himself. When an arc of hot water sprayed across his low body he jerked and yelped in surprise.

"Sorry," she giggled. "I wanted to wash you, too. Like you did for me."

"Probably not a good idea," he said between gritted teeth, reaching for a bar of soap.

"Why?"

"I'm trying hard to be good and not take you again. If you touch me, *hard* is precisely what I'll be."

Her golden eyes widened and shot straight to his groin. "Really?"

TWENTY-FOUR

Curiosity had Delanee straightening, her legs still spread, her body perched on the edge of the marble bench. His shower was glorious, not that she'd expected anything less in his perfect house. And the man? Stars above, she had no idea a man could be so fascinating. As she watched, his penis grew. Thickened and rose toward her as if seeking her touch or her body. Lust sizzled in her veins. Not only belonging to him.

She couldn't stop from reaching for him. Thankfully, he didn't prevent her. Didn't seem capable, his hips shifting to meet her seeking fingers. The shower head disappeared from her hand. Breath sawed from her lungs as her fingers encountered steel wrapped in velvet. A deep ingrained instinct she couldn't deny had her leaning forward and rubbing her cheek across the broad head. Her lips brushed his glistening tip, her tongue flicking out to taste the salty offering. His strangled groan echoed in the spacious stall. She repeated the process, rubbing and tasting until her own body ached with an unsated need.

Through her exploration and yes, she couldn't deny a claiming, Ryan stood near motionless, his heavy panting breaths joining the harsh rush of cascading water. At some point, he'd braced both hands on the smooth marble wall at her back, his feet between her parted ones. When Delanee could no longer stand the sensual tension, she took what she could of his length into her mouth and sucked. Hard. His hips bucked, and he shouted. His fingers speared into her hair, holding tight. And then he moved, slow at first, and she followed the shallow roll of his hips, wrapping a hand around the base. Oh yes, the decision felt right. Natural. He was *her* man, and his body was *hers* to please.

The comprehension emboldened her further, and she licked and sucked until a string of curses, sounding more like pleas, fell from his lips. Then he jerked from her mouth, his hand replacing hers, and she cried out in disapproval until hot liquid splashed across her chest and over her breasts. Echoes of his pleasure flared through her and she gasped. Surprised, she glanced down and watched the rest of his release leave him. She glided her fingers through the slick fluid in wonder.

"Probably a little more intense than you were ready for," he said, breathless.

"I'm ready for everything," she blurted, looking up at his flushed face, her fingers still playing in his release.

He chuckled and reached for the removable shower head again. "Not quite. But soon. Adventurous, aren't you?"

Delanee blinked. Was she? An unexpected possible development for her. "I don't know. Am I?"

He grabbed a bar of soap and slid it across her chest, washing himself away. Delanee frowned, surprised the action bothered her. She *liked* wearing him. Enjoyed the way she'd felt marked by him.

"No one else had ever done that for me. I never really wanted it before," he said.

"Why?"

He shrugged and finished rinsing her. "It was rather personal, wasn't it?"

She nodded, her gaze falling to his now shrinking member. "But you liked what I did?" she asked, uncertain.

The pressure of his knuckle under her chin lifted her gaze to his handsome and very satisfied face. "Oh yes. Very much." He replaced the showerhead and then dropped to his knees before her, spreading her thighs.

Delanee grabbed his shoulders to keep her balance. "What are you doing?"

A wicked smile tilted his lips and glimmered in his pale eyes. "My turn."

Then her legs were thrown over his shoulders, her butt gripped in his palms, and her sex fully exposed to his—

"Oh, my stars!" Delanee shrieked as his tongue licked down her clit and speared into her tender opening.

Intense pleasure zipped through her, and her arms windmilled around in a frantic attempt to grab hold of something. Anything. The wall proved useless, her hands slipping and sliding down the wet stone. His forearms were too low. The recessed shelf above proved a good option, and her hands wrapped around the subtle lip. Bottles toppled onto her shoulders, rolling and clattering to the bench or the floor. Nothing broke, so she didn't care. He didn't seem to, either. His tongue flicked and flitted in and out of her in a maddening rhythm her hips ground against his face to chase. He tasted every intimate inch of her before returning to the maddening shallow penetration.

Delanee struggled to breathe and couldn't stop from watching his head move between her spread legs. Water spiked the short length of his hair, so much lighter than her skin. His arms banded around her legs provided another tantalizing contrast. One she'd only imagined and now, upon seeing, couldn't get enough of. They were beautiful together.

He glanced up, his eyes illuminated by the white striations of his talent. A faint haze wrapped around him. The manifestation of his gift seemed to ebb and flow with his emotional state. All for her. Only for her. Delanee brushed her fingers across his mouth, covered in her desire. He sucked a finger into his mouth, his gaze hot and full of lust. Again, for her. Delanee almost climaxed. Never in her life did she envision this moment would happen. Had, in fact, worked so hard to ensure such passion wouldn't be hers. What a mistake she'd almost made.

He released her finger, and his touch glided between her butt cheeks and up to her core. "Do you like what I'm doing?"

She nodded.

"Say it," he demanded.

His fingertips traced a faint path around and over her clit, enough to tease and make her hips rise for more. He lifted higher onto his knees and took a nipple between his lips. Sucked. Delanee moaned and arched her back as need shot straight to her center, making her inner muscles clench with the demand for release.

"Please don't stop," she implored.

"Don't stop what?" he asked, nuzzling her breast with the prickly growth on his chin.

"Ryan," she whined, drawing his name out in a plea.

He chuckled and dipped low again, licking her bottom to top. "I find I enjoy this, too."

How could he speak? Coherent thought left her as he returned to the pleasurable torture. Delanee grasped for the shelf again, and needing more, she braced her feet on his shoulders and spread her legs as far as possible. He groaned, his grip tensing on her butt, spreading her wide to almost the point of pain. The new position increased his ability to lick deeper, and soon, Delanee's cries of need filled the steamy shower. She gripped the marble ledge tighter and ground against his face, not caring how wanton the action made her. Ryan seemed to love it, growling and devouring her like a man starved.

The orgasm slammed through her, causing her back to arch and her inner muscles to spasm. She squeezed her eyes shut and rode the storm, which Ryan kept at its height, prolonging the onslaught until she almost passed out. When the pleasure finally slackened, and her body sagged, she opened her eyes to find the two of them enveloped in his energy. The mist from the shower curled around them, adding to the intimacy.

"You are mine, Delanee Ralston," he growled from between her legs, his words whispering across her flesh, still pulsing from the climax.

"Delanee Voklane," she whispered, her fingers spearing into the short length of his saturated hair.

Another deep rumble left him and his mouth returned to her sex, devouring anew. She moaned and held on for the ride, letting him do whatever he wanted. Turned out he wanted to do a lot, and by the time he finished with her, he'd had to carry her to bed, she'd been too boneless to move on her own.

Delanee had been clueless about the intimate acts available between lovers that didn't include actual sex. And what would she allow to be done in the heat of the moment? Again, a bit shocking. Yes, apparently, she was rather sexually adventurous. Ryan said he couldn't wait to explore that side of her and watch her flourish with confidence. As exhaustion pulled her under, she wondered if she could look at him in the morning without her face burning with mortification. Confident? Not quite yet.

A masculine groan and the sensation of wet heat and need throbbing between her legs dragged her from sleep. Desire teased every nerve and stole any emerging thought. Her own? His? Did she care? Barely awake, she turned toward the warmth of Ryan's naked body pressed against her. He kissed her throat and licked her collarbone.

Inhaling deeply, he grumbled, "You smell so good."

She managed to murmur sounds, but nothing intelligible, her hand seeking the hard length jutting into her hip beneath the sheets. Her legs spread without hesitation, and he mounted her as if they had always started the morning hungry to join. The haze of sleep still fogged her mind and as he pressed into her with slow, unhurried motions, each lazy roll of his hips sending him deeper. She arched to meet him, the pain of last night barely registering in her subconscious.

He shuddered, his face buried against her neck, his nose bumping her ear. "You feel good." He inhaled deep again. "And why do you smell so amazing?"

Delanee wrapped her arms beneath his and clutched his flexing shoulder blades. "I... don't know. Maybe... your soap," she managed to groan out as he slid all the way into her.

He didn't stop, kept moving, each languid thrust heightening her need in a way she could never imagine. Different from last night, when he'd been forced to go slow. This was relaxed. Comfortable. Her inner muscles quivered around him, and he shivered, reaching to grab the headboard. The action elongated his torso and allowed him to shift and move deeper. Delanee pulled her knees in and tilted her hips. Their rhythm increased until the bedframe squeaked, and the harsh breathing of their coupling filled the room. Sweat soon dampened their bodies, and the blankets still covering them became almost too hot, but neither stopped to remove the layers. They rocked together, chasing the pleasure just out of reach.

The pressure for release mounted within her, a combined demand since his need warred with her own. Desperate cries rose from her, a begging she couldn't communicate in words, but he seemed to understand all the same. His pace increased until his pelvis slammed to hers in a hard grind, sending her over the edge. The room sheeted white, and she threw her head back, every muscle seizing as euphoria swept her away. He bucked, thrusting deep, the heat of his release filling her and catapulting her into another orgasm.

Panting, they collapsed together. Her legs slid along his, and her arms flopped to the mattress. His weight covered her, and he continued to gently rock inside her, sending tiny waves of pleasure with each shallow movement.

"I wish we never had to leave the bed," he whispered, kissing her neck, jaw, and mouth.

She returned the tender kiss, her fingers sliding into his damp hair. "That would be amazing."

He smiled against her mouth, still moving within her until the need she'd been released from began to build again. How did he do that? Last night, when he'd come, he had needed some recovery time. Now? That did not seem to be the case. He took her again, slow, until she practically clawed his shoulders apart. He kept the pace leisurely, tormenting them both, and when they finally reached their climaxes, the intensity brought tears to her eyes.

"*Ryan,*" she cried out, clinging to him, overwhelmed.

He held her close, stroked her hair and her shoulders. Kissed her temple and whispered hot words into her ear. Trembling, Delanee fought to catch her breath. He rose above her, a troubled expression pinching his face.

"What's wrong?" she managed to pant.

He shifted, his hard length still buried deep. "I'm not sure. I can't seem to get enough of you."

She bit her lip. "Is that bad?"

"Well," he breathed out, chuckling. "Unless you want to stay stuck together all day? Might be a problem."

Her inner muscles clenched. "I might not mind."

He kissed her. "You might not be able to walk afterward."

Excellent point. She wiggled and paid attention to the subtle twinges and aches of never-before-used parts of her body and others that had been used in new ways. Ryan groaned and dropped his head to her shoulder.

"I am a little sore," she admitted.

"That's what I thought," he whispered and kissed where her shoulder met her neck. A current of need sizzled through her, and she couldn't stop from lifting her hips. "You have to stop."

"You stop," she moaned.

He moved his hips, and her eyes nearly crossed. His head dropped back to her shoulder, where he licked. "Maybe once mo—"

Cold air wafted into the room a split second before the happy sing-song voice of an elderly woman broke the haze of lust clouding Delanee's mind.

"Up, up, up, says the Inara," Evelyn, or maybe Ava, crooned. "Up, up, daddy! Isn't that ri—Ryan Aleysk Voklane!"

"What is all this fussing ab—Oh my. Well. I guess the boy didn't learn his lesson the first time, Evie."

"Take her. Take the baby into the other room."

Ryan rolled off Delanee and yanked the sheets up over her. The sudden emptiness made her wince. "No, that won't be necessary. Bring our daughter here, please."

Evelyn's shrewd gaze narrowed on Delanee as she shifted against the headboard, the pillow rolling behind her back. Delanee knew she looked like a thoroughly loved woman. Crazy hair, sweaty skin, and breathless. She tried not to be embarrassed. But really, what else was there when caught literally in the act?

"*Our* daughter?" Evelyn asked, hugging Inara closer to her shoulder.

Ryan glanced at Delanee and smiled. "Yes. Delanee and I married last night."

"And wasted no time consummating, I see," Ava sang. "Ah, the romance of marriage. I do believe I want to get married, Evie. Do you think her grandmother could help me?"

"Who would marry you? You'd break a hip on your wedding night."

Ava harrumphed.

Delanee blinked. "You know who my grandmother is?"

"Yes. We learned," Evelyn stated, walking to Ryan's side of the bed. "We can keep her another day if you'd like."

"Thank you, but we have an obligation with Delanee's family today," Ryan said, reaching out his arms for his daughter. No, *their* daughter.

"We do?" she asked, frowning.

"Yes. Lucianna is bonding today. Madeleine told you last night, remember?"

Delanee flushed. While she remembered much of last night, none of it had to do with her grandmother. "Oh, that's right."

He chuckled and cuddled a happy infant to his chest. "You don't remember, do you?"

Delanee flushed a deeper shade of red and picked at an invisible string on the navy comforter. The quiet snick of the door closing made her glance up, realizing they were alone in the bedroom. Inara burbled and kicked. Ryan set her on her feet between them, supporting under her arms as she bounced up and down. Her tiny hands slapped at his, and joyful noises left her. Delanee scooted closer and laid her head on Ryan's shoulder. She pressed a finger to Inara's hand, smiling when the baby held tight.

Ryan set Inara down. The baby plopped onto her behind and then rocked until she toppled forward onto her hands and knees, then scooted herself back into a sitting position and grabbed fistfuls of blanket.

"She'll be crawling any day," Delanee said.

"I have gates in my storeroom to contain her to the living room when that happens."

Delanee snorted. "Are you prepared for everything?"

"I want her to be able to explore a safe area when she's mobile. I read she can begin crawling as early as four months, and wanted to be ready," he said.

"Of course you did." Delanee shook her head. "I bet you have all her clothes for the next year, too."

He glanced over at her, blinking. "Do you know how many times I've put something on her that fit two days prior and couldn't even fit the buttons together?"

Delanee laughed. "Yes, babies do grow incredibly fast. But fashions change, too. Even for babies."

"No one sees her."

Delanee smoothed a hand over Inara's downy platinum curls. "They will now."

He stared at her and then blinked. "Maybe. But I couldn't care less about infant fashion."

"It is silly," Delanee agreed. "Did you know ten years ago, ruffles were the main style? Ruffled skirts. Ruffled shirts. There were even little ruffled socks."

"And what are we in currently?" he asked.

Delanee tweaked the bright red bow sown into the neckline of Inara's yellow onesie and then patted her little knee, clothed in knitted blue and red striped pants. "Bright colors and patterns. Washed-out pastels are a no-no for the fashion-forward parent."

"Huh. The twins must read fashion periodicals. They've been buying or making all her clothes for me."

Delanee looked over the garish outfit, which was made entirely of primary colors. "Yes, they do. From the seven-seventies."

Ryan laughed. "That explains a lot, actually." He plucked at the fabric covering Inara's round belly. "So, how would *you* clothe her?"

If not for her nudity, Delanee would have swept off the blankets and shown him. After all, what hadn't he seen, touched, or— heat blossomed across her cheeks at the memory— tasted? Ryan seemed to realize her dilemma, scooting to the edge of the bed before reaching for Inara.

"You can show me after we shower," he said, plucking her off the mattress and tucking her against his side.

"But, what about—"

"She sits in her crib just fine." He bounced the infant and nuzzled her nose. Inara giggled and patted at his cheeks. Delanee's heart about swelled free of her chest. "At least, she has for the past six months."

Ryan went around the bed and deposited Inara in her crib. She fussed, reaching for him the second he stepped away. He caressed her head and handed her a stuffed toy. She grabbed at the fluffy animal, making noises only she knew the meaning of. Ryan stopped at Delanee's side of the bed and held out his hand.

"Come on, we need to get going. Your family lives outside the city, don't they?"

"Yes, in Whispering Ash Woods." She kept the sheet clutched to her chest until the last moment.

"The city or the actual woods?"

"Not far outside the city, but deep enough in the woods for all the various beasts we had in our house at one time or another. My father wanted to make sure my mother had easy access to necessities if he needed to travel. She'd only lived in Haven City until they bought the house, and she doesn't ride a horse or know how to drive an Ariot, so she needed to be able to walk for groceries or ride a bike if the weather warranted."

He helped her stand, tossing the blankets away,

completely comfortable in his state of undress, while she worried in the light of day, he'd realize what he was stuck with... for a very long time. The chill in the room caused her to shiver and gave her an excuse to shield her breasts. Ryan frowned and went to the fireplace.

"Go ahead and hop in. I'll get the fire going again," he said, crouched before the fireplace.

"Why I prefer woodstoves." She glanced around for a robe but had never seen him wear one and hadn't gone to her room to gather any of her things the night before. Plans had shifted into a new, much more pleasurable direction.

He glanced over his shoulder, grinning. "I don't normally sleep so well. I wake up enough in the night to put wood on the fire to keep the room warm."

Alone in the shower, Delanee let the hot water cascade over her body and wondered how she would tell her family she'd married... and become a mother. Anxiety spiked through her. What was she thinking, taking on such a responsibility? She knew nothing about parenting. Had never imagined she would be able to have a child of her own to raise. She hadn't even asked Ryan if he was okay with her hasty decision.

Strong arms banded around her from behind and hugged her close. "What are you worrying about?"

Delanee sagged against his chest and wrapped her hands around his forearms. "Are you mad about Inara's birth record?"

He rested his chin on her shoulder and squeezed his arms. "No. I'm thankful and awed that you'd do something so selfless for a child who isn't yours."

Delanee twisted in his arms and took his face between her hands. "She *is* mine."

"And yet you worry."

"I may be a terrible mother," she whispered.

"You will love her." A statement, not a question.

The faith he had in her tore at her insides. "Yes."

"Then you'll be as good a mother as I am a father. If anyone is unqualified for this life position, it's me."

Delanee disagreed. "You're an amazing father."

He leaned close and smiled against her mouth. "And you'll be an amazing mother."

TWENTY-FIVE

RYAN HELD Inara while chaos surrounded them. His daughter twisted left, then right, her silvery-blue eyes wide, not knowing where to look or who made what sounds for her to focus on. Ryan sympathized. She'd fallen asleep on the ride to the township of Whispering Ash Woods, and Delanee's mother, Bella, had shown him to a nursery suite still set up in their bedroom suite for when the grandbabies visited. Inara had slept through Lucianna's bonding ceremony and had let the whole house know when she'd awoken. He had walked downstairs to the gathering that had been quietly sitting when he had left, now engaged in conversation and a few antics.

A little girl, maybe around five, hopped, her dark curls bouncing. Her arms were lifted in front of Dominik Ralston, who had a huge bird perched on his shoulder. The raptor twisted its head and regarded the child, film blinking over the fiery golden eyes. The light caught on the feathers as Dominik squatted enough to reach the girl, showing a rainbow of colors on what had looked dark brown seconds before. Fascinating.

The falcon lifted its wings when Dominik straightened

with the little girl on the opposite side of his body. Her small fingers reached for the creature, and Ryan's breath lodged in his throat. A myriad of bad scenarios flashed through his mind, all of them ending in blood and screams. His hold tightened around Inara's legs until she grumbled. But the falcon didn't nip or treat the small fingers like food being offered, rather stretched toward her to be petted. The child grinned and used one finger to smooth the feathers atop the bird's crown gently. The falcon opened its beak wide and released faint, high-pitched chirps, and the girl pulled her arms into her chest, giggling in delight.

A teenage boy inched closer with his gaze locked on the falcon. The bird chittered and shook its feathers, angling toward the teenager. The falcon did to the boy what it hadn't done to the girl, snapping its beak in warning. Dominik said something low, and the boy backed off, his gaze never straying from the animal.

"Dmitri is drawn to Alstair," Markus Ralston said, his arms crossed over his chest, clothed in a dark green shirt.

During Cia's bonding ceremony, all the Ralston beast master males were shirtless, their unique tattoos on display. Delanee had sat in the back with Ryan, and he wondered if she felt the pull to be part of a ceremony that was her birthright. Cia had worn a flowing open-backed gown, showing off her bonded marking.

"I don't blame him," Ryan said.

"Someday, he will have a predatory bird of his own, and he is desperate to know the experience." The Ralston patriarch surveyed his home in silence for a few moments. "So. You are the man who married my eighth daughter. The stubborn one. How, exactly, did you manage that?"

"I...." Ryan blew out a long breath. "Have no idea."

Markus laughed and patted Ryan's shoulder. "Your lost expression is about what we expected to see on her spouse's face often. We usually have it ourselves where she's concerned." He clapped his hands in front of Inara and then plucked her from Ryan's arms before either could object. He settled her to sit on his forearm, bouncing her slightly, his golden eyes shining with delight. "Did you know," he began, ticking under Inara's chin, "that your *makyshka* wrote her first article when she was nine?"

Inara stared at him, eyes round, and babbled softly. Markus smiled and nodded.

"That's right," he continued. "She'd noticed a man and woman carrying on an affair in her *baki's* building. But that was not the big deal, however. Oh no. Your ma discovered the woman had been stealing from the man's spouse. She wrote up a big public service announcement, as she called it, warning everyone to be careful with their belongings, and tacked it on everyone's door. When the woman showed up to confront Delanee's accusations, your ma hissed at her, told her to keep her thieving hands away from her *baki's* apartment, and slammed the door in her face." He tickled Inara's belly, making her laugh. "*Dak*, she did."

The exchange fascinated Ryan. Both the information being given about his new wife, and the way Inara accepted Markus's embrace despite him being a complete stranger. Delanee was the first person she'd been exposed to outside of people on the street or at the market the twins shopped from and often took Inara. He'd expected tears and tantrums anytime someone came too close. Then again, the man had enough experience and confidence holding an infant. Inara probably had some ingrained baby instinct about her safety in Markus's arms. Ryan still hovered.

A cacophony of dog barking broke out in the next room. Markus sighed and bounced Inara. "Let's take the wolfies outside before your *baki*—"

"Markus!" a woman shouted.

"We're coming, *krahet'sna!*" Markus replied and then

smiled at Inara. "Have you met our wolves yet, *ser drapresi*?"

Markus pushed between the guests, past the foyer, and into the room where the wolves were apparently misbehaving. Ryan went to follow, but Delanee intercepted, her fingers intertwining with his, and tugged him back into a secluded corner.

"Let my father have this time with her," she said softly. She glanced at the doorway he'd disappeared through and then back to Ryan. "She is part of our family now, and he feels a strong need to establish that bond with her. All my family will, but my father most of all."

A sudden burst of anxiety made his palms sweat. "What if she... you know, starts glowing?"

Delanee smiled. "Like she did with me?"

Ryan glanced around, rubbing his hands on his legs. The alluring scent of her teased his senses and fought for dominance over his insecurities. If he could get lost in her again, he would. "And just like that, your entire family will accept her?"

"You mean like your parents did when they found you?"

She grasped his hand again and pressed it to her chest above the solid beat of her heart. The heat of her skin soaked into his palm, and he had to keep from angling his fingers to touch her breast. She didn't seem to realize the temptation she offered. One Ryan needed to ignore before he embarrassed them both.

Her hand tightened over his, drawing his attention back to the conversation, not his internal musings. "Did they not take one look at you and decide they were your parents, and you were their son?"

Ryan had often tried to imagine when an exhausted and overwhelmed group of archaeologists, historians, and explorers realized live infants were among the items collected from the ancient research facility upon which they'd stumbled. How all of them ventured into an icy wasteland and had emerged as parents. To hear them tell the story, Ryan's father had picked him up, snuggled him close, and looked at his wife. No words had needed to be exchanged. In an instant, Ryan had parents, no different from any other child.

Inara was experiencing the same, only she was a bit older. Instead of the welcoming arms of a huge family waiting to meet her hours after birth, they were meeting her now, six months into her life. No, Ryan would not deny her the opportunity at family. Especially since his own parents never had the chance to meet her. She'd never know how much they would have loved her. An ache Ryan would live with forever.

"Okay?" she asked, squeezing his hand.

Ryan took a deep breath and nodded. "Okay."

Smiling, she patted his chest, and he resisted the urge to yank her against him and hug her tight. Just to feel her body pressed to his. "Good. Come on, time to meet everyone."

By *everyone*, she meant a boisterous group of siblings, in-laws, and close family friends. Some he knew, others he'd never met. A handful of small children raced between the adults. One, barely a year old, struggled to keep up and was swept into the arms of Darius, the Ralston with whom Ryan had worked the most. The boy squealed and kicked his feet as Darius held him upside down and pretended to shake out his pockets. When he flipped the little one around and positioned him on his hip, he held a glimmering object in his hand. The boy quieted, his pale brown eyes wide, his small hands reaching for the item. Darius bounced a polished wooden horse up and down like it was galloping to the boy's nose. Squealing in delight, the child grabbed at the horse. Darius released the toy and then set the wiggling boy down. He toddled off, prize held high, into an adjoining room.

Darius noticed Ryan and closed the distance between them. He clapped Ryan's shoulder and then shook his hand, grinning. Dark gray strands broke apart Darius's deep wine-red hair. All the Ralstons except two appeared to have inherited the color from their father. More gray defined his beard.

"You look lost." Darius released his hand.

"I guess I never really considered the sheer size of your family before," Ryan admitted.

Darius squeezed his shoulder. "You're family now, too. Welcome to the Ralstons." He shook his head. "I still can't believe Delanee married. And to you? Never saw that coming."

That made two of them. "It was rather impulsive."

Darius barked out a laugh. "Her curiosity has always led her."

Information Ryan wished he'd known before not only housing Delanee but giving into temptation and kissing her. Again and again. Yet, would he have changed anything? Markus returned inside, Inara babbling up a storm perched in the crook of his arm, her little hands reaching for the outside disappearing behind a closing door. She fussed at him, opened her palm, and then pointed, repeating the gesture obviously meant to communicate she wanted to go back out.

"Ah, *mie ser drapresi*, no more outside, it's getting too cold for you." He pressed a loud kiss to her chunky cheek.

"Na-ba-da-da-da!" she shouted and pointed again.

"*Vye*," Markus said and tickled her belly.

She grumbled some more, twisting in Markus's hold. The elder Ralston ignored her fussing, handing her off to... Ryan narrowed his gaze. Which sibling? Ah, yes, the oldest sister, Dalila. The woman cooed and touched her nose to

Inara's. And yep, a faint, white haze shimmered around his daughter. Ryan froze. A little girl gasped and tugged on the woman's plum, tunic-style shirt. Like Delanee, Dalila seemed unaffected by Inara's emerging talent.

"Momma, she's glowing," the little girl, Rose, proclaimed in a loud whisper. "I wanna glow! How can I do that?"

"Uh..." Dalila glanced around.

Delanee swept in, scooping Rose into her arms and propping the little girl on her hip. "You know how your momma helps people find love?"

Rose stuck a finger in her mouth and nodded, her gaze never leaving Inara.

"The glow is part of Inara's gift."

"Will my gift glow?" Rose asked in awe.

"Maybe," Delanee said.

Darius slowly turned his head to look at Ryan. He batted his lashes in a curious yet mocking *gotcha* way. "What does the glow mean, Mr. Voklane?"

TO DELANEE, the question her oldest brother posed hung like an undetonated bomb in the midst of her family. Chances were high that Ryan had used his talent on a brother or two in her family. He needed to know who to trust, and she knew he trusted Darius and Deklan, which meant they had passed the questions he'd asked without their knowledge. Her alpha, never-challenged brothers would have a com- apart if they knew the truth. She wouldn't blame them; an invasion of privacy was just that. She also couldn't blame Ryan. His position and the respon-sibilities he bore came with a high cost.

Ryan opened his mouth, and Delanee spoke first. Her ears burned from the sudden attention on her. "The trait is familial. We won't know Inara's talent fully until she's a little older." She looked at Ryan. "Right?"

The internal struggle to not lie to his new family and yet protect himself and his child filtered along their bond. Delanee would support his decision, regardless of which one he made. Reveal himself and deal with the fallout, or let his secret remain between them. And really, Delanee wasn't telling a complete falsehood. They *wouldn't* know the full extent of Inara's genetic ability until she was old enough to learn how to wield the talent. Would she be as powerful as her father? Or had her mother's weaker genetics allowed the gift to become somewhat diluted?

Take it, Ryan. Take the out, Delanee silently beseeched. Today was about Cia and her bonding. Not the crazy talented man Delanee had brought into the mix of Ralstons. Her family's power had just increased, but would her brothers see that at the start? No. Because they were her brothers, their testosterone would blind their critical thinking skills at first.

"Right," he said reluctantly.

"So, this is from her mother?" Dalila asked slowly.

Delanee sniffed and lifted her chin, hiding her relief at his response. "I don't know what you're talking about. I'm her mother, and her gift is all her own."

Donovan, the brother born after her, number nine in the Ralston line of children, slung his arm around her shoulder and hugged her into his side. Rose held her arms out to him, and their niece climbed between them, grabbing Donovan's neck and wrapping her legs around his waist.

"Keep your secrets," Donovan whispered, hugging her tighter into his side. "We'll figure them out eventually."

"If my mate has secrets, they're mine, too. You'll never figure them out," Delanee vowed.

"Oh, yeah?"

"Yeah." Delanee lifted a brow. "Have you found Mr. Wolfsy, yet? Hmm?"

Donovan narrowed his eyes.

Delanee smiled. "That's what I thought."

Donovan's glare increased, then eased into a smile. Concern flared through her.

"Ma!" he shouted.

Delanee gasped in outrage. She yanked from his hold and punched his bicep.

"Hey," Donovan barked, turning away from her fist. "Don't beat me in front of your niece. Tell Auntie Lanee she's bad, Rose. Bad, Auntie Lanee, bad!"

Rose snickered, covering her mouth.

"Are you two being bad influences on my sweet Rose again?" their mother, Bella, asked, plucking Rose from Donovan's arm.

"Will I glow, Grammy?" Rose asked.

"You glow now, sweet girl," Bella answered, hugging her.

Rose beamed and squirmed to be put down. The instant her feet touched the floor, she raced off, shouting for her father.

Bella turned her attention to Delanee and Donovan and they both froze at the disapproving stare she cast them. Fists on her hips, she looked between them. "What are you two fighting about now?"

Delanee pointed at her brother. "He said he was going to—"

"She stole my Wolfsy," her brother said over her words.

"Only because he put mashed potatoes in my tea at dinner," Delanee defended, glaring at her younger brother. "And you're nineteen. Nine. Teen. You don't even need Wolfsy anymore."

"He's mine. I want him back."

"Delanee," her mother sighed, rubbing her temples.

"Get the stuffed toy and give it back to your brother." She lifted her hands and muttered, "Why am I saying this to my grown children?"

Delanee pressed her lips together and looked away.

Donovan growled. "You lost him, didn't you?" He pointed to her and then at Ryan. "That's it. Every secret will be mine. Every single one."

The talent Donovan carried within him was unknown enough that he might very well be able to make good on the threat. Delanee squealed and spun away, beelining for her daughter. She gathered Inara from Dalila's arms, her sister protesting the loss of the baby, but she ignored the grumbles and continued to Ryan.

"Time to go," she proclaimed, rushing past him.

"Wait, what?" Ryan asked, following close behind her.

"Coward!" Donovan shouted.

"Extortionist!" Delanee shot over her shoulder, continuing toward the front of the house.

"What is going on?"

"Find my Wolfsy, Delanee!" followed them out of the house and into the cooling day.

"What is a *wolfsy*?" Ryan asked.

"It's my brother's favorite childhood toy that I stole when he made me mad that I may or may not have lost."

Ryan paused on the front walkway. "What?"

Delanee huffed and adjusted Inara's position on her hip. "Donovan put garlic creamed potatoes in my tea cup at dinner last fall. I took a drink. I vomited all over my brother-in-law. Donovan had that stupid wolf in his pack, and when I saw it, I just grabbed it, okay?"

"And what happened to it?"

"I put it in my room."

Ryan groaned and ran a hand down his face.

"Exactly," she stated, spinning and heading toward the parked Ariot.

"Wait, I needed to—"

Delanee backtracked, grabbed his hand, and tugged him down the brick path. "Whatever it is, you can radio or go to where they work tomorrow after you drop me off at the paper."

He grabbed her elbow at the Ariot and turned her to face him. "The paper?"

Inara gurgled and yanked on one of Delanee's errant curls. Wincing, she shifted the baby to her other hip and tilted her head away from questing fingers. "I have to turn in my article from the blooming party, or I'm going to lose my job. I'm already behind on my article quota."

Ryan sucked in a breath, and she knew, just *knew*, he was going to argue about her returning to work. Delanee turned and opened the vehicle. "I know what Mr. Ingerman said last night freaked you out." Was that only last night? Delanee opted not to ponder how much had changed for her in less than twenty-four hours.

"Delanee—"

"However," she continued over him, leaning inside to secure Inara in the back and talking louder, "nothing has technically changed. He's unaware of his confession, so I'll be as safe tomorrow as I have been all along."

Inara kicked her feet and waved her fists, but thankfully, she went into the seat made for her without issue. Delanee twisted around to sit and found two brothers staring at her through the open door, arms crossed, brows lifted. Despite fourteen years between them, the two were unmistakably brothers. Their parents' offspring hadn't deviated too far off the genetic path. Darius flexed his jaw, his beard ruffling in the wind. Donovan smirked. His wolf, Zhenya, sat at his side. Inara leaned forward and babbled happily.

The wolf whined and sought a way to climb into the small vehicle. Since Deklan had brought him home and a very reluctant Donovan had bonded with Zhenya, no one in the family could deny the damaged and healing canine much. Delanee wasn't immune. Sighing, she climbed out and motioned at the interior. Zhenya yipped and pushed his nose in first, then his entire upper body. Inara squealed with delight.

"Um," Ryan started, rushing around to the other side.

"He's fine," Donovan said, his gaze still locked on Delanee. "He loves kids and, since joining our family, can't seem to get his fill. No pun intended."

Delanee opened her arms and spun in a slow circle. Her long, knit skirt and jacket fluttered in the wind. "I obviously don't have your toy on me."

"That's not...." Donovan shook his head and sighed. He motioned at Darius.

"Deklan mentioned you were with Ryan to begin with because of a threat against you. *Baki* said you're still in danger. What's going on?" Darius asked, glancing at her and then at Ryan over the top of the Ariot. "And is the Mr. Ingerman you're talking about the same one who followed you around like a puppy a month ago? What does he have to do with anything?"

Oh no, she did *not* need her ultra-over protective brothers interfering. "Everything is under control, right Ryan?"

"Inara's fingers are in the wolf's mouth," he said, eyes wide, pointing inside the vehicle.

Donovan pushed Delanee to the side and squeezed into the front seat. He popped out a second later. "It's fine. He hasn't eaten anything he shouldn't have, and I brush his teeth because he sleeps with me. Zhenya says she's just curious about how his teeth feel. All the babies stick their fingers in his mouth, nose, and ears. He's incredibly patient with them."

A dog sneeze and baby laughter sounded from the interior. Must have been time to explore the nose.

"See," Delanee beamed, shoving her brother away from the vehicle. "Fine."

Darius sighed. "Delanee—"

"No." She pointed at them both. "I am married now. Trust my husband to handle whatever the problem is. If there is one. Which there isn't. Everything is fine."

Husband.

The word once again caught Delanee by surprise. She was married. And mated. An external sense of being overwhelmed joined the dazed sensation stealing her thoughts. She blinked and glanced at Ryan. Her statement must have also reminded him of the whirlwind changes not only between them but in their lives.

Neither of them knew how their relationship would affect their careers. Her family wasn't exactly low-profile, which was a requirement for his position. Her job kept her in the spotlight by necessity. How could she continue to follow her professional aspirations without jeopardizing his? Not that Ryan had any desire to further his career. He was happy being invisible. Irreplaceable to the arch guardian he served, yet unknown to the country he helped protect.

She would continue writing as D. Ralston, and no one would be reporting on her marriage since it had happened in secret. Although Delanee found she *wanted* Sziveria to know she'd claimed him. An odd realization considering she never wanted to acknowledge, let alone utilize, that aspect of her genetics. Knowing Ryan carried her mark did funny things to her insides. Made her want to tear his clothes off and take her fill. Trace every line and continue to explore the body she knew could make her combust in pleasure.

Ryan cleared his throat and braced a forearm on top of the Ariot. "I'll come by the SNID tomorrow. What time do you normally get to your office?"

Darius glanced at Donovan. "Before traffic gets heavy, around seven."

"I'm going to work with him tomorrow. I'm helping on a case," Donovan stated, glaring at Delanee.

"I won't be with him," she clarified. "I'll be at my own job, thank you very much."

Donovan's smile didn't reach his eyes. "That's fine. You can swing by the apartment and find my Wolfsy on your way to wherever home is now. Your *husband* can bring it with him tomorrow."

Delanee inhaled to argue and question why he even needed a stuffed toy anymore as a grown man, but the shadows in his eyes made her nod. "I needed to grab some stuff anyway."

"Have you seen her room?" Ryan asked slowly.

Darius sighed.

Donovan rubbed his forehead. "Yeah, I know I'm being overly optimistic, but a guy can hope."

"Hey," Delanee snapped, looking at the men surrounding her. "I'll find the wolf, okay?"

"Are you going to tell *Ahty* and Ma goodbye?" Darius asked.

"Ma saw us leave. She knows. She will tell our father, thank you very much," Delanee said.

Donovan snickered. "Saw you flee, you mean?"

Delanee nudged Zhenya from the vehicle. "Goodbye, dear brothers."

Darius laughed, the action melting years from his handsome face. Delanee's heart clenched. She wished her eldest brother had more to be happy about, but his smiles were few, and his laughter even rarer. He grabbed her door and leaned down to kiss her cheek.

"Be careful, sister mine. This group, if it's the one I think is causing all the issues, they're nothing to play around with," he whispered.

"I know," she said softly.

He rapped his knuckles on top of the vehicle and straightened. "Take care of my sister, Voklane."

"Already have been, Ralston."

Delanee sighed, half of her surprisingly delighted Ryan could hold his own against her brothers, the other half annoyed that they required such from him. Darius closed her door as Ryan climbed inside. Inara babbled, and Delanee glanced at her, smiling.

"Did you have fun, baby girl?" she asked, reaching back and grabbing her sock-covered toes.

"The apartment?" Ryan asked, carefully maneuvering down the uneven dirt and gravel driveway.

"Yes." She turned and looked out the window. "I should probably grab some more of my stuff."

"And find the wolf thing."

Delanee chuckled. "Yes, and find the wolf thing." Her humor faded, and she chewed on her bottom lip. "When should I pack up everything?"

"I don't know," he said. "We should wait until we're sure no one is watching you."

The reason was sound, yet insecurity made her hunch her shoulders. Her room was a disaster, which meant packing said disaster and relocating all her, well, junk to his immaculate home. Where would all her balls of yarn and unfinished projects go? And her clothes? Did he have room for her books in his study? These were all things they would have discussed like normal people if she hadn't jumped into a marriage with him.

"Where are all my things going to go?" she asked quietly.

"I have some ideas," he stated, turning off the drive and onto the main road.

The rhythmic sound of the Ariot's wheels moving over brick filled the interior. The gentle motion lulled Inara until she murmured and dozed. Townhouses and shops made up the majority of Whispering Ash Woods proper. A few buildings held signs for lawyers, investors, and even a small paper, where Delanee had published her first article at thirteen. She still wrote pieces for them when they asked, visiting the township enough to know the ebb and flow of the people who called the quaint suburb home.

"Do you think they know?" Delanee asked, still looking out the window. The afternoon sun streamed between trees, casting light rays on the road.

"Know what?"

"That I was the one who discovered the identity of their assassin? Do you think they know, and that's why they sent Mr. Ingerman after me?"

"No. I think Mr. Ingerman's pursuit of you is unrelated to the assassin. It could be related to your other missing articles, however."

Delanee snorted. "And let me guess, they just want to *talk* to me at that warehouse he was supposed to bring to."

"It is concerning, which is why—"

"No. Nope," she quickly cut in. "I'm safe at work. We have already established that. You can drop me off at the back door like last time and pick me up when I'm finished. I can't miss any more days, Ryan."

He sighed. "Is there a radio at your work?"

"We're a newspaper, of course there is."

"If you feel unsafe at any time, call immediately. I'll leave you a list of all the places I expect to be and the radio numbers to reach me."

"And you'll just drop everything to come and get me?" she asked, shaking her head.

"Yes," he said. No hesitation.

Delanee blinked and turned to look at him. "Ryan—"

"No arguing. You are more important than anything I'll be doing or anyone I'll talk to tomorrow."

Delanee wanted to contribute his protective behavior to the mating bond, but she couldn't. No, his reaction was all Ryan, all for her, and the knowledge made her glow a little bit inside.

"Promise me if at any point you feel uncomfortable or something concerns you, you'll call," he said, splitting his attention between her and the road.

"I promise," she said. "Though I won't need to. You'll see."

TWENTY-SIX

Master Guardian Raiventon's residence

RAINA MERRICK LEANED back in her desk chair and released a long sigh, rubbing her belly where her baby kicked and twisted. She glanced at the clock above the fireplace mantle. One more customer meant two hours at the most, and she could end her day.

"Janice, who are we waiting for?" she asked her assistant, whose office was located just outside her own.

Janice popped into the doorway, a thin book in hand with a pen perched above the pages. Dark brown curls were styled perfectly around her face, her makeup understated. A navy pencil skirt down to her calves paired with a cream satin blouse. A sapphire brooch sparkled in the center of a wide, cream bow tied at her neck. Despite having a closet-sized office overflowing with files, Raina's young assistant had always taken her position seriously.

"A Mr. Aaron McRiv... McRiverarcr...McRiverir?" Janice huffed and dropped the schedule to her thigh, exasperation on her face. "I have no idea how to pronounce his name. I'm sorry."

Raina held out her hand. "May I see, please?"

Janice rushed into the office with the book held out. "Of course."

Raina looked at the entry, which was written in neat block letters, and frowned. "It is a rather odd name, isn't it?"

"Yes. I don't recall scheduling him, but the name must have been spelled out for me."

The ink color and writing were different. Raina tapped the page. "This must have been scheduled earlier in the week when you had your sister come fill in for you."

Janice touched a finger to her temple and tsked. "That's right. I can't believe I didn't notice it wasn't even my hand-writing."

Raina stretched her hand across the desk and patted in understanding. "You have a lot going on, don't be so hard on yourself."

A faint blush rose along Janice's neck and into her cheeks. She cleared her throat and picked up the schedule book. "Yes, well, I'm afraid I have to be, all things considered."

Raina sighed with sympathy for her employee and her friend. "Everyone makes mistakes."

"That's kind of you, but we both know I'm lucky to have had the embarrassing itch issue and not a deadly one." Janice glanced over her shoulder at the open office door. "I'm thankful for both of you trusting me to make better decisions in the future when I put this entire house at risk."

Because if Janice had become sick with human rabies syndrome and went into the active state while working, she could have killed or infected everyone in the house. To say Raina's husband had been livid was an understatement. But Raina had been in the room when Janice had realized her current lover had transmitted a sexual infection to her and how close she may have come to becoming an HRS victim. A hard lesson to learn between the fear and sense of betrayal. Scared of the worst, Janice had visited the containment facility for a health assessment to ensure the awkward and uncomfortable rash was the only thing that had been transferred to her. They'd treated the infection and sent her home. Her sister had filled in for her during the ordeal.

"You did the right thing by going up north. Kevin appreciated your responsibility," Raina said.

The flush in Janice's cheeks deepened. "I never plan on allowing it to be an issue again. Marriage contracts only for me from this point on. I listened to bad advice and... well, it doesn't matter." She took a deep breath and straightened her spine. "I will let you know when Mr. Aaron arrives for his appointment. Is there anything else you need?"

"A snack would be lovely." Raina knew Janice needed something to do to erase the difficult conversation and reminder of her mistake.

"Perfect. I'll find Mrs. Taft and have one sent right away."

Raina organized her desk and files from her last client while she waited. The snack arrived at about the same time as her new patron. She hastily stuffed her face while Janice saw to Mr. McRiverir's outdoor wear and collected the basic information Raina would need to begin working with him. At least, that's how it was supposed to happen. A bite of cheese and cracker with some strawberry jelly on top, because her cravings had taken an odd turn, was halfway to her mouth when a man stalked into her office, Janice chasing after him.

"Mr. Aaron, wait, please, I need this—"

The man slammed the door in her assistant's face. He seemed to search for a lock, and when he didn't find one, he turned, his light gray coat flaring, and leaned his body against the door. Silver flashed, and Raina found herself staring at the barrel of a pistol.

"Refuse to answer my question, and only one of us is going to walk out of here," he growled, his dark eyes hard and angry. He looked like any other client she assisted with their business's logistical needs. Well dressed and groomed.

Raina set the food down slowly, never taking her eyes off the man. "I strongly advise you leave my home, Mr. Whoever-you-are."

"Not until I have the information I've come for."

Raina waited. Silent. Janice would already be on her way to find Kevin.

Perspiration glistened along his combed hairline and dotted his cheeks. The gun trembled in his hand. "Where is the prince?"

"Which one?" Raina asked calmly despite the pounding of her heart and folded her hands on the table. "There are two."

He shook the gun, and Raina winced, her hand falling to her distended stomach without thought. "The youngest one!"

So, Prince Jaiden was indeed in trouble, as her father had feared. What lengths had he taken to secure the boy? Knowing her father, extreme would look mild. "I don't know why you think I know where he is."

His face darkened with anger, and he took a step from the door, hesitated, and pressed himself back against the paneled wood. "Don't play stupid with me. We—I mean, I need to know where the boy is."

Raina caressed her belly. The baby kicked and pushed in response to the flood of adrenaline in her system. "I have no idea. I do not work with the royal family, let alone know where the youngest member is."

The weapon trembled so hard in his palm the metal pieces clanked together. Sweat trickled from his shaven jaw to splash on his shoulder. "I'm not going to ask again, Master Guardianess Raiventon. Where is the boy?"

The fear she'd been trying to keep control of surged through her blood. "How am I supposed to know if he isn't in the palace?"

"The arch guardian knows."

"Which arch guardian? There are six of them," Raina felt the need to point out, knowing it was a risk to toy with her captor but needing to give Janice time to reach Kevin.

Aaron growled, his already hard eyes blazing with a deeper anger. "You know *exactly* which arch guardian I'm referring to."

"Perhaps, but I am not the arch guardian," she reasoned, anxiety making her shake.

"He will have told you— he tells you everything."

Raina blinked and suppressed the urge to laugh at the ridiculous statement. "I can assure you my father tells me nothing. You have wasted your time coming here and threatening me."

He squeezed his eyes closed. His grip tightened on the gun until his knuckles turned white. "No. No! They said—"

The door burst free of its hinges and knocked the intruder forward. The gun went off, and Raina screamed, falling from her chair to the floor and curling into a ball to protect her unborn child. Glass shattered. The weight of the heavy door slammed into the floor.

"Raina?" Kevin bellowed.

"I'm fine! We're fine!" she quickly assured, rubbing her belly to soothe herself as well.

A pained scream followed by sobbing made her cautiously peek around the corner of the desk. Her husband knelt on her would-be attacker's spine. Kevin held Aaron's wrist between his shoulder blades, his arm bent at an unnatural angle. Aaron's booted feet kicked and thrashed along the carpeted floor. Snot poured from his nose, and tears streamed down his face.

"Do you not know who I am?" Kevin asked, punctuating the question with a faint twist.

Aaron shrieked and attempted to bow his back, but Kevin's knee pressed harder. "I didn't know! I didn't know!"

"Who sent you?"

The man cried, a puddle of drool and snot forming beneath him. Raina wanted to feel sympathy, but the cold air from the bullet hole in her office window took any compassion right out of her.

"N-no one sent me. I overheard a conversation and d-decided to act. My s-superior likes a man of action."

"Who is your superior?"

Aaron gagged and whimpered. "I don't know."

Kevin increased pressure on Aaron's back and arm, his expression one of furious determination. Once, that look had terrified her. Raina hadn't known her quiet husband had been capable of extreme violence. Now she knew the real man. The one who would allow nothing to harm his wife or children, no matter the cost to him.

"I don't!" Aaron screamed. "He uses the name I gave, okay? That's all I know."

Kevin looked up and met her gaze. She no longer wondered how he seemed flawlessly aware of everything around him. "Are you okay?"

She nodded.

"Radio your father, please."

"No, wait, wait!" Aaron screamed.

"Now, Raina."

Raina pulled herself up using the desk edge for leverage. "What do you want me to tell him?"

"I have someone he may be interested in speaking to."

Twenty-Seven

Satisfied with her work, Delanee leaned back and pulled the last page of her article from the typewriter. She'd already turned in the beginning to her editor to ensure his approval of the direction. Curtis loved what Delanee had gathered about the mother attempting to lift the family's social status through a much-too-young daughter. An old tale, but one readers never grew tired of, the shallow content something worth snickering and gossiping over. Delanee included lavish descriptions of the party itself and all the flowers. She even managed to throw in a bit of a side snippet about a certain new guardianess and her foray into the maze with a man who wasn't her new husband.

Petty of her?

Maybe.

Did she care?

Nope.

Papers in hand, she pushed her chair back and stood. The newsroom bustled with activity. Couriers rushed between cubicles, and printing assistants leaned over the tops of partitions with page samples in hand. The volume was loud, the energy hectic. Delanee bounced from her space, unable to stop smiling. She might be relegated to fluff and scandals, but she loved being a writer for one of the most prestigious publications in Sziveria.

Curtis's office was empty, so Delanee fished a paperclip from her skirt pocket and set the article in the bin he had for final drafts. While her article required his edits, he'd handle the final aspect. The social pages rarely needed rewrites. Delanee checked the time on the return to her desk. In about two hours, Ryan would arrive to collect her. What could she do to pass the time? She gathered her notes and the newest fashion quarterly delivered in her absence and opted to sit upstairs with Sarkis in his artist lair. He always had hilarious opinions about what constituted fashion for the elites and even funnier predictions of how the budget seamstresses would interpret said styles for the everyday consumer.

After lifting her messenger bag off the back of her chair, she waved to fellow cubicle buddies and headed toward the corridor off the right side of the large newsroom. She glanced up long enough to ensure she wouldn't bump into anyone while putting her things in her bag.

A mistake.

She failed to notice the man lurking in the shadows of a storage room doorway. He leaped into her path and grabbed her arm, dragging her into the dim, chilly room full of old periodicals and editions waiting to be archived. Before she could scream, a damp palm slapped over her mouth and yanked her back into a solid form.

"Miss Ralston, I deeply regret doing this, but you've left me no other options. After the other night, I realized you would never allow us to be alone long enough for me to convince you to leave anywhere with me," a familiar voice said softly into her ear.

Barnaby Ingerman! Panic blossomed through Delanee, robbing her breath and skyrocketing her pulse. She tried to speak through his hand, but her words were muffled and useless.

"No, I'm sorry, it matters not what you say. I have been tasked with securing you and won't fail again. I can't."

A tremor of fear laced his words and increased Delanee's. Whoever held his reins in the V Alliance had obviously threatened Ingerman if he didn't come through. Ryan had mentioned several members who hadn't survived their failures. Bad news for her.

Delanee attempted to struggle, but he'd learned his lesson from the maze, keeping his body angled to prevent her attacks while ensuring he kept a firm hold. He dragged her toward a rarely used door into the back alley. Using his butt, he pressed the bar in, and the door latch released.

"About time," a gruff male voice grumbled.

"I had to wait," Ingerman snapped, dragging her into the cool afternoon. Bright sun blinded her and she struggled to see who else was around them. "I couldn't just grab her from her desk."

"What do you think's so special about her?" the unknown man asked.

"I've not a clue," Ingerman said, his words strained as he tried to contain her. "A little help would be nice."

"Oh, yeah, that's right."

Fabric rustled, and Delanee increased her attempts to break free. The grip on her arm and the one banded around her chest and covering her mouth tightened to the point of bruising. She tried to talk again, but only useless sounds emerged.

"Now, now Miss Ralston, if you had remained calm, we wouldn't have to use this on you," Ingerman said.

A flash of pain in her upper thigh preceded liquid fire burning through her veins. She screamed behind Ingerman's tightened hand. Blackness dimmed across her vision. *Ryan* whispered through her mind....

THE FIRST HINT of something being wrong stopped Ryan mid-word of filling out paperwork for one of the intel teams conducting a mission outside the country. An uncomfortable sensation of panic teased his senses. He straightened and examined the emotion. Not being prone to spontaneous anxiety, he knew the sentiment wasn't his own, which left... *Delanee*. Ryans surged from his seat, the pen falling forgotten from his hand.

He went to the radio beside his office door and set the frequency for Delanee's office.

"Haven City Chronicle, this is Amy speaking, who may I take a message for?"

"I need to know if Delanee Ralston is still in the office."

"Miss Ralston? Let me check for you. Hold one moment, please."

Empty static sounded, and Ryan tapped his foot in impatience. A faint crackle sounded seconds before the woman's voice returned.

"Miss Ralston is not at her desk. What message shall I take for her?"

"No message, thank you."

Ryan slowly flipped the radio switch off. He ran a hand down his mouth and beneath his jaw. Over the years, he'd had to help several of his intel teams save their spouses. Never did Ryan think he'd be the one in the situation, needing someone he loved rescued. He had no doubt someone from the V Alliance had run out of patience and found the opportunity to grab Delanee.

Everything in him stilled.

Loved?

He blinked. Delanee's smile, her boldness laced with innocence, and her unwavering acceptance of his daughter and of him flashed through his mind. Yes, loved. Nothing could happen to her.

Ryan grabbed his hat out of habit and rushed from his office. The corridors were crowded but flowed well, allowing him to get downstairs and to his Ariot without much delay. Inside his vehicle, he tapped the steering column and considered his options. Her brothers, or the team he trusted the most? Her brothers knew their personal situation, his team... he sighed and started the ignition process in the Ariot. His team would require some explanations.

Despite the potential fallout from the secrets he'd be forced to divulge, Ryan found himself pulling down the narrow drive to Sean Blackbain's house. The primary guardian holding the Wintersfall seat lived in an elegant two-story brick home with a spacious greenhouse rising two additional stories above the roofline. Late afternoon sun glinted off the angled glass panels and reflected the golden light. Ryan stared at the glittery panes for far too long, warring with the decision to knock on Wintersfall's door. Every internal safety mechanism he'd erected to keep himself, and his talent, safe urged him to back out of the driveway and... do what? He couldn't rescue Delanee on his own. He needed help.

Taking a deep breath, he opened his vehicle door and climbed out into the brisk afternoon. After closing the door, he leaned against the side and forced himself to straighten and take the necessary steps to the front of the house. The door opened before he could knock. Of course,

Davis, Sean's butler, would have known the instant Ryan arrived on the premises.

"Mr. Voklane." Davis executed a perfect bow and stood to the side to allow Ryan entrance. "I have informed the primary guardian of your arrival. He is in the library."

Ryan pulled his hat free and smoothed strands of hair back into place, relieved his hand didn't tremble. "Thank you, Davis."

Davis held out his hand. "If I may?"

Ryan relinquished his ivy cap. He stared at the open library doors. A firm grip squeezed his shoulder. Shocked, Ryan glanced at Davis.

Davis offered an encouraging smile. "It'll be all right, whatever it is. Go on."

Perhaps Ryan wasn't as collected as he believed. He crossed the short distance through the foyer to the library. The spacious yet cozy room was where the Blackbains chose to live out their lives while at home. Bookshelves rose two stories from the floor to the ceiling. A rolling ladder on either side allowed access to any of the titles. Stairs flush to the left side led to a loft. A couch adorned with discarded blankets and stuffed toys sat before a large, grated fireplace. The impressive desk toward the back of the room was where Sean saw guests, but his work area was upstairs. Papers rustled from above, and Ryan glanced at the loft.

"I'll be down in a second," Sean called.

Ryan went to the couch and sat. Bracing his elbows on his knees, he held his head. The stairs creaked, and he straightened.

"Must be bad if you didn't send a note with instructions," Sean said, joining him on the couch.

"I'm not here in an official capacity. I mean, I could pull resources if necessary, but this is personal." An understatement if he'd ever said one.

"All right, what's going on?"

Ryan took a deep breath. "The V Alliance has kidnapped my wife."

Sean's brows raised. "Wife?"

"Newly contracted," Ryan said.

"Ah. I didn't realize you were promised or even courting anyone." Sean tapped his thumb on his thigh. "Then again, we know very little about you, don't we?"

"I'm not meant to be anyone important," Ryan said softly.

"And yet, you are perhaps the most important man in the Sziverian government, correct?"

"I really am just a liaison for the Arch Guardian Synintel."

Sean smiled, though any jovial emotion didn't reach his amber eyes. "One thing at a time, yes?"

Ryan took a deep breath and nodded. "Yes."

"Good."

Ryan managed a shallow smile. "I can see why Synintel chose you as a team lead."

"Tell me about your wife."

Ryan stood and began pacing in front of the fireplace. "I married Delanee Ralston."

"Delanee Ralston? Wolvenguard's sister, Delanee?"

Ryan nodded.

Sean chuckled and shook his head. "I wouldn't have imagined her to be a fit for you, she's...."

Sean seemed to struggle to find the word to describe Delanee, so Ryan supplied it for him. "Life," he whispered. "She is life."

Understanding laced with sympathy lit Sean's gaze. "Yes, that is what we call our wives, too. Tell me what's going on."

"I'd prefer to tell everyone what's going on all at once."

Sean rose. "The whole team, or...?"

"The whole team, along with Wolvenguard, Darius, and Dominick Ralston."

Sean snorted. "As if I could keep Wolvenguard away when he learns from his wife why she's heading our way."

"Yeah, probably not." And Ryan wasn't looking forward to any of the Ralston brothers learning he'd failed in protecting their sister.

TWENTY-EIGHT

Nausea rolled through Delanee. Groaning, she rolled onto her side. The cold, hard surface beneath her pressed into her hip and shoulder. The queasiness grew in strength until she lifted herself up enough to vomit the contents of her stomach without choking.

Loud clanking reverberated through her brain and made the protesting of her stomach worse.

"Girl, hello, girl," a haughty, female voice said between the clanks. "I am not paying for you to be sick." The hard clanks sounded again, followed by a huff of exaggeration. "Manilek, do something."

Bleary-eyed, Delanee lifted her head, blinking to try to bring anything into focus. Metal bars surrounded her and a woman, draped in a red gown, tight from breast to hip and flowing in a beaded train held off the ground by two servants, stared down at her with disgust in her chocolate brown eyes. Red lipstick coated her full lips, and smoky black eyeshadow drew attention to the faint upturn of her eyelids. High cheekbones and a delicate jawline were framed by straight black hair.

A man clothed in a red tunic and slate pants joined the

woman at her side and wrapped an arm around her waist. "Patience, my darling. You shall have your precious pet, but the girl is clearly getting over the effects of the sedative. We were warned."

Their accent was unfamiliar, lyrical, and smooth.

The woman tsked and smacked the bars with a metal rod again. "I do not want to wait. This country is cold, and the food is weird. Too much sweet. Where is Adeelya?" She straightened from the bars, tucked the rod under her arm, and clapped her hands. "Adeelya!"

A small, older woman shuffled forward, a scarf tied around the top of her head and braided into her long, dark hair. Her brown dress brushed the floor but lacked the train. Her arms were folded and her head downcast. When Adeelya spoke, Delanee didn't understand the words.

The woman barked a response, pointing at the cage. Adeelya shuffled closer until her bony hand could reach through the bars. She grasped Delanee's chin between cold fingers. Nausea rolled through Delanee's stomach again, and she struggled to swallow against the flood of saliva in her mouth.

Adeelya spoke in their rapid language. What country were they from? Whatever Adeelya said made her mistress unhappy, for she stomped her foot and snapped at the man. He beseeched Adeelya, who shook her head and hobbled away from Delanee's cage.

And why was Delanee in a cage, anyway? She forced herself into a sitting position, backing her butt up against the bars. Another wave of nausea doubled her over, and she heaved, coughing against the lack of stomach contents to expel. Panting, she straightened and lifted a weak hand to wipe the undignified drool from her chin. Her eyes still struggled to focus, but she forced herself to look around.

She was indeed in a warehouse. The same one Ingerman had said he needed to take her to? Men loitered around, some carrying weapons, others sitting in groups playing cards or dice. They all wore black uniforms with red accents and a marking on the left arm of a pyramid with a sword going through it. Where had she seen the patch before? Her fuzzy mind refused to draw forth the memory.

Shifting her attention to the cage she was contained within, her breath lodged in her throat as her gaze settled on a cowering white ball of fluff. Boot heels clicked on the cement floor, and Delanee dragged her focus from the cat to the man heading in her direction. He stopped at the couple, offered a shallow, formal bow, and then adjusted his cuffs and looked at Delanee.

The smug satisfaction on his face told her she'd get no help from this particular primary guardian. Not that the man deserved the title any longer, or the position he resided over within Haven City Enforcement Services. Over the years Delanee had covered ranked society, Primary Guardian Hedleston had steadily gained favor among elite. Now she understood why, the scab. Despite the nausea still rolling through her belly, Delanee managed a glare.

The woman waved her hand at the cage. "Make her do something."

Primary Guardian Hedleston smiled indulgently. "I told you not to give her any medication, did I not, *Ahasi'ma Kaliya?*"

Kaliya lifted her chin and clicked her nails at Hedleston. "You told us to tell the men you hired to use it if she were, what is this word, not to agree. They said she fought."

Hedleston sighed and sauntered closer to the cage. "Of course you fought, Miss Ralston."

Delanee wrapped a hand around a bar. "Let me out. You know my brothers are going to find me." She didn't mention her mate, who was perhaps a bit more dangerous.

"It is an unfortunate situation, but you are required. By the time your family realizes you're missing, it'll be far too late to do anything. People go missing in this town all the time. The Ralston family won't be immune. Considering your job and recent predisposition to investigate dangerous topics, well..." He held his hands open in a helpless manner. "Perhaps you should have stuck to the safer gossip columns."

If Delanee's rebellious stomach weren't a distraction, her breath would have caught. "What do you know about my articles?"

"Miss Ralston, we can't have lies being written about our country. I hope you understand."

She swallowed. "H-h...." Her words stuck in her throat. She coughed, squeezed her eyes shut, and tried again. "How did you even know about them?"

He sniffed and wiped under his nose. "Let's just say a concerned citizen brought them to my attention. I make it my business to stay informed about any suspicious behavior within the city. You had a great many suspicions. I was doing my duty, you understand."

Delanee's nostrils flared. "And my investigations will somehow be revealed to my family after I go missing?"

"Such a shame. You must have offended the wrong people."

"As the First Prefect over MagnaRail Avenue's HCES location, you will ensure the investigators do everything they can to find me, right?" Delanee said between swallows to hold back another wave of queasiness.

He crouched before her and clasped his hands between his bent knees. "That is the plan, yes. You will be given a choice after you assist the lovely House Mother of House Desaidai. You can decide on a quick and painless death, or to live but be placed on the last ship the SNID hasn't been able to discover transporting people."

Delanee's breath caught in her throat. Panic made her lips dry. "A slave ship, you mean?"

He shrugged. "Sure."

"How could you?" she asked, tears burning her eyes. "You're a guardian."

"Believe it or not, most people boarding the ship do so of their own free will." He smiled. "The promise of access to their addiction makes them most agreeable."

Hedleston stood, pushing his hands into his pants pockets. "Now, if you'd please tame the lynxia there for Kaliya, we can get on with whatever choice you make."

Right, because death or slavery were such stellar options. Delanee closed her eyes and reminded herself her location wasn't a secret. She just had to stall. Her mate and her brothers would arrive soon.

Her attention moved to the cowering feline in the opposite corner. "I don't know anything about lynxias."

A pistol cocked. Delanee snapped her focus to Hedleston, who had the barrel of a gun trained on her. "Don't play games, Miss Ralston. I happen to know you're a beast master and your beast is a Ruthenarc lynxia."

What? How had he learned? No one knew except her family. She had even chosen her design and had her beast master mark inked in Ruthenia, not Sziveria. An appropriate choice since when she stepped foot from her father's native land, she left that part of herself behind, the only acknowledgment a design she never thought to see again. But, in the chaos of the situation she found herself in, she doubted she would ever find out the truth.

Her best hope was to make him believe whatever he had discovered was a rumor or an outright lie. "No, that's—"

A bullet pinged off the bars above her. She shrank and screamed, covering her head. Adrenaline flooded her already stressed body. The cat backed deeper into the corner, head raised, and hissed, exposing long, white canines. Silvery, sage-green eyes with huge pupils stared out.

Men shouted, and the relaxed mood in the warehouse shifted to tense expectation.

"*Don't* bother to lie to me," Hedleston stated, his gaze hot and slightly unhinged.

Instinct took over, and Delanee held out her hand to the terrified animal. The feline slinked to her, curling into her hip, and hissed at the bars again. Delanee wanted to do the same but swallowed the urge.

Satisfaction lit his blue eyes. "Good. Very good. Now, that wasn't so difficult, right? Do the next step, tame the cat, and we'll all carry on with our day."

Delanee sank her fingers into the thick fur at the nape of the lynxia's neck. "It d-doesn't work that w-way."

Hedleston waved the gun around. "I don't care what way it works. Just get the cat to obey its owner." He pointed a finger at Kaliya. "Right there."

Kaliya stepped closer to the cage, and the entourage carrying her train followed. "This cat will bring honor to House Desaidai." She lifted her chin and waved a dramatic hand. "We will be revered, awed, for we alone will have a lynxia in the land of Cairo."

Cairo? Delanee blinked. That meant... her attention shifted to the men standing at quiet attention in the warehouse. Cairoen Sentinels. Oh, bad. So, so bad. What she knew of Cairo was limited, but she knew enough. The Sentinels were a mercenary force, available for a steep price to anyone who could afford them. If the V Alliance had access to them... Delanee's grip tightened on the lynxia. The House Desaidai must be the house who owned the contingent in the warehouse, and in exchange for the use of the force, Hedleston's people had agreed to tame a lynxia.

"How did you even get the cat?" Delanee asked.

The feline's massive white paws with ghostly gray spots tightened on her thighs. Ruthenarc lynxia, like Ruthenarc wolves, was a species specific to Ruthenia. They weren't allowed to be exported under any circumstances. If Delanee had wanted to bond, she'd have needed to do so in Ruthenia, and only then could she leave with her animal. Someone had stolen the hopefully unbonded feline. Delanee could do nothing if the cat already had a beast master.

Hedleston sniffled and retrained the gun on her. "Questions are irrelevant. Tame the beast."

"I... can't," she admitted, breathless.

He stomped forward and shoved the barrel of the pistol through the bars. "Do it!"

"It doesn't work that way!" she screamed, hugging the cat's head. The fluffy black tips of its ears brushed underneath her chin. "I have to bond, and once it happens, it can't be undone. The cat will be mine, and mine alone. They aren't tamable."

Kaliya shouted in Cairoen, waving her arms around. Her husband rushed to Hedleston and demanded Delanee do what had been promised. In the chaos, tears tracked down Delanee's cheeks because she and the cat had only one chance of surviving the debacle before Ryan could arrive.

They needed to bond.

A crazy plan formed in her mind, and she took a deep, centering breath, digging her fingers through fur until she encountered the feline's skin. A purring rumble vibrated beneath her hands, and the lynxia twisted under Delanee until they faced each other. Nose to nose. Gazes meeting. The cat's nostrils flared, and it released a soft hiss. Not in anger or alarm but in expectation. Every muscle tensed beneath Delanee's touch. The gentle currents of energy she had failed to notice when bonding with Ryan pulsed from her fingertips. The cat licked a rough tongue beneath her chin in encouragement. If the lynxia was willing to bond, it didn't already have an alpha.

"I don't want this," she whispered, unable to stop more tears from spilling.

The feline head-butted her jaw. Outside the cage, arguing continued to ensue. Loud, angry shouts and accusations flew in a mixture of Atlantic and Cairoen. Delanee sniffled and buried her face in the soft fur of the large cat's neck. Purring rumbles vibrated against her cheek. If Delanee had ever decided to bond on her own, she would have been surrounded by her family's support and love, as Cia had been while bonding with Izia. Now, all she could hope to do was mitigate some of the trauma of the experience from the lynxia.

"*Dsi pry'jesh zhatek mie?*" Will you accept my bond? She whispered the vital question. One Ryan had deserved to be asked, and one she would not neglect for this moment. The request was punctuated by a faint flow of her beast master talent. A physiological knock.

The lynxia growled, and the connection singed through Delanee's veins. If anyone had been watching, they would have witnessed the astounding phenomenon of the bond flaring into existence. The cat's eye flashed Delanee's golden shade while Delanee's transitioned into a beautiful pale gray-green of the cat's irises. In a blink, the colors returned to their original hue.

I would very much like to be free of this metal room. A soft, feminine voice filtered into Delanee's mind.

Me as well, Delanee admitted.

Then, allow us to leave.

Delanee smoothed a hand over the top of the cat's head and around her ears. *I'm afraid we are locked inside, and I don't have a key. What should I call you?*

I have never been named.

Do you have a preference?

The cat pushed her head into Delanee's shoulder and rubbed. *Something beautiful, for I am beautiful.*

Well, Delanee couldn't argue with the statement. The cat had a thick, long tail and tufted ears in slate gray. Healthy, defined muscle tone rippled beneath white fur adorned with ghostly gray spots.

How did they capture you?

Stole me from my home in the middle of the night.

Delanee considered the response. *From an alpha's home or a forest home?*

An alpha. My mother and father are bonded to a couple. I was of their first litter.

How long ago?

Almost a year.

Young then. Cubs to eventually be paired with a beast master remained with their host family and parents for two years before they were registered as bondable. This feline was unregistered. Old enough to survive without parents, but still learning the appropriate social queues. Which would now fall to Delanee and her family. The traffickers had done their research, ensuring the host family could only describe the feline, as no registration number would have been inked into her ear yet. The news of a Ruthenarc lynxia in Cairo would have eventually spread, and someone from Ruthenia would have investigated. Perhaps the House of Whoever had enough political clout not to fear any repercussions of such an investigation.

Kossa, Delanee tested out for a name.

Kossa is regal. A queen's name. I accept.

If the situation were different, Delanee would have laughed. But they were still prisoners. A lethal, foreign force was on her homeland's soil.

We're going to have to pretend to get out of this cage. Can you do that? Can you pretend?

I will do what I must to help us be free.

All right. Delanee could do this. She straightened, ignoring the rolling in her stomach, and let her hands drop from Kossa. She sagged against the bars at her back. "Hey," she croaked and then tried again, louder. "Hey!"

The warehouse descended into silence. Everyone's attention shifted to her.

Pretending to be too weak to do much more than slouch into the bars, not too far from the truth, Delanee waved a limp hand at Kossa. "I did what you asked."

Kaliya inched closer to the cage. "You have tamed the wild cat?"

"She was never wild," Delanee said before she could stop her response. She cleared her throat. "I have calmed her, yes."

Kaliya's eyes slitted in suspicion. "She will not bite?"

"No," Delanee said. *Do not bite her when she attempts to touch you.*

You ask me to suffer.

Delanee kept from rolling her eyes. *The woman will only pet you. No suffering.*

Kossa's tail flicked hard. *I do not want her to pet me, so I will suffer.*

Well, how could Delanee argue with that logic? Kaliya stuck her hand through the bars, chin lifted, while her husband sputtered in their language.

"Come to me, cat," Kaliya ordered.

"She only knows Ruthenian," Delanee said.

Kaliya tsked and lifted her chin. "Such a barbaric language. She will learn Cairoen."

Delanee kept her mouth closed. Kossa didn't budge as Kaliya stroked the top of her head. The feline growled low, but the sound must have been mistaken for a happy one because Kaliya beamed a proud smile at her husband.

"She is happy of me," Kaliya said, stepping back. "I will have her now."

Hedleston remained quiet during the exchange. He stared at Delanee. "You said the cat couldn't be tamed."

"It's wrong," Delanee said.

Hedleston shoved a hand into his pocket. "Ah. Wrong, not impossible. I see." He watched both her and Kossa, and then edged around to the front of the cage.

Move to where the man is going and sit and wait, Delanee instructed Kossa. She said the same aloud in Ruthenian for the benefit of those around.

Kossa's tail swished along the cement floor. She stood, stretched, her thick claws flashing before retracting. She moved at a slow pace to the front of the cage. Sat. Lifted a paw, licked, and then ran her tongue along her mouth, showing off her thick canines. Hedleston watched, his hand with the key frozen halfway to the lock.

"The cat is under control, right?" he asked.

Delanee swallowed against a new wave of queasiness. How would she manage to get out even if she and Kossa pulled off the impossible? "Yes."

The hopelessness of their situation became very clear as she glanced around again. Even if she managed to escape the cage with Kossa, where were they supposed to go? They couldn't take on a guardian, a contingent of Cairoen Sentinels, or their... owners? Leaders? Delanee didn't understand the relationship between Cairo Houses and those indentured to them. Too many obstacles were between her and freedom. While she could possibly get Kossa safely out, what then? The cat was hers to care for and to protect.

Wait, Delanee ordered along the bond.

I am doing what you asked.

No, I changed my mind.

Kossa turned her head, looked at Delanee, and hissed. *I am not a puppet.* Her ears twitched, and she growled low in her throat.

We can't escape the way I planned. We're safest in the cage, for now.

How is this right?

My mate is coming for us.

Kossa flicked her tail, crouched low in front of the door, and growled. She swiped at the bars, shaking the door on the hinges.

Hedleston leaped backward, palming the key. "What is this? What's going on?"

In response, Delanee twisted and heaved, gagging on bile.

Disgust sounded behind her, followed by a loud rap of metal against the bars. "She never had control of the cat. She lied!"

The arguing picked up force again. Delanee sagged back against the bars, any energy she'd managed to draw forth from the adrenaline rush quickly fading.

I don't know if I can stay conscious for much longer, she admitted to Kossa.

Kossa bounded over to her and laid across her lap. *I will keep you safe.*

No, Delanee immediately objected. *If you get the chance to escape, go. I will find you.*

Kossa licked a rough tongue beneath Delanee's chin, cleaning off the nasty drool and stomach acid left behind. *Silly alpha. I will go nowhere while you are in danger.*

Delanee didn't have the strength to argue, even in her own mind. She wrapped her arms around the cat, thankful for the companionship, and succumbed to the darkness edging her vision.

Twenty-Nine

Ryan accepted the scope Katria Blackbain handed over to him. She swiped wisps of black hair from her face, her vivid blue eyes aglow with excitement and humor.

"You'd think they would have bought a new warehouse after we raided," she said, shifting over to the rifle case laid out next to her on the flat roof.

Ryan adjusted the focus for his vision. "It has been a couple of years, and the ownership *did* change hands."

"But not the building."

"No, they didn't purchase a new building, apparently they just sold it to another Alliance member." Ryan pressed the button on the MagnaCom secured at his hip. "Scythian, what does Alstair see?"

"*No ground movement,*" came Dominik's deep voice across the airwaves.

"Raiventon?" Ryan asked.

"*I'm inside,*" Kevin whispered across the link. "*At least fifty Cairoen Sentinels.*"

Not the best news, but considering the last kidnapping done years ago by the group within this very same building had been conducted with Sentinels made it unsurprising. Ryan glanced at Katria. "Can you see inside from here?"

"No. I handle any strays," she said, flashing a dangerous smile.

Ryan quickly assessed the situation. He had Wolvenguard's three wolves, Donovan's wolf, two interceptors, a raptor, and a sharpshooter. Of course, the rest of the team had come along and knew how to shoot and fight, but Ryan didn't want the conflict to reach such critical heights. He wanted a clean extraction and a peaceful surrender.

"What about Delanee, can you see her?" Ryan asked into the com unit.

"*Affirmative. She's in a cage with...*" Kevin's words faded and a whispered curse cut across the line.

Ryan tensed. He hadn't sensed anything from Delanee for almost a half hour. Prior to that, an alarming flood of anxiety and fear had sent him to his knees. Deklan had caught him before he'd face-planted and helped him breathe through the worst and identify what didn't belong to him to separate himself enough to continue functioning.

"*With what?*" Deklan asked at the same time as Dominik.

"*The largest cat I've seen in my life,*" Kevin replied.

Oh no. Ryan had to fight against the urge to immediately climb down from the roof and get to his wife. "What is the cat doing?" Ryan asked.

"*It's lying across her lap. It seems to be protecting her,*" Kevin answered. "*The Sentinels are relaxed, not on alert.*"

Ryan considered the situation. "Kynhaven?"

"*Is there a way to get Miss Ralston—*"

"Voklane," Ryan cut in.

Mason's throat clearing came over the line. "*Right. Is there a way to get Mrs. Voklane from the enclosure without going through the Sentinels?*"

"*Negative,*" Kevin answered.

"Do you recognize anyone in there?" Ryan asked.

"*Negative. I'm not much on the social scene. Maybe you, Sean, or Mason will.*"

"*Not me*," Mason chimed in.

"*I only go to anything social when forced*," Sean said.

"*And even then, he doesn't engage much*," Katria said, her voice an odd echo with her being so close.

Ryan maintained his patience and waited until the line quieted. "Someone from Sziveria is present, then?"

"*Oh*," Kevin said, "*yes. There is a man dressed in Sziverian guardian style and hair. He has a gun. The others are definitely from Cairo and appear to be unarmed.*"

"Delanee will know who it is," Ryan said.

"*That could make things more difficult*," Sean's static-laced voice said across the line.

"*If he eliminates Miss—Mrs. Voklane before he flees, she won't be able to identify him*," Mason said, his tone grim.

"*That's not going to happen*," Deklan growled.

"No, it's not," Ryan agreed, maintaining calm. "But we have to be sure Delanee's safety is guaranteed when we make our first move."

With Mason's assistance, they formed a plan. Ryan climbed off the roof using an access ladder. Mason waited at the bottom to take his place beside Katria and continue coordinating the efforts from an elevated position. Ryan shielded his eyes and tried to find the falcon soaring above.

"Incredible," he muttered when he failed to spot the predator against the bright blue sky.

There were a few kinks in his plan. Such as how to protect Delanee once she was rescued. But that was a problem for *after*. After he had her back in his arms. After he had her home.

Sean stood waiting around a corner in the shadow of another towering warehouse, a medical bag slung over his shoulder. They'd debated having Wolvenguard's medical scientist assist, but Sean was equally qualified. And since the operation was technically under Ryan's command, his team sufficed. Ryan didn't anticipate anyone needing medical treatment besides Delanee. Not if all went according to plan.

They met Deklan and Cia at a now unguarded side door. The Sentinel lay sprawled just outside the door, his black uniform with bright red markings unmistakable in origin. Beside Deklan, the wolves licked their muzzles, their muscles quivering in anticipation. Their exceptional training shone through as they ignored the unconscious stranger, their attention rapt on their master. Kevin ushered them inside quickly, leading them to a dark alcove off the main floor. Box-like offices were built nearby, forming a hallway of sorts, with storage space constructed above them. The space between the offices was dusty and poorly illuminated by the high windows and few lit lanterns. They all crowded into one corridor. The low hum of conversation was broken by a loud bang of metal against metal.

"There's a woman," Kevin whispered, "she's been trying to awaken Miss Ralston."

"Voklane," Ryan corrected.

"How about we just call her Delanee," Cia suggested softly. "How's that work for everyone? Good? Great."

"There's been no movement from the cage," Kevin continued. "We'll have to move fast and secure her. Her being unconscious might be a problem. She can't hide from harm if whoever it is out there decides to use his gun before he takes off."

"I'm hoping he'll be too focused on self-preservation now to worry about what might happen to him later," Ryan uttered.

"That would be ideal," Kevin agreed.

Ryan flattened himself against a wall and peered around the edge. The contingent of Sentinels was indeed relaxed.

Their signature knives were at their hips, but no other weapons appeared to be on them. A woman in red slammed a metal rod against the bars again and appeared to rant at a short man at her side. He motioned at the cage, his voice rising with each spoken word. Ryan searched around them for the supposed guardian.

"I don't see the guardian," Ryan said softly.

"He's pacing behind the cage," Kevin said.

Indeed, the man was dressed as a guardian should be. In fact, Ryan bet the man had arrived in an issued Ariot, and his HCES jacket was slung over the seat. "Hedleston," Ryan muttered.

"You know him?" Kevin asked.

Ryan glanced at Kevin, then Sean. "Primary Guardian Hedleston. He's the First Prefect for the MagnaRail Avenue HCES."

Sean hissed a curse. "How in the arctic do they keep getting these high-ranking guardians on their side? What are they promising?"

"We'll learn soon enough." Ryan kept his voice pitched low. "He can't be allowed to see me."

Deklan wrapped a hand around Ryan's shoulder and squeezed. "Don't worry. He won't notice much of anything except the nearest escape route."

Kevin pulled Cia to the back of the narrow hallway. Their conversation was near silent, conducted by mostly using an abridged version of signing the team utilized when communication had to be stealthy. Since Cia was fluent in full Atlantic sign language, she followed along, nodding and adding a few quick and deliberate motions of her own. Ryan knew enough to catch the meaning of the conversation. Kevin wanted to ensure Cia understood how the Sentinels fought with their knives.

Cia returned to Deklan's side. One of the wolves, Izia, separated from the small pack and sat beside her. Deklan rubbed a hand along her back and leaned in close, kissing her temple. She smiled up at him, love shining in her gaze.

The simple intimacy had Ryan looking away. Yet he could not stop himself from wondering if he and Delanee would ever reach such trust between them. Yes, Delanee had bonded with him, but the act hadn't been from her heart. They had time to forge something greater if they wished. He was shocked to learn he did, in fact, want love from the adventurous beast master. He wanted everything from her because she was *everything* to him. A confession he wished he'd made before he dropped her off at the paper this morning. Standing there, looking at her cage, containing the fury igniting in his blood, he hoped she never doubted his coming for her.

"Might want to calm down there," Donovan whispered behind him.

Ryan blinked and glanced down at himself. A faint white haze surrounded him. He cursed and shook out his arms. "Sorry."

Donovan patted his shoulder. "Interesting manifestation. I can't say I've seen it before in anyone but you or your daughter."

Ryan frowned and asked before he could stop himself, "Not even in Ruthenia?"

Donovan shook his head and looked at Deklan. "No, not even there. You?"

Deklan shook his head, too, but remained silent.

Was it possible whatever talent he held had died out? Or perhaps never existed because he, and others like him, had been trapped so many centuries ago? He often chose not to think about his actual age in reality or the very inhuman way he'd come into existence, and now certainly wasn't the time to contemplate his bizarre past.

"What are you?" Donovan asked quietly enough to keep the question private.

Ryan shrugged. "I don't know."

Donovan patted his shoulder again. "Welcome to the club. I'm not quite sure what I am, either."

Ryan drew his brows together. "You're not a beast master?"

Donovan's smile didn't show his teeth. "I'm a bit more."

Well, all right, then. Delanee hadn't been trying to make him feel better when she'd said her family was full of powerful Gen-Heirs. He sought out her cage again and tried to find any hint of their bond within himself. Only silence met his efforts. He needed to touch her. To verify the strength of her heartbeat beneath his palm.

"Is everyone ready?" he asked the group and into the MagnaCom unit.

Hushed confirmations sounded.

Ryan took a centering breath. "Good. Let's go."

THIRTY

Comfortable softness surrounding her awoke Delanee. On a gasp, she launched herself upward, her hands touching every inch of the blanket pooled in her lap and around her hips. She blinked, taking in her surroundings, her heart pounding a painful rhythm.

"Shh, you're okay. You're safe," a calm, familiar male voice said to her left. Gentle fingers brushed along her curls. "Delanee, look at me."

Swallowing against the acrid dryness in her mouth, she slowly turned. Ryan sat against pillows, a sleeping Inara on his chest and a huge cat curled against his left side. Kossa's fluffy tail twitched and flicked over his knees. Her head lay on his stomach beneath Inara's feet, hiding the baby's little toes in fur.

"It wasn't a dream," she half croaked, half whispered.

"I'm afraid not," Ryan said softly.

"I'm disgusting. I need a shower," she blurted.

"I know. Your father and Sean said you'd request one the second you woke up. Apparently, they both have experience with how Ruthenian's react to sedatives." He brushed her curls behind her ear. "I would have bathed you if I had a tub, but I don't. I considered the pool."

She decided to focus on her condition and not... everything else. At least for now. One thing at a time. "I can't believe you laid me in bed still wearing these nasty clothes."

When she went to throw off the blankets and leave the bed, he gently grabbed her arm. "Wait, let me lay Inara down, and I'll help you."

"I can do it myself."

"Please."

She swallowed and nodded. "All right."

Ryan eased out of bed, cuddling Inara to his shoulder. Kossa grumbled and rolled into the warm spot he left behind. Without realizing, Delanee stroked her fingers through the silky fur along the lynxia's flank.

You were right, the cat hummed through her mind. *We were rescued.*

I'm sorry I missed it.

Your mate is very gifted.

Delanee watched as Ryan carefully transferred their sleeping daughter to her crib. Her little fists quivered, and when she went to fuss, he popped a pacifier into her mouth. She took several quick pulls on the binky and settled. He brushed the baby fine curls from her forehead. Despite all the turmoil rolling around inside her, Delanee's heart almost swelled straight out of her chest.

He really is, she agreed.

Kossa licked her paw and purred a loud, rolling vibration of sound. The gentle rumble soothed Delanee on a level that let her breathe a little easier. A reaction she didn't want to contemplate now. Sniffling, she allowed Ryan to help her from the bed. Her legs wobbled, and she realized she wouldn't have been able to do much on her own even if she had wanted to. Ryan helped her shuffle to the bathroom, one frustratingly slow step at a time. Nausea slammed into her, and she gurgled in alarm. Ryan swept her into his arms and made a frantic rush for the toilet, lifting the seat and getting her into position the second her stomach rebelled. Not that anything was left, but she heaved, choked, and drooled all the same.

Once the spasms in her stomach ceased, she clutched at the toilet bowl, weakness reducing her to a puddle of herself, and burst into tears. The rush of water hitting tile filled the bathroom. Ryan gently lifted her from the floor and removed the filthy clothes from her body. He adjusted the shower head to flow over the bench and set her down. A toothbrush overflowing with paste was pressed into her hand.

"You're g-getting all w-wet," she chattered, her body shivering under the heated water as she clutched the brush.

"I won't melt, I promise."

The woodsy scent of his soap surrounded her. While she managed to brush her teeth slowly, he tenderly worked the suds into her hair, over her throat, and along all her limbs in a clinical fashion, cleaning every inch of her. Delanee's focus fell to his bare feet. Water plastered the legs of his sleep pants to his ankles. He grabbed the removable shower head and rinsed her.

"How did you rescue me?" she asked when he turned off the water.

He slipped out of the shower, grabbing two towels. "Very calculated. Scythian waited outside with Alstair to follow Hedleston. We didn't want to alert him that we knew of his presence."

She accepted a towel and pressed it to her face. He used the other one to squeeze out the water from her hair. "You recognized him?"

"Yes. I know all the First Prefects in this town. He wasn't aware of our relationship?"

Delanee shook her head and dropped the towel to cover her torso, tucking it under her arms. "No, he had no idea."

"Good." He helped her stand, tossing the damp towel on the shower floor and then helping her to wrap hers around her still trembling body. "Wolvenguard sent his female wolf...."

"Neva," Delanee supplied.

"Yes, Neva, to guard you. The second she appeared, chaos erupted. The younger wolf...."

Delanee couldn't help but smile. "Nikita."

"Yes, that one, he treated it like a game and started randomly chasing Sentinels around the warehouse. Izia and Lucianna cornered the stragglers and subdued them while Wolvenguard and Raiventon handled the others. It was interesting. And noisy."

"Wow, I'm kind of sad I missed all that. What about the Cairoen couple?"

"I questioned them. Not much we can do at this point without creating an international incident. I obtained the information I needed."

Delanee stilled and met his calm stare. "In front of... everyone?"

"Yes."

She clutched at the towel. "And how did that go?"

Ryan shrugged and guided her into the bedroom. "Someone here in Sziveria learned the woman, a house mother over a Sentinel unit, was desperate to get a Ruthenarc lynxia. She'd seen a Ruthenian dignitary with one almost a year ago. After discovering Ruthenia doesn't allow them to be given to anyone except Ruthenian beast masters, she tried to find someone willing to steal one for her. Then she learned they were pretty much feral *without* a beast master, and so began a quest trying to figure out how to convince a beast master to tame one for her."

"And someone here in Sziveria approached her?" Delanee asked, sitting on the edge of the mattress.

"Correct. In exchange for the use of fifty Sentinels, they would get her the cat she wanted." Ryan went to the dresser and pulled out a lounge set and a new pair of pants for himself. He quickly changed before bringing the clothes to her. "I think you know the rest."

"How did everyone react?" She pulled the soft bamboo silk blend from his grasp, wondering if she'd ever wear her own clothes again when she had nowhere to be except their living room. Probably not.

Ryan took the clothing from her hands and set it somewhere on the bed. He crouched before her, bracketing his arms on either side of her thighs, causing the mattress to dip her closer to him. "How are you, Delanee?"

The easy path would be to say she was fine. Everything was fine. Being forced to bond with the giant cat lying behind her was fine. Being drugged and kidnapped hadn't made her feel vulnerable in a way she had never imagined possible. Not with the strength of her family. A shield she once considered impenetrable. But now the illusion had been shattered. Though she *could* act like none of the awful occurrences mattered. She found herself really, really wanting to pretend she wasn't a complete mess inside.

Ryan patiently waited. He didn't force her to answer. He watched her, his gaze full of... love. The emotion flared across their bond and drowned out all the negative anxiety trying to overcome her. A tear escaped, sliding down her cheek and dripping off her jaw. He didn't brush it away, just continued to watch her in that silent, calm manner of his. All the composure she had managed to conjure in the shower evaporated. Poof. Gone. The safety of his love provided the sense of security she needed to be honest with not only herself but also with him.

"I'm really scared," she whispered. More tears raced down her cheeks.

Ryan shifted his weight onto his knees and swiped his thumbs beneath her eyes. He kept her cheeks cupped gently in his hands. "They won't get the opportunity again."

Delanee sniffled and wrapped her hands around his wrists. The towel sagged to her waist. Chilled air beaded her nipples and caused goosebumps to spread across her skin. She ignored both and continued to meet his concerned stare. "I'm not worried about that."

"No?"

She shook her head and sniffled again.

"Ah," he whispered, his gaze shifting to look over her shoulder before returning. "The cat, then. What is her name?"

"Kossa," Delanee said softly.

"Your tattoo hinted at how a lynxia looked. I was unprepared for how stunning Kossa truly is," Ryan said.

"They're unique in all the world," Delanee admitted. "Much like the wolves."

"And why are you scared?" He gently urged her to the edge of the bed until he knelt between her parted thighs.

The temptation to throw away the towel, lay back, and allow him to drive away all her fears and anxiety with pleasure had her hand dropping to the plush fabric. Ryan stilled her efforts, lacing his fingers through hers and bringing them to his chest.

"Why?" he asked tenderly.

Beneath her palm, his heart beat a steady, comforting rhythm. Her fingers flexed into the soft fabric covering the supple muscles of his chest. Saying she never wanted the responsibility or the animal that was her birthright seemed wrong with Kossa lying not feet from her. Whether she wanted the feline or not no longer mattered. Kossa was with her until one of them left the earth.

"You didn't ask for any of this," she whispered, a fresh tear sliding down her cheek. "A bonding. A cat attached to your wife."

Ryan smoothed his hand over hers to her wrist and squeezed. "I could argue the same for you."

Delanee shook her head and leaned forward until she rested against his chest. He hugged her, his fingers tracing the line of her spine. "I, at least, knew I had the potential, even if I never expected to use it. I should have shared it with you, and I'm sorry. Now you're stuck with both of us."

Subtle pressure on her shoulders urged her back enough to meet his pale gaze. He brushed curls from her forehead and kissed her. "I never expected life with you to be anything less than an adventure. You are not disappointing my expectations," he said, smiling.

"We have a giant cat," she whispered.

Ryan took a deep breath. "We do."

His acceptance unraveled a knot in her chest. They were in this together. She didn't have to navigate her weird talent alone. Her brothers may have accepted their genetic inheritance, but Delanee had been happy leaving hers behind. Growing up in a country where being gifted did *not* include an animal bond, she had so carefully crafted what she presumed would be her ideal future. All of it had come apart at the seams. Some because the man in front of her had changed her perception of what a relationship meant. And others because the choice had been taken from her. Either way, the imaginary life she'd fantasized about no longer existed, and Ryan had become a shelter in her personal storm.

Delanee launched herself at him, wrapping her arms around his neck and burying her face in the warmth of his throat. His scent invaded her senses, and his strength enfolded her. He hugged her tight to his chest. One palm pressed flat between her shoulders, and his other hand gripped her hip.

"I love you," he whispered into her ear, his fingers burying into her damp hair at the nape of her neck.

Gasping, Delanee leaned back and stared at him. "You do?"

He leaned close until their noses touched. "So much it hurts."

A better kind of tears stung her eyes as happiness burst free inside her. She couldn't stop herself from kissing him. The need to seal those adoring words with another type of intimacy too much to ignore. His lips parted immediately for her, his tongue sliding to tangle along hers. Delanee struggled to get closer, the towel a lump of wadded fabric between them.

He pulled his mouth free and rained kisses along her jaw. "We can't."

"Sure we can. I'm feeling a lot better." *So, so much better.*

"No," he said, his tongue licking a heated path down her throat.

"I'll beg," she moaned, scooting so far to the edge of the bed he had to wrap a hand under her butt to keep her from falling.

"As much as I want to hear that, we can't because your entire family is here."

Delanee blinked and sat back. "Here? As in, in the house?"

Ryan nodded.

She tilted her head and listened. Her family didn't know the meaning of the word *quiet*. Silence just didn't exist in their presence. Muffled sounds she hadn't noticed before became obvious. Dishes clanging together. Voices.

Delanee's grip tightened on his shoulders. "When you say the entire family...."

"Grandmother, parents, brothers, sisters, in-laws, and the littles. They're all here. My greenhouse has become an animal sanctuary. Kossa refused to be in the same space as the wolves."

They're obnoxious, the wolves. Always with the barking and the mouth-breathing. Not for me, Kossa purred through her mind.

Delanee looked over her shoulder and the lounging feline. *Two of my brothers and my father have wolves. You'll have to accept them at some point.*

Her eyes opened to the barest of slits. *I will not.*

"Great, I'm arguing with a cat," she muttered.

Ryan chuckled. "If her behavior has been any indication, I think she'll be content to stay home when you go to work."

Delanee took a centering breath. "I hope so."

"And if not," he said, shrugging, "I don't think she'll be a burden at your desk."

Delanee chewed on her bottom lip. "That depends on how cat-ish she's feeling. If she pounces all over everyone's desks, that could be a problem."

He laughed. "Okay, that's true. We'll figure it out."

Delanee slid her fingers into the short hair at the back of his head and kissed him again, not caring about the potential audience beyond their bedroom door. She opened her mouth, satisfied when he did the same, and accepted the deeper kiss she craved. Their lips mashed together, their tongues tangled and explored, and fire slid through her veins. She craved his touch and desperately wanted to feel the weight of his body moving over her. To get lost in sensation and allow them to focus only on each other for a sliver of time. Didn't they deserve the reprieve?

A heavy knock vibrated the door.

Apparently not. Delanee growled out her disappointment. Ryan pulled free of her embrace.

"Get dressed. I'll see whose impatience could no longer be contained."

Rising, Delanee grabbed the clothes he'd tossed behind her and stalked to the bathroom. Kossa hopped off the bed and followed. She padded across the tile and into the closet. Delanee stepped into the pants and drew the drawstring tight. Pulling the shirt on, she joined Kossa in the huge closet and discovered that Ryan had set up a nook for the cat. Two bowls were set on a rug, one with water, the other empty, and another thick rug lay not too far away. The gesture was nice, but Delanee figured Kossa would spend most nights on their bed and much of her days in the greenhouse. They'd need to plant some sturdy trees for enrichment and plan regular visits to her parent's forested property. Delanee took a deep breath. She could handle the changes. She could. She *would*.

When she returned to the bedroom, she found her husband had been replaced with her younger brother. Donovan sat in the rocking chair, a sleeping Inara cuddled in his arms.

"She was fussing a bit. Ryan said it was okay for me to hold her," he whispered.

When he looked up at Delanee, genuine happiness shone in his gaze, and her heart clenched. Slowly, she sat on the floor at his feet, not wanting to break whatever peace he'd managed to find.

"She's so... perfect," he said.

Delanee nodded. "She is."

"And you get to be her mother."

"I do."

Kossa ambled from the bathroom, her long, thick tail flicking. She sat next to Delanee, lifting a paw to lick, and then suddenly jerked around to bathe her back while fur twitched and spasmed frantically.

"Whoa," Donovan said, eyes wide. "That's a big cat."

"Says the man with a giant wolf," Delanee quipped.

Donovan used his toes to rock the chair gently. Inara pursed her lips and flared her nostrils but stayed asleep, snuggling against his chest. Her brother pressed his big index finger against her small palm, smiling the sweetest smile Delanee had ever seen him give when the baby gripped his finger tight.

Kossa headbutted Delanee's arm until she lifted it. The cat laid her body across Delanee's lap, her nose buried in the soft fabric gathered between Delanee's legs, her giant paws kneading Delanee's other thigh. Sharp claws flashed and massaged into her leg, but never enough to cause pain. Delanee petted the silky fur between the feline's fuzzy ears. The loud, vibrating rumble of a happy cat rolled through Delanee.

Donovan laughed in surprise. "That is oddly soothing."

"I know, right?" Delanee joined in the laughter.

They sat quietly, the subtle creak of wood from the rocking and Kossa's purr surrounding them in otherwise comfortable silence. Donovan brushed Inara's curls, stroked her chubby cheek, and watched her sleep.

"She's not the first baby you've held," Delanee said.

"No, but she will be the first to truly understand the responsibility of a power greater than others can fathom. She was born for our family to help raise her," Donovan said softly. "And I get to be her uncle. How lucky am I?"

Delanee smiled, tears blurring her vision. "How lucky is she?"

Donovan chuckled. "That, too." The smile faded from his face, and when he looked up and met her stare, all humor had fled. "How are you, Lanee?"

She dropped her gaze to Kossa, scratching behind her

tufted ears and around her jaw. Kossa rolled her head to give Delanee better access to under her chin. The purring intensified, and affection swelled for the cat. "I'm okay."

"Yeah?"

Delanee nodded. "Yeah, I think so."

"Good. I was worried. When Deklan brought Zhenya to me, I didn't want him."

"But you needed him."

"I did, for multiple reasons, and now I can't imagine my life without him. Your feline will be the same."

Delanee smoothed the fur along Kossa's sleek flank. "And if I had asked you to take her from me?"

"I wouldn't have," he whispered. "You don't understand what that's like for either of you, and you wouldn't allow your beast, as her master, to suffer the fracturing of a bond."

"It's painful then?"

"For the beast master and the beast? Yes, especially if one party is unwilling. Zhenya's situation wasn't as traumatic as it could have been when Deklan forced the bond from his previous master to himself because Zhenya no longer accepted his old master. But the trauma was still there from the actual breaking of the connection."

"And when he came to you?" Delanee asked. No one had been present for Donovan's bonding with Zhenya, only Deklan. The wolf had been too distressed for a ceremony.

"Deklan released him. The hold was tentative anyway. Deklan's max wolf pack is three. Having four was hurting him."

Delanee wanted to ask what had happened to Donovan that taking on a broken wolf had been therapeutic. For them both. But she figured if he ever wanted to share, he would, and until then, she'd support him the only way she knew how, by being his big sister. Sometimes annoying, sometimes supportive. He required both because both were normal, and Delanee had a suspicion he wouldn't share because he didn't want to lose *his* normal. She would respect that.

"I guess I need to go out and show everyone I'm not going crazy," she sighed.

"Yeah, I'm surprised Ma hasn't barged in here. She's probably the most anxious of everyone, next to Deklan."

Delanee raised a brow. "Not *Ahty*?"

"*Ahty* said he raised a strong daughter and that you're fine. He was certain of it enough to hang out on the couch and read a book while everyone else paced and argued about when to break down the door to your room."

Delanee laughed. "I love our father. So much."

She rolled Kossa from her thighs. The cat grumbled a throaty meow and jumped onto the bed as Delanee stood. She adjusted her pants, grimacing at the wisps of cat hair floating around. Ryan would not appreciate the layer of fur about to cover absolutely everything.

"I'm going to stay here," Donovan said, continuing to rock the infant.

Delanee smoothed a knuckle down Inara's cheek and smiled. "All right."

A wall of noise met Delanee the second she opened the bedroom door. She blinked and carefully closed it behind her, not wanting to awaken Inara. After creeping down the hall, she tested the waters by poking her head around the corner of the entryway. At least half her family crowded in the kitchen and dining nook, which meant the rest of the Ralston clan occupied the living room. Deklan perched on a barstool, Cia wrapped in his arms, her back to his front. She laughed at something Dalila's husband, Torian, said. Their son Rowen was asleep, his head on Torian's shoulder, where a puddle of drool darkened the fabric beneath his mouth. The commotion didn't faze the toddler one bit.

Deklan noticed her first. He hopped up, making Cia

squeal in alarm. Cia moved from the circle of his arms before he could run her over in his haste to get to Delanee. He yanked her into a tight hug.

"You scared all of us," he whispered, then pulled back and cupped her cheeks in his hands. His eyes, the same shade as their mother's, searched hers. "Are you okay?"

Delanee wrapped her hands around his leather-covered wrists and squeezed. "I'm fine. I promise."

He searched her gaze, then nodded and released her. "Make sure you go see the wolves, Neva especially. I haven't seen her that upset in a long time."

"I will."

He nodded and glanced at the archway to the hall. "Where's Donovan?"

"With Inara."

Deklan kissed her temple. "I'm glad you're okay."

"I am, thank you."

He squeezed her arm and then brushed past her, heading to the bedroom. Delanee contemplated following and eavesdropping, but someone new noticed her, and the process of assuring the next sibling she was fine and not going to break apart into a million shattered pieces started over again. A barrage she accepted with a thankful heart because not even one of her family members was willing to let her endure a traumatic event alone.

She worked her way into the living room, where her father sat, an ankle braced on his knee, a book resting on his leg. Reading glasses were perched on his nose. His long hair fell in a braid over his shoulder, the late evening light glinting off the silver strands throughout the dark red. Ryan was beside him, quietly talking to her mother. Drayke sat on the coffee table across from them. They all looked up when she stopped in front of her father.

Markus slowly closed the book and removed the glasses. "There you are, *mie duceraka*."

He held his arms open, and she didn't hesitate to climb onto his lap, laying her head on his strong shoulder. He hugged her tight, rocking gently, and kissed her head.

"*Tsa drago'va dsi, Ahtyshka*," I love you, Father, she whispered, wrapping her arms around his big chest. "Thank you for believing in me."

Her father rested his cheek on top of her head. "How could I doubt my own blood? Or your mother's, for that matter."

Bella leaned forward. "Our children aren't invincible, Markus."

"But they are ours, are they not, *krahet'sna*?" he asked, his voice a deep rumble in her ear.

While she couldn't see her mother, Delanee imagined the eyeroll accompanying Bella's answering scoff. "What am I going to do with you?"

"Hopefully, the same thing you have been doing for thirty-four years," Markus answered, chuckling.

Delanee looked up enough to see Ryan watching her with concern. The warmth of his love continued to hum through her veins. She stretched her hand toward him, pleased when he slid his palm along hers and entwined their fingers.

The whole family crowded into the living room. All the kids piled onto the couch, trying to cram between the adults and fit onto whatever lap would take them, including Delanee's. Even Ava and Evelyn were present, wearing ludicrous outfits, their hair styled high and weighed down with so many baubles, Delanee didn't know how they kept their heads upright. They hovered around Madeleine. Her poor grandmother. Delanee couldn't stop a snicker from escaping.

"This is good, laughing already," Markus said.

"Look at them," Delanee said, motioning at the women with her free hand. "They're ridiculous."

"*Dak*," Markus agreed. "They are hoping your *baki* can find them husbands. But they have not left, and they made food for everyone."

Delanee smiled. "They're family, too."

Ryan squeezed her hand, and she settled into the chaos of her family, allowing their love and concern to begin to heal the distress of her abduction.

THIRTY-ONE

LATE IN THE EVENING, the last family member willing to leave walked out the front door. Darius and Donovan both asked to stay, taking the two guest rooms. Darius disappeared into the room Delanee had once occupied, and Donovan took the smaller room, which would eventually become Inara's bedroom. Ryan hadn't made much progress in decorating, but a few feminine touches had been added, thanks to the twins. A pale orange blanket with little white knitted flowers covered the bed, and matching lace curtains hung from the window. A large rug in the shape of a flower took up the center of the floor. Zhenya and Donovan both looked a little out of place.

"You don't have to stay," Delanee felt the need to point out. Again.

"I went to work with Darius this morning. He's my ride home," Donovan said with a sideways grin. Then he sobered. "But even if he weren't, I still would want to be here. The man who kidnapped you is still out there."

"I have Ryan, and now Kossa," Delanee said, lighting a bedside lamp with little glass flowers as the cover. The lamp itself was a round bubble made of swirled glass in pink, green, and pale blue. The glass shade protected the flame and dimmed the light to a comfortable level for resting.

"And your husband's talent of being able to stop someone in their tracks literally is impressive, but he can't do much with that ability alone. If we hadn't agreed, Dominik, Deklan, or Drayke would be here. Just accept you're stuck with your family for a little while."

Delanee sighed. The mention of Ryan's talent made her meet her brother's gaze. "Were they mad when they learned what Ryan could do?"

"There was some tension," Donovan said cautiously. "But Primary Guardian Wintersfall reminded everyone we *all* have done things with our talent that not everyone would approve of or understand. Your husband is in a difficult position. He's been tasked with pretty much ensuring everyone he encounters in a professional capacity is trustworthy enough to not only do their job but be in the presence of those with national secrets. It's a lot for one man to carry. I think Deklan understood that more than everyone else."

Delanee searched her brother's golden gaze and shook her head. "How are you so wise for being only nineteen?"

Donovan went to the narrow bed and sat, resting his hands on his knees. The bedframe groaned from his weight. Zhenya followed, standing between his legs, tongue hanging out and eyes beseeching to be shown affection. Donovan smoothed both hands into the fur beneath the wolf's ears. "It took a lot of courage to use his talent in front of us on that couple. Took even more trust."

Delanee joined him on the bed and waited for Donovan to continue.

"He didn't know we could be trusted, not really. He also had no idea how any of us on whom he's potentially used his talent would react. But he loved you enough to risk it. I respect that, and I think everyone else in the warehouse who witnessed what he's capable of did as well."

Pride filled Delanee, and she bumped her shoulder on his. "I *knew* everyone would accept him."

"But Ryan didn't know. And that he went ahead and used his gift anyway? Yeah, everyone took a deep breath and let that sink in, I think."

"How do you know it was love that made him use his gift and not just wanting the information for Arch Guardian Synintel?" Delanee asked, knowing Ryan's sense of duty may have been mistaken for his affection for her. Not that she doubted his love, not when she'd experienced the emotion along their bond, but her brothers didn't know how seriously he took his covert intelligence position.

Donovan stared at her for a long moment and softly said, "I think you should ask your husband that question."

RYAN RINSED THE LAST DISH, shaking off the water before laying the bowl on the towel he'd spread across the counter. A pile of plates, silverware, and cups were neatly arranged and drying. He'd put them away in the morning. Going to bed with the kitchen a disaster had been a solid *not going to happen*.

Delanee ambled into the kitchen, her hair still an uncombed mess of frizzy curls, his pants and t-shirt hanging from her thin frame. And she was stunning to him. He turned off the water and braced his hands on the counter's edge. She paused when she noticed him watching her, a pretty flush darkening her cheeks.

"What?" she asked when he continued to stare at her, tucking hair behind her ears.

"I'm glad you're home," he said quietly, very aware they weren't alone in the house. Not that much could be heard in the other rooms, which is why Inara still slept in the same space he did.

"Me too." She stopped on the other side of the counter, climbing onto a stool. "You sure you're okay with my brothers staying?"

"I'm surprised only two of them are. I think they drew straws or something," Ryan said, grabbing the soapy washrag he'd used for the dishes and wiping down the counters.

Delanee chuckled, and the sound warmed him. "They might have done *something* but not drawn straws. They're not that civilized."

Ryan laughed and continued washing the marble. "I'm okay with them being here, yes. I don't think anyone will try anything, and if they do, they're more likely to try your apartment or even Deklan's residence. They won't know you're with me, we were very careful. Dominik is staying with your grandmother. Deklan and Lucianna can take care of themselves."

Delanee snorted. "Breaking into Deklan's house would be a mistake I'd pay to see someone attempt."

Ryan tossed the rag back into the sink. The damp fabric landed with a *plop*. Delanee stared at her hands and fiddled with her fingers. Ryan leaned forward, resting his weight on his forearms. "What's wrong?"

She barked a sarcastic laugh. "If that isn't a loaded question."

"Delanee."

She took a deep breath and still wouldn't meet his gaze. "Donovan told me to ask you something."

"All right."

"And I'm working up the courage," she admitted.

Ryan straightened and rounded the counter. "You? Working up the courage to ask a question? Perhaps you aren't as fine as you've been letting everyone believe."

"Ha, ha," she mocked.

Ryan took her cooler fingers between his and urged her from the stool. "You can ask me while we're getting ready for bed."

"Is Inara asleep?"

"Fed, fresh diaper, story read by your sister, Dalila, I think? No, wait, the one who is pregnant," he said, trying to recall which D name belonged to which sister.

"Damira," Delanee supplied. "She will also answer to Mira."

"Like you will answer to Lanee?" he asked, dousing all the lights in the kitchen and making her tag along.

She smiled. "Yes. It was easier for the littles to use shortened versions of our names where possible. Most of them stuck."

"But only within your family?" he asked, noting that the siblings referred to themselves by the full version of their names when introducing or talking about each other.

"Yes. I like my name. I know Damira feels the same. And Donovan vetoed Don immediately, and Dominik hates being called Nik, or Nikkie as we tease."

Darkness encompassed the quiet house. He guided her to the hallway to their room. "Hmm, I'll have to remember that."

She gasped and paused in the middle of the hall, causing his arm to pull tight. "Don't you dare call him either one. He'll know I told you, and he *will* retaliate."

Ryan recalled how all the Ralston siblings seemed to call out one name and one name only when they reached the end of their patience with Delanee. "I'm not afraid of your mother."

"And my father?"

"Maybe," he said, tugging her back into motion.

She laughed. "All my brothers will discover your weakness and plan an attack accordingly. Most of my siblings know Ma's disapproval of anything I do is like a stab straight through my heart."

Inside their room, he checked the fire and lowered the lamp's intensity on his side of the bed, casting the room in heavy shadows. Delanee closed the door and sagged against it before straightening. Kossa lay curled at the foot of the bed, a pale blob of fur against the navy bedspread, her head face down, only the tufts of her ears visible. The tip of her long tail twitched, but otherwise, she made no indication their entrance had disturbed her.

Ryan waited, hoping their comfortable conversation had given Delanee the time she needed to ask whatever it was her brother had felt she needed to ask of him.

"Donovan said you used your talent in front of them because you loved me, not because you wanted to gain information for Arch Guardian Synintel," she said quietly, still hovering near the door. "I asked him how he knew."

Ryan crossed his arms. "And he told you to ask me."

"Yes."

Ryan huffed out a long exhale and sat on the corner of the bed. The vulnerability of using his genetic talent in front of so many—especially those who'd been on the receiving end of his questions and would witness firsthand what he could do—returned. This time, however, it wasn't because she might reject him but rather because she would discover the power she now had over him.

"I only questioned them about you," he said.

She took a step from the door. "What do you mean?"

"I didn't ask if they knew what the Sentinels would be used for. I didn't ask how long the Sentinels were expected to be in our country. I didn't ask if they had contacted anyone except Hedleston. I didn't ask about anything except... you."

"Ryan," she whispered, crossing the room to stand before him. She threaded her fingers into his hair, and he met her stunned gaze. "They're probably already on a ship bound for who knows where just to escape Sziveria."

"I know." The chance to learn information from the source supplying foreign mercenaries to the V Alliance had now evaded him. "You were my only priority."

Her mouth closed over his. No warning, just a sudden, desperate kiss. Ryan wrapped her in his arms, yanking her to his chest. She came without hesitation, climbing onto his lap, her knees bracketing his hips. He cupped her rear in both palms and opened his lips for her questing tongue. She didn't hesitate, kissing him in a manner he wouldn't have considered her capable of prior to tonight. Her innocence and inexperience had transformed into a passionate and confident woman. Ryan was all in for the change. The anticipation of helping her learn new sensual aspects of her nature, and even his own, excited him in a way he never thought possible before her.

"Are you—"

"*Yes,*" she said into his mouth, framing his face between her hands. "I can't say yes enough times. I *need* you."

Ryan glanced at the crib. Inara still slept with her face turned away from the bed. Now that his bedroom was no longer his alone, they would have to add a nursery or move her across the house into her own room. An issue for another time. He returned his focus to his bride, helping her toss away her shirt. Then he stood, supporting her weight on his forearms. She wrapped her arms around his neck, and her bare torso pressed to his chest. Ryan carried her into the bathroom, using his foot to close the door. Not the best, but privacy mattered. He almost continued into the closet. A vertical surface was a vertical surface, even a carpeted floor.

But Delanee tugged at his shirt and squirmed in his arms. The live current of her desire threaded through his veins, further enflaming his own, creating a desperation he needed to appease. For them both. He set her on the counter, his mouth claiming hers in a heated, open-mouthed kiss. Something clattered and fell into the sink. Dense darkness heightened his other senses and made him impatient for the one he didn't have. Sight. He *needed* to see her.

Tearing his mouth free, he patted the wall where he kept matches on a small ledge for the lamps on either side of the huge mirror. His hand bumped the ledge when Delanee yanked his shirt over his head, and he tugged the fabric free. The box rattled to the counter, the matches shaking around inside. He searched the cold surface while Delanee licked and bit at his neck. She tugged at the drawstring, fumbling in the darkness to undo the tie while he did the same, attempting to isolate a match. He leaned around her to grasp the box to strike.

Before he could ignite the stick, Delanee managed to get his pants loose enough to reach inside. Her cool fingers wrapped around his length, and he dropped the match, his hand clenching around the open box. Matches popped out and scattered. She stroked him, her thumb sliding through the moisture gathered at his tip. Her touch glided across sensitive nerve endings and delivered enough pleasure to almost send him to his knees. Cursing, he dropped the box, the need for light forgotten. Another demand rode him far too hard now. He grasped the waist of her pants and pulled. She lifted her butt, and the fabric easily slid free and fell to the floor.

Grasping her thigh in one hand, Ryan reached between her spread legs with his other to find the heart of her. She gasped as his fingers encountered her sensitive flesh, first dipping into the slick heat at her opening and moving higher to tease her swollen nub. He helped her position her leg, grasping her ankle and bracing it on the counter surface. The action changed her balance, and she released her hold on him long enough to brace her other foot. Ryan wished he could see her open to him. Then again, the erotic sight of her feet perched on the ledge, knees wide, butt hanging off the ledge, allowing nothing to be hidden, might be more than he could handle in his current state.

Ryan leaned over her, his mouth seeking hers while he pushed a finger into her tight opening, adding another when he slid in and out easily without causing her discomfort. She rocked beneath him, making desperate little sounds deep in her throat. Her inner muscles clenched and slickened further from his touch. Ryan kept hold of her open thigh to ensure she didn't fall from the counter. He pulled his fingers free and smoothed them up her belly to her breasts, tweaking and caressing her pebbled nipples. Her hips rose against his, her wet heat beckoning him.

Once again, her fingers found him, and she tried to guide him to her opening, but she was too rushed. Ryan stilled and let her learn how they fit together. Her first attempt had his tip slipping high, and her second try went too low. She yelped and squeezed, and he gritted his teeth and forced himself not to take over.

"I'm not doing this right," she whispered, her breath panting heavily between them.

Ryan flexed his hips, pushing his length, still in her control, along her swollen folds. "Try again, but slower."

She took a deep breath and gradually eased him into her body, her hips lifting to take him deeper while he gently rolled his own. Ryan groaned at the sensation of her accepting him. She maintained hold until her hand could no longer fit between them, and he shuddered when he felt her explore their joining, her touch skimming around his girth and touching her stretched flesh.

"I wish I'd lit the match so you could see us," he breathed into her ear.

"Next time," she panted, wrapping her arms around his back.

Knowing there would be many, many more opportunities to explore their sexuality together had him thrusting to the hilt. He pulled out and glided forward again, soon becoming lost in the sensual rhythm they forged. Her nails dug into his back, and her small whimpers turned into outright cries. Her high-pitched moans filled the bathroom, and Ryan drove harder and faster, wanting to hear her scream in pleasure. Beneath him, her body arched and writhed in an attempt to get closer, to take more. Ryan straightened, grabbing both her legs and holding tight while slamming into her, giving her the hard and fast she wordlessly beseeched from him.

She gripped his forearms, her nails biting deep. Her inner muscles fisted around him, and her thighs clenched and quivered in his hold. Her deep, throaty cry echoed off the tile and marble surrounding them. She begged him to keep moving, and Ryan couldn't form the words to tell her that even if one of her brothers burst in, there was no stopping. Soon, any coherency to her words faded into indiscernible wails, her orgasm reaching the height that triggered his. Ryan let go and allowed the pleasure he'd been holding back to consume and pour from his body. Groaning, he held her thighs tight and ground deeper into her, liquid heat spilling free.

Spent, he collapsed on her, and she wrapped him in her arms, her legs sagging to frame his, sweat sticky between them.

"I love you," she whispered, breathless, hugging him tight.

Anxious to see her, Ryan scoured the counter for the discarded matches and box. He lit the lamp and dropped the smoldering stick into the sink. The sudden burst of light made him squint and blink. He straightened enough to see her. Framing her face between both his hands, he met her shy stare. "Say it again."

"I love you," she said softly. "So much."

Through the haze of lust still burning hot within him, her love glowed like a comforting balm. Ryan kissed her and rocked within her, hard and desperate for her all over again. She met his gentle motions, her ankles locking at the base of his spine, her whole body wrapped around him. Ryan braced his hands on the marble beside her and lifted enough to allow him to lengthen his thrusts. She watched him, searching his face and then sliding lower. He followed her gaze down over his shifting muscles to where he moved in measured motions, gliding in and out of her welcoming body.

Breath coming in hard gasps, her eyes widened as she watched their coupling, looking first at him in shock, then back down. Ryan kept a grin of masculine pride to himself. Yeah... he was way turned on and stretching her wide. To show her what that did to her body, he gently slid a finger along her clit. She jolted and cried out in surprise. He'd done this for her the first time he'd taken her, but the attention had been as a distraction to increase her pleasure from her discomfort. Such was not the case now.

"Again?" he asked.

"Stars above, *yes*," she managed between heavy pants.

Ryan worked her nub and kept his thrusts long and slow. Her breathing increased, and she never looked away. And when she reached to take over, he let her, moving his attention to her breasts. While their lovemaking wasn't as frenzied this time, he found it no less erotic. Exploring her body, finding what made her squirm and demand more and what didn't elicit much response at all, delivered a new sense of excitement. He knew each time they came together, new discoveries would be made, and he had never looked forward to the future more than he did at this moment.

Between her touch and his methodical movements, she reached another climax. But Ryan still wasn't done. He gathered her in his arms, turned on the shower, and dragged them both under the water, discovering the stall was his new favorite place in the house. And he intended to make it hers as well.

THIRTY-TWO

RYAN SET a heaping plate of seasoned roasted potatoes in the middle of the breakfast table. Darius made silly faces at Inara, holding a spoonful of yogurt an inch from her laughing mouth. The faint glow of her talent fuzzed the air around her. Neither Darius nor Donovan seemed to care. Donovan read a paper, scooping scrambled eggs like he hadn't eaten in days. Zhenya lay at his feet beneath the table, his eyes so mournful Ryan had to stop himself from tossing the wolf kitchen scraps.

At the stove, Ryan flipped the bacon and stirred more eggs. A plate with potatoes and cut fruit waited for the protein. He'd take the food to Delanee and attempt to awaken her for the second time that morning. She'd roused long enough to prove she could be on top and enjoy the experience before promptly falling back asleep on his chest and refusing to leave the bed when Inara had awoken them with a shout.

Noise from the main part of the house had urged him up with his wide-awake daughter. The two brothers had been in the kitchen trying to figure out where he kept the items to make coffee or tea. They didn't care which one so long as they had some form of caffeine fix. Darius had shoved Donovan out of the way when Ryan had emerged from the hall, Inara on his hip. The oldest Ralston brother had plucked Inara from his arms, spun her around while she squealed in delight, and then stuck his tongue out at Donovan. Ryan had watched the exchange with fascination, not having had any siblings to understand the interaction.

"We won't fight anymore," Darius had said, bouncing Inara in his arms, "if you get on with making us another niece to adore."

"Or don't," Donovan had said while continuing to dig through cupboards, "because gross, I don't need that visual in my brain."

The vision of Delanee pregnant with his babe excited and terrified him. How would they handle another baby, their new relationship, and a huge cat? The lynxia was currently exploring the greenhouse, a space Ryan already knew Delanee would want upgraded to suit the feline better. One of the many changes he'd need to make to the house. Sometime soon, they'd need to pack up Delanee's disaster of a bedroom and move her completely into their home.

"What did Synintel say?" Darius asked, holding a slice of strawberry for Inara. She grabbed the bright red fruit, her eyes nearly crossing to focus before shoving it into her mouth and gumming it with a happy garble.

"Nothing I didn't already know," Ryan admitted.

Kevin had told him of the encounter in Raina's office. The master guardian had immediately called his father-in-law. Much to Ryan's shock, he had learned the young prince of Sziveria was, in fact, the son of the man he'd been working for his whole adult life. The sense of betrayal still stung. Ryan's parents, and by default Ryan, had trusted Henry Edmond with the secret of Ryan's talent. Had trusted the arch guardian to be responsible with the gift Ryan used for the greater good of the country. That Synintel hadn't trusted Ryan in return hurt on a level that still stunned him.

Henry had radioed after Ryan had pulled out the stovetop coffee maker, the beans, and the grinder. Donovan had taken over while Ryan ran to the study to answer the incoming missive. The conversation had been short and to the point, Ryan too agitated to say much to his superior. Henry had imparted the information about Jaiden, swearing Ryan to secrecy. Ryan hadn't mentioned Raiventon had already revealed the secret. Kevin, like Ryan, was a bit disgusted with the entire situation. The only thing that made Ryan feel marginally better was Raina, Henry's own daughter, hadn't learned of the relationship until recently.

"He didn't have any information about Hedleston?" Darius asked, brows raised in surprise.

"Nothing except Hedleston, along with seven others, will be attending the same party tomorrow night."

"And you already knew this?" Donovan asked, flipping the paper to a new page.

"I did and was already planning to attend."

"What sort of party?" Darius asked.

"It's actually a low-key affair, which is why when I noticed the guest list, I opted to attend," Ryan said.

He removed the cooked bacon slices and placed them in a dish with a thin towel to soak up the excess grease. He then added raw slices to the skillet. After washing his hands, he set the plate on the table. The brothers devoured the meat in minutes. Darius popped off a piece of fat that would easily dissolve in Inara's mouth and offered it to her. She leaned forward and took the fragment from him. She munched, then made a shocked O with her mouth and eyes wide.

"Yummy?" Darius asked, offering her another. Her little feet kicked, and she waved her arms, leaning forward, mouth open to take another small piece.

Ryan laughed. "Well, I guess she likes bacon."

"She'll like it more when she has teeth," Darius said, joining in the laughter.

"How do you get into any social gathering you want?" Donovan asked, an elbow propped on the table while he bit into a bacon slice.

"If I haven't been ordered to attend already, I tell Synintel, and he gets me an invitation," Ryan answered.

"The host or hostess doesn't care?"

Ryan shrugged. "They don't usually know."

Darius frowned, setting a few strawberries in front of Inara for her to eat at her leisure. "And they don't notice an uninvited guest?"

Ryan smiled. "If they notice me, I'm not very good at my job."

Surprise and respect flashed across Darius's face. "Nice."

Donovan gave him a skeptical look. "How exactly do you blend? You're over six feet of pale."

Ryan laughed. "I have my ways."

Donovan narrowed his eyes and snapped up the paper. "Mm-hmm."

"It's true," Delanee said through a yawn. She shuffled the rest of the way into the kitchen. A pair of his gray sleep pants and a t-shirt hung from her slender frame. "I smelled coffee. And bacon."

"Your brothers ate what just came off the stove."

She wrapped an arm around his waist and leaned toward the cooking food. The easy comfort of her touch spread warmth through him. "That's mine. I'm laying claim now."

"All of it?" Ryan asked.

"Every slice," she said without humor. "Mine."

Ryan went to the ice drawer, a large insulated drawer with ice to keep goods refrigerated, and pulled out another butcher's wrapped pack of bacon. "I guess I'll be making more."

He scraped the eggs onto a plate and replaced the empty bacon dish. Delanee motioned for Donovan to scoot down the bench. Her hair was a disaster of tangled curls that would require both of them to unknot at this point. But, like yesterday, she didn't care how her family saw her. Donovan pecked a kiss on her cheek, and Darius reached across the table for her hand, squeezing her fingers before returning his attention to Inara.

Using her fingers, she popped a seasoned potato into her mouth. "So, what party do you need to be incognito at?"

Donovan set a plate in front of her, along with a fork, and made a *voila* motion. "Ma raised you to be more civilized than that."

Her gaze found Ryan. Naughty mischief danced in the golden depths of her irises. An unspoken reminder that there was absolutely nothing *civilized* about what had happened in his bathroom last night. Ryan quickly looked away before he embarrassed himself. Her delight at his forced restraint zinged along their bond, making him smile.

"I'm attending the Irondales' annual wine sampler," he said, flipping bacon.

"Ah, an invitation people actually watch their mail for this time of year," Delanee said.

"Have you been?" Ryan asked, picking up the plate he'd begun for her and then pushing the empty one out of the way.

She beamed a smile up at him and grabbed the fork. "Of course, I have. Aside from the Terravine Wintervail party, it's *the event* to cover for the social pages. It's the only party I'll stay long enough to brave drunk people and observe. By the end of the night, I have so much written down that it always takes two days for my editor to help narrow down what should be included in the article. We sell out of that edition every year."

Ryan took a deep breath and maintained her stare. "Hedleston will be there."

Her focus shifted to her plate. "Ah."

"Along with seven others I've been watching closely. This is the first event at which they're all going to be gathered."

"And you don't think that's a coincidence," Darius stated.

"No, I don't," Ryan said.

Delanee forked fluffy eggs onto her utensil and chewed, contemplation pinching her forehead. She pointed the fork in thought. "I'll have to attend, but if Hedleston sees me, he may bolt."

"Your boss knows you were kidnapped. He'll excuse this party if you want," Darius said.

Delanee adjusted the fork's position and pointed it at her oldest brother. "I don't want, thank you very much."

Ryan sighed. "Delanee."

"No. I'm not broken. I'm not even hurt. There's no reason I can't attend the party. No one is going to snatch me from there."

"Just like no one was going to snatch you from work?" Ryan asked.

She flushed and returned to poke at her eggs and potatoes. "Mr. Ingerman went unnoticed because he had been by my office a handful of times."

Ryan removed the bacon from the stove. "His persistence continues to surprise me. Something will need to be done about him."

"Don't worry, it will," Darius said, his smile predatory.

"You still shouldn't attend, Delanee," Donovan said, returning the conversation to its original track. "Your kidnapper may bolt with information your mate could gather, or you could be giving them the opportunity to grab you again. Neither are worth the risk."

"They don't need me anymore," she said, popping a strawberry into her mouth.

"The maniacal woman could still consider the cat to be hers," Ryan said, setting the plate of bacon next to Delanee.

Delanee snorted. "I wish her luck if she tries to take Kossa."

Donovan snickered. "Would teach her a valuable lesson, and maybe she won't attempt to have another one stolen."

"Will Ruthenia require Kossa to be returned?" Delanee asked.

Her question made Ryan pause in laying fresh bacon into the sizzling pan. He glanced at the now quiet table.

"No," Darius answered. "You've bonded. If they discover what happened, and that's a large if, you might have to compensate the breeder, but that will be all. There are enough official witnesses to confirm you had nothing to do with the theft."

"I bet Hedleston won't care I'm present," Delanee said, munching on bacon. Inara pointed and babbled in a demanding manner. "He seemed confident nothing would happen to him and I doubt that mindset has changed."

"I would be inclined to agree," Darius began, "if it were anyone but you. If you were to level an accusation against him, it would be taken very seriously."

"Which I haven't." She placed a small piece of bacon on the highchair for Inara. "And won't unless I'm asked to."

"She may have a point," Ryan conceded, hating the idea of her in a room with so many potential enemies but not wanting to stifle her freedom. "The group's arrogance to date has been one of the only reasons I've managed to make any progress. They think themselves so superior that when they do make mistakes, they don't consider it to be a problem."

"You think she should go?" Darius asked in disbelief.

"No," Ryan said slowly. "I would obviously prefer she stay home. But she won't be in any further danger at the event."

"I'll act like nothing happened," Delanee said, making a clean-slate motion. "And if more than Hedleston behaves in a nervous fashion, it'll only help confirm Ryan's suspicions. Win for everyone. I get my story, and he gets his information."

THE TRANQUIL *SHOOSH* of flowing water and the occasional trill of birdsong created a soothing environment, allowing Delanee to take a deep breath. Darius stood beside her, arms crossed, looking out over the manicured greenhouse. Ryan cut a path through the water, his body sleek, muscles rolling. Kossa lay at the pool's edge, pawing at the ripples formed from Ryan's workout. The bright sun glinted off her pale fur, revealing ghostly spots.

"That's a pretty mark on your mate's back, Lanee," Darius said, bumping their hips together.

"Ha, ha," she mocked. "I didn't ever think a man would wear it."

"I think it looks good," he said softly.

Delanee glanced up at him and noted the seriousness in his expression. "Yeah?"

"Yes. You're very lucky."

Inside, Donovan and Inara napped on the couch, the infant snuggled on her uncle's chest. Delanee had never wished she'd had the gift of drawing more than at that moment. She wished she had a way to capture the memory for Inara and Donovan. In the quiet, Ryan had slipped outside without a word. An internal chaos had been plaguing him all morning, thrumming along their bond, and compelled Delanee to follow. She'd found him doing laps in the pool.

"I'm going to be there tomorrow," Darius said softly.

Delanee raised her brow and angled her stance to see him better. "At the tasting?"

Darius nodded.

"Why? I mean, do you even have an invitation?"

He seemed to hesitate. "I do."

Delanee narrowed her gaze. "Do you or not?"

He took a deep breath. "The lovely Willemina Irondale personally asked me to attend."

"The married Mrs. Willemina Irondale? That one?" Delanee asked, agitated.

"Yes."

"And you said you'd attend?"

"I said I'd think about it."

Delanee sighed. "Darius, you deserve more than a married woman using you."

"I said I'd consider going to her gathering, not gracing her bed, Lanee."

Gaze narrowed on her brother, she considered his behavior and his words. "What is Mrs. Irondale suspected of doing?"

He cut her an amused glance. "Thievery."

"And she still invited you?" Delanee asked, shocked. "Arrogant."

"Very. The case is eerily similar to one *Ahty* and Ma worked decades ago." He made a noise of frustration. "I just haven't been able to find the personal connection yet."

"No relation to the original criminal?" she asked.

"Not that I can find. The woman was a very skilled forger *and* grifter. The cases are fascinating."

"And she's no longer alive?"

Darius shook his head. "No. She died in Glass Fields Correction about a decade ago. No one was even notified of her death outside of the posted reports for all the national publications, as required."

Sziveria required all inmate deaths to be posted, along with the cause. The prisons in the Northern Boundary often had brutal conditions, and without accountability, those environments could lead to many inhumane situations. *Haven City Chronicle* was one of the means of providing the public with the information. From there, anyone could request an inquiry if they had suspicions about a facility.

"Did you ask *Ahty* or Ma about the case?"

"Not yet. I have the file and their notes. I'm going to visit Glass Fields in two days."

"And attend your suspect's party."

"I'm curious. She invited me, I'm assuming, to help prove her innocence."

"You don't suspect the husband?"

Darius ran a hand over his face. "At this point, I believe anything is possible. Man or woman, whoever is pulling off these heists is a logistical genius."

"A Gen-Heir, then," Delanee said softly.

"Yes, but recorded or not? Jermaine Irondale is a financial talent, and Willemina is, as far as anyone knows, gen-common. She's a remarkable socialite, however. By hosting parties and developing friendships with the spouses of Irondale's clients, she's grown his business and carved a place out for them in high society."

"I don't disagree. She set a trend last Wintervail season of wearing silver and blue to all the parties. Silver and blue! Colors usually avoided at all costs because they remind us of the coming colorless season. But she glittered and sparkled, and after that everyone was wearing a shade of silver and blue." Delanee shook her head. "I don't think her party will be as low-key as Ryan hopes."

"It's not some fancy ball with huge gowns, hair, and guest list," Darius said.

"It's not casual, either. Ranked guardians and some of the most influential in the finance and merchant industry will attend. The women will dress to be seen, and those needing to increase their connections will try to impress. All while everyone attempts to get drunk at an equal rate so as not to embarrass themselves too early." Delanee rubbed her hands together. "I love this party."

"I'll be doing what Willemina Irondale will expect. Watching her and finding nothing suspicious," he said.

She rolled her eyes. "And watching me."

"I know you believe no one will try anything, but let's make sure, okay?"

"Are you staying again tonight?"

"Yes, Donovan and I both are." He consulted his watch. "I'll run to my apartment here in a bit to get clean clothes and something for the party tomorrow."

"The twins will be annoyed when they realize their job has been taken for a second day."

Darius grinned.

Delanee returned the expression. "You can be the one to tell them."

The smile faded into a frown. "Why are you so mean?"

She pointed at her chest. "I'm not the one encroaching on their self-appointed position in this house."

Darius glanced at the greenhouse door on the other side of the structure. "Maybe they won't care."

"Maybe," Delanee chirped.

Darius grumbled and headed back into the house. Delanee chuckled, moving to the edge of the pool. She rolled up the baggy legs of her cotton pants and sat, sticking her feet into the warm water. Gentle waves lapped at her calves from Ryan's circuits. He did two more rounds before he noticed her. Kossa moved into a sunny spot on the brick and flopped down within reach. Delanee dug her fingers into the thick fur covering the cat's flank and scratched, rewarded with a rumbling purr.

Ryan folded his arms on the stone ledge beside her and looked up. Water beaded down his face and spiked his hair. His skin glistened, highlighting all the muscled planes of his chest and shoulders.

Delanee clasped her hands between her knees to keep from touching. "What has been bothering you?"

"Besides the constant danger you seem to find yourself in?" he asked, floating closer. A puddle of water followed him and slowly seeped into the fabric of her pants.

"Yes, besides that."

Indecision crossed his face and brushed across their bond. "Synintel...." He took a deep breath and swept dripping water from his eyes.

Delanee grasped his pruning hand and laced their fingers together. "What? What did he do?"

"Kept something really important from me. And I shouldn't even be mad because he kept it from his daughter, too."

"Not mad," she said softly. "Hurt."

His pale gaze cut to her before looking elsewhere. "Yeah, that too. Which is stupid because he's my boss, not my friend."

"But you've known him almost your entire life. You've trusted him with a part of yourself you didn't trust anyone else with."

"Until you," he said, his gaze catching hers again.

Delanee tugged, and he floated until he slid between her legs. She was already wet. More splashed or dripped water wouldn't hurt. He braced his arms on her thighs, and she slid her fingers into his soaking hair.

"And it was my parents who trusted him first. I just followed blindly because what other option did I have?" He dropped his forehead to her chest, his shoulders moving with his deep breath. "I'm frustrated, for Raina, for myself. I feel like we deserve better, but we don't. Not really."

"Why not?" she asked, a sense of vindication rising. A need to challenge the authority set by an arch guardian because her mate was hurting.

"Because if I look at it from a different perspective, if I take away the personal aspect, he was protecting the queen's progeny. A prince. Familial relations don't matter at that point. The child's safety is the only important thing, and he decided to protect the child by hiding his identity."

Delanee blinked, completely lost. "What are you talking about? Is Jaiden not the prince?"

"He is." Ryan lifted his head and flexed his jaw. "Swear you won't repeat a word of what I'm about to say to anyone, including your brothers."

Delanee stared at him, frustrated. "I've kept my promise so far. Why would that change now?"

"Please."

"All right, I swear I won't say anything."

"Prince Jaiden is Henry Edmond's son."

Delanee processed the revelation and the implications. "Are they still—"

"I have no idea. I don't care or even really want to know."

"He was born not long after the king's death, everyone just assumed...." She released a long breath. "Wow. They were lucky with the timing of his birth."

"Yes, they've hidden the truth from everyone. I imagine if Raina didn't know, then the queen-elect's children probably don't know either."

Delanee didn't know the arch guardian over the intelligence teams well, but she did know he required a sense of control over everything he managed. "Learning the prince was in jeopardy must have freaked him out."

"Yes. Just the idea of his daughter in danger led to her arranged marriage to Raiventon. That there was a legitimate threat against his son?" Ryan shook his head. "I'm shocked I wasn't told about the kid sooner."

"Or told to start questioning every potential lead you have."

"That, too." Ryan framed his head in his hands. I just... I spent a lot of time at the palace because Synintel works from there most days. Many of his habits make more sense now, as does the prince's frequent interruptions."

Delanee smiled at the visual of a young child disrupting the arch guardian's day. "How did he not let it slip?"

"I have no idea. Maybe he doesn't call him father or anything like that in public. I know Henry would insist on being part of the child's life, but to what degree?" Ryan shrugged. "No one even suspected the relationship."

"The gathering of the V Alliance members tomorrow is really important, isn't it?"

"Yes. I *have* to learn something."

"I'll help in any way I can," she said, the urgency and pressure to find new information forming a bubble of excitement. The thrill of the hunt and the exhilaration of discovery were not something she could ignore.

"You can help by staying safe."

THIRTY-THREE

THE CONSTANT HUM OF CONVERSATION, laughter, and clinking glasses filled the Irondales' house. The open floor plan allowed all the guests to mingle in the various spaces, from the kitchen, where finger foods were being served, to the dining room, where the wine-tasting bar was located, and the spacious living room, where every seat was in use.

Doors leading to a paved and lamp-lit path were open, and many guests wandered into the brisk night and continued to a functional greenhouse. While the space was inviting, it wasn't cultivated for visitors, but rather used for food, with fruit trees and vegetable beds. The curious ventured to see what the Irondales grew and Delanee imagined a few modifications would be made to a few greenhouses in the days to follow. Some plant nurseries would see an uptick in sales. Willemina prided herself on the immaculate condition of her greenhouse. Every plant was labeled, and not a weed or stray ornamental flower could be found.

Delanee took a casual sip of her wine. The sweet, almost woodsy flavor made her brows raise. This year's offerings came from Noreden, an arid, desert land. Description cards had been set up in front of each bottle. Delanee had carefully noted each for her article but hadn't paid much attention when she'd selected a bottle and poured the drink to pretend to participate. Now she wished she had at least glanced at the label, the sample surprisingly delicious.

Somewhere on the property, Ryan observed. His ability to fade into the background still amazed her. Darius chatted with someone Delanee didn't know, his gaze constantly roaming the crowd. Hedleston had seen her and promptly disappeared elsewhere. Delanee didn't think he'd left, just moved out of her sight. At least, she hoped such was the case. No one else seemed nervous about either her attendance or Darius's. Which meant the V Alliance was *that* confident, or they weren't present in the numbers Ryan suspected.

Delanee mingled, participated in meaningless conversations, and then found a quiet, unobtrusive location to observe when inhibitions started to loosen. Wine continued to flow. The consumption led to most forgetting about her and, therefore, forgetting to behave themselves. Most would become amusement for the city in the society pages when the summary of the night's events printed. She bit the inside of her lip to refrain from grinning in unapologetic glee. The first round of entertainment did not disappoint.

Key Guardianess Jenicek tripped over her too-high heels, laughing hysterically while dumping wine down the back of Chloe Abenroth's sage green and peach embroidered gown. Chloe shrieked and launched herself forward in an attempt to get out of Jenicek's way and collided with Primary Guardian Lanion. The two tumbled to the floor in a flurry of arms, legs, food, and more flying wine. Primary Guardianess Lanion took one look at her spouse beneath the beautiful and unmarried Chloe and burst into dramatic tears, airing the couple's very private grievances for all who would listen. Delanee flipped open her notebook.

The night devolved from that point onward. More wine spilled. More angry words flew. Attempted seduction took place, with some managing to be more successful than others. Delanee hoped, as puddles of wine and discarded food formed on almost every surface, that the Irondales hired a cleaning service to help with the mess.

Darius sidled up next to her, a half-full glass of wine in his hands. He hadn't refilled the entire night. "You come to this every year?"

"Since I took over Cora Dandridge's position three years ago, yes," she answered, noting a couple slipping out the back door, shushing each other, and laughing too loudly to be covert. The woman's husband was passed out in a chair, wine dripping from an overturned glass dangling from his limp fingers.

Darius followed her gaze and sighed. "It's no wonder human rabies syndrome continues to plague our civilization."

"Not like it once did," she said. "But yes, still around because, well, temptation isn't something everyone can ignore."

"Especially not when inhibitions disappear."

"Some of them won't even remember doing anything," Delanee said, saddened at the knowledge.

"And won't know if their one-time partner becomes sick." He shook his head. "Such a terrifying risk."

"Did you get any leads on your thief?"

"No, and this would be an excellent party to grift the unsuspecting. But if it is one or both Irondales, they'd be foolish to steal at their own house and bring attention to themselves like that." Darius's attention shifted over the room. "Neither of them has spent much time in the company of the ones wearing the most outlandish displays of wealth tonight, either."

"Ah, yes." Delanee consulted her notebook. "How any

of us could possibly ignore the thousands of raimarks' worth of charms glittering in Master Guardianess Taravella's hair."

"Or covering her entire chest."

Delanee snickered. "Something needed to because her dress certainly hadn't."

Darius watched the party continue to slip into depravity with her until, apparently, her older brother had seen enough. "I'm done with this. Nothing productive is going to happen tonight. If your husband's suspects are here, they're too drunk to plan much of anything."

"Including kidnapping me?" she asked.

"They'd fall on their butts before they reached the front door if you did anything more than walk meekly at their side."

Which they both knew would never happen. "I'll see you at the house?"

He leaned over and kissed her cheek. "You know you will."

Delanee watched him cut through the crowd of seeking hands and stumbling bodies and tried not to laugh at his struggle to not be groped. Amateur. He should have left out a back or side entrance. She was so busy being amused by the awkwardness of his departure, she almost missed the small group that left, single file, out the door leading to the greenhouse. Minutes after the last man disappeared, Delanee glanced around, noting no one seemed to notice or care. She handed her drink to a woman searching for something. The woman beamed a bleary smile at her and downed the rest of what Delanee had in the glass.

Outside, an icy breeze fluttered the leaves of shrubs and ensured no one remained in the elements for long. Of course, those too drunk to notice may be in some trouble if the Irondales didn't do a sweep of their property. Wouldn't be the first time someone had frozen to death at a function.

A sad reality in their arctic world. While the nights were no longer dangerous for outdoor activity due to summer creeping in, they were if one neglected to get to the shelter in time or wasn't dressed appropriately for an extended period in the dropping temperatures.

The group moved at an increased rate once they were halfway to the greenhouse. Delanee kept off the brick and out of the limited glow of tealights illuminating the path. Clouds drifted above, blocking the faint glimmer of moonlight, making all the shadows dense. She tried to squint in the darkness, wanting to ensure she didn't stumble onto any salacious activities. A silhouette moved, separating from the depths, and Delanee sucked in a breath and stumbled backward.

"This way," a familiar voice said in a low tone.

Delanee clutched her journal to her chest and tried to calm her racing heart. "You scared me."

"Sorry. I couldn't let you keep going. Someone will glance back before entering the greenhouse," Ryan said, taking her elbow and guiding her through the grassy yard, already damp with dew, and toward the faint glow of the conservatory.

"I wasn't on the trail."

"They would have seen you. Your yellow gown doesn't exactly blend into the night."

Yellow wasn't Delanee's best color, but options had been limited with most of her belongings still at the apartment. The yellow silk gown with a sheer overlay of gossamer thin silk embroidered with dark amber threads had been clean and hanging in her closet when they'd collected a few of her belongings. The same could not be said for the majority of her clothes. She brushed a hand down the fitted bodice and sighed. If she had known she'd need to be clandestine tonight, she would have dug around for something more appropriate.

Ryan led her around the glass building to a side door already propped open enough for a person to squeeze inside. He motioned for her to enter first, pointing to the dim space beneath a tree. Delanee picked up the skirt of her gown to avoid making excess noise and softly walked to the space, crouching behind a raised bed full of tall, leafy vegetation. Ryan used his foot to ease the door closed and then joined her.

Hushed voices soon filled the space. Leaves rustled, and mulch shifted beneath shoes. The whisper of the door swooshing closed changed the environment enough to make the male voices increase.

"Where is Kyle?" someone asked.

"Saw him disappear with a woman hanging off his arm."

Someone scoffed. "Typical. We'll let the boss know."

Beside her, Ryan tensed a bit. A sliver of disappointment trickled along their bond. If the boss wasn't present, did they even need to stay and listen? Since they made no move to attempt to sneak back out, Delanee figured Ryan hoped to glean something. At this point, anything new would be worth skulking in the shadows.

"Are we secure in here?"

"No one has entered since I stood at the door."

"And the side door?"

Another scoff. "Are you kidding? No one is sober enough to know where to find that, let alone in the dark."

Delanee pressed her lips together and wondered if she could somehow take notes. The pen seemed to burn against her palm, and the empty journal pages beckoned. The conversation continued to center around one man assuring another they were safe. Delanee very carefully shifted onto her rear and eased open her notebook. Ryan cut her a glance. She blinked at him. She knew he wanted to argue but couldn't, and Delanee poised her pen above the paper.

When he didn't snatch the book or the pen from her hands, she gingerly began to journal the clandestine meeting.

Only the occasional trousered leg, polished boot, or ornately embroidered coattail was visible from their hidden location. All the men were dressed in expensive clothes. None of them seemed to have partaken in the endless supply of wine like the rest of the guests. No slurred words or confusion from an impaired mind. They had obviously waited until everyone else was incapacitated to have their meeting, ensuring no one noticed they were missing or cared about their disappearance. In the seclusion of a greenhouse not belonging to any of them, no one would ever know the secret gathering had taken place. A brilliant plan.

Then again, perhaps Mr. Irondale was indeed present. Delanee couldn't see any of their faces to know, and now she wished she'd paid closer attention to everyone's clothing. She bit her tongue to keep from asking Ryan if he'd paid attention to all the men who had left the party. Hedleston was certainly among them, Delanee figured.

"What is the update?" a man finally asked, breaking through the argument about their security.

A throat cleared, and yep, the voice that answered was familiar. All Delanee's muscles tensed in remembrance of hearing his coldhearted words through the bars of a cage. Ryan's hand smoothed up her shoulders to the nape of her neck, where his warm fingers settled against her skin.

"We were unable to secure the Sentinel team."

"You assured our queen-to-be the Sentinels were as good as ours," a voice said, quivering with anger.

Hedleston cleared his throat again. "We underestimated the Ralston family."

"I knew it," a new man stated, anxiety clear in his high-pitched voice. "And now they know. What are we going to do?"

"They know nothing," the man who first spoke

snapped. "For all they know, the Cairoen woman brought her force along because she wanted the cat that desperately. No one has harassed Hedleston. He made a clean escape as promised, and the Cairoens didn't give us up, or we'd have been visited by Darius Ralston at the least, or the Wolvenguard."

Feet shuffled at the mention of her powerful arch guardian brother. Pride made Delanee's lips quirk in delight. They were wise to fear Deklan. But what was this *queen-to-be* nonsense? No vote had taken place to elect the next queen or king of their realm. Delanee wrote down the information, underlining the question.

"We knew it was a risk," the apparent leader continued. "The Ralstons are a powerful family. But we all agreed on the necessity of the Sentinels."

"Which we still don't have," someone pointed out.

Delanee really wanted to shift the foliage aside and place faces to the voices. But the movement would alert to their presence. She'd never been undercover before and wondered how Ryan handled the suspense of not knowing. Or perhaps he knew, being more involved in the guardian world, who was in the act of admitting treason. His gentle touch on her neck hadn't changed, and no new intense emotions had filtered across their bond. The whole situation seemed like a standard day for him.

A heavy sigh sounded. "No, we do not. However, we do have a rather impressive local force." Alarmed grumbling ensued. "I know, I know, none of us wanted to call on them just yet, but we don't seem to have a choice. The princess is concerned someone is aware of the threat against Jaiden—"

A creepy chorus of *never my prince* arose from the gathering. Both Ryan and Delanee tensed.

"And we need to act immediately," he finished.

"Only one ship is in port that they don't suspect and haven't searched," Hedleston stated. "As I assured our princess at the emergency meeting, the Ralston woman doesn't remember her capture, or the ship would have been boarded. If our princess is going to enact the plan, she needs to do it before the ship departs."

"I agree, and I've told her as much. But she needs our support."

They all acknowledged their unwavering support and dedication. Ryan glanced at Delanee, and she bit her lip. In the post-chaos of her bonding to Kossa, Delanee hadn't told him any of what Hedleston had revealed to her while held in the warehouse. She quickly scribbled their plans for her and showed him the paper. He read over the words. White striations sparked through his irises when he lifted his gaze. His anger flared hot across their connection.

The anger morphed into horror, then to a rage that almost overloaded her consciousness. The pen and journal fell from her grasp. Little arcs of energy sizzled and popped in her veins. His talent, she realized, from where he still touched her. Then, without notice, he launched himself upward, arms open, his authority flaring from him like a living force. Delanee squeaked in alarm and jumped up, taking in the scene. Awe and panic— not from his gift but his being caught using it— made her mouth dry.

Only she had nothing to fear. The group stood immobilized, each caught in the tangling web of lightning Ryan had created. Their eyes bled white, and their faces were relaxed in an emotionless state.

"*Who is your princess*?" Ryan asked in a voice so dark with emotion she barely recognized the cadence.

"Verica," they answered as one.

Goosebumps covered Delanee. Princess Verica, the queen-elect's oldest child. *She* was the mastermind behind the group? Delanee's mind buzzed as she squatted down and gathered her dropped items. There were more important things to her at the moment than a traitorous royal.

Rising, she couldn't help but look toward the entrance. If anyone were to stumble in, Ryan's secret would be revealed. There was no hiding the remarkable power emanating from his very person. Delanee swallowed and grabbed his arm.

"Stop," she urged.

"I need to know more," he growled.

"We know enough. We know it all now, Ryan. And you'll be able to figure out what we don't with the evidence you already have."

Still, he continued to hold the men captive, his fury feeding his talent in the most beautiful, yet terrifying, way. No one could know about the capability to unleash his genetic skill in such a manner. Not even Synintel. Perhaps *especially* not the arch guardian. If even one person witnessed the spectacle... Deeper anxiety knotted in her stomach. Delanee tugged on Ryan's sleeve.

"Ryan, your ability is too important for you to give it up now," she beseeched. "Sziveria can't afford to lose you."

He slowly turned his head and looked at her. None of the blue remained in his irises, only the silver interlaced with white. Delanee brushed her fingers along his jaw and kissed his chin. She took a deep breath and, on the calm exhale, allowed only her love for him to remain within her. None of the fear of being caught or the anxiety over the future of their country remained.

"Please," she whispered.

The tension remained coiled in his frame, but the wrath burning along their bond dissipated. Delanee rested her forehead on his chest in relief. His heart pounded, and she flattened her palm over his pectoral.

"Leave," he whispered.

Startled, she shifted and met his gaze. "Ryan...."

"I'm going to have to delicately remove my talent from them. There won't be time for both of us to leave unnoticed."

She hesitated, glancing at the incapacitated group.

"I promise I will follow," he said softly.

The truth of his assurance was like a salve to her frayed nerves. She nodded and clutched the journal and pen to her chest. She kissed his lips quickly, unable to leave him without the simple intimacy. "I'm going to be right outside here waiting, where they won't see when they come back to their senses."

"I won't be long."

"Be careful, Ryan."

"I will."

And still she hesitated, wanting to say so much more. She nodded and eased around him to the side door, conveying everything she couldn't place into words along their bond. Offering her support, strength, and especially her love. She needed to trust he indeed had everything under control, and they'd leave the party with no one knowing their secrets were never safe if her husband was in the room.

Thirty-Four

She had saved him.

The realization was no less impactful as Delanee walked beside him through the wide palace corridors. Colorful marble gleamed in the early morning light. Potted plants and hanging flower baskets added a much-needed natural beauty to the pristine shine covering every surface. Meant to impress, the main part of the palace had the level of sophistication and wealth the public area lacked. If one managed to make it to this section, one was privileged and meant to feel as such.

The folder stuffed to capacity seemed like a load of bricks in Ryan's hand. Never, at any point, had he or anyone else contemplated the possibility of the *V* in *V Alliance* standing for Verica. A princess of their country. Someone who, over the years, had seemed to be doing much good for their nation. Only the efforts had come *after* the need had been engineered by her very hand. A catastrophe of drug addiction and kidnapping was created just for her to show the masses she cared and to one day conceal her ulterior motive.

Remove the youngest Nirromar from the country.

This would, therefore, allow the election that had been put off until his eighteenth year, to occur. An election that would have happened four years ago without the birth of Prince Jaiden when Princess Brienne came of age. Now, the election wouldn't occur for another eight to ten years. Not until the prince reached legal age could the people of Sziveria decide between *all* the Nirromars. If he wanted two years to go before the public and campaign, the election would be withheld that much longer. He would be allowed to earn the trust of the people his siblings had garnered for themselves during his youth. Being the oldest, Verica would be well into her thirties before the process came to fruition.

All the proof of the massive scheme, from the money trail to the illicit secret deals between businesses and, even in some cases, foreign powers, had been carefully collected over the past two weeks now that Ryan knew what he was looking for. The sale of slave labor from their prisons to New Columbia, Ravenna, and even Cairo. The trading of human cargo through Mark Inland. The smuggling of magic lily dust was the only one he couldn't trace. The ships that brought in the addictive drug came from all over the world, and where the pink powder originated from continued to elude every investigator across all the national services.

And still, through it all, the night he'd lost control kept creeping into his consciousness. Without Delanee, he might not have discovered much more than Princess Verica's secret, one she may have fled from without being held accountable. If anyone had witnessed his outburst, he'd never work in the city again. No one would ever be caught alone with him, let alone allow him to attend one of their functions. Upon learning of his genetic ability, the princess would have likely hopped aboard the ship where she had planned to place her youngest brother. A country would have harbored her. Ryan didn't even want to contemplate the political nightmare such a situation would cause. Delanee had prevented it all, the entire potential catastrophe.

Ryan spotted Arch Guardian Synintel up ahead, waiting for them. No hint of emotion showed on his face. At a discreet distance, one of his many guards stood at attention, the pressed dark green uniform with large silver buttons right at home in the elegance of the palace. As usual, the arch guardian himself was also immaculately dressed and groomed. A burnt orange, long-sleeved silk shirt was paired with a pale brown wool vest, accenting the fit physique he still maintained. His short, salt-and-pepper hair needed little styling to appear neat. An onyx stone gleamed at his throat instead of a necktie.

The long folds of Delanee's navy skirt swished and whispered with each step. Her boot heels clacked a steady, confident rhythm. His steps were silent; his clothes were unassuming, no different from his attire on any other workday. Queen-Elect Arnita never cared much about formal clothing, and Ryan preferred not to leave an impression. As an assistant to the arch guardian, his appearance would convey his average position.

"She's waiting for you," Synintel said quietly once they reached his side.

Ryan glanced around. "We aren't meeting her in the Audience Hall?"

"No." Henry clasped his hands behind his back and headed to the left. "She preferred the comfort of her private sitting room for this meeting. The guards aren't required to remain in attendance."

Ryan looked at Delanee, whose lips were pressed tightly together. Her irritation zipped across their bond. Knowing her, she had jumped to a conclusion she didn't like and somehow managed to keep her strong feelings to herself. Ryan brushed his fingers along hers, the subtle contact a means to ground them both. She inched closer, and the messenger bag slung over her shoulder bumped between them.

An attendant waited at a door almost two stories in height. Elegant filigree in gold, teal, and lavender accented the white wood. Stripes in the same colors were painted around the frame. The female servant wore a tunic gown in the same shade of lavender. Golden and teal threads in the same filigree pattern adorned the outfit, making it worthy of any social function. The woman's hair was perfectly coiffed atop her head, the faint sparkle of glass beads in the dark strands glittered in the natural light filtering in the side windows.

She bowed her head. "Arch Guardian Synintel. Guardians Voklane. Queen-Elect Arnita is pleased you can join her this morning. A prepared breakfast in buffet style has been set out for your eating pleasure. Please, follow me."

The woman opened the door, and delicious scents immediately wafted into the corridor. Synintel's guard stopped at the entrance and took up position, nodding to the arch guardian as they filed past. Like the rest of the palace, the room was a study in white, with the royal colors sprinkled throughout. Colorful pillows on the white sofas. A woven rug on the marble floor. Paintings of Sziveria in all the seasons on the white paneled walls. The chandelier hanging from the ceiling sparkled with faceted crystals. The colorful stained-glass panels in the windows cast a rainbow of colors along the floor and walls.

Delanee gasped. "I think I want stained glass windows in our house," she whispered, her steps slowing as they ventured deeper into the spacious room.

"The effect is magnified due to the white room and tall windows with unobstructed sun," he answered quietly.

"Most of our windows are a view into the greenhouse or are covered by the front porch roof."

Our windows. He still marveled that he had someone sharing his home and his life. Someone he loved.

A side door opened, and a middle-aged woman swept inside. Loose black cotton pants and a flowy dark yellow shirt fluttered around her thighs. A teal scarf with black flowers hung loosely from her neck. No shoes were on her feet. Her black hair hung in a loose braid past her waist. She smiled when she noticed them.

"Good morning." She motioned to the food piled on a side table near the entry she'd come through. "Please, no need to wait for me to get a plate."

Synintel crossed the distance to take her hands and kiss her cheek. "My queen."

Queen-Elect Arnita lifted her chin to accept his kiss. "No need for formalities, Henry. Not in here."

He kissed her forehead and smiled, making Ryan blink in shock. "I know, but we aren't alone, so it's a habit."

Arnita turned to face them, one hand still holding Henry's. "Ryan, good morning."

Ryan nodded in greeting. "Good morning."

Arnita turned her attention to Delanee. "And you must be Ryan's wife, Delanee. I have heard much about you, my dear girl."

Delanee's cheeks flushed. "It has been an eventful couple of weeks."

Sadness tinged the queen's smile. "It has been. But your adventures alone aren't how I know of you. Deklan has spoken of you, as well, as has Dominik the few times I've met with him. I enjoy reading your articles and always ask if they happen to know what entertainment we're due for next." She chuckled. "Of course, they never do."

"She reads my work *and* knows my brothers by name,"

Delanee breathed, eyes wide. Then she blinked, her cheeks darkening further. "I said that out loud, didn't I?"

Arnita laughed. "Don't be so surprised I know your brothers. They are the only ones who can do what they do for our country. I am indeed a lucky queen to count them as allies and guardians."

"Thank you," Delanee said.

Arnita's focus shifted to the folder Ryan held, and her smile faded. "Let's eat, and then we'll move on to... more unpleasant conversation."

Ryan set the folder on an end table between couches and then pressed a hand to the small of Delanee's back, guiding her to the buffet table. Everyone filled a plate and found a place to sit on one of the four couches arranged around a rectangular ash table. Two small vases filled with bright flowers were arranged in the center on glass coasters. Henry and Arnita sat together across from Delanee and Ryan.

"How conclusive is your evidence?" Arnita asked halfway through the meal.

Ryan glanced up from his plate, brows raised.

Arnita dabbed at her mouth with a cloth napkin. "I'm sorry. I know I said I wanted to wait, but I can't. My stomach is... well, I'm very anxious."

Henry caressed her back, concern etched on his face. "Even without the evidence Voklane gathered, I already told you—"

Arnita held up a trembling hand. "I know." She sighed heavily. "I know, Henry. I just, I need to see it. The evidence. I have to see the proof one of my children was capable of such awful things."

Ryan leaned across the distance and collected the thick folder. He slid it across the table to the queen-elect and arch guardian. "Take your time."

The two pushed their plates away and leaned close

together over the folder. Arnita slowly opened the file. Henry separated several pages, pointing to areas on the papers and mumbling softly. Arnita nodded and shuffled through the evidence, isolating pages herself. Her cheeks and neck flushed red. From anger, mortification, or a combination of both, Ryan didn't know, as she remained silent in her perusal. The arch guardian showed no emotion as he read over the documentation.

Finally, the queen-elect cracked. Papers fluttered from her hand, and she sagged into the couch cushions. She pinched the bridge of her nose. Tears trailed, glistening tracks down her cheeks.

"How could she have been doing all this, and none of us suspected? I've had you chasing the V Alliance for years. All the while, their leader was right under *my* roof." She pressed a fist to her chest. "She made a fool of everyone."

Henry laid papers down and picked up a new set. "It's a shame she felt the need to create an entire subculture of drug addicts and kidnappers, to forge illegal partnerships, and smuggle resources from our allies. The entire scheme was nothing short of brilliant."

Arnita's jaw clenched, and she straightened. "She was running my country under my nose in the worst way, Henry."

Henry set the papers down. "I did say it was a shame."

Arnita hopped up and hustled around the couches, quickly disappearing in a rush of fluttering fabric through the door she'd entered from earlier. Delanee turned to watch her. Ryan kept his attention on Henry. The arch guardian remained sitting, reaching for his plate. He popped a strawberry in his mouth, his expression thoughtful.

"I think she would have run this country if she'd been patient enough," Henry said.

"But would she have been a good leader?" Ryan asked.

Henry shrugged. "I think she would have made Sziveria prosperous. Imagine what she could do with official connections if she could create this level of a trading network with smugglers."

"Smugglers don't require as much in exchange politically for their trade agreements."

Henry dipped his head. "True. We have no idea how she managed to garner such relationships. She could have made as many enemies as allies."

Arnita returned. The tears were gone. The calm composure of a queen had replaced the anxious hurt of a betrayed mother. "Bentlie is bringing Verica to us." Her gaze cut to Ryan. "Guardian Voklane."

Ryan straightened, his stomach clenching. "Yes, my queen?"

"I do not want to exchange any trivial conversation. Please proceed with your questions when my daughter takes your hand in greeting."

"What do you want me to ask?"

"Anything." Arnita huffed out a breath and waved her hand. "Everything. If either Henry or I have anything specific we wish to know, we will have you ask her."

While whatever Ryan's talent uncovered couldn't be used to convict Verica— after all, she would have no memory of her confessions— they would still learn the ultimate goal from her lips. With the information, Ryan could verify the criminal evidence gathered and level accusations. Against her and anyone who had been working alongside her in Sziveria. Ryan also knew Henry would want the names of the contacts she'd been working with in the countries she had set up smuggling operations. The implications if they were government officials for those nations... Ryan and the intel teams would be busy for some time.

The knowledge Verica would reveal could potentially uncover weaknesses other countries weren't even aware they possessed. What Synintel and Queen-Elect Arnita did with the information wasn't something Ryan could worry about.

The door to the room opened. "... had to be pulled from my chambers and dragged to my mother's. This is ridiculous. I am a grown woman."

"Queen-Elect Arnita, Princess Ver—"

"She knows very well who I am," Verica snapped. The princess swept into the room, the long length of her orange and red skirt fluttering behind her. A flowy cream top draped from her shoulders to her hips, a red undershirt visible beneath. Her dark hair was swept into an elegant twist atop her head. Behind her, two female attendants followed at a far enough distance to keep from stepping on the short train of fabric gliding across the floor. "I don't see what the po—"

Ryan stood. Verica stopped so suddenly that the nearest attendant following bumped into her, sending the princess stumbling forward, her skirt yanking tight enough to strain the fabric. Irritation flashed across her face but was quickly masked by a gracious smile. The attendant skuttled backward and attempted to fix the silk now sporting an obvious shoe scuff. Verica waved her away, her smile never faltering.

The queen-elect rose and waved a hand at the door. "Please excuse us, ladies. This is a private breakfast."

The two women hastily bowed before exiting, closing the door in their wake. Verica remained where she'd stopped, fixing her skirt, her gaze moving between Ryan and her mother.

Arnita motioned at Ryan. "Verica, this is Guardian Voklane."

Verica raised a brow. "Guardian? Unranked?"

The rustle of fabric sounded behind him. A sharp jab of anger, not his own, cut across his nerves. Ryan gave a subtle wave behind his back, hoping Delanee remained on the couch.

Verica's cordial smile faded. "Why does an introduction to an unranked guardian warrant my morning being interrupted?"

"Did I raise you to be so discourteous?" the queen-elect asked, lifting her chin. "Greet a guardian of our realm with the respect he deserves."

Ryan almost believed the princess would refuse. Then she forced a smile and a step forward, her hand held out, fingers down, to be taken in a gentle greeting. Ryan obeyed the unspoken command, grasping her hand just enough to transfer the tendrils of his ability.

"Guardi—" The dark green of Verica's irises flared white. Emotion dissolved from her features.

"Why a nasturtium?" Ryan asked. The symbol of a nasturtium flower growing between wings had been found tattooed on several V Alliance members. Nasturtiums were also known to be left behind at the scenes of what the V Alliance considered major accomplishments. The emblem was unique to the group, and if the group indeed belonged to Verica, she'd be the only one to know the answer to such an elusive and random question.

"I like the color purple," Verica answered without infliction.

Arnita gasped and covered her mouth with a shaky hand.

"Why wings?"

"For the day I'll be free of constraints."

Arnita moved to stand beside Ryan. "Ask her what constraints."

Ryan obeyed.

"Time," Verica answered.

The answer wasn't a shock to Ryan, but the queen-elect

frowned and looked at him, then behind to Henry. "Time? What sort of an answer is that?"

Henry glanced at Ryan, the corners of his mouth pinched, then back to Arnita. He slowly stood. "Princess Verica no longer wishes to wait for her turn to be voted into the highest position in our land."

Arnita wrapped her arms around her waist. "Brienne turned twenty-one three weeks ago."

"Jaiden is only ten," Henry whispered.

"Oh... Jaiden," she murmured, taking Henry's hand. "His upbringing has been so very different from my other children. I never considered his future beyond whatever he wishes or the opportunity he will one day have to belong to the people." She offered a small, sad smile. "I guess perhaps I should have. It is our way."

Delanee joined the small group. "Princess Verica did not forget. No one can be voted into the elected queen or king position until the youngest prince reaches age."

"Ask her that specifically. I need to hear her say the words," Arnita said.

Ryan took a deep breath and stared at the immobilized Verica. "What are your plans for Prince Jaiden?"

"He will disappear on a ship bound for Mark Inland, with all the other boys his age who look like him in description," the princess stated, emotionless.

"When?" Ryan asked.

"The second I learn where he's being kept."

Arnita gasped a sob. "That's why he's been with you. Why you didn't tell me where he's been staying."

"Yes," Henry whispered. "However, I didn't know the threat to him was so close."

"Oh, Henry." She turned to face him, clutching both his hands to her chest. "I have been so mad at you."

A weak smile twitched at Synintel's lips. "You weren't upset this morning."

A tear slid down her cheek, and she quickly dashed it away before grabbing his hands again. "Only because I saw no need in arguing before an audience." Her gaze cut quickly to Delanee. "Especially *this* audience."

Delanee's cheeks blossomed a pretty pink. "I would never gossip about you."

Arnita snorted. "Please. A fight between the queen-elect and one of her arch guardians—"

"Happens all the time," Delanee interrupted. "I know my brother."

Arnita laughed and shook her head. She glanced at Ryan. "Keep her."

"I plan to." Warmth blossomed in Ryan's chest, threatening to break his concentration and, therefore, his connection to the princess.

"While that may be true," the queen said, "my relationship with Arch Guardian Synintel would certainly interest all the gossip circles in ranked guardian households. Any nuggets you divulged would be consumed with great delight. Your editor would probably increase your salary to ensure you remained with his publication until the day you retire."

Delanee's grip tightened on her pen until her knuckles bleached. "I'm not interested in reporting gossip. Your personal life is safe with me."

Arnita sighed. "And yet, my personal life led to this entire disaster, didn't it?"

"No," Henry said. "An obsession for power is what led to this. Not anything you did."

Arnita stepped away, another tear slipping free. "How many lives has she destroyed? My daughter, the architect of so many terrible memories and shattered hopes. I can't believe this." She turned her back to everyone, shoulders trembling, and waved a hand. "Please, just send her away."

"You need to compose yourself, and everyone needs to return to their seats," Ryan said.

"Right." Arnita sniffled and accepted a napkin Delanee handed to her. Difficult seconds passed, and sweat gathered along Ryan's hairline. Finally, the queen took a long, deep breath and sat. "All right, I'm ready." She patted the cushion next to her. "Henry."

The arch guardian returned to his seat, and Delanee took hers, concern etched on her face. Ryan winked, and she relaxed, giving him a small, encouraging smile.

The wisps of Ryan's talent released Verica from their hold. Color returned to her irises. "—an Voklane," she finished greeting, the returning false smile tight on her lips.

"Princess Verica." Ryan let go of her hand.

The princess looked at her mother, a brow raised. "Is there anything else?"

"No," Arnita said tightly. "You're free to leave."

Verica glanced at everyone in the room, confusion, and a hint of discomfort clear in her stiff frame. "Right, well, wasn't this a waste of my morning."

"Guardian Voklane works very closely with each of my arch guardians. He's meeting all my children," Arnita stated, still refusing to look at her daughter.

Verica straightened her shoulders. Her gaze skittered from Henry to her mother. "*All* of them?"

Arnita adjusted a saucer and teacup. "Jaiden is a bit young to worry about adult things, don't you think?"

"I think it's odd he's been gone from his home for almost a month. We are all getting very concerned about our little brother," Verica said.

Teacup in hand, Arnita relaxed back into the couch. She took a sip before addressing her daughter's statement. "I felt it was time he toured the country. You remember doing so when you were his age, don't you?"

"I do, yes. Where is he on his tour now? Is he enjoying himself?"

"I believe they just finished with Port Anchor and will be venturing by train to the Tabrias next," Arnita said easily. "Jaiden loved the beach, so Margaret is considering taking him further down the coast to visit Southern Pointe Tower Station. That will add a few more days to their trip."

"You must be missing him terribly," Verica said, though her voice conveyed she wasn't exactly believing her mother's explanation.

"Of course I miss him. But he sounded fine on our last radio call."

"Will they stay at our mountain residence while touring the Tabrias?"

"They will do just as all you children did. One night at Rimewind Tower Station and then a week at Highfrost Manor, where he will learn about the local wildlife and mountain customs."

"Some of my fondest memories," Verica said. "I'm pleased he's safe. I wish you would have told us."

Arnita made a noncommittal sound. Verica glanced around the room again, said her goodbyes, and left, closing the door louder than necessary. Arnita set her cup on the table with such force pale amber liquid sloshed over the rim.

"I thought I was going to be sick," she proclaimed, pressing a hand to her stomach.

"You did very well," Delanee said.

"Yes," Henry agreed, "I don't believe I've ever heard you lie so convincingly."

"Jaiden's life is at risk," the queen said, her gaze serious. "I will do what I must. If lying is the worst of it, easy enough."

Ryan returned to his place beside Delanee. "I may need to meet with her one more time to get the names of her leaders. I think they were all in the greenhouse two weeks ago, but I can't be sure. I need names to ensure a thorough investigation. Enough for those who are ranked and betrayed their seat to be taken before the Endowment and Revocation committee."

Arnita nodded. "I'll see that it happens."

Henry shifted. "Speaking of the E and R committee...." He glanced at Arnita, and she nodded, taking his hand.

Ryan gazed over at Delanee, and she gave him an *I-don't-know* look before poising her pen over the notebook. Ryan remained quiet, the environment turning to one of heavy anticipation. More so than before Verica had been expected.

"I have decided," Henry said slowly, covering Arnita's hand with both his hands. "To accept Arnita's request to contract."

Delanee gasped and then beamed a smile at them. "Congratulations."

Ryan wasn't quite as excited as his wife. He frowned. "Who will take over your position?"

Henry glanced at Arnita again. "Well, we are hoping you will, Voklane."

Ryan blinked. Perhaps he'd misheard. "Excuse me?"

Arnita smiled, hope in her gaze. "Ryan Voklane, will you honor Sziveria by becoming the next Arch Guardian Synintel?"

EPILOGUE

ARCH GUARDIAN SYNINTEL Residence
Two months later...

DELANEE SCRATCHED between Kossa's ears. A loud rumbling purr sounded from the cat. Inara sat on the floor, trying to catch the feline's flicking tail. She squealed in frustration and scooted closer, her small hands waving. Delanee glanced at the infant to ensure she hadn't moved again and then returned to the calendar she'd been reviewing, counting days. Kossa headbutted her when she stopped scratching.

"Stop it," Delanee sighed.

Pet me, Kossa demanded.

"Wait a minute, I'm trying to figure something out."

What is more important than me? Kossa rubbed her head along Delanee's hip again, grumbling.

Over the past two months, Delanee had found she preferred to talk to Kossa aloud. Speaking mind-to-mind, having to think words instead of speak them, made communicating feel like an extra step, and the cat understood her either way. If the guards and attendants who wandered around the residence thought it weird she conversed with a cat, they didn't allow it to show.

Delanee sighed again and slid her hand along the feline's fuzzy ear, up to the tuft. "I'm trying to figure out when my last cycle was. I haven't been tracking in all the chaos, and I feel like it's been a long time. Too long."

Kossa twisted her head until Delanee's palm landed between her ears. *Why does this matter?*

"Because I—"

Wish to know if you are having a kit? Yes, you are.

Delanee blinked. Her hand froze. "What?"

Purring, Kossa rubbed her head along Delanee's palm and pushed herself between the desk and Delanee. *Now, you do not need to look at anything. Pet me.*

Delanee stumbled backward. Inara crawled after Kossa's tail swishing along the carpeted floor. Babbling, Inara eased herself back into a sitting position and tried again to capture the elusive fluffy appendage. Shock had Delanee reaching for the desk chair. Encountering only air, she gave up and plopped onto the floor. Inara squealed in delight, and chortling happily, she crawled to Delanee and climbed into her lap. The baby clapped and then stood, grabbing fistfuls of Delanee's shirt to keep her balance as her little feet wobbled on Delanee's thighs.

Excitement warred with a sense of panic within Delanee. A new life grew inside her. Not once had Delanee worried about pregnancy. After all, she was half Ruthenian, and the possibility of conceiving without a Ruthenian mate... Never in her wildest dreams did she think she would be a mother beyond Inara. Yet, perhaps she should have because Ryan was more than Ruthenian. The original genetic material that created her father's nation formed her husband. Neither of them considered how easily they could apparently conceive. In seven months or so, she'd have *two* babies. Two. She blinked. Could she handle two little ones?

"Hello, neighbor!" a familiar female voice called out. When Delanee didn't reply, Cia called out, "Delanee?"

"Down here," Delanee shouted, taking hold of Inara's hands and helping her stand. She bounced, warbling incoherent words only she knew.

Cia rounded the desk, her gaze softening. "Deklan wants one."

Delanee blinked. "A baby?"

"Well, he doesn't want a cat," Cia said, hopping onto the desk.

Kossa hissed. *She reeks of wolf.*

Cia hissed back.

Kossa growled low in her throat.

Cia glared and returned the sound.

"Hey," Delanee snapped.

"What?" Cia asked innocently.

Since her annoyance was at both woman and feline, Delanee rolled her eyes and sighed. "Nothing. Is my brother here?"

"Yeah, he's with Voklane and the rest of the team. I came to get you."

Delanee lifted Inara. Cia moved off the desk and grasped the baby under her arms. She flipped Inara around and made a funny face at her. Inara giggled and patted Cia's puffed cheeks. His brother's young wife was only a few years Delanee's junior, yet advanced maturity had come to Cia at a high cost. Someday, when her fears no longer ruled her decisions, she would make a wonderful mother.

Delanee shifted onto her knees and used the edge of the desk to stand. She smoothed her skirt down, her hand briefly resting on her flat belly. A tiny life was snuggled and growing within her. The knowledge brought the burn of tears to her eyes. How much longer would she have before she needed to wear different clothes?

Cia settled Inara on her hip, frowning. "I guess I need to get used to referring to him as Synintel now instead of Voklane, don't I?"

Delanee sighed internally. Would she ever get used to their new social and political ranking? Or the amount of responsibility that rested on her husband's shoulders? Her editor almost peed himself when the Endowment and Revocation Committee results were posted in the paper, and Ryan's name was listed as approved and endowed with the Arch Guardian Synintel rank and seat. There had been a great many revocations, as well. The council would be busy as the queen-elect, former arch guardian, and the current arch guardian over intel teams investigated the recommended new blood for the seats vacated by traitors.

Curtis hadn't been able to contain his excitement over the new social opportunities Delanee would now have access to and, therefore, the elevation in the gossip content. His reaction had been all she'd needed to know about her future at *Haven City Chronicle*. With Ryan's encouragement, Delanee had turned in her notice. With the queen-elect's assistance, she'd begun writing the biggest story in Sziverian history. The betrayal of a princess. Queen-Elect Arnita was deciding where she wanted the story printed. A popular, unbiased lifestyle magazine was the current front-runner to be approached.

They headed across the vast foyer to one of the many gaming rooms in the downstairs part of the house. Aside from the spacious office, the ground floor was dedicated to social use. From the ballroom in the center, separated from the foyer and rooms by huge pillars, to the three game rooms, two formal dining spaces, and even a small theatre room, the house was meant to entertain the elites and dignitaries Ryan would be expected to welcome. Delanee often stood on the grand staircase branching off from the upstairs and tried to imagine either she or Ryan being a gracious host to the most important people in Sziveria, let alone the inhabited world, and failed. Every time. If she contemplated for too long about the pressures on their new relationship, from family to leadership, she'd break down. One day at a time had become her new motto.

The hum of conversation filtered from somewhere beyond the ballroom. Delanee led the way through one of the game rooms. Four dark green velvet-lined hexagon-shaped game tables were arranged around the room. Woven rugs in dark green, maroon, brown, and cream were beneath each table. Velvet dark green drapes pulled back to reveal cream and dark green-striped wallpaper and made the room feel opulent. Artistic paintings of dice, cards, tiles, and tokens brought an expectation of entertainment. An open door revealed the billiard room and she entered. She continued past the pool tables, the gleaming colorful balls arranged in perfect triangles ready for the next match, and into the theatre room. Comfortable padded chairs were arranged eight across and nine deep in an arch formation on a faint decline. An oval stage at the front of the room was empty. Only one of the almost dozen chandeliers hanging from the vaulted ceiling was lit.

Ryan stood at the front of the room, talking to Vayden Dossett. Vayden had been tasked with most of the investigations for the recently vacated ranked guardian seats and those recommended to go before the Endowment and Revocation Council to fill the positions. After the queen-elect and former arch guardian approved the selections, Vayden conducted the investigations. When Delanee crossed the threshold, Ryan glanced up, his pale gaze zeroing straight to her.

Delanee's stomach did the little excited flip it always seemed to do when he looked at her, regardless of the emotion in his gaze. Heated lust, unbanked frustration, tender love, or, as now, concern, his undivided attention never failed to weaken her knees.

He mouthed, "Are you okay?"

She nodded. He stared at her for a second more, seeming to assure himself she spoke the truth and then returned to his conversation. Delanee wanted to be selfish and drag him away from one of the many teams he now oversaw, but this meeting was too important for their personal life to intrude. A new normal, she figured.

Kossa pushed past her and Cia, sauntering into the room, finding a chair, and springing onto the padded seat. She immediately set to grooming, her loud purr joining the hum of conversation.

"What is the cat's purpose again?" Cia asked, adjusting Inara's position on her hip. "Because all she ever seems to do is lay around sleeping and shed all over the place."

"Ruthenian lore says during the Primal Years, the lynxias helped patrol settlements by finding people who didn't belong, and they also provided small game for food. They were better hunters for rabbits and such than wolves. They were also crucial in spy operations after the Primal Years, as they can remain silent and motionless while their beast master listens to conversations."

"You can bond like Deklan does with his wolves?" Cia asked.

"I'm sure I can. I haven't needed to, so I haven't tried," Delanee admitted. There was a lot she hadn't attempted regarding the cat. Being bonded and able to communicate seemed enough for Kossa, so Delanee also figured it was good enough for her.

Inara spotted her father and immediately began to fuss. Cia set her on the floor, and the baby took off, her hands and knees carrying her down an aisle. She babbled excitedly. Still talking to Vayden, Ryan met Inara halfway, scooping her off the floor. She squealed in delight, laughing, and gazes turned their direction, smiles on every face. Delanee's heart swelled.

Inara had been another secret Ryan had revealed to his closest team with some trepidation once he accepted the arch guardian recommendation. After all, keeping Inara a secret no longer mattered, and Delanee didn't want their daughter to grow up in isolation. The family no one knew he had become the one everyone accepted with congratulations and excitement. Inara would have playmates and more family if Delanee had to guess. Wintersfall's team didn't seem one to allow Ryan to do life alone, and she was thankful for the extended support.

Ryan moved to the front of the room. Mason Dandridge stepped forward and took Inara from him. She fussed, and Delanee immediately moved to intercept, but Mason's beautiful wife, Jessi, clapped her hands and made happy sounds at the baby. Inara settled, her hand reaching for Jessi's red hair. Jessi's very round belly made settling Inara on her hip a bit challenging, but she managed, her expression soft as she looked at her husband. Soon, they'd be holding an infant of their own.

Kevin's wife, Raina, was home with their newborn son. Kevin was no longer the son-in-law to an arch guardian but rather to the consort of the queen-elect. He seemed to have taken the change in stride but, according to Ryan, refused to go to the palace to see his in-laws.

Jonathon Hunter and his wife Sylphine were seated up front, talking to Jonathon's sister, Ramsey, and her husband, Caidon Survaine. The first time Delanee had met the shipping heiress, she'd felt wholly inadequate. The Italyssian beauty's confident grace was what every Sziverian woman attempted to achieve and always managed to fall short. Delanee often wished she could be as comfortable as Ramsey, who saw Sylphine as nothing more than a sister. Ryan had requested her presence due to her insights into imports and exports. Raina would have also been included as a logistics expert if she hadn't recently given birth.

Ryan called everyone's attention, and Delanee moved to the front while Cia sought Deklan, who sat near the back with Izia. Bonded to them both, the wolf never seemed far from them anymore. Delanee wondered if he whined through their bond when they left him behind. She wouldn't be surprised.

Ryan shoved his hands in his pockets. "Thank you, everyone, for coming."

"As if we had a choice," Sean said, smiling. "You are the boss now."

"I still appreciate your presence," Ryan stated. He leaned back against the edge of the stage and looked over the room. "What I'm about to say isn't public knowledge, and depending on how Queen-Elect Arnita chooses to handle the situation, it may never fully be revealed."

Delanee squirmed in her seat. What the public should learn was a point of contention between Delanee and everyone else involved in approving what she included in her story. Ryan told the gathering about the V Alliance and Princess Verica's connection and failed intentions. The room remained silent, though a few shocked gasps sounded, and Izia growled at some point, no doubt a reaction to Cia's heartache and anger.

Ryan crossed his arms over his chest. "The queen-elect has decided to send her daughter to Imperial Qu'in."

Vayden, leaning against the left wall, asked, "Why there?"

"Communication is limited, as are ships departing," Kevin answered. "While further evolved as a society beyond the Primal Years than Mark Inland, they're still far behind the rest of the inhabited world. She won't be able to do more damage to Sziveria or the nation that has agreed to host her. What were their requests?"

"A working radio communications network within their capital city and the right to woo the princess to marry one of their many princes," Ryan said. "Queen-Elect Arnita wished them luck and gave her blessing on any marriage, providing Verica agreed without coercion."

"Women in their culture only have power if they're married to a powerful man. I imagine she'll agree before the year ends," Kevin said.

Vayden raised a brow.

Kevin smiled. "Raina handles accounts for a few merchants who trade with Imperial Qu'in. Through her work over the years, I've learned about a lot of cultures."

"There's still a lot we don't know," Ryan continued. "Verica made a lot of deals that she didn't know the outcome of."

"The prisoner exchanges," Sean said.

Ryan nodded. "That was one, yes. The drug trade is another. She had a contact at the beginning of the plan, but as nefarious enterprises tend to do, competitors arose, and so long as they paid their tariff to her organization, she didn't care who distributed. Her initial drug broker was apparently killed in an altercation with one of the new dealers. We also haven't figured out who has been poisoning the drugs to make them a means of assassination when a V Alliance member no longer served their purpose. The person she asked to make those deaths occur has disappeared."

"Great, another murderer on the loose," Katria said.

"We've given the SNID all our information to open investigations. The queen-elect is leaving that at the discretion of Master Guardian Perrella for which ones get assigned and what may not be worth pursuing." Ryan shifted on his feet, bracing his hands on the stage floor behind him. "International operations will also be increasing. I'm informing you of this so those who wish to step aside have the time to do so before assignments come down."

"Are other teams being given this option?" Sean asked.

"Some. Syn—" Ryan shook his head, pressing his eyes closed for a moment. "Sorry, *Henry* had a few other teams with whom he was close and wanted to ensure they knew overseas missions may be more frequent in the coming months. We have a lot of political cleanup to help with."

Delanee refrained from looking at the teams who had families or were in the process of growing one, and would have to make difficult decisions about careers, rankings, and family duty.

A commotion outside the theatre room had everyone's attention shifting to the entry. Ryan straightened and began down the aisle, only to halt. A flustered attendant chased an all-too-familiar and very unwelcome woman. She wore cream-colored silk pants, a matching jacket, and a bright teal shirt adorned with a sparkling gold and crystal beaded necklace. Bright teal beaded slippers completed her outfit. Her hair was piled in an elegant twist atop her head, with little sparkling crystals worked into the braided strands. Perfectly applied makeup accentuated the beautiful curves of her face and the startling blue of her eyes. She hesitated when she saw the rapt audience watching her entrance but she lifted her chin and ventured on. Delanee jumped up, fisting her hands in annoyance and anger.

"I've come to visit my daughter," Renelle announced.

A SLEW OF EMOTIONS, none of them positive, cascaded through Ryan. He should have anticipated this moment, knowing what he knew of his ex-lover and her clear obsession with power and influence. Should have known she'd show up and attempt to lay some claim to the child she'd abandoned. Almost six weeks had passed since the arch guardianship had been endowed to him, and in the chaos of the transition, Ryan hadn't given Renelle a single thought.

A mistake.

Red-faced, the attendant gulped in the air and grasped the door jamb for support. "My guardian, I tried to stop her, but she forced her way past me."

Mason stood, moving to shield Jessi, who was holding Inara protectively to her chest. Delanee slipped behind Ryan, her anger a red-hot sizzle along his already frayed nerves. When she reached Jessi, she gathered their daughter in her arms without speaking. Inara remained silent, eyes wide. The tension in the room was a palpable thing even the baby could sense.

Renelle's gaze scanned the room, stopping on Delanee. A false smile twisted her face, and she clapped in mock excitement. "There she is! My precious baby!"

A dangerous low growl sounded among the vacant chairs to Ryan's left. The flash of a white tail appeared over the tops of the seats behind Renelle. Kossa stalked out from between a row, her huge claw-tipped paws moving silently along the carpeted aisle.

Color leeched from Renelle's face, leaving the blush applied to her cheeks a harsh pink. She blinked and rubbed her palms along the loose fabric of her pants. "I, um, I need to see my child."

"You don't have a child in this house," Delanee announced, coming to stand beside Ryan.

Needing to touch her, Ryan slipped his hand along her back and pulled her to his side. Inara whimpered and reached for him. Delanee released her with reluctance, and Ryan settled her against his other side. Kossa crouched behind Renelle, ears flat, tail flicking in a wild, annoyed pattern.

Renelle's gaze dropped. She seemed to change her mind about looking behind herself, as if she were afraid of what she would see, her frame going still. "I'm sure everyone in this room can see I do, in fact, have a child."

"Everyone in this room can see the Arch Guardian Synintel family," Deklan stated, rising. "Of which you are not a part."

Renelle laughed, the sound nervous and lacking the confidence she had exhibited when she'd entered the theatre. "Oh, please. To anyone looking, it's clear that babe is mine. I won't make a big deal of this unless I must. I just want my rights as a parent."

Ryan kept his anger leashed. "What parental rights, Renelle? How can you ask for those when you aren't her parent?"

Renelle scoffed and rolled her eyes. She glanced around the room, her smile faltering some when all she encountered were frowns and glares. She cleared her throat and twisted a finger in the beads draping down her torso. "Oh please, who else would be her mother?"

"What is *her* name?" Kevin asked, moving down the row.

Renelle blinked and looked at Kevin. "This doesn't concern you, mister..."

"Not mister, Master Guardian Raiventon," Kevin corrected, his stern expression never changing.

Ryan removed his hand from Delanee and motioned to the couples around the room. "You will find no allies here, Renelle. I suggest you leave before you further make a fool of yourself."

Renelle lifted her chin in that haughty way of hers again, her gaze going hard, the color returning to her face. "It's Primary Guardianess Chatom. And I'm not leaving until we come to some sort of an agreement about the child."

Ryan huffed, unable to stop a sarcastic smile of disbelief. So, she wanted to play the name game. Very well. "Allow me to introduce the Primary Guardians Wintersfall, the Primary Guardians Kynhaven, the Key Guardians Asherwick, the Master Guardians Survaine, and I'm sure you've heard of the Arch Guardians Wolvenguard."

Every couple stood, closing in around and behind Ryan and Delanee. Vayden, the only civilian in the room, went to stand near Deklan and Cia in the back.

Renelle's jaw flexed, and the confidence again fled her features to be replaced with uncertainty. "I just want—"

"I know what you want," Delanee sneered, and behind Renelle, Kossa growled. "And it's not going to happen because you are the mother of no one in this room."

Renelle pointed a trembling finger at Inara. "She is mine, and I will have my rights observed."

"According to who?" Delanee asked. "Because on her birth record, I'm her mother. I'm her *only* mother. I don't know why you felt the need to come here and tell these lies."

"I—" Renelle twisted, looking at all the people gathered, and smirked. "Oh, come on, as if anyone is really going to believe *you* are her mother?"

"Who, exactly, is going to believe she isn't?" Cia asked. "Delanee Voklane is the baby's mother."

At some point, the attendant had gathered property guards, who stood awaiting orders at the back of the room. Ryan lifted his hand and motioned. Two of them nodded and made their way down the aisle. Kossa glided past Renelle, hissing on her way to Delanee's side, flashing long, sharp incisors.

"Oh, summer sun!" Renelle shrieked, jumping out of the aisle. "What is that?"

"Your escort from my property, which you are never

welcome to step foot on again," Ryan said as the guards stopped at the row where Renelle had leaped.

"Now, wait, *wait!*" Renelle shrieked as a guard took her arm and began to force her from the room.

"I have this," Deklan stated, intercepting, and taking hold of the squirming woman. Izia moved to stand in front of her, growling. Renelle stopped resisting. Deklan forced her to turn and face Ryan and Delanee, pointing. "Do you see that family?"

Renelle whimpered and nodded, her gaze moving over them, to Kossa and back. "Y-yes."

"That's my brother-in-law, my sister, and *my* niece. Do you understand?" Deklan asked.

"Y-yes," Renelle whispered.

"Good. Trust me when I say you don't want the team surrounding them for an enemy, and you definitely don't want the Ralston family as one, either. I suggest you never attempt this scam again." Deklan released his hold on her. "Do you need to be seen out?"

"I know the way," she said and fled the second Izia moved from her exit path.

Cia whooped the moment she disappeared, and a loud chorus of cheers and applause joined. Someone clapped Ryan on the back, and another person squeezed his shoulder. Overwhelmed, Ryan glanced around the support system he never realized he had and was suddenly humbled. Delanee pushed under his arm and wrapped her arms around his waist, hugging him. A bright smile lit up her face when he glanced down at her. Unlike him, she didn't appear surprised by the outpouring or the end result.

For the first time since accepting the arch guardianship, Ryan felt as though he could manage the position successfully. Doubts had clouded his mind and affected his confidence. He'd risen to one of the highest positions from an unranked guardianship. A rank he never wanted but had accepted because Henry convinced him he alone could be trusted to do the job and do it with integrity. As far as any of the men and women he'd worked with knew, he was a nobody, and the sudden change wouldn't be accepted by everyone. Yet the only people he *did* care about accepting him had already done so, and he hadn't even been aware until this very moment. Emotion clogged his throat and burned the backs of his eyes. Nope. He would *not* cry.

Inara disappeared from his arms, her babble of excitement letting him know whoever had her was a welcome change. Ryan blinked and glanced around, shocked to note the twins had arrived and were carrying Inara from the excitement. They'd made the household move with him and Delanee, proclaiming wherever the baby went, they went, too. Neither Ryan nor Delanee had bothered to argue. The house was big enough for a staff of nannies, and their words would have been useless anyway.

The excitement eventually wound down, and Ryan concluded the meeting. After everyone left, Ryan went out to the greenhouse, lamenting the loss of his pool to help release the jittery remnants of Renelle's confrontation and his first official team meeting. Delanee found him standing in the middle of one of the many stone-paved paths, arms crossed, staring at nothing.

Her hand on his back pulled him from the racing thoughts. "Are you okay?"

"I'm fine."

"Ryan."

He ran a hand down his face, sighing. "Renelle isn't going to give up. If nothing else, she'll start a rumor about Inara's parentage."

"She doesn't even know Inara's name."

"She'll learn it as soon as she requests the birth record."

"Then we'll deal with that when it happens. She can start all the rumors she wants. The document tells the truth, and she isn't on it. This isn't the same as a father. As far as anyone knows, a mother can't be faked."

"Everyone who knows you knows you weren't pregnant a year ago, Delanee," he said.

"Okay, that's true. But, really, what else can she do? Cause some trouble? Let her. All we have to do is turn down a few invitations we know she's accepted and as soon as hosts realize the conflict, they'll pick us every time over her. She'll lose all social standing if she pursues her ambitions to insert herself into Inara's life."

"We'll have to tell Inara before her first social function," Ryan said, hating the drama both his wife and daughter would be exposed to due to his bad choices.

"Yes, but I'm confident in our family. She'll be okay, Ryan. Inara will be a strong, grounded young woman, raised by two people who love her."

Ryan laughed. "And will tell Renelle what she can do with her claims?"

"Probably."

Ryan hugged her tight, swaying with her in his arms. "Stars above, but I love you. So much."

She clung to him. "I love you, too. And... I have something to tell you."

He leaned back and took in her now serious expression. "Is this about what had you so upset earlier?"

"Not upset," she clarified and tried to pull away, but he strengthened his hold. "Surprised."

When she didn't continue, he said, "All right, I'm listening."

"I, well, see, I learned earlier after looking at the calendar, and then Kossa confirmed— how the cat knew I had no idea, but she did, and now I'm wondering if she'd known all along and—"

"Delanee," Ryan interrupted, laughing.

She took a deep breath and then blurted, "I'm pregnant."

"You're... wait, what?" he asked, surely having misheard.

"Pregnant," she said, taking another deep breath. "Another baby is on the way."

He wanted to ask how, but really, he was an active and enthusiastic participant in all the many opportunities she'd had to conceive. "When? How long... how far along?"

"I have no idea. I wasn't tracking my ovulation phase at all because, well," she shrugged helplessly, "you know."

She hadn't ever anticipated needing to track the information beyond monitoring her monthly for health reasons. Which wouldn't have included an ovulation window because she'd had no intention of having an intimate relationship. And he couldn't help but wonder if it would have mattered when they'd first contracted. Neither of them had been concerned with her fertile period two months ago.

"Are you upset?" she asked softly.

"What?" He shook his head and hugged her closer. "No. Absolutely not. Surprised, though I shouldn't be. We haven't exactly ever stopped, have we?"

She laughed. "No. I think if things were less chaotic, we would have realized we hadn't ever *needed* to stop to wait for my monthly to pass."

"Which means we'll probably have another baby in six or seven months."

"Seven at the most," she agreed.

He searched around, spotting a bench, and pulled her to it. Sitting, he tugged on her hands until she sank down, straddling his lap, her hands on his shoulders. He ran his palms up the silky fabric over her thighs to her waist.

"Are you okay?" he asked.

"I'm really nervous, but I think all first-time mothers are," she admitted, color rising in her cheeks. "I asked Jessi before they left how she took learning of her pregnancy, and she said despite her and Mason having tried for years, she cried because she was so scared when she first made the discovery."

"You're already a great mother," he said.

"But my attention will be split, and Inara deserves—"

"To be loved. That's it. We can love more than one child, and Inara won't feel less cherished because of a brother or sister. I promise."

"She might get jealous."

"And we'll teach her how to handle that if it happens."

Delanee snuggled into his chest, laying her head on his shoulder. Ryan hugged her, resting his cheek on top of her curls.

"I can't believe I found a mate, became a mother, am a soon-to-be mother, bonded to a cat, and became an arch guardianess, quit my job... all in a few months," she whispered, her warm breath teasing his throat.

"Any regrets?" he asked quietly.

When she didn't answer right away, his chest constricted.

"No," she whispered. "Do you have any?"

He, too, had a list of life changes. Bonded husband, ranked guardianship, a pregnant wife.... All of it incredible because he had someone extraordinary to share all of it with. Because he'd taken a chance and finally trusted. No, Ryan had no regrets. Life would never be boring, but he'd never want anything else. Smiling, happiness suffusing every cell in his body, he said with absolute conviction, "Not a single one."

About Sarah

SARAH WESTILL lives in Alabama with her US Army-retired husband. They have two sons – one they've successfully raised to adulthood – the other is still a work-in-progress, navigating high school. As a full-on creative, Sarah lives to write, crochet, teach, and meet amazing people while doing portrait and wedding photography. A veteran in the publishing industry working as a cover artist under the name Elaina Lee, she has been blessed to help hundreds of authors to achieve their own publishing goals for over a decade. To learn more about Sarah, and about her Guardians, please visit her at sarahwestill.com or follow her on Instagram @authorsarahwestill